FRAGMENTS OF
A BROKEN LAND

Borgo Press Books by ROBERT HOOD

Fragments of a Broken Land: Valarl Undead

FRAGMENTS OF A BROKEN LAND

VALARL UNDEAD
A FANTASY NOVEL

ROBERT HOOD

THE BORGO PRESS
MMXIII

FRAGMENTS OF A BROKEN LAND

FIRST EDITION

Published by Wildside Press LLC

www.wildsidebooks.com

DEDICATION

For my father and mother,
Bob and Nora,
for their unconditional love
and gentle humanity.

CONTENTS

"...The Eternal Man is seal'd, never to be deliver'd.
I roll my floods over his body, my billows & waves
    pass over him,
The sea encompasses him & monsters of the deep are
    his companions.
Dreamer of furious oceans, cold sleeper of weeds &
    shells,
Thy Eternal form shall never renew, my uncertain
    prevails against thee."
        William Blake, *Vala, or the Four Zoas*, 4.132–136

"The true existential struggle is not between Good and
Evil, but between Form and Chaos. The one makes
Society possible, the other shapes Existence itself. Yet
the desirable outcome of this conflict is not dominance.
In the struggle between Form and Chaos *neither* can
conquer, for if either does so, Life is distorted into a
monstrous parody of itself and its continuity rendered
problematic."
        Hugo Drakenswode, *An Existential Exploration
            of the Physiognomy of the Monstrous*,
                Ergo Press, 1927, p. 59

CHAPTER ONE
ALIEN PLACES

i.

Remis felt soiled just being in this rat's nest. Its patrons were as loud as the poorly embroidered hanging that dominated the barroom wall. The wood of the table, stained and pitted, mimicked its owner's complexion. Remis even fancied she could see tiny creatures in her wine glass. It was a foul place, yet it was here in *The Night Binge* that the representative of Lanaris Commercial House had insisted on meeting her.

"Lady! Ya want another drink...or ya just gonna take up table space, eh?" The landlord leaned over her, his face scowling. It wasn't personal. He carried an air of resentment with him from table to table and inflicted it on all his customers.

Remis thrust her glass at him. "I haven't finished this one, as you can see. There's rather too much body in it for my liking." The man glanced at the specks floating—even swimming—in the wine.

"What'd you want of me?" he managed at last.

She pushed the glass into his hand. "A replacement, please."

"Replacement?" He frowned. "You must be joking."

Remis stared at him coldly.

Muttering to himself, the barman shuffled toward the bar. He paused to talk to a thin, raggedly bearded man, who looked at Remis and laughed.

Choices are rarely free—that was what Remis Sarsdarl

had come to realize. The spilt beer on the floor, the ambient smell of sweat and sickness, swearing voices—she resented all these things as she would a personal slight. Nevertheless she sat there enduring it, a martyr to her sense of the inevitable. Lanaris House was an important force in City-life—and since it also controlled a significant proportion of the world's traffic in magical artifacts, it was in her interest as a novice spellbinder to listen to its proposals. That she knew what was wanted, and had no intention of working for Lanaris whatever was offered, didn't matter to her. Humility was all part of her initiation into the world of commerce and had to be endured. Newly graduated from the Aram-Halas Seminary—the largest and most prestigious magic-training college in Vesuula—Remis wanted to be accepted as a colleague, not an underling. Advancement in the commercial environment of Vesuula's political capital, Koerpel-Na, demanded such gamesmanship.

When at last Lanaris' lackey arrived, he didn't utter one word of apology. Remis had pictured him just as he turned out to be: a neat man, officious and slightly sinister, squatting like a toad over his glass. "So you see, my dear," he croaked condescendingly, "without us you will flounder in poverty, struggling vainly for a mandate. Neither the House Lanaris nor its *insignificant* rivals will aid you. The manufacture and sale of magical artifacts is no frivolous venture—"

"I know about magical artifacts."

"So you do. But what will that avail? You have only recently come from the Seminary, where you did tolerably well in your studies. But you have no friends, and it is these who will help you thrive. Put your talents to the best use. To work for my Lord Deern Lanaris is no degradation. He would make a useful ally."

"I worked for your House under acolyte bond, but the apprenticeship is over. I want to remain free of direct ties, thanks just the same."

"Such freedom is illusory. You're too vulnerable."

"Is that a threat?"

He smiled and the bend of his lips told Remis the truth of it.

"Surely there's room for everyone," she said.

The little man smiled again, more tightly this time. "Idealism is an admirable trait...in the young." He leaned toward her and his voice lowered. "May I speak frankly?" Remis shrugged, as he clearly had no intention of remaining silent. "Your acquiescence is inevitable, because the alternative is not to work at all... and hence not to live. You have surpassed all your peers in the development of spellbinding arts and this fact alone is enough to bind you to Family service." His head cocked arrogantly before continuing his lecture. "Profits are the key to political power in the Merchant State—and as Vesuula is the world's commercial center, it little tolerates either the idealist or the democrat. Should you work in opposition to us, for yourself or another Family, you will be draining Lanaris' custom and influence, however minutely. My Lord Deern would not readily condone such a thing."

Remis stared at him. It was unbelievable that her simple wish to be self-dependent should lead into conflict with the rulers of Koerpel-Na. But she saw that that was where her training had consistently been taking her. Magic studies bore on how the world was fashioned, not on the vagaries of society. Now she felt alone and abandoned, no longer part of a vast supportive family. She had no friends and was acquiring enemies quickly.

"I see you understand our position." The man glanced away, as though hearing something that interested him much more than Remis. Tension along his jaw line, however, told her he was waiting more keenly for a response than he was letting on.

"I understand that you think I can be influenced by threats," Remis said, drawing his attention back to her.

"We never threaten. Commercial intimidation is forbidden by Ruling Council guidelines."

Remis leaned forward slightly. The man half-turned from her, as though sensing something that repulsed him. "What if I said I could wither your heart as easily as I could spit on the floor at your feet?" She glared at him, intending to convey a delicate instability. "The Deep Power is more primal than your bureaucracies." The man cleared his throat, pushing his chair away from her.

"You dare threaten me?" he said shakily.

"Of course not. As you yourself pointed out, it's forbidden." Remis sat back. "But I won't sell myself to you either. There's no law says I have to. Having commercial power over me doesn't make you right."

Suddenly the little man rose. His scornful superiority had returned. "Sooner or later we all must choose to whom we will sell ourselves. Look around you. Learn the lesson of this place. Would you be slave to such a life, or would you be its master?" He bowed minutely. "I take my leave. If you change your mind, send a message to me. I'll understand." His smile was sour. "Out of charity, I'll assume your insolence is merely the folly of youth."

He bowed again and left. Remis watched him push through the crowds as though they were not there, every movement a denial of the tavern and its common inhabitants. She rubbed at her forehead, feeling the tension growing into a headache. Damn it!—she felt as though the ground had shifted uneasily under her feet.

Roars of drunken abuse from across the room gave her no chance to recover her equilibrium. At a nearby table, even the publican stopped scrubbing with his greasy rag. A dark-complexioned, exotically dressed man was engaged in a scrap with a rather weedy crewman from one of the commercial ships, the pair of them threatening, shoving at each other like adolescents. It ended when the sailor lost his balance and crashed into a table. Spilt beer did nothing to dampen the roar of conversation in the place, but it did inspire a chorus of shouts from several onlookers.

"Watch your tongue, fancy-boy," the sailor's attacker slurred, staggering slightly as movement raised the alcohol in his head, "or you won't keep it long."

"I'm of the Shippers Confederacy," sneered the crewman

from his pained crouch among the ruins of a table, "and of honest parents. I won't apologize to a slaver's bastard." The dark man went for him, but the sailor was away before he could be caught. He pushed a path to the door, turned and spat. "Have that as a favor, horseshit!" The door swung shut. The dark man bellowed something incoherent.

Enough is enough, thought Remis, *it's time I went home.* Meeting with Lanaris House had been a mistake, more damaging to her than she could have imagined—at the very least it signaled an end to any complacent acceptance she might have had as to where her future was headed. Certainly there was no reason to endure the tavern's acrid smells and coarse violence further. She shoved past the table and headed toward the landlord and his cronies. They watched as she approached, as though they suspected her of some sinister intent. "You forgot my replacement wine," she said petulantly, when she reached the landlord.

He shrugged.

"I know you're busy," she continued, her tone flattening. "Perhaps too busy. I'll mention it to my uncle. Perhaps he could help."

"Your uncle?"

"Councilor Nabalen. He's a sympathetic man...at heart." Nabalen was Head of the Waidenar Family, which owned most of the taverns in this part of the City, and was a leading member of the Ole'eth-Aluk Ruling Council—the State's elite political body. He was no relative of Remis's, of course, though he'd once instigated bankruptcy procedures against her father, when failing wheat crops had spoilt some minor entrepreneurial endeavor of the Waidenar's. But Remis's clothes and superior manner would add credence to her claim, enough to unsettle him perhaps. "I'm sure he'll be fascinated by your plight," she added for effect, mustering as much sarcastic self-confidence as she could manage.

The landlord scoffed, though uncertainly. "Nabalen wouldn't piss on the likes of you," he ventured.

Probably true, thought Remis. But she mimicked a sort of mock surprise. "You think so, do you?" She smiled nastily. "Well, we'll see." And turned away, feeling that if she evoked momentary doubt it would be sufficient. A petty revenge, yes, but the afternoon had made her feel petty. He called to her before she reached the door. She ignored him and swung out into the night. Street air was cool. A strong wind blew in off the unseen harbor and carried ocean tangs and other stenches from the docks. Only the windows of *The Night Binge* showed any light. The tall stone warehouses and surrounding shops were dark and few people walked the streets.

A cacophony broke through the night as the door of the tavern opened. The publican staggered out, trailing shadow and smoke. "You don't frighten me, lady!" he yelled, his face betraying his anxiety.

Remis waved dismissively and strode off down the main Dehum-Rewi thoroughfare before he could say more, her boots clicking dully on the paving stones and sloshing in the frequent patches of mud. Wide and long, the road disappeared into darkness around the edge of a black-stone edifice. There were no oil-lamps there. But she didn't intend to be frightened of the night and she didn't look back either.

A voice shouted from beyond the buildings, one of the workers on the main dock. It was bleak and forlorn. *That pompous Lanaris fool was right in one thing*, Remis thought, *I need friends, or nothing will thrive. But I'll pick them myself, no matter how unlikely the choice may seem.*

The ground about her flickered under the pale movement of residual day in the clear, but always starless, night-sky.

ii.

Sevthen Ulart-Tashnark made it home—or rather, made it back to his mother's home—without much trouble. Sure, his head hurt, his memory was fuzzy and he had no real awareness of his surroundings, but none of that could be considered unusual. For many years, he'd been able to negotiate the short walk—or, more accurately, *stagger*—along the port district's muddy streets without the help of conscious thought at all. It was like a groove he was in and the most that ever happened to him was a bruised elbow or two acquired from bumping into the sides of the rut.

His mother, ever trustful, had left the back door unlatched so there was no need for him to deal with the impossible task of locating keys and then manipulating them into the lock. Instead Tashnark pushed on the plain wooden paneling and let the door swing open by itself. He staggered into the kitchen, tripped over a chair and admonished himself rather loudly to keep quiet. Somehow he found his bedroom at the end of a dark corridor that should have defied navigation.

"Tashnark? Is that you?" came his mother's voice, echoing dimly through the night like an overfamiliar memory.

"No," he shouted grumpily, "it's just a burglar!"

As he fell face down onto his bed, he allowed himself a moment of regret. There wasn't time to define the nature of the regret, however, before his abused body and mind withdrew into darkness.

This had become a familiar pattern. Nearly every night, it seemed, Tashnark would drink enough cheap beer to deaden the most intense depression. Its effect would sit on him like a fog, blurring the edges of memory and dulling his fears. Sometimes it made him aggressive, as it had earlier tonight.

But it never kept the night and its darkness away. And the darkness scared him. Lately it had been offering up strange and vivid dreams—dreams that took him to another place, another time....

And on this night, too, as he slept, reality shifted—and he became someone else.

He was Bellarroth and Bellarroth was travelling. He had been travelling for...he couldn't tell how long. Though he was aware of progress he had no sense of history. His memory was only the memory of present-past—moments slipping into an obscurity that had no form, offered no imagery. He did not question; he just traveled.

But time filled him with thoughts.

When the wind grew bad, he sought shelter. Its sudden intensity and the way it screamed around the crevices and ridges told him that the Great Monster Tammenallor was moving, making Its way through the void. Memory of Tammenallor came suddenly, a herald of other knowledge. Tammenallor was the world on which he lived, he knew that much—a living being like himself, but one so far beyond Bellarroth's conception of life, and so much larger, that he had no terms in which to think of It. Bellarroth looked toward the horizon and let his mind understand the heaving movement visible there.

Soon he reached the Serpent Acres themselves. The twisting trees, snakeheads raging, made a fearful silhouette against the sky. Beyond them, mountainous Koroom—as he had euphonically named Tammenallor's noisy head—loomed above him and momentarily drove other thoughts from his mind. Every so often light would spark off the gargantuan fangs protruding through the flesh of the Koroom-mouth, spearing Bellarroth's heart with pain and blanching the sky with its horror. Only this distracted him from the danger of the trees themselves. He would watch Koroom's huge mouth open soundlessly and it would numb his more immediate fears, replacing them with primitive terror.

Vapor hung like torn skin in the space around it.

<Come to me. Hurry, hurry.>

The urgency had taken on a voice now, so clear that Bellarroth started, thinking someone had approached him. He steadied himself, and listened. <Hurry,> it said, <Hurry or the way is lost.>

The voice was not from outside. It trembled through the interior of his head like uncontrolled thought.

Is it Hanin? he wondered. Is the voice my teacher's?

The ground shook.

* * * * * * *

Tashnark would respond by tossing aside the images that crowded through his restless sleep. He'd open his eyes and the night, broken into shadow-patterns on the plaster roof above him, would coalesce into something familiar again. He'd be in his mother's home. Her house stood on the edge of a large park on the seaward side of the City of Koerpel-Na, in the merchant-state called Vesuula. His father was a state-sanctioned slaver. He himself was drunk too often and a great disappointment to his family. Heavily built and, on occasion, oafish with it, he occupied his time in taverns and gaming houses, working for money only when his father indulged in the sort of parental moralising that had frustrated many a fine layabout.

Why then was he plagued by the dreams? They were more frequent now than they had ever been, so barely a night passed that was not full of their bizarre imagery. Tashnark felt the dream...no, it was more than a dream...he felt the *memory* growing clearer and clearer nightly. Yet it was impossible. He was Sevthen Ulart-Tashnark and he lived in Koerpel-Na. There was no Tammenallor, no Hanin, no Bellarroth.

He'd turn in his bed and pull the blankets around his shoulders.

Can dreams supplant reality? he'd wonder—but would not want an answer.

* * * * * * *

In the morning he had a hangover. His memory of its causes was blurry to say the least, though oddly enough what he remembered most about the night before was not whatever conversation he may have had with acquaintances in *The Night Binge*, nor how much he drank, nor the fight with the ship crewman (which he only knew about because of a note from the publican he found in his jacket pocket, billing him for a busted table). Rather it was a woman he'd noticed sitting at the back, as though waiting. He'd watched her for a while, fascinated by her, and had seen some self-important bastard from one of the Commercial Houses come in and sit with her. As a liaison, however, it looked to be about as welcome as a bacterial infection in places best not mentioned in polite company. The woman was intimidated at first, but then rallied, putting the wind up him by something she said and sending him on his way with only a show of scorn to cover his annoyance. What happened then got a bit hazy, but Tashnark did recall that the next time he'd looked for her, the woman was gone.

He'd been attracted to her, that was certain—irresistibly drawn in fact. He'd admired her face and figure to be sure, but was even more entranced by the manner in which she carried herself. Dark hair, tied back firmly, compact body, ornately decorated clothing, piercing eyes. Though her face was delicately and finely featured, giving a suggestion of being lost, there was no hint that this fact demoralized her. In her determination, which was plain to him even from a distance, she reminded him of his mother. Tashnark might have approached the woman, hoping to prolong an acquaintance that didn't even have a starting point, except he'd been sober enough to realize he was in no state to impress. He was incoherent and morbid and drunk. His shirt and rough cotton pants were filthy with spilt food and beer stains. No doubt he stank. So he'd kept away and all that was left now were a few recollections. It was strange, though, that despite the alcoholic amnesia that inevitably settled over him, memories of the woman should linger.

Both his mother and Ishwarin, his brother, had breakfasted by the time he made it to the kitchen. He forced himself to eat some eggs and a plateful of cereals covered in thickened juice—he had no idea what kind of fruit the reddish green sludge had once been—then was sick into a large washbasin he was using to splash the throbbing out of his temples.

His mother didn't appear either to comfort or berate him, so he assumed she'd left for her workplace—the Hassur Libraries. She spent an inordinate amount of time there, much more than her job required. It was as though she were desperate to track down some important scrap of information hidden in the thousands of volumes written by men and women long dead—a truth that would make her content. She wasn't content, Tashnark knew that. Under her veneer of easy acceptance was a spirit tormented by longing. Tashnark didn't fully understand the source of that longing, but his awareness of it made him uncomfortable. Part of him wanted to help her, though he had long ago given up any pretence that he knew what could be done for her.

And he was conscious of his own responsibility. Once, looking for money, he'd violated the sanctity of her room while she was out. On her desk lay piles of paper and his eyes had scanned them lazily. One sheet was an old fading leaf covered in the archaic square pen-craft of Hassur-scholars. It was a 'Meditation on Worthiness' by Halek-Sinor, one of the College's founding fathers. Next to it was something written in a recent and more flowing script: his mother's, without a doubt. There was a date at the top, that of several days before. Strangely compelled, Tashnark had picked up the paper and read it.

How can we see Halek-Sinor's Worthiness, with its relentless pursuit of Truth and correspondent Morality, in the Hassur of today? Godliness seems further and further removed from every part of intellectual life. Nor can I, on a personal level, keep my own life pure and free of ambiguity. What is my son? I cannot admit what I know in my heart, that my son is dead, and that a stranger has taken his place. Hassur records, but does not evaluate. Is this worthy? I remember the past, as does Hassur, but resist the memory in favor of blind hopes and ignorant assumptions. In that, I'm like the Temples. If Ur-Teth the God called upon us today, how far from truth and willingness would we find ourselves to be, I and my Hassur?

...that my son is dead, and that a stranger has taken his place.

What did she mean by it? Tashnark hadn't known, and still didn't, but memory of her doubt and sorrow made him afraid— for her...and for himself.

He heated water over the stove, carried it through the house in a large pot and poured it into the expensive metal-wrought tub that graced his mother's bathroom. After the third trip, he stripped off his smelly clothes and soaked himself for a while. He tried to cut off his thoughts, which were too often spoiled by a self-pity he didn't let anyone else see. Post-binge melancholy didn't help. Such self-indulgence struck him as pathetic and made him feel worse. Instead he watched the whirling phantoms molded from steam from the hot water and listened to the muffled sounds of the outside world. At one point he found himself wondering again who that woman in the tavern had been—her dark hair tied back, her gray-green eyes glinting clearly even across the smoky taproom, the way her hands moved with an elegant expressiveness as she talked.

If I search hard enough, he wondered, *will I be able to find her again?*

As his mind numbed and his eyelids got heavier, Tashnark heard his brother singing gently in the room above. The words filtered into his mind as an undercurrent to thought and settled there like a sediment over his day-dreaming.

> "Where are you going?" spoke a man I met beside the
> bay.
> "Along the road and out of town," at once I tried to
> say.
>
> "Where are you going?" again he pressed, that man so
> thin and gray
> "Beyond the last house, out the gate, still further on
> my way."

The tune was slow and measured, soothing on the surface yet somehow unsettling at a level below Tashnark's conscious thoughts. Verse after verse described the determined questioning of the thin, gray man. More, it charted the narrator's growing terror as the stranger's words took on darker meaning. Tashnark found his mind drifting into a landscape full of hazy light, as the song's narrator begged the strange man to leave him alone....

> His "Where are you going?" laughed at me, his eyes
>   said plainly "Nay!"
> His hand stretched out and touched me, and he wraith-
>   like went away.
>
> The winds sigh "Where are you going?" Dark waters
>   in the bay
> Breathe the words like sleeping beasts; "Where?" the
>   brambles say.
>
> Trees whisper "Where are you going?", "Where?"
>   chirps the lonely jay.
> A cursed soul, I wander lost, in exile, old and fey.

The accompanying lute mimicked the sound of wind. Tashnark stirred restlessly in the cooling water as, again, something monstrous formed in the empty spaces of sleep. He felt it coming and groaned, tossing about in sudden terror.

Words burst from his lips. "Hanin! Hanin!" There was an intense red glow that blinded him and stunned his mind into dullness. He squeezed his eyes shut.

* * * * * * *

When he opened his eyes, a vague uneasiness came upon him, making him feel displaced and lonely.

He was called Bellarroth. He remembered that.

He remembered the name 'Tashnark', too. But who was Tashnark? Bellarroth had no idea.

What was he doing then? Bellarroth couldn't remember that

either.

He looked around at the near-dormant serpent-trees and the grainy haze of the sky beyond, and another name came to him. Hanin! He was searching for Hanin—that was what he was doing.

The first signs of the Fire-beast Lucishnor had appeared on the few scraps of horizon visible to him. Lucishnor's imminent arrival heralded a new day—and the possible awakening of the trees. A touch of fire in the sky silhouetted their still forms. Bellarroth began to run, his awareness of Hanin's call renewed and strengthened. But the sky flared suddenly as the monster Lucishnor sped into view. The heat of its closeness battered him.

Movement made him glance up. A shadowy mass towered above—a mountain moving with life. He was close to the base of Koroom, so close the monster-head lost appreciable detail and was simply a solid, incomprehensible hugeness. Hanin's call hounded him on. <Hurry, hurry!>

Bellarroth's breath came in gasps and his chest heaved against the rough, hair-woven garment he wore, while the heat of Lucishnor burned across the back of his neck like a swung fire-brand. Sweat rolled off him and thirst tore at his throat, but he didn't stop beneath the shade of denser forest nor when he came to water leaking out of Tammenallor into a gentle rivulet. The water began to steam.

And then the winds grew fierce. There was movement among the serpent-trees that was not a product of their perpetual squirming. It threw them into a simultaneous swing to one side and their hissing swept into Bellarroth's ears as though they cried out in alarm. Hair-grass whipped about his feet, making him stumble as a blast of wind hit and scalded his already-reddened skin. He fell to his knees.

Now the sky was on fire. As he glanced up, Bellarroth's flame-blurred eyes discerned in that instant the shape of Lucishnor's fiery wings even through the forest of serpent-silhouettes between him and the sky-beast. He turned away, praying that the monster would fly around behind the enormous head of

Tammenallor, so that Bellarroth would be running in shadow. Battle between the monsters seemed inevitable and this perception fueled the panic already barely under control in him. If the monsters were to fight, there would be no possibility of survival for him on Tammenallor. Gigantomachy would annihilate the delicate balance of existence, his life consumed in the holocaust.

He knew instinctively that time was shortening. Yet it was not despair that rose in him, but determination and heightened awareness of the urgency sent from Hanin. Fatalistically, he stumbled on through the mounting chaos, crouching low to reduce the push of the winds. Heat ate at him like a predator.

How long it was before he reached the limit of his endurance he didn't know, but reach it he did. And acknowledging that limit brought a swift and unwelcome end to his flight. The call speared into his mind with a sharp, almost hysterical intensity. He saw ahead a tangle of shapes materializing in the stark glare—his mind grasped to that tangle as though linked by some ethereal bond. Momentarily the haze on his eyes cleared, showing him a thick mesh of smaller, vine-like serpents and clinging, fibrous strands. In the midst of this, held and shredded by insensate fingers, lay Hanin—a bloody corpse being shorn of its flesh. A moan escaped from Bellarroth's lips and his limbs stiffened with sudden fear. Darkness overwhelmed him.

* * * * * * *

Tashnark awoke to the sound of dim voices, chattering frenziedly in dark. A hand gripped his arm, pulling him up. *"Hanin!"* he cried, weak with ghostly terror, *"I saw you dead."*

"Dead, no." The thin, wrinkled lips released words as though they were precious jewels, *"but you find me dying. Tammenallor has broken my defenses and Its body takes me to Its own. Soon I will be dead. You, Bellarroth, have been born to save. Act now! Awaken!"*

His skeletal finger bent to Bellarroth's forehead and touched him there.

The contact jolted him, filling his bones with fire.
"I'm not Bellarroth!" he yelled.

Tashnark's voice echoed in the small bathroom, rebounding like a shattered vase from the tiled walls. The water, cool now, lapped against his chest, spilling over onto the floor. His fingers gripped the smooth-beaten metal of the bath rim. Someone was pounding on the door. "Tashnark! Are you all right?"

The door creaked open and the smooth, ascetic face of his brother, Ishwarin, squeezed into the gap. "What the hell are you yelling about, brother?"

"Nothing. Sorry. I fell asleep and had a nightmare."

Ishwarin opened the door fully and came in. He was dressed in the formal purple and gray coat he always wore when attending the Courts. "You yelled something about Bellarroth."

"Did I? I've never heard of him."

"The thing is...." Ishwarin leaned down, full of his usual earnestness—a peculiar stance that always accompanied displays of erudition. His plucked eyebrows curved into a questioning frown. "Bellarroth is a rather esoteric name. Where did you come across it?"

Tashnark shrugged. "This water's cold. Do you mind?" He stood in the bath, letting the water slough off him.

His brother stepped back to let him get at his towel. "It's part of an ancient tale."

"Tale?"

"About the end of the world. Do you know it?"

Tashnark dried himself, shoving Ishwarin aside whenever he got in the way of his elbows. The floor tiles felt cold and unpleasant under his feet.

"It's a very obscure thing. Legendary. Bellarroth was said to have undertaken a great journey to confront the world's tormentor. No, wait, I'm wrong. It was not something done, but an action foretold. A prophecy—"

"Brother!" Tashnark gestured in front of Ishwarin's face to silence him, sensing danger. "I don't want to know this, thanks. Save it for your better educated cronies." He strode out, heading for his bedroom. "I don't know anything about it and I'm quite happy to leave it that way."

"It's interesting."

"I'm sure it is. But I don't care."

Ishwarin didn't follow him, taking his frustrated attempt to further Tashnark's education through into the hearth-room. Tashnark dressed quickly. His mind was numb, still disturbed by fragmented images of serpent-headed trees, a roaring mountain and a fiery monster that lit up the sky. He tried not to think about it.

Then striped light falling from outside across the crumpled surface of his bed invoked the specter of a bloodied corpse cut by vines.

"Ishwarin!" he yelled.

"What is it?" came his brother's distant voice.

"What about the name *Hanin*? Does that mean anything to you?"

Silence took over for a moment, until Tashnark thought that Ishwarin hadn't heard him. He was about to withdraw, when Ishwarin appeared at the end of the corridor.

"There was a Hanin in Cormidthal's court. One of the Warlord's Inner Circle spellcasters, I think."

"Cormidthal?"

"The last ruler of Mikhalin—which, in case your history's as poor as your manners, was a great empire on the southern landmass, before it was fragmented in an apocalyptic war, oh, perhaps a thousand years ago. The Greatest War, some call it. Surely you learnt something of this from your tutors."

"What I learnt from my tutors wasn't what they were trying to teach me."

Ishwarin's gaunt features became more stern as they reflected his disappointment. "You've wasted your time, Tashnark. You always were disrespectful."

Tashnark held up his hand. "No lectures."

Ishwarin shrugged.

"Is that all you can tell me about Hanin?"

"I could look it up. Why? What's your interest in him? Has this to do with Bellarroth?"

"Just something I heard." Tashnark waved him away. "It doesn't matter. Hadn't you better get going? You're late for work."

"The Court sitting doesn't start till mid-morning." He walked toward Tashnark, a gaunt shadow in the dimness of the hallway. "You look like you could use a drink. Want to visit the Refectory?"

"I drank quite enough last night."

"Something non-alcoholic then?"

Dream-residue struck Tashnark suddenly and he staggered, leaning against the wall so that Ishwarin wouldn't notice. *Heat and tempest around him. The corpse of Hanin a bloody skeleton, little flesh remaining on the bones. Even as he watched he could see that the mesh in which Hanin was trapped sucked the moisture from what remained of his body. Too late! Too late!*

"Are you still drunk?" asked his brother.

The image of dead Hanin was replaced by that of a living woman. The woman from the tavern last night. *She reached out and beckoned to him.*

Tashnark shook the visions aside. Damn it! "No, just a bit dizzy. Listen, there's something I want to talk to you about anyway. Maybe you can give me some advice."

"Me? Advise you?" Ishwarin raised an elegantly curved eyebrow. "This is a turnaround."

"Don't get cocky. The world's aging and so am I. Come on!" He grabbed his brother's bony arm and bustled him toward the front door.

* * * * * * *

The Refectory—originally established by the Shaa-Derthperrit Temple as an eating place for magic-workers who, for one reason or another, had fallen on hard times, but long since having become a fashionable secular meeting-place for locals—wasn't very busy at this time of the day. Its high roof and compartmentalized architecture, however, created complex patterns of light and shadow that always gave the impression of quiet occupancy. Ishwarin never objected to coming here, even though the richness of his purse predisposed him to more upmarket venues. On the other hand, it had always been a favorite of Tashnark's. It suited him when the louder egotism of the district's innumerable taverns didn't appeal, or when he felt like talking. He liked the way its internal skeleton of wooden pillars and carved ribbing evoked a living presence. Even when there were musicians playing, it was a quiet, contemplative place.

Ishwarin called for hot drinks made of crushed ocar beans and nuts—to Tashnark it was an anemic scholar's drink, but he accepted the gesture. Suddenly hungry, he added bread, cheese and crispy bacon to the order.

"So what's on your mind?" Ishwarin started right in, once the attendant was gone. His curiosity was patent. "Is this something serious?"

"Serious? Have you ever known me not to be serious?"

"It's about our mother, is it?"

Ishwarin had always had a profound love for Eresteyin that he never offered to his real mother, their father's current wife. Strictly speaking, Tashnark and he were only half-brothers, though they didn't think of themselves that way. Ishwarin's actual home was far across the City, in the Old Gorim district—the historic center of Koerpel-Na—but he spent most of his time in Eresteyin's house. It was always plain where his loyalties lay.

"No, she's fine," Tashnark said. "This is about a...different woman."

Ishwarin laughed. "What? You're asking me about your love life?"

Tashnark frowned. "I don't have a love life."

"I noticed."

"For god's sake, just listen."

"Sorry."

"I want to find a woman, a particular woman, and I don't know how to go about it. You're good at all that bureaucratic horseshit. You got any ideas?"

Ishwarin grinned at him stupidly. It irritated Tashnark.

"Well?"

"I'm amazed, that's all." Ishwarin swiveled his eyes in a dismissive gesture. "Who is she?"

"I don't know. She was at *The Binge* last night. I watched her, on and off, for maybe half an hour. Now I can't get her out of my mind."

"Love at first sight, eh? I didn't think you had it in you."

An old woman in a long brown robe materialized with their drinks. Tashnark took a heavy gulp and let the smooth bland liquid course down his throat. Was it love at first sight? Or perhaps lust? No doubt there was a sexual side to it, but that wasn't what it was about. He met many women, felt drawn toward their shapeliness or their long, inviting legs. Yet he rarely pursued them. What was different with this one?

"I don't know," he said. "I felt...." He shrugged. "Actually I don't know what I felt, but she got in my mind and now worries at its edges like a damn cat with a mouse."

Ishwarin stared into his eyes thoughtfully for a moment. It was a disconcerting habit and one that normally irritated the hell out of Tashnark. Today, however, it unsettled him instead. He glanced away.

"What is it you want, brother?" Ishwarin almost whispered.

"Want? You mean, from this woman?"

"From your life. You have to admit, it's not in the best shape."

Confusion flowed through Tashnark, numbing his arms, hollowing out his chest. Something he recognized as a sob ballooned into his throat, but he cut it off before it could be expelled into the air and give him away.

"I want to find this particular woman at the moment, that's all. Is it too much to ask you for simple help, without a cross-examination?"

Ishwarin would have recognized this response as evasion,

but he let it pass. He nodded. "Seriously, though, this is just what you need, Tashnark. An obsession."

"Can you give me any useful advice?"

Ishwarin let his broad mouth smile knowingly. "Her name? That'd be a start."

"I didn't talk to her." When Ishwarin's face produced a look that contained both amazement and scorn, Tashnark added: "I was drunk at the time. I kept my distance."

Ishwarin gazed at him with an amused smirk.

"She was dressed well but in clothes that were slightly out of fashion. Too much pattern." Tashnark frowned, concentrating. "And she moved her hands when she talked in a very studied way, but beautifully, like it was a dance."

The bread, cheese and bacon arrived and Tashnark ate it while he told Ishwarin what he could remember of the encounter, such as it was. Thinking of it must have distracted his stomach from its earlier disquiet, for the food stayed down.

"Maybe the publican knows her," Ishwarin suggested.

"She was totally out of place. Her first and last time in *The Binge*, I'd guess."

"Her unwelcome companion then, the Houseman? Could you track her through him?"

"The emblem on his cloak was a round object—a ring perhaps—with three wavy lines in the center—"

"Lanaris Family. From your description—especially the hand movements—she's probably a magic-worker. It fits. Lanaris's interest would suggest a spellbinder. No doubt newly graduated. Lanaris aims to maintain a monopoly on the employment of the Seminary's best students. They want her and she's resisting." He waved his hand like a street performer. "Simple."

Tashnark squinted at his brother. "You'd make an excellent legal advocate, if you could just learn to be suitably corrupt. So how do I find her?"

Ishwarin swallowed a mouthful of ocar, unaccountably yet obviously savoring the light creaminess of the beverage. It left a scum of brown foam on his upper lip. "Ask Lanaris House," he said.

iii.

Despite her sense that bridges had been burned behind her, Remis continued with plans to find independent work. In the morning, she woke bleary-eyed and lethargic and had to force herself to wash, have breakfast, dress and head out from her thin, cluttered rooms into the City. Everywhere it was the same: officials who had previously welcomed her enquiries now turned her away without explanation, agreements nearly signed were found to be faulty and lapsed or were discarded, no new custom approached her door. Over the following days, she would go to the docks to meet incoming ships, hoping to keep ahead of the spreading conspiracy that isolated her from her future, and there approached captains and foreign merchants, offering her skills. Some would express interest. But within the hour a richly attired figure would come to them with whispers and nods, and they would send her away.

"I'm sorry. We can't use your services," they'd say.

"Why?" she'd ask. "I can be competitive and guarantee the result."

"I'm sorry."

Once, pushed beyond self-pity into anger, she let go her restraint and accused a fat merchant's agent of conspiring with Lanaris House to ruin her. The man laughed and had her removed from his office by force. When she threatened to go to the Ruling Council, he gestured carelessly for her to do so. He knew as well as she that it would get her nowhere.

Her shop, so lately a symbol of her new, expanding life, suddenly felt like a prison, its dark narrow workrooms cold with discouragement and failure. She spent some time binding minor power-spells into worthless trinkets, which she then hawked at a nearby market. One sold, but word got around somehow and before she knew what was happening, she was jostled and items were stolen in the crush; thugs appeared to channel passersby away from her. When she complained to a Sumis law enforcement officer, he commented that the markets were like that—not a fit place for someone of her status to peddle their wares.

"It's more than that," she insisted. "This is organized intimidation. I've been threatened by Lanaris House."

The officer studied her intently. "You do have a permit to sell in open market, do you?"

"I'm a trained spellbinder. That gives me the right."

Darkly, he insisted she accompany him back to the main Sumis offices at Mallos House, where he checked her credentials. After a delay of about three hours, she was told that her license could not be confirmed.

"I'm a graduate of the Seminary," she said, astonished.

"I'm sure someone has misplaced the documentation, that's all. It'll get sorted out. But until it does, you must refrain from practicing your Art commercially. I'm sorry."

Argument was useless. In a rage, she went to the Faen-Hassur Shas'torarb, which housed the Seminary and had been for so long her only home, and told the Dean her story. He was sympathetic, but it was clear that neither his jurisdiction nor his outlook extended much beyond the walls of the school. She talked to some of her teachers to the same end. It was her problem, they said. If she chose to resist the system, there was little they could do to help her.

It made her isolation all the more apparent. What friends she'd made during her years of study were scattered across the world now; only one had remained in Koerpel-Na—Seran, a young woman born far outside Vesuula and adept at various minor commercial magics. Accordingly, Remis sought her out and they went for a drink together, but already their paths had separated. Their talk was superficial, emotional connections weak. It left her feeling morose. More and more she thought of the family she'd left behind many years ago in the mountain plains just outside the northern Vesuulan border. Her father hadn't wanted her to go, had instead wanted her to marry the son of a local landowner and thus cement the family's local fortunes. "What else are girl-children for?" he'd yelled. They'd fought about it, long and hard; Remis had left home in a storm of argument and regret. She hadn't seen either her father or his wife for over five years, though once her mother had written—a tense, clumsy missive which Remis had too easily discarded. To whom or to what was she connected? She'd abandoned her bloodline and the society she'd adopted was abandoning her. Perhaps it had been a mistake to place so much hope on a vision of the future. Of what real worth was it anyway?

"You must ask yourself what it is you want out of life, Remis," one of her old teachers offered her. Right now, she didn't know.

Walking home that afternoon, she passed the forge of a smithy whose skills she'd used on occasion when her own non-magical technical abilities hadn't been up to the metal-working required for some particular object she was devising. The smithy was named Arhl Mogarni, and his ultra-pale skin and border-land accent branded him as much an alien in this cosmopolitan city as she was becoming herself. Koerpel-Na wasn't as open a place as it pretended to be, she reflected. It was closed-off and unfriendly, greedy for foreign trade but subtly exclusive in its practices, even to those it had beckoned into the fold.

As she approached, she saw that the smithy was standing in his front yard, leaning against the large open door of his work-room—obviously seeking momentary relief from the interior heat. He noticed her and waved. On an impulse, she veered closer.

"Hello, Mogarni," she said.

He acknowledged her with unexpected eagerness. "Please, it's Arhl," he said. "No formality necessary."

"Taking a break?"

"Not entirely by choice." He smiled a touch wryly. "Work is scarce."

"For me, too. It's hopeless."

The look of concern that spread over his pale, bony features seemed overstated—she should have been more careful what she said. He had always adopted a fatherly air in her presence.

She shrugged. "It's all right. I'm just feeling a bit sorry for myself. I'm finding it harder than I imagined. Independence, I mean."

He nodded dumbly, as though he'd been close to revealing too much and had suddenly realized the fact. "You deserve better," he mumbled.

"I'm sure things will improve."

She wished him well and continued on her way, vaguely disappointed. What had she expected? There had been some sort of connection between Arhl Mogarni and herself, but it had felt distant and awkward. They hardly knew each other—and not personally—so how could it be otherwise?

* * * * * * *

Her nights, lying alone in her rooms, filled with dreams and omens. These gnawed at her incessantly, like rats at a hessian grain-sack. She shivered in her bed, desperate to throw them off. But they gathered about her mind in ever-thickening clusters, finally coming together into shapes of terrible significance.

One night a few days after her abortive meeting with Lanaris House's lackey—finding herself on the verge of acquiescence—Remis lay on her bed in the semi-dark, staring at the ceiling, wishing she could find some resolve. After a while the shadows seemed to move toward her. She blinked to steady them, but they only drifted closer, wrapping themselves around her.

She was standing before a creature of corrupted flesh, a death-being whose eyes were black and lifeless in their sockets. Its limbs were shrunken, but the muscles on them were bound like thick twine about its bones. Fearfully she offered this creature a bronze-edged coffer and watched as it took the offering in its hands. It stared mutely at the object that lay inside: a spiky, jagged-limbed artifact that made her think of a candle-gleam caught in stone. Although she only vaguely recognized the shape, it created in her a strong urgency and a sense of awe.

There was greed, too. She indicated for the creature to place its hand upon the object.

At that moment the skin of the creature's face tore like volcanic ground splitting apart under vast subterranean pressure; its hand became a knife that cut out her heart in one bloodless stroke. She screamed as pain twisted her muscles. The candle-gleam artifact sprang from the cut and its pointed, undulating arms grew swiftly, flowing outward and around, engulfing her, binding her, one with her body and spirit, utterly consuming her every thought. Then the artifact began to rise away from her and it drew her life with it, leaving her crying out in despair and torment. There was fire in her chest and it supplanted the hollowness of her body, flowing through her like blood. Desolation overtook the world. She cried out: "Where are you going?" but the evanescent artifact gave no reply. Its departure left the world ablaze.

Remis was tossed into wakefulness. She stared up at the ceiling still, re-living the nightmare in an effort to secure it in her memory. She was a student of the Deep Power, and in the philosophy of the Magic Arts dream-imagery held mysteries it was worth making an effort to solve. The meaning of this one escaped her.

The night was quiet, and her surroundings suddenly unfamiliar. Her wooden casements had been transformed into threatening alien relics.

A storm pelted heavy rain drops against her tile roof, creating a rumble that vibrated through the baked-clay walls. Wind swept over her. She shivered and dragged herself from her bed, realizing that a door or window must have been blown open in the sudden tempest. Sure enough, as she emerged from her room into the central corridor, she could see along it to the square of liquid dark that should have been the closed front door. She cursed. Her feet padded across the gritty sandstone floor toward it.

Lightning flared, cracking the night apart. There was something there, in the doorway. Two vivid green eyes, low to the ground, pierced into hers, surrounded by a compact gray shape. A cat?

For a moment, while storm-light lingered in the air, and as the building trembled with the concussion of lagging thunder, she stood as though paralyzed, staring at this specter. Then darkness engulfed her.

She moved forward again. The cat was no longer there. Remis leaned out into the storm, glancing up and down the street. Nothing but the detritus of the night.

She shut and locked the door and in the resulting stillness went back to her bed.

iv.

Ishwarin claimed it was simply because Tashnark was so bone idle, and had nothing better to do with his time, that he had become so focused—but something more drove Tashnark to visit the main offices of Lanaris House, seeking information about the woman he'd seen in *The Night Binge*. Call it obsession, call it lust. He didn't care what it was called. He simply wanted to know who she was and felt a growing urgency to find her.

Lanaris House was less than cooperative. The insincere fool he was allowed to talk to was suspicious of his request for information and sought guidance from above. Whoever his reply came from, the answer was the inevitable one: such a meeting as Tashnark described could not have taken place—it would hardly be appropriate for a commercial Family of Lanaris's eminence in the Supreme Council to conduct business in a grubby dockside tavern. Tashnark must have been mistaken.

"Maybe it wasn't official business," Tashnark suggested, "but I'd like to speak to the Lanaris official who was there. He was wearing the House emblem."

He described the man, but still received no satisfactory answer. If he hadn't been so physically imposing, they would have thrown him from the building. The experience confirmed the prejudice he harbored against Family bureaucracies and made him suspect a conspiracy.

That night he must have dreamed of Hanin, for when he woke his head was filled with memory of the man. How could such memories suddenly exist where before there'd been nothing? Moreover the memories were from the point of view of Bellarroth, who haunted his nights with greater and greater frequency....

* * * * * *

"Who are you?" Bellarroth had asked.

Hanin's old eyes flayed him, as though the issue were one that should never be raised. He had not answered.

But Hanin had taught Bellarroth many things—how to cook and sew and hunt and survive. He found him shelter where there was none, fed him when vermin was scarce, and gave him thoughts beyond those of simple survival. The old man always appeared whenever he was needed.

"What's does my name mean, Hanin?" Bellarroth had asked once.

"It means nothing, as now you mean nothing." Hanin smiled ironically, his weathered face creasing into a complex pattern. "One day—in another place—you will be more important than you can imagine and then you will have a new name. Until that time, you are nothing."

Hanin spoke of the 'other world', the world he called Tharenweyr, born out of the dream of the fallen deity Errellinarth. He spoke to Bellarroth of many things in that other world—of great magic and the Deep Power, of greed and of ambition and how these evils had brought destruction; and he told Bellarroth of the exile of his mother, who was named Korrenea, onto Tammenallor's shoulders. "Tammenallor?" Bellarroth would declare. "What is Tammenallor to me?"

Tammenallor was a great cosmic monster, Hanin explained,

a living world...one of the mythological Kharathahul who were said to inhabit the spaces outside reality—manifestations of the deepest of human emotions. "You live upon its shoulders. It's no natural dwelling for men and women, rather a tomb and a prison...we're simply parasites and die in futility like the vermin we parody, trapped in the guilt we have ourselves provoked."

Bellarroth protested. "Guilt? I have nothing to be guilty about."

Hanin smiled at him with affection. "Not you, my son—no, you are born of this place. The guilt is not yours. It belongs to those who brought it from the first world." He sighed melodramatically. "But you inherit the consequences of their actions."

Bellarroth never understood the purpose of Hanin's teachings, nor did he question the source of the old man's knowledge. Only once had Hanin come close to that subject. "My son," he'd said, "you are my expiation. Responsibility lies heavy on my soul and somewhere a world laden with pain by my indulgence. I will pay the debt."

Bellarroth knew from this that Hanin had been one of those whose guilty acts had created Tammenallor and exiled them both onto the monster's vast shoulders. He did not understand what to do with the insight.

Once they talked of death, Bellarroth asking whether it was true that life did not end, that each person was formed around a grain of the Immortal Being. But Hanin spurned his questioning. "I'm neither a god nor a prophet. Don't ask me to delve beyond my mortal knowledge." He lowered himself into a crouching position and stared at Bellarroth with his disturbingly lambent eyes. "This I can tell you, son. I am a dealer in the arcane and I live in power. To one such as I life consists less of surface and matter than it does of spirit, and though I have spent many years and much error learning the cause and the course of things, it is still the unpredictable, the mystery, that most forcibly defines my experience. If I chose I could draw my life into the smallest part of me, and it would survive there, invulnerable to blade and disease. I can't be killed by mere attack upon the flesh. Something as malleable as the life that sustains me is not confined to flesh and space...truly it can resist the demands of time and the tyrannies of fate."

* * * * * * *

These thoughts were in Tashnark's mind when he awoke. He felt threatened by them. It was mid-morning, as he discovered when he approached the window, the street beyond its imperfect glass still damp from storms that had raged across the City during the night. Early light reflected in sharp yellow patterns from the wet stonework. He heard someone, probably his mother, moving about below.

Unwilling to risk communication at that moment, he dressed and left the house silently. The Skywave lay less than mid-firmament northward, its long scar of crackling energy sizzling the blue expanse white. Scattered clouds created bands of shadow. Around him, Koerpel-Na hummed—but suddenly it wasn't his city. It seemed an alien place, its densely packed building-squares, its park lands, and bustling streets and markets as bizarre as anything that haunted his dreams. More so. At that moment, it was as though the strange landscape that Bellarroth trod was more familiar, more a part of him, than this place where he lived his real life.

He trudged across the park behind his mother's house, then over the central Dehum-Rewi thoroughfare just north of the Temple of Shaa-Derthperrit. That building's imposing marble façade was expressionless and silent. A path wound past the Temple's vegetable plots and several large storage buildings, ending among a tussle of bushes and windblown trees on a small cliff overlooking the harbor. Tashnark sat at the edge and stared across the deep blue water, which only gave way to an illusory strip of gray land far off on the other side of the bay. Several merchant ships and a scattering of smaller craft glided over the choppy surface. Sometimes all Tashnark wanted to do was get on one of those ships and travel to somewhere else. He didn't know where.

Later, when his stomach told him he should eat, he headed back the way he'd come, dodging the produce carts going to and coming from the docks along the main street. His mother waited for him.

"Are you ill, Tashnark?" she asked. She was a small, compact woman, absurdly slight considering her son was so large. Tashnark looked at the delicate curves of her cheek bones and the fragility of her arms and wondered how the two of them could be related.

"Bad dreams last night," he said.

"Again? Won't you tell me about them?"

He put his arm around her shoulders, which were on a level with his chest, and squeezed gently. It was an affectionate gesture but also dismissive. "They're nothing," he commented.

She wouldn't let it go. "Dreams are never nothing. You need to understand them."

He moved away, toward the kitchen. "I know what they mean." She followed him; he could hear the skittish whisper of her feet on the boards. "My mind's restless. I think I've been here, doing nothing much, far too long."

"We've all told you that." She pushed past him as he grabbed a loaf of bread, taking it from him. The bread quickly became sandwiches filled with cold meat and a cold vegetable stew she'd obviously made sometime during the night before. She glanced up at him, her eyes hard and unforgiving among her fragile features. "I don't want to lose you, Tashnark, but you mustn't be consumed by this City's essential wastefulness."

"You want me to be a scholar, like you. But it's not in me."

"I want you to find out where you belong, that's all."

He took the sandwiches and retreated to the hearth room, where the atmosphere was closed off and shadowy. She didn't follow him. No fire was lit, but he sat in front of the hearth anyway, as though the memory of flame could warm him in places the real fire left cold.

CHAPTER TWO
ANCESTRAL CALL

i.

The alley was a dead end.

At first, the inebriated fat man hadn't noticed this fact. Shock had cleared some of the fuzziness from his head, but not enough to neutralize a full afternoon's drinking. He'd stumbled upon the opening and plunged in, desperately hoping it could hide him from his pursuer. The dagger he clutched in his hand had seemed little defense in the open street, but the alley's darkness reassured him.

Echoes of his padding feet, their rhythm fractured by a weakness in his left leg, came back to him from the rough brick walls to either side. By the time he realized his way was blocked, it was too late to hide. He glanced back. A dark shape slid toward him against the lighter background of the outer street. "What do you want?" Zeth-han cried. His gilded robe rustled loudly, his sandals scraped on the rocky dirt of the road, but the shadow said nothing. It was almost on top of him now, losing its outline in the darkness, growing larger as it joined with other shadows to become one terrible, formless mass.

"I have no money!" His words rebounded hollowly.

Out of the gloom, fingers like steel ropes clamped on his arm. Zeth-han screamed as his attacker's bulk clarified and the amorphous shadow became a face made of darkness. Gaunt and wasted, it looked like a thing long dead.

"No, please!" Zeth-han groaned. Pushing outward with his hand to fend off the attack, he struck the flesh of his attacker's chest. The skin was rough and cold, and gave way along the edge of a ragged cavity—as though the thing's heart had been torn out. For a moment, synchronicities reverberated in Zeth-han's mind and in his bones, even while fear fractured his thoughts. He remembered something...a living heart. But the cold memories slipped past him without clarifying. Night roared in his ears.

Zeth-han screamed again, thrashing out in a mindless panic, wanting to cut away the darkness and prove these events a nightmare. But though there was no awakening for him, there was reprieve. More by luck than design, the dagger he still clutched in his hand found the thing's cold flesh and plunged into it. The impact was hard, but the blade penetrated to the hilt.

As the dagger slipped from his fingers, Zeth-han was suddenly free. He staggered backward, hearing the heavy thud of his attacker's body on the stones and dirt. Hysteria churned in his throat and choked him, the wall shifted under his weight, and his empty hands scraped on the rough bricks. The metallic ornament he always wore on his wrist felt heavy and dragged at him, as though compelling him to follow his attacker to the ground. He forced himself in the opposite direction.

Long minutes passed before he escaped from the alley. He felt himself pulled back continually and had to fight for every step. His gimpy leg ached and his lungs were weak with exhaustion. Sweat dripped onto the damp road, as though the shadows were clinging to him. He glanced back once, but the alley was still.

In that moment of peace, memory of the disembodied human heart returned—a heart found beating in a funereal coffer on the penal island of Reyad. He had tried to forget he'd ever seen that object, for thought of it drove ice into his gut. Now, rebelliously, his memory held up one nightmare from his past against another in the present. This creature lacked a heart—he had found a beating heart on Reyad. Could they be connected? But his mind revolted from the idea. Too many years had faded behind him for the terrible discoveries of those days to find some fearful culmination now. Desperately, he drove the revelation deep into the dark beneath memory. Once, he recalled, he had been a penal governor, a man of power afraid of no one. Now, every shadow was his enemy.

He waited until he caught his breath, then got back on his feet and staggered for support against the wall on the opposite side of the main thoroughfare. An old sign there read 'Telfith's Mast'. Zeth-han looked into the night-sky for a hint of dawn.

He feared he would not survive to see it.

ii.

Remis found herself within another's body, a cold dead body that she could not control. It confined and oppressed her as it stepped through night-shadows, the damp of the streets stagnant at its feet. Now it had entered an alley, the brick expanse of walls to either side rough and dirty, abandoned to years of weathering. Remis...or the undead corpse she had become...leapt along the lanes, grabbing at the burning imprint that scored the air, the pain in its limbs driving them into fits of rage. But wherever the shape was when the corpse snatched at it—light before a darkened wall, glittering in a shaded doorway—it was gone as the thing reached the spot. It spun away like a fog-wisp before the corpse's grasp. Each time it grabbed at emptiness, the creature cried out, silently, in mingled despair and anger.

Then before it was a man whose eyes were wild with fear. He staggered, perplexed in misery and terror; when the corpse roared the man cried out and ran. A jagged glow lent its flame to his escape. In a frenzy of pain the undead corpse scrambled through Remis's dream, following the man, aching for explanation, aching for the thing that dogged his path. The roughness of the road went unnoticed beneath the corpse/Remis's feet. The man limped around a corner as the undead thing reached out, smashing the worn timber of a narrowing fence-line.

"What do you want of me?" the man yelled.

Corpse-Remis roared. The man held out his hand and there appeared between the creature and the man a specter, burning with unseen flames as its fingers snatched at the corpse's empty chest. It stepped back, afraid.

In sleep, Remis went rigid. Her muscles twitched as though her body were pricked by pins of fire. When the tension dissipated, the peacefulness of night infused her.

Her eyes flickered open. For a moment she saw only the night-dimmed forms of furniture and the wood-frame of the room. She puzzled briefly over the strange vividness of the dream, searching through her study-memory for some way to interpret its meaning. But movement swept these conceptions away before they were formed. A dim figure stood near the door, barely visible among the shadows. Remis gripped her blanket tightly, but the shade did not move. Remis blinked, doubting her eyes. Clear contours were lost in the speckled darkness.

"Who's there?" she asked it.

No answer. She sat up, straining to focus her eyes on the place where she imagined the shape to be. Was it possible it was just an after-image of vivid dream?

Then the figure was near her, leaning. She had not seen it move. She stifled a scream in the base of her throat. "Please!" she whispered instead, fearful that her voice might goad the phantom into some ghostly act.

In the faint light that drifted through the window, carried on a breeze that chilled the sweat on her skin, Remis could see the phantom's face, white and bony, framed in a distinctive square-cut beard, the lips moving in silent speech. When she saw the opaque whiteness of its eyes she knew it was no mortal visitor. Numinous terror tightened her neck muscles. "What do you want?" she whispered.

The specter said something, but it was dim and without force, not driven by fleshly lungs. There was pain in it. Her shock and involuntary superstition dissipating, Remis realized that this was no ghost either, but rather an image sent to her from elsewhere. It was a message. "You want my help?" she said. It nodded. "Why did you come to me?"

The figure made hand-movements in the air, speaking in study-signs. It spelt out the words, "You are Valarl—blood-link." What did that mean? Was she related to this phantom? But there was no time; she let speculation pass. Later. The sending was barely visible in the gloom.

"How will I find you?" she asked.

The figure reached out a translucent hand and touched her. In her mind she gazed along a darkened alley, the road-stones wet with dew and mist. Beyond the alley ran another, larger thoroughfare. A painted sign, unclear in the distant fog, read: "Telfith's Mast".

"I'll come," she said. Instantly the image faded.

Remis rubbed her eyes, which were sore and strained. Her mind felt dried out, as though its edges had been brushed by the passing of some dusty desert wind. She wondered whether she had dreamt the encounter, though she knew quite well she hadn't. Someone was in an alley off the Street of Telfith's Mast; they had called to her, psychically, seeking aid. They were, or had once been, her kin. These things seemed clear.

Quietly she slipped out of bed and dressed.

iii.

Night in Koerpel-Na was generally a dreary, sordid thing—a poor substitute for the clean expanse of natural darkness that night became in the outer lands where he'd been born. Arhl Mogarni lay on the flat baked-clay roof of his workrooms and let nostalgia and sorrow take him.

Life had not been easy of late. Talking to his neighbor, Remis Sarsdarl—even if briefly and without much engagement—had brought the difficulty of it to the forefront of his mind again. Now he was having trouble sending it back into a darker place where it could be accepted without morbid self-loathing. What was his life? Little work, no money, few prospects. His landlord was threatening to have him evicted. He'd had to lay off his apprentice, though he'd kept the lad on beyond his ability to pay proper wages, hoping the situation would change. It hadn't, and fulfilling his obligations to the youth had been hard. He had to face the truth: his business was almost dead. All in all, Arhl felt strongly that he had failed, as he always failed, and could see no clear way forward. This fact saddened and infuriated him.

Yet he knew that thinking this way was pointless.

Despite himself, however, he let the worries and self-doubt continue to surge through his thoughts, giving them free rein. Sometimes it was necessary to experience the full gamut, to allow emotions to grow, to rage against the inevitable, even though in the end such indulgence might be a sign of weakness. Arhl was tired of being strong. In that, too, he was a failure. So, for a while, he would let himself be weak; he would succumb to self-indulgent recriminations and pathetic complaint, and after a time it would pass, returning him to his life of stoic acceptance.

Wind guttered through the eves below him and rattled at some loose metal sheeting there. A dog barked in the distance, the sound wild and ominous. Above, the sky grew suddenly clearer than usual, free of smoke and the filth of local industries. Residual light snaked through the blackness, forming into patterns he couldn't decipher.

Breathing slowly and more easily now, Arhl felt his body closing down toward sleep.

But something—a movement nearby—jerked him awake again. Skin across his scalp tingled. The night seemed thicker about him, its breath plucking at his face.

"Who's there?"

Silhouetted against the sky, a figure sat on his roof with him, knees drawn up, staring out across the City. How had his visitor climbed up without Arhl noticing? Instinctively he made to draw himself further away, but some familiarity in the size and shape of the figure stopped him. It was a woman, he saw.

Her hair was long and plaited, and her clothes made of fur and roughly woven dyeless fibre, after the tribal fashion of his own people. Leather strapping around her waist and over her shoulders were the accoutrements of a hunter. Arhl sniffed at the air, which should have carried her human scent to his sensitive nostrils. But there was only the smell of coming rain and smoke residue from his own forge.

He swallowed back a groan. He knew this woman and he knew what her appearance here, now, might mean.

"Mother?" he whispered.

The woman turned. At that moment night-light shimmered above and lit her features dimly. She had the hard, pale youthfulness Arhl remembered from so long ago. Within her eye sockets, however, there lay an ancient darkness.

"You've come to me again," Arhl remarked, his voice weak with ghostly anticipation.

You are my son. The bond between us is infinite. Why wouldn't I come to you when danger stirs about you and your world is threatened?

The fear Arhl harbored grew more resonant in the hollow of his chest. Mogarni had come to him like this before, several times, since her hunting death long ago when he had been a mere cub. Each time, the comfort she offered had done little to bring him peace. Were others haunted by their dead kin like this? He didn't know, because he was always too afraid to ask them. He suspected it was not common. There was a strain of psychic doom within his people that would have marginalized him even further had the inhabitants of this City known about it—a link to the Deep Powers of the world that led, inevitably, to death or madness. It had destroyed his father...in the end it had fractured his tribe. Perhaps, too, it had driven Arhl himself to come to Koerpel-Na, seeking a purpose that was tangible and this-worldly. Why must his past haunt him like this?

"What do you want?" he snapped, annoyed at the injustice.

I know what you fear, my son. I know I am not welcome in your life—not like this, not as a ghost. But I'm in you and can't be ignored. I'm a part of you that lies so deep in your soul you rarely hear its whispers. Yet I'm more in tune with the currents of the world than you can imagine—and I see what's around you, ache with the pain of it. I won't be silent.

"Say what you must say then."

She smiled gently, like a memory from his infancy.

Watch the one you care about, the woman with Power.

"Remis Sarsdarl? What are you talking about?"

She is at the center of a storm. She will need your help.

He pushed himself up and crawled toward his mother's ghost, forgetting his fear now. Strangely the movement brought him no nearer to her. "What do you mean? How is she in danger?"

Ancient currents are converging. Vast, dangerous currents. At such a time, even the simplest of actions may be vital to the survival of all. You must be alert. Watch her! Stay near to her.

"Can't you tell me more? What's happening?"

I have no more to tell. That is all I can see, and all that you can know. Guard her and you guard your own future.

And suddenly Arhl was alone on the roof, lying in the spot where he'd been all along, staring into the clear, flickering night sky. He sat up and looked about himself wildly.

"Remis!" he whispered, speaking the name as though the sound of it would bring her to him. When nothing happened, he frowned but continued to scan the darkened city, his breathing labored in the aftermath of the visitation.

iv.

The night was clear and still. Winds gathering earlier had swept away the clouds and then gone with them into stillness. The dark firmament twitched with light-residue. Remis watched a brighter trail weave its dim pattern and spend itself as soon as formed. "Now where was Telfith's Street?" she whispered to herself, trying to remember. She had a vague recollection that it was near the southern docks.

She headed in that direction, assuming an easy running pace. Uncharacteristically, the City was quiet and still. As she entered Than-Rewi, the main road through to the largest bridge to cross over the City-dissecting Antelon river, she found its emptiness unnerving. Her boots were noisy on the hardened surface, creating strange and sometimes distant echoes that made her feel as though she were being followed. The first time a human figure appeared ahead of her—in all likelihood a worker headed home from the inner harbor docks—his featureless presence sent fear like ice into her heart.

When the Than-Rewi thoroughfare reached the Circle, she followed its eastern branch toward the Antelon crossing. This led her past the Yucartel Chambers where Family members and their political visitors slept peacefully—no lights burned in street-facing windows and the forecourt was empty. The ornately filigreed Law Courts, too, remained silent and apparently unoccupied, except for a partially visible guard, standing in the umbra of the stone archway that defined the Courts' main entrance. Remis approached cautiously, trying not to startle him. "May I ask you a question?" she said, unsure of the protocol.

His eyes were not visible in the shadows under his plumed headgear. "What do you want?" his low voice rumbled.

"Directions to a street called Telfith's Mast. It's very important." She felt absurdly concerned to justify speaking to him.

"Telfith's?" His left arm rose. "Continue along here till you reach a square. There's an open grassed area in its center—with a statue...ugly thing. Some hero or other. On the other side of the square, take the road veering south-west. Telfith's leads off this road. Look for a large mast."

"Thank you."

"My pleasure." He leaned closer suddenly, so she could see his eyes. They were benign. "You shouldn't be wanderin' about down there this time of night. It's not safe."

"I'll be careful."

He grunted, then stood upright again.

* * * * * * *

Some time later Remis entered an old-fashioned dirt-covered street, dark brick storage buildings squatting silently along its length. Further on there were more decorative façades indicating shops and an occasional tenement, but at this time of night the street was deserted. The Mast could be seen at its far end, over Telfith's, the shipwright.

During the visitation, she had been shown an alley, opposite a painted sign. She walked further along, peering into the few alleys that disappeared into dark shadows off the street. At last she stopped beneath an old, weathered board, on which some careful hand had written 'Telfith's Mast'. There was an alley opposite. She turned and gazed into the tenebrous murk of the alley's depth, straining her eyes to see through the gloom.

She couldn't blunder in blind. The alley was so thin the overhanging shingles of buildings on each side effectively blocked out what diffused light came from the night-sky. Thick shadows made her nervous.

Standing before the alley's mouth, Remis made a few discreet ritualistic gestures with her hands. She began to recite the Lunist-Kan Chant for night-vision—and after a moment, as her words focused the Deep Power in her, her eyes acquired a steely aura. Darkness slipped away for her, as though sucked into the surrounding brickwork. Now she could see what appeared to be a body lying at the alley's rear, perhaps a hundred paces from where she stood. Beyond it the alley ended abruptly at a rough stone wall.

Maintaining clear vision by the continued recitation of the Chant, Remis walked slowly down the alley, concentrating power through the channeling crystal she wore around her neck—the *cerenil* that had been formed over the whole period of her magical training, a solid reflection of her own advancement. It took a lot of concentration, for the Chant drained her and demanded a large proportion of her attention. To minimize the weakness she felt stealing over her, she modified the spell, though this diminished the clarity of her vision. Darkness crept over the alley again, as though a gray twilight were falling. A grainy sheen further dirtied the stones and walls.

Lines of blackness that were probably some clinging vine covered the dead end stone-block wall ahead. Glimmer showed that its base was damp, watered by drainage from the roofs. Piles of refuse were scattered all around. They stank. The loose rocks and dirt beneath her feet seemed broken and decayed.

Her legs tingling with weariness, Remis stopped a pace from the body she had already seen from the distance. It was a man, sprawled on his back and naked, limbs twisted into a caricature of some epileptic spasm. The hilt of a dagger protruded from the corpse's chest. She was too late to help him. She glanced around nervously, fearful of spying the murderer.

But the alley was empty apart from herself. She knelt. The shadows became deeper as her will faded. Her spell muttering continued as an undercurrent, blurred further by echo from the walls.

The first thing she noticed was that there was no blood around the blade in the man's chest and none pooling on the ground beneath him—none that her failing vision revealed anyway. Admittedly the dirt was wet, but she saw no evidence of a thicker, bloody pooling. Where his heart should have been was a large dry cavity. His heart had been removed, it seemed, and without a drop of blood spilling out around the wound.

She reached forward, running her fingers over the man's skin. It was as cold as the dirt he was lying on. Not an hour had passed since she received the Call and the caller hadn't been dead then. How could he be so cold and bloodless now? This thing reminded her not of the phantom that had called her, but of the undead corpse that had raced through her dream—only this one did not move.

This was no time to ask such questions, she decided at last. Her sight had darkened to the extent that the alley was nearly as obscured as it had been originally. Remis' muscles ached with the effort. Moreover, to be found bending over a murdered man in this part of the City was to be found guilty of the crime. She wondered what the guard at the Law Courts' entrance would think, if he caught her here like this.

There was nothing she could do. But the experience required study and given her expertise, it was the dagger in the man's chest—the murder weapon—that was most likely to yield some answers, however tentative. She had to study it. She could look into its substance and read its history. Ceasing her chant, she took the dagger by the handle and tried to pull it from the body's chest. The corpse shifted, but the knife remained where it was.

Adjusting her stance in order to get better leverage, she placed both hands around the hilt and pulled. Still the blade refused to release the dead flesh. Full darkness had returned now, though she could see better in the dark than she'd been able to before utilising the chant. Details were lost and the dead man was a thick shadow, but she wasn't blind.

She concentrated and forced a release spell through her oddly reluctant lips.

The knife slid out abruptly. The suddenness caused Remis to stagger back. She regained her balance, staring at the strange snaking double-blade that she held. It was too dark for her to make out details. Night seemed to congeal, as though the air was alive with movement. It concentrated directly in front of her. Remis felt a chill that was almost solid stab into her chest.

The corpse rose stiffly, flexing its arms in the snake-thick air.

Remis tried to edge away—wanting to run from the fear and unreality of her dream realized—but instead found herself motionless, mind numb with cold. The creature's hand jerked out and thudded against her shoulder. She staggered, though it hadn't been a hard push. Almost a touch after all. Its body was sinewy with tense muscle and suppressed power.

"Who are you?" Remis asked it.

It remained mute. Remis found herself staring into eyes devoid of life. Deeper within them perhaps, further than she could see unaided, a life was trapped in the decaying flesh.

"Are you the one who called me?" She tried to send the words on a psychic level as well. Still it neither answered nor ran from her. Movement like an involuntary twitch shivered through its limbs.

"Please—"

Its hand pointed. The dagger. Remis gripped it before her, unconsciously prepared to use the weapon. The creature might have been staring at it, conveying a message she didn't understand. Was it dangerous?

"This...knife...." Remis raised it and the creature drew away, "...did it hold you? You needed it to be taken out of your flesh?"

The dead man stood unmoving.

"The man in you, who you once were, before undeath claimed you, is he here? Can I speak to him?"

There was no answer, as she knew there wouldn't be. The man this corpse had been—the man she'd seen in her sleep—was visible in the hard lines and stony lifelessness of the dead face, but what had come for her help had been a shadow, the last traces of a trapped spirit. The dagger, which had to be an enchanted one, would be a talisman designed to simulate true death in the corpse, to hold it immobile. Yet the creature had desired release so that the false death with which it was cursed could achieve some end unknown to her. Once she'd taken the dagger from its chest, the creature's undead life had returned.

And with that realization, its gaunt hand touched her again. In a moment the undead creature was roaring—soundlessly. As though there was nothing in it to come out.

Then it turned and sped down the tunnel of darkness into the open road beyond. Turned left. Was gone. Ahead of it, and in its wake, surged a wave of power that almost overwhelmed her. It had told her what it had wanted her to know, and now it had returned to whatever business obsessed it.

Remis' knees buckled. She sank to the rocky dirt of the alley, its irregular surface somehow reassuring. Her heart was pounding and blood hissed in her ears. The runic pattern on the dagger felt like a warning as she pressed her fingers against it.

"I don't know what you're after," she whispered, staring into the night, "but I intend to find out."

Remis was not overly superstitious, but nor was she fool enough to lightly dismiss the weirdness of this night and the awful reality of the unliving corpse. Was it coincidence that all her plans—the vision that had governed her life for so long—had in the lead-up to this moment been all but squeezed from her? On the Rheateeshan Continent children were instructed that all were caught in the net of Junsar's Curse. Junsar's Curse was Fate, the inevitable deterioration supposed to have resulted from the actions of the primeval God, Junsar. Remis knew the tale well: Junsar was one of the original creators of the world, set to define the world's end limits, and hence the shape of being. But doubt and fear had entered his heart and Junsar, hoping to build a safer place for himself with its power, stole a husk of the cosmic Seed from which the world had been grown. The Seed-husks, or kartoranth, were to be placed at the opposite ends of the world to define a space in which the fallen god Errellinarth could be re-made. This was the world, Tharenweyr, as they knew it. The Far Kartoranth, which Junsar stole, was intended to fix the lower limit of Tharenweyr. Instead of saving himself, therefore, Junsar warped the world, and the result was Fate.

Now, in these events that had touched her life, Remis could smell more than a whiff of Fatefulness.

v.

Remis had not been alone with the undead corpse that night. Another had been watching from back in the shadows—a tall, strong figure dressed in the robes of a sorcerer: Aridor—senior Acolyte of the Yanuran Lord Worjaren Rehemon. He was an intense, thoughtful man, and soon his thoughts would be turned toward Remis.

At first, however, standing under Telfith's Mast, Aridor had seen nothing out of the ordinary, despite the omens that had brought him there. He'd thought he was alone, as he preferred it. The street ran before him into darkness, empty and damp with rain. On one side there was a stone wall; on the other, brick warehouses and slat-fronted shops. Smears of blackness along the way were alleys and lanes leading nowhere.

He began to walk down the street, staying close to the shop façades for protection from the rain and watching eyes. His breathing was slightly labored. He was very tired. This day, like many of his days before it, had been spent in an outer-circle reading room of the Hassur libraries, where he sought to refresh his memory of undead lore. For according to his master Lord Worjaren Rehemon, an undead creature lay at the center of their search for the legendary artifact known as the Cerendar. They had heard whispers of its presence, tales of the disturbances that attended its arrivals and equally sudden departures—always hints of the all-powerful Cerendar were found in its wake.

"Whatever this thing may be," Lord Worjaren had said to Aridor, "this much is clear: it is pursuing the Cerendar, mind-lessly, as the birds pursue the Spring, with a perception no other being in all the world can claim. The Cerendar is hidden even from the searches of the bright gods of Tharenweyr—the Guardian Raashyr—but this creature sees it. It will find the artifact because it must, and we must be there when it does. Of that you can never doubt."

Lord Worjaren Rehemon was clearly obsessed with finding the artifact called Cerendar. Aridor knew that, had known for many years—but he had never before seen him this intensely insistent. It was as though he smelled the nearness of the legendary object on the wind.

Why did Lord Worjaren want it so much? For the incredible power it was said to wield? Wasn't such foolish avarice a weakness?

Lord Worjaren's authority within the Yanuran court, and the sorcerous influence he controlled, ensured that Aridor would never allow his dedication to flag or his mouth to utter treachery, whatever his mind might whisper. But the doubts were there nevertheless, gnawing at his belief.

Tonight, returned from the Libraries, he had lain in his room within the Yucartel Chambers and indulged his pessimism. A year had passed since Eblamthezaik, the Ormsinir of Dark God Lord Huedaik, had come in his demonic glory and purged the royal Court of Dagest-Yanu of those harboring treachery in their hearts and, dare he say it, doubt in their souls. The demi-god had spoken of the victory possible through the Cerendar and urged all Huedaik's disciples to join the search for it. With many others, Aridor and his master Worjaren had sniffed out the clues. But where had it led them? To this decadent city. To stagnation. To despair.

Yet, tonight, his dreams had been of an undead creature and of the Cerendar. It was nearby—of that he was sure. Just out of his reach. He woke with the images in his mind. He knew the time had come. He felt it. From a guard at the front gate of the Chambers, he learned of a woman who had passed in the night, looking for the Street of Telfith's Mast. Though it seemed irrational and insignificant, he had known at once that his search must focus on that woman. He stood now in the Street of Telfith's Mast in order to prove his intuition true.

"Are you the one who called me!" The voice was clear and strong—too strong to be only in his ears. Someone was drawing upon the Deep Powers.

A shadow moved in the shifting darkness. Aridor ran forward a pace, but a continuation of the movement he had already seen caught him unawares. It was like a tidal-wave in a rock canal, pushing the sea into furious eddies. He saw it sweep out of an alleyway ahead of him and knew instantly it was too late to avoid it. When it hit him he staggered physically, though the wave was no material disturbance. It was a thing of the spirit.

His mind reeled. He was afraid. Burning pitch was foul in his nostrils.

Something struck him a blow to the side of his head. It felt like a fist.

"Shut up, boy!"

He was kneeling in the dirt. A large, warty face leered at him. One of the raiders that had appeared from the sea.

"Tanuul!"

It was important that he ignore his father's voice. They were killing the old man and Aridor could do nothing to help him. To hear the pain would only harm himself.

"Help me, Tanuul!"

There were blows and his father screamed. Aridor collapsed face down, covering his ears with his hands.

But his arms were grabbed and the sounds flooded back.

"You'll hear," a voice snarled. "You'll hear it all."

The images of his own past—the death of his father at the hand of raiders—collapsed into darkness. Aridor leaned against rough stone as the night fractured again.

"Take it!"

A creature like a man stood before him, its flesh dry and decayed. Aridor knew it was dead—no longer a man, but merely the animated shell of a man.

"Take it!"

The undead creature reached out, its fingers scraping Aridor's face.

It was in his mind, but he cringed and suddenly was in the street again.

Light flared. For a moment, clearly, he saw a bright, jagged shape burn out of the darkness—as though the night were a gray fabric that had been shredded by the creature's fingers. The light was coming from a place far beyond the world he knew. It was from outside, where the real and the imagined blended together and became infinitely powerful.

He recognized the shape of the light.

Cerendar! he cried. His voice echoed in the street. A creature was before him for a moment, real this time, looming out of the darkness of the alley's mouth. Grotesque. Decayed. It did not see him. He fell back and collapsed onto the cobbled road. When he looked up it was gone.

The night fell silent, though there had been no real sound made, apart from the scraping of feet on stone and dirt. Aridor blinked into a mist of fine rain. The Street of Telfith's Mast was empty. He made himself stand, his body weak. The wave of Deep Power had come from the alleyway—not an attack upon him, but a spell-residue to which his sensibilities had made him vulnerable. The creature, too, had come from the alley.

Aridor reached the wooden fence at the corner of the alleyway and peered cautiously into its shadows. Gathering the last vestiges of his strength, he extended his sight to push aside the darkness.

He saw a woman. She walked along the alley, studying something held in her hands, too distracted, hopefully, to notice his magic.

In that instant Aridor's knees began to buckle under him, but he forced himself to stay upright. The woman had to be followed.

His consciousness drifted in and out of shadows. With an effort he made it into a doorway before he lost control. He fell heavily and for a while there was nothing.

When he woke, mere moments later, the woman was far down the street, but still visible. Aridor staggered up.

A dull stream of rust-blue whiteness was draining out across the firmament, catching fire on the damp air and igniting clouds in the north. Behind it, in about half an hour, would come its source, *Taal-Numid*, the Skywave that brought day with it, a pulse of intense iridescence that stretched in a cosmic bow from the west to the east and moved steadily southward over the world toward the home of his Dark Gods at the end of the world. Soon it would be full dawn, and the City would wake.

Aridor stood, his head throbbing. Images of the undead creature and of the Cerendar were clear in his mind. He took a step. It was difficult, but the one that came after was easier. Then another. He began to run, staggering unsteadily, before the woman disappeared from sight.

He knew the importance of this effort he was making. The undead creature. This woman whom he assumed could control it. Surely in them was the secret to finding the legendary

Cerendar. The connections seemed obvious.

His Master would be pleased.

In this way, the woman's fate and that of Aridor—and beyond him, that of his master Lord Worjaren Rehemon—had became entwined. There could be no turning back from this.

Gathering his determination, Aridor hurried on.

CHAPTER THREE
SKIRMISHES

i.

Once again Bellarroth stood before Hanin's body, which lay tangled in a mass of serpent-weeds. Despair numbed Bellarroth's limbs.

Torn and bloody, bones stripped of flesh, his mentor appeared to be dead.

But, as Bellarroth had often found yet frequently failed to remember, appearance counted for little in this mercurial place.

<Take the skull. There is little time.>

When he heard Hanin's voice, Bellarroth did not pause to contemplate what it might mean. The old man had trained him well. Instead he wrenched aside the strands of hair that had begun to grip his own limbs. He swung his blade like a scythe and, avoiding any futile attempt to free Hanin's now-useless bones, let it sever the bony cartilage of the old man's neck. It was an intuitive act and felt right. Serpents turned toward him as though awakened by an alarm he couldn't hear. He grabbed the gored skull and scuttled out of their reach. The heat of Lucishnor ripped across his face like a burning wind, he fell, felt a stab of pain as a small serpent-weed sank its fangs into his arm. Wind roared as he rolled away, a larger serpent crashing to the ground where he'd been. It writhed, but the heat and its misjudgment had broken it.

"Where to, Hanin? The storm is fierce."

He gripped the slimy hardness of the skull, feeling thick liquid dripping down his arm.

A gust of wind lifted him from the ground. Patches of old, dried hair were smoldering in the heat. He struggled up yet again, seeking a place to hide. Much depended on respite, but there was nowhere safe in a living forest, attacked by monstrous winds and escalating firestorm.

Soon the forest-growth grew so thick that passage seemed impossible. Bellarroth was close to the base of Koroom-head now, aware of a pulsing beneath his feet, evident even through the winds—the life-blood of Tammenallor, spurting upward to feed the monster's brain. Bellarroth made his way around the obstruction, keeping his distance from the tendrils of the forest-mass, but found no end. It went on and on, encircling the neck of Koroom in a protective collar of serpent-trees and living mesh.

"I must rest," he groaned, collapsing onto the rough skin. Hanin's severed skull regarded him silently. He gripped it and held it before his face. "Hanin, what is to be done?"

Answer, if any, was obliterated by a shattering thunder. The sound rushed out of the sky and ripped through the forest, drowning all other noise and plunging deep into Bellarroth's soul. He cried out in pain. A tremendous wall of flame disintegrated the distance and raised blisters on all the exposed parts of his body. Lucishnor had attacked.

The ground rose under Bellarroth and threw him violently across its corrugations. Above him, screened by a haze of fire, the Koroom-head was roaring its agony. Ripples of contorted flesh swept through the forest, tearing down serpents and opening cracks in the skin. Bellarroth was aware of a moment of torture and a flood of thick, liquid heat, then his consciousness lapsed into a realm of dream.

He dreamt of Sevthen Ulart-Tashnark.

* * * * * * *

"Tashnark, Tashnark, wake up!" Someone was shaking

him. He glanced through early-morning light, tossing aside the images of darkness—serpent-trees, a monstrous landscape, the inevitability of destruction. "You were screaming," said Ishwarin.

"Was I?"

"Mother said you dream a lot."

"So what if I do?" He shoved his brother aside and stood. His bare skin stung as though burnt.

"So maybe you should talk to someone about it."

"It's mind-shit, that's all," Tashnark said. "Dreams and fantasies." He strode from the room, bumping into the wall as he did.

"It's a mistake to ignore such things," Ishwarin shouted after him.

"Don't harass me!"

He splashed cold water over his face, relishing the sharp muscular spasm it brought on. Tension began to dissipate.

"So you're telling me I should mind my own business." Ishwarin stood behind him, startling him with the sudden intrusion.

"Yes, damn it!"

"On all matters relating to you?"

"For god's sake, leave me alone."

Ishwarin nodded in a self-conscious, smug manner that indicated he had something else on his mind. "Okay, I guess I wasted my time chasing up that woman you wanted to find."

"You found her?"

"Pity you don't want to know about it." Ishwarin began to turn away, but his brother's large hand shot out and collected a loose fistful of his shirt. Tashnark slammed him against the bathroom wall. Ishwarin laughed, careless of Tashnark's aggression, even though his lean stature made him appear frail. He reached into his pocket. "Her name's Remis Sarsdarl—and she's on Lanaris's want-list right now." He handed Tashnark a scrap of paper. On it, in his rigid handwriting, was an address.

"Arlon's Rest? Where the hell's that?"

"Near the Inner Harbor. It's a tavern. Surely you know it.

Haven't you been thrown out of every alehouse in the City?"

Tashnark let him go, ignoring the insult. "She lives in a tavern?"

"On the street named after it."

"How'd you find this out?"

Ishwarin tapped the side of his nose smugly. "Contacts. What else?" He chuckled. "I figured she was a recent graduate. The Seminary was able to identify her easily enough."

Tashnark suddenly felt dizzy. He sat down and clutched at his forehead.

"Are you sure you're okay?" Ishwarin's hand rested on his shoulder. His tone was no longer ironic.

Tashnark glanced up at him, but he said nothing.

* * * * * * *

Arlon's Rest was a pleasant enough tavern—cleaner and more up-market than *The Night Binge* at any rate. At the moment quieter, too. Tashnark downed some of its more potent spirits, seeking courage. Or conviction. Perhaps both.

There was a lazy hum of conversation that wandered from group to group, gathering a word or two at each. It was very ordinary, a daylight scene with no unwonted overtones. Tashnark found it annoyed him—partly because he was alone and the communal noise emphasized the fact, and partly because his ordinary life seemed to be disappearing behind a fog of obsession and weird dreams.

He remained there for several hours, brooding over what to do. Logic and past experience told him to go home and forget it. That he had tracked down this Remis Sarsdarl was bad enough—that his brother had helped made him feel worse. And was it coincidence that the dreams of Bellarroth were intensifying?

Somewhere in a dimmer corner of *Arlon's Rest* a singer was playing a lute and sending his high counter-tenor voice drifting through the failing light:

"Olden storms, ageing wind-lust,
Sugar bitter, sweetness tart;
Where lies that maiden turned to death-dust,
Whose winsome ways have slain my heart?"

Tashnark listened for a while and the song made him melancholy. When he became aware of the emotion, he ground his fingers into the wood of the table. What in god's name was this Remis to him? *I don't even know her*, he thought. *At my age, is the mere sight of a woman good enough reason for this sickness of the heart?*

He began to mumble a different tune under his breath:

"A maiden's heart, a maiden's bed
Is all the bliss I'll need:
And when I've got her maidenhead,
A mug of sturdy mead."

A fat woman at a nearby table looked at him with a frown. He growled, not at her but as a sort of general defiance.

ii.

The dagger proved to be ancient and complex. Reading its past was difficult. Remis concentrated an analytical web of Deep Power into the substance of it, drawing her magic through the metal and back into herself, and thereby experiencing something of its history.

The knowledge was harsh. It burned in her mind.

* * * * * * *

There was a corpse.
She was the corpse, the corpse was her.
Darkness. Silence. These two sensations interwove and lay

heavily on her. It was tomb-like, though Remis/the corpse knew nothing of tombs.

There was a sense of struggle as well, as though she fought something, pitting her strength against a desire to move. Pain spilt on her. No direct experience, this, but an infusion from elsewhere.

Vibrations rattled through the impossibly viscous substance surrounding her. Light, a dim shade that tinted the dust. The air moved. Humans had come. They spoke.

"What's this about, Theor-Wal? What've you had us doing?"

"Never mind. Just follow orders."

"I ain't goin' into no death-house. The rock stinks of ghosts."

Grumbles of assent. Scraping sounds and a tremor of movement. Remis/the corpse began to struggle against the bonds that held back her strength.

"We go down now or you can spend a few weeks in the lock-up."

"You're a damn belly-scraper, Wal!"

More vibrations, scratching heard as though under water. The light was artificial.

"What's that?"

"Seems like a corpse."

Harder movement, growing into the heat of proximity.

"What the hell's it doing here on the floor? How'd it get out of the coffin?"

"Grave robbers maybe."

"Heart's been cut out."

"What?"

"I said the damn heart's been cut out!"

"I don't like this."

"Still got the bloody knife stuck in it."

"How long you reckon it's been here?"

"Who knows and who cares? Leave it. We've other stuff to find. It'll rot fast enough now the doors are opened." Movement. The light shifted. "Check the coffins!"

"Not me."

"Check them, you goddamn coward—or the Warden'll have your guts."

"He can have 'em."

"Okay, okay. I'll look in the fuckin' coffins m'self, you damn coward."

More movement. Curses. The voices of men as they found substances in casks—powders, ashes, the detritus of ancient lives.

"Nothing, damn it."

"What about the dagger? Looks fancy enough to be worth something."

"Good idea."

The touch of living warmth. She felt a panic that had no human immediacy, but was the cold, material feeling of rightness violated.

Suddenly the pressure of struggle was gone. Now there was the pain of loss. Remis/the corpse moved.

"Wal! It's alive!"

Desire and pain mingled into a cry that echoed soundlessly through air and stone. Matter screamed. So did the human voices. There was violence and blood.

* * * * * * *

Remis recovered slowly from the Spell-casting, her mind re-arranging images of wall and bench and apparatus into a form that made sense. Her cluttered workroom surroundings became familiar once more.

Analysis of the dagger had led her deeper and deeper into esoteric Spell-lore. Layer upon layer of visionary matter unraveled, and a terrible history that the substance of the dagger itself was loathe to recall. Determinedly she had pursued the knowledge, utilizing at last a barely familiar series of divinations called the Lore of Open Matter. This lore delved into the deep substance of an object and allowed the diviner to experience any memories the object's matter held. It was a grueling and dangerous use of the Deep Powers—and it had drained her.

The rites had, however, uncovered a well of visions, intermeshed patterns of sense, emotion and spirit, as though some elemental moment had been forced to open itself utterly and spill, like water onto thirsty soil, upon a timeless wasteland of histories. Her efforts revealed one thing for certain: the dagger's past was complex and tumultuous.

But more than that, her delvings had revealed patterns that she recognized, human patterns that represented an infusion into the substance of the dagger itself. Such a thing was rare. It was a level of power binding that her studies had touched on and dismissed as possible only in some distant past—perhaps indeed merely as myth. Yet, she was sure she had evidence of it here before her. And what amazed her was that she knew the pattern, had come across it before—in her dreams. The vision that had led her to the undead creature in the alley had contained elements in common with the pattern she was seeing in the substance of the dagger itself, as though...she wasn't sure. Could it be that the dim, undying sentience that had called her—the undead creature—was also an integral part of the dagger? Were the two somehow bound together by their nature?

It seemed so. But what really scared her was another level of recognition, a wispy thread of identity that suggested her own ancestral make-up. The creature and the dagger were intricately connected, but she, too, was tied to them both, as she had suspected. Tenuously, it was true—she was not bound in the same way, not as directly, and the indications were slight. But it was there. *You are Valarl—blood-link*, the vision had signaled to her. She and the undead creature were related, perhaps over centuries of time. If this were true, it explained why the creature had been able to send its spirit to her over such distance. Their blood was a bridge that connected them across time and space.

Somehow, she was meant to have this dagger.

And *that* was a sobering thought.

Wearily Remis staggered from the room, wondering vaguely what time it was. Day had faded under wintry weather. Seeking to relieve her throbbing head, she wandered out the front door. It was only midday, but the street had become windswept, chilling gusts spiraling down the cobbled way and driving citizens into sheltered corners. The air was rich with brine. Remis imagined the dark, crested waves churned up in the Inner Harbor, the merchant caravels moving in agitation.

A gust battered her coldly, like pin-pricks on her skin, and worried hair into her eyes. She returned inside, very sleepy and very hungry. The afterglow of lightning flared on one of the skylights of her workroom as she entered it, and a moment later dim thunder shook the air. Large rain-drops splattered heavily on the roof.

Remis found some bread and drew water from her storage barrel, then she sat at her workbench to eat and drink. The dagger was there, and an open volume of spellbinding lore. She read the words:

> New patterns must be sealed into the inner form of the object, stamped with the signature of the Worker. That none other than the one with knowledge of the binding may release the Deep Power hidden there it is vital that the Worker understand the manner in which the forms of original matter and imposed pattern interweave, and seek in his formulation to obscure evidence of Locking.... Secrecy maintains a maximum hope of correct usage, though the danger remains that an incomplete fulfillment of the Unlocking conditions may result in disaster....

Remis shut the book. Natural locking could be as tricky as the locks imposed by a Worker. To some degree, untouched matter was tougher to break into, insofar as the patterns that kept it bound did not necessarily follow the logic patterns of humanity.

Yet in the world's beginning, when magic was spontaneous, there would have been no secrecy, she thought. Once, the world had been open. It was deterioration, the movement toward the world's end, that locked knowledge away from curious eyes and made magic a discipline rather than a natural ability.

She picked up the dagger and examined the intricate lines etched into its surface. Were the clues to its secrets there? Remis knew that in opening this dagger to her mind-probes she had touched the edge of something profound and dangerous. What the nature of that something was, she was only beginning to guess—but it had to do with necromancy, and that was a Deep Power usage not simply forbidden to her, but repugnant as well. Undeath perverted both life and death—a secret born of corruption. That it intrigued her nevertheless, at the same time as she had uncovered indications of her blood link to the necromancer, was something she preferred not to think about.

iii.

When he tired of the tavern and himself, Tashnark went into the gloomy afternoon and wandered along the street. It was futile, stupid, conducive of melancholy, but easy, too. It allowed his mind to explore a landscape of pointless details—wind that gathered in alleyways and thrashed at stone cornices, dribbling its residue down supporting brickwork; edgeless shadows that joined and spread from shop fronts and under the awnings of houses, threatening to consume the whole street; seabirds struggling to stay aloft, as though the earth dragged at them. He wandered along the Street of Arlon's Rest, pausing before Remis Sarsdarl's place. It was narrow, old and made of wood and clay bricks. Nothing pretentious about it at all. A light flickered far within, possibly a fire. He moved on.

"Tashnark!"

For a moment he didn't recognize his own name. Hearing it shouted like that, in the midst of his deepening uncertainty, he found it alien and strange.

"You don't ignore me, do you?"

The speaker came close. He was tall, ropy and pale, but gave an impression of heaviness. Tashnark knew the face and the air of displaced wildness.

"Arhl Mogarni!" he said. "What the hell are you doing here?"

The white-skinned easterner laughed. A gust of wind scattered his long dark-red hair about his neck. "You always were forgetful. I live here. My forge." He pointed further down the street and over the top of buildings clustered there. He was indicating where his smithy was situated, presumably, though he might have been gesturing at the roiling sky. Lightning flashed some distance across the city. "Question is more what *you* are doing here."

What indeed! Tashnark thought. But he said, "Just clearing my head." The rumble of thunder punctuated his words.

"Are you well?"

"Well? Yes, I suppose so. How's business?"

Arhl shrugged. "Non-Family enterprise is not encouraged in this city. Perhaps I will have to leave soon."

"The city?"

"The country."

"Is it that bad?"

"The Families are strong. They want it all." Arhl Mogarni's hand clamped onto Tashnark's shoulder. "You're not here by chance. I've been watching you. Why are you studying Remis Sarsdarl's house so intently?"

"You always were an observant bastard, Arhl. And nosy." Tashnark looked up into his pale-blue eyes, which squinted against minute shards of rain carried on the wind. "You know this Remis, do you?"

Tentative nod. "We have spoken. She is a neighbor. I do work for her at times." A deep wrinkle scarred across Arhl's forehead. "Day before yesterday I saw her harassed by Family bullies. In the market. I broke one thug's head open for him."

Tashnark laughed. "I'll bet you did. Surely she'd be grateful."

"There was a large crowd. I don't think she saw."

Tashnark nodded absently. Did Remis Sarsdarl inspire such

silent devotion so often? He sensed there was more to Arhl being here, watching over her, than his old acquaintance would admit to, but clearly Arhl intended to say nothing about that reason, whatever it might be.

"You are not the only one spying on her," Arhl added. "Early this morning I noticed men standing in the shadows." He gestured back over Tashnark's shoulder. Tashnark glanced around and saw nothing but empty street. Gray bluster swirled in the distance. "Another at the rear. In Unelan Lane. There is a pack-leader who is dark and wizardly. All of them—carrion-dogs. I don't like it. This district is no underworld slum, to have secret wardens watching our every move."

"And they've been watching this Remis Sarsdarl's place?"

"Watching. Waiting for some signal. Come!" He grabbed Tashnark's sleeve and pulled him further down the street just as heavy drops of rain began to fall. Tashnark found himself shoved into an alcove. Thankfully it afforded some shelter. "I thought you might be with them," Arhl continued ominously. "Had to find out."

"I'm with no one." Tashnark looked into Arhl's eyes. "What's this about?"

"More Family plotting perhaps. I think the woman needs help. They will move soon."

"How can you tell?"

Arhl spoke in a low, sibilant whisper, pointing at his eye. "There is something...important here. Hunters read the wind."

It was probably true, but such aphorisms made Tashnark impatient. He leaned around the edge of a rough stone wall, catching rain across his face, and glanced down the street toward the tavern. There might have been men there, in the gloom, moving closer. A sheet of rain swept toward him out of the murk. No one was in it.

Remis Sarsdarl's front door opened. The woman herself came out. She seemed puzzled. Through the silhouettes of tossing shrubs, Tashnark watched her study the street, her attention roving over him without pausing there. Wind swept around her.

"What's she looking for?" he hissed at Arhl, though there was no way for his friend to know.

"Perhaps she senses trouble."

After a moment, Remis retreated indoors, huddled against the cold and rain. Lightning flashed, nearer this time. The door slammed shut.

"Are you sure about this?" Tashnark asked, drawing back into the alcove.

"I'm sure."

What was it with this man? Could he be trusted? Tashnark had known Arhl Mogarni for all of a decade, though it must have been nearly a year since he'd seen him last. They'd become acquainted during the course of one particularly demoralizing summer, working as laborers on a wall-construction project along the coastal lands west of the City. Both had been desperately broke. They'd hung out together; Tashnark had liked Arhl for his solid earnestness and integrity, his great drinking prowess and, oddly, for his lack of kinship with Vesuula and its society. Arhl had seemed to enjoy Tashnark's company, too. Why hadn't they kept in touch? He couldn't remember.

Was it just coincidence that this Remis had now brought them back together?

"I hope this isn't some whim of yours," he commented. "As I recall you were prone to whimsy."

Arhl said nothing, just looked serious. Rain scoured over Tashnark's face again as he leaned around the corner to check the street. This time there were three men. One of them was tall, with a long-tailed coat that flowed about his legs like a cloak.

"They're the ones," said Arhl, and added: "Some of them." He watched with Tashnark as the three men hesitated in front of Remis Sarsdarl's door. The tall man said something. His two companions split off to either side of the building-front.

"They're up to no good all right," Tashnark commented.

The leader stood silently outside Remis' door, as though listening. The others hid. Tashnark moved out into the storm, to intervene, but Arhl's large hand clamped on his shoulder and restrained him.

"Shouldn't we stop them?" Tashnark growled.

Arhl gestured for quiet. "There are others," he whispered. Sure enough, two more figures had materialized in the shadows and rain-mist, apparently emerging from the alley at the rear of Remis's long narrow building.

Impatiently, Tashnark struck his companion's hand aside. Then he said: "Several of them have swords. What about you? Any weapons?"

"A knife, is all."

"Then we'll have to improvise, I guess."

* * * * * * *

Someone knocked on the door, sharply. Remis let her thoughts drop away. Could it be a customer? She found she hoped it wasn't, but went anyway to check.

The man standing against the troubled sky was tall and dark and was wearing a thick brown coat. His face was angular, with prominent cheekbones and a long, thin moustache defining the line of his mouth. His eyes questioned her. There was a sharpness to his glance and a turn to the way he held his long, slender fingers that told her that he drew on the Deep Powers, though she could not tell to what purpose; for a moment longer they stood across the threshold from each other, frozen in a tableau of enquiry.

"Yes?" Remis said at last.

The stranger smiled, a brightness sparking from his eyes. He gestured a greeting with his hands. Remis noticed the silver rings that he wore on several of his fingers. They were beautiful—tokens of great wealth.

"Pardon this intrusion, siris!" 'Siris' was a polite epithet common within magical circles and suggested a willingness to be deferential. Yet his voice was strong and spoke more of power than humility. "If it's possible, I should like to speak with you." His use of Lesser Goduulan, the common commercial language of the central states, mitigated the accent in his speech. She couldn't place it.

"On what business?"

He didn't answer, but hunched his shoulders against a light spray of rain. "May I come in?" he asked.

Distantly, thunder rumbled and wind above her in the misty air made her suddenly unnerved and suspicious. "I'm not open for business," she said, pulling her clothes tightly about her. "Not today at least. I'd prefer it if you made an appointment to see me another time. Perhaps tomorrow?"

The stranger gestured casually. "This is urgent," he said. "I have a commission that impels me—" His careless hand movement became a purposeful sweep and he pushed the door aside. Several men appeared behind him in the rain.

"What is this?" Remis cried, backing away.

"Be silent and you'll not be hurt." The stranger gestured to his men. Remis watched them move past her and enter the rooms beyond. Thuds and scrapings told her they were searching for something. What could she have that these men would want?

"I'm not wealthy," she commented.

The leader slammed the front door against the wind and the open street, and waved Remis into the most distant corner of the room.

* * * * * * *

The sound of wind and dripping water was deafening; Tashnark had heard nothing of the conversation that took place on the other side of the street. When the tall man forced the door back upon Remis—signaling at the same time for his hidden thugs to surge forward—Tashnark decided he had to act. He shoved at Arhl and stepped out into the street.

Arhl had no intention of letting him go. He gripped Tashnark's arm and pulled him further away, keeping to the walls and out of sight. "We can come at them from the back. That'll be better. Surprise."

"The back?"

"Go straight in here, front on, and we face swords and the leader's magic—you can see he's strong. From the other side perhaps we can pick them off before they realize they are attacked."

Remis's door slammed shut. "We should hurry," Tashnark suggested.

* * * * * * *

"What are you after?" Remis stood defiantly before the intruder.

"There is an inevitability to events, as you well should know." The man had an air of superior knowledge. "Though perhaps the compulsion is deeper than you realize. If you have what we seek, then you know the answer to your question already. If not, then it is better you remain ignorant."

"Who are you?"

"There is no escape from this, siris. The gods are rarely kind, even those who claim charity as their nature. Your Power crystal. May I have it?"

Remis clutched at the icon around her neck, her fear burgeoning now. What was to happen? Without her *cerenil* she would be weakened further, and even with it she wasn't trained in combat.

A voice came from the workshop: "Sire, she's been working tricks. The place reeks of magic."

"Bring me her books!" the leader ordered, careful to remain between Remis and the door. Then he smiled to himself or to Remis, and added in a low voice. "They're fools, and understand nothing."

There was a crash from the workroom and a series of rushed movements. One of the men cried out—a cry of pain. The leader frowned darkly. "What have they done?" he muttered.

Someone yelled, and the cry was followed by a loud thud. Remis gasped involuntarily. The man glanced at her, his eyes blazing as though his passions were catching fire. His lips began muttering control-words. Remis started up, but he flicked his hand at her and something stuck her a blow from head to foot. She reeled, collapsing at the knees, as the room flared into bright numbness.

Desperately she summoned what she could of her inner strength, thrusting it outward to break the man's hold on her. The creeping progress of his grip halted, but she could not toss him aside as easily. Then, with sudden ferocity, he altered the words of his chant and a stab of mind-pain tore her resistance away. She slumped, conscious of the energy being drained from her. Her mind, her memory, vision of the room—these all splintered. She was left with an overwhelming feeling of helplessness, and a disturbing image of a man she didn't know shredded by the dark stranger's power.

Her lips tried to reproduce the words her mind was forming, but nothing came. Nausea splashed her thoughts into a confusion of images. Then a figure appeared through the threads of hanging suspended from the door-jamb....

"No!" she managed.

* * * * * * *

With efficient familiarity, Arhl led Tashnark to the rear of Remis' tenement. A narrow lane ran along the back and Arhl identified a high brick wall with a wooden door in it as belonging to Remis. It was locked, but Tashnark had it picked and open before Arhl could finish commenting on the fact. Easing through a tangle of overgrown bushes, they reached the back door, which looked like it hadn't been used for some time. According to Ishwarin, Remis Sarsdarl had only taken up residence in this building a few weeks before, so perhaps her interests and life-style hadn't yet compelled her to brave the wilds of her own backyard.

"Can you open this one, too?" asked Arhl, pointing at the rust-coated lock.

Tashnark felt that the time for subtlety had passed; there were noises from within the house—a clattering sound, scrapings—and a voice shouted. Remis's? He couldn't tell. He raised his boot and pounded on the lock. The doorframe splintered.

"What?" someone exclaimed, revealed as a thick-set man of about Tashnark's height, whose demeanor went from surprise to anger in an instant as the door caved in. His sword was sheathed and his hands full of magical paraphernalia. He tangled himself up trying to grab the hilt of his weapon. Tashnark rushed through like a battering ram and smashed him in the chest before he could react. The man expelled a nasal groan as he crashed backwards into one of his comrades. They both fell in a heap.

Tashnark didn't give them time to regain their composure. He grabbed the hair of one and used it to pound his skull on the stone floor. The other pushed himself away in a panic, but his friend's weight pinned him to the ground long enough for Tashnark to back-hand him square on the nose. The bone splintered with a dull crack and he went quiet.

From the rear, Arhl blinked in astonishment at the speed and ferocity of Tashnark's attack. A third man was drawing his sword, obviously intending to use it in defense of himself if not his comrades. Tashnark hadn't noticed. Arhl roared for the man's attention and ran at him. It worked. He swung his blade away from Tashnark, aiming for Arhl's chest instead; Arhl leapt back quickly and the tip of the blade feather-touched along a fold of his shirt.

"Missed," he said.

The man barked some angered monosyllables, kicking at one of Arhl's legs and connecting painfully. Arhl buckled. Before he could regain his balance, the man had raised his sword for a clear strike at Arhl's head.

"Won't miss this time," he snarled.

But the blow never came. A sword blade sprouted suddenly from his chest. Mingled astonishment and pain replaced aggression in him and a sigh escaped from his lips as though he'd had an unexpected revelation. He toppled as blood sprayed from the wound. Tashnark stepped into view.

"You should be more careful," he said to Arhl.

He crossed the room at a run and in an instant was along the corridor and through the door-hanging that separated the two parts of the house. Arhl caught a glimpse of Remis's horrified expression and a tall, dark man snarling. Then the hangings fell back into place and a rush of fire and scalding light stabbed through the gaps.

* * * * * *

In the explosion of power that met him as he pushed through the door-hanging, Tashnark could see eyes. Gray, yet compellingly vivid. The pupils were almost clear, as though absent from the orbs.

In the ecstasy of combat, and assaulted by Deep Power from a source he could not yet identify, he felt himself being transported...somewhere....

Hanin?

To be watched by Hanin's eyes was an unsettling experience. To gaze into them was to court madness.

Tashnark felt the threat of madness now.

He was somewhere else.

Someone else.

* * * * * *

Bellarroth had stared into Hanin's eyes once, obeying the old man's injunction. Something snatched out of them with violence and conviction. His mind went numb and in that instant he saw a terrible vision. It was a vision he knew was History. That was the worst of it. This had happened.

But not to Bellarroth—to Hanin himself, long ago in a different place.

There was a darkened chamber. A circle of cowled figures, faceless in the shadows. Chanting began, the chanters raising their hands, drawing Power from above or deep within. A dim image formed before them, like a gleam stretched through a haze, swirling masques of momentary effulgence flashing and retreating into bands of gloom. Hanin had felt a growing effort as he, too, began to voice the words and move his hands in intricate, arcane patterns. Power surged through his fingers.

"More! More!" cried a voice in transforming anticipation. His master's voice. Cormidthal's (or so the knowledge leap into Bellarroth's mind, though he did not understand what it meant).

The hand movements of the chanters became more frenzied and more determined, the pattern they formed more coordinated. And the voice rang out again—"Begin Garnez-ev Harrid!"—calling for a ritual sequence designed to establish an interweaving of all the diverse currents of Deep Power being drawn into the room by the chanters.

The words changed. These were old and barely familiar. Hanin had felt his flesh tingling and scalding with the influx of more and more power. An image hardened in the center of the circle. Its shape, still unstable, remained there longer, as though it was becoming more and more tangible.

"Hor-mir Tarthelnis!" bellowed Cormidthal's voice, signifying an opening spell, seeking to create a gateway for something deeply hidden. Again the chant changed and the circle began to move, Hanin with them. It was like a dance. In the center of the floor light exploded like tiny fire-bombs, each detonation adding substance to the elusive image. Pain wracked Hanin. "Can this continue?" someone near him whispered, but before he could answer, their master's voice, louder and more authoritative, cried: "Acolyte Korrenea, you disturb the Rites with your babble."

The chant and the dance grew in intensity. Somewhere a drum beat a deep and bone-throbbing rhythm. The conjunction in the midst of the circle was firm now, a thick silver glow, so bright it burnt the eyes, sucking as if to drain away their ability to see. The voice shrieked "Ca'Shal-er Azharan!" and again the chant was transmuted into a new and more intense form.

Hanin had barely been able to stand, but somehow he had continued to move with the others. The central glow grew until it encompassed them all. Then the voice said: "Enough! The Cerendar is ready to speak to us."

The circle of figures stood waiting, consumed by light; Hanin had imagined it tearing his flesh from his bones. Then the voice said: "This company, long seekers of the Ultimate Power, stand now at the brink of a new world...the world of infinite desire fulfilled. All-Power will be ours—gods we will be in the sight of lesser men. Speak the secret Names assigned you, and each in the unity of our Circle will release unto all the powers of the Kharathahul, the Great Ones who wander the hills of Heaven alone, bound into their fate by the symbol of the star-object known as the Cerendar. Summon the power of each by name and They will reward us by granting our wish."

One by one each of the cowled figures spoke a name. Hanin had pronounced the syllables "Tammenallor"—which meant 'compliance' but was here the name given to a powerful deity supposed to exist just outside the world. In coordination with the other Kharathahul whose names were spoken around the circle, Tammenallor would open the Cerendar to Lord Cormidthal and his chosen acolytes.

"Tamm-en-al-lor!"

As the syllables left Hanin's lips the room exploded into light and dark fragments, pain ripped through his muscles, alien perceptions bursting from the rents, grabbing him and flinging him toward darkness. It was a darkness more terrible and unending than he had ever imagined possible and it was filled with his guilt.

Compliance became infinite culpability.

As life ceased, Hanin had reached out in panic, muttering Words of Stability and Joining in an effort to resist the loss of everything he knew. For a heartbeat he was spinning through space, his eyes filled with images—monsters of unspeakable shape, immense and terrible. One grew larger until Bellarroth's eyes throbbed with Its presence, as though It were too huge to be contained by them.

The Monster had a gnarled head atop a deformed inhuman body, its neck ringed by serpents that sprouted from the skin, the body a knotted hulk, ghastly and many-limbed, wings growing from Its back and spreading wide to encompass all of Space. It grew and engulfed him. This was Tammenallor, given form.

Hanin had collapsed as if struck dead.

Bellarroth collapsed with him now.

<Tashnark! Awake!>

Tashnark opened his eyes. Before him he held a sword, but it was not the sword he had taken from the man in the other room. This one was rough-beaten, with symbols gouged into the metal. The handle was an interwoven mass of serpents into which his fingers were molded. It felt familiar, part of him—yet he had never seen it before.

Then his ears were filled with roaring, and fire—a fire that did not burn—swept around him, swirling like a tornado. The eye of that tornado was the sword in his hands.

* * * * * * *

Force like lightning cracked from the space contained within the sorcerer's fingers. The room shook and lost all definition in a iridescent flare. But the dark-skinned newcomer—whose black hair was woven into plaits against the back of his head—held his sword between himself and the fire, and the Deep Power was sucked away, as though absorbed by the blade. The sorcerer cried out in amazement. For Remis, the world wavered, like a reflection on a lake surface suddenly broken by rocks thrown into the water. The newcomer might have been different at that moment—larger, with blazing red hair and a thick burnt-umber beard. His Vesuulan clothes seemed rougher, more tribal, like poorly treated leather. His eyes were black holes. Illusion, surely. Remis's senses gave way.

With a speed that made him dream-like, the newcomer leapt and struck forcefully with his bared fist, knocking the sorcerer back against the door. There was stillness then. Remis felt an irresistible weakness grow in her legs. Her head was so light it was drifting away, caught in a gust that suddenly swept through her house but touched nothing except her mind.

The newcomer was standing over her. "Are you all right?" he asked.

His face: dark, skin-pocked. He was clean-shaven, though it had been carelessly done. Black hair. Plaits. Eyes a vivid green.

"I...I feel very weak," she said.

He let his sword drop to the floor, reached out and held her. His grip was strong. "It's over now," he said. "We're friends."

Friends? Did she have friends? She couldn't recall a single name, let alone that of this man. Yet she had seen him before. Where?

Perhaps in a dream.

"Who are you?" she managed.

"Sevthen Ulart-Tashnark," he replied. "And this is Arhl Mogarni. He's a neighbor. You know him." Another man had appeared now. He was tall. Pale. Balding. He hovered behind the speaker shyly. She'd seen him, too, but couldn't recall where. Then it came to her through the fuzziness in her head: the blacksmith—Arhl. Of course she knew him. "We were passing when we saw these scum force their way in." He gestured contemptuously at the unconscious sorcerer.

"You stopped him," she said still unbelieving.

"Yes," he replied. "Did he hurt you?"

"He...wounded me...inside." Remis felt what remained of her strength bleeding away. To heal the psychic injuries, she needed to let herself go. But could she trust herself to this man's care, leave herself utterly vulnerable to him? She tried to focus on his eyes, caught and held them at last, and saw concern there. Something else, too, something distant and dangerous—but, she sensed, not a threat to her. A threat to someone, but not her. The fact that he knew Arhl reassured her.

"We'll look after you," the stranger said. "You're safe."

Implicitly Remis believed him. She couldn't have said why

it seemed so impossible that this man should be an enemy, but as he spoke all suspicion drained from her. Darkness wavered above her, trembled and retreated, breathing wind across the shutters in a departing frenzy. Somewhere above, lost in the storm's refuse, hung the screech of a night owl, and the sound passed like an afterglow into memory. Lightning flickered through cracks in the window-shutters.

She had no choice.

"Must sleep," she whispered and the world went away.

iv.

Like wind thinning veils of fog and bringing tree-shapes into gradual view, a mind-force tugged at power that nested around Aridor's slumbering thoughts. He was drowning in a sea of ill-formed impressions. What was solid here? His mind, unable to find assurance in the present, reached into the past.

* * * * * * *

When Aridor enter the room, his Lord, Worjaren Rehemon, was gazing out a window, staring southward. It was full day.

The Lord had been absent for many months, on a journey the purpose of which Aridor had never understood. Lord Worjaren had just returned, but as usual there were no pleasantries to bridge the gap.

"There were rumors on Cantalcis, Aridor," he said, without turning. Cantalcis was a large continental island in the seas to the north of Rheateesha, Aridor knew. "...Rumors concerning a creature that could not be killed. It was violent and wanton. A witness told me it had no heart, for she saw the empty cavity in its chest. Yet even so it lived. I believe we may have its heart here, in this box, and having this, hold the key to something greater."

He had followed the trail of rumors, he explained, and had eventually arrived at one of the islands of the Cantalcis chain—Reyad, an insignificant place that had once been a penal colony for the Vesuulan state authorities. There he had found a weird treasure: a living heart. He produced a box and showed Aridor its contents. The heart, though disembodied, pumped bloodlessly, even now, in a small, ornate case—a necromantic miracle that filled Aridor with both wonder and fear. It had come, the Lord said, from the tomb of a family named Valarl.

"It seems impossible, my Lord," Aridor had replied.

"Such a thing was once possible." The Lord began pacing the room like a man possessed. "Perhaps it still is. The Art was in the displacement of the heart—as symbol of life—from the breast of the subject, without dispelling the living qualities of the corpse itself. It was a symbolic gesture, but one that arose out of a specialized use of Deep Power."

"And a symbol could lie at the core of such a miracle?"

"A symbol. Yes." He moved impatiently. "I refer now, acolyte, to times so distant that even the records of Hassur have forgotten the knowledge. But legend tells of an age when magic permeated every aspect of worldly effort, and symbols lived. The Power then was not so deeply buried. Our own arts are a debasement of these primeval skills."

"A pity, Lord."

"Pity?" Stark lines tightened over the Lord's face. "We strive for debasement. As the world winds down toward the fated death we worship, so magic dies and the Gods are locked away from the lives of men. Don't forget, Aridor, we can contemplate victory in the struggle against life only because the Guardian Raashyr are crippled and weakened. Not all the Dark Gods combined could stand for a moment against the unbounded wrath of a single Guardian Raashyr, even the weakest of their ranks."

"My Lord, you shouldn't speak this way. It smells of blasphemy."

Lord Worjaren Rehemon gazed at Aridor slyly, the chamber falling silent. "You're right to caution me, of course, Aridor," he said at last. *"The Raashyr are weak, life is cruel. Only death is strong. But magic is made possible by the life that still remains in the world and, when we use it against life, we pave the way to its own destruction."*

Aridor had wondered why the Lord was saying these things. The expression of such thoughts, however true, made one's position doubtful and laid one open to accusations of treason. Yet he was sure Lord Worjaren knew this and had calculated the risk for his own ends. Perhaps it was a test.

"These are thoughts which encourage me, Lord," said Aridor and left it at that. "But what of this living heart? And the creature it came from? Did one of the Valarl Family practice necromancy? And, if so, why did he ensure the survival of an undead creation into these years so far from his own death? What has it to do with the ancient artifact we seek?"

"Questions, Aridor. But I can offer no clear answer. Guesses are all that sustain me."

"Guesses?"

"That the undead creature is the result of an ancient attempt to unleash the power of the Cerendar. Such attempts have always had unexpected results." He scowled as though at a private and unwelcome thought. *"Now the creature is bound to the artifact by its own torment. Is that guess enough?"* He sounded annoyed. *"Never mind guesses,"* he went on. *"This I can say for certain. No necromancer had the power to achieve such a deed. No one has been capable of utilising symbolic magic in this way for ten times the two thousand years that lie between us. A greater Power would be needed."*

"Cerendar, as you say."

"Cerendar, yes. The Cerendar misused and ill-understood. Once the artifact lay in that tomb on Reyad. I know this, no matter how. But it has disappeared yet again and the creature without a heart is the only clue we have to locating it. I want this search to be over, Aridor. I desire rest."

* * * * * * *

In a murkier present, new awareness struggled upon Aridor, forcing the memories aside.

"Aridor!"

It was pain, the suddenness of awakening. He tried to answer, but words were impossible in the web of incoherence that engulfed him.

"Aridor, *ruthlim*! *Ruthlim*!"

The magic trembled. Memories faded completely. The spirit in him responded to his Lord's words, strengthened by them, and at last he could grasp the vision.

"Forgive me, Lord, forgive me," he said. "I have failed the Godling we worship and abused our joining." How was it, he wondered, that he had lost all awareness of his body? There was only thought, memory, and the echo of his Lord's words. A tremor shook his spirit, washing a film of imaged thought over his intellect. He experienced the shifting as a stroke of anger. Lord Worjaren Rehemon materialized before him.

"You are taken?" The images broke apart like the facets of a kaleidoscope, and were reformed. They shook, stabilized. The Lord curled his prominent upper lip and rubbed his hand smoothly over the curve of his right eyebrow. "Taken? By the Unliving Spirit, acolyte, I didn't think you so weak."

"Lord, I am humbled."

The Lord's voice was mocking, but not hard. "I have no desire to humiliate you, Aridor."

"Someone...something strong attacked without warning—"

"There is a force wielded against us, yes. I can feel the bruises caused by its arrival." A terse smile quivered on his lips. "Never underestimate the resourcefulness of your enemy. Even the weak are capable of winning against the odds. All Deep Power, my Acolyte, must be understood and contained— weaker souls subjugated, stronger ones ruthlessly destroyed. The strongest among us are weak; find that weakness and there's an end to your problems." He shrugged. "Even I am not invulnerable, amazing as that may seem to you." He waved his hand in a turn like a dance, then his fingers contracted into a

fist. "This stronger enemy has simply caught you unprepared—that's your error."

"But what is his power?"

"The cunning to force you into sleep, at least."

"Sleep? Am I dreaming?"

"I am speaking to you in a dream, Aridor, guided by our joining. Your enemy is very strong—"

"Is he from the Raashyr?"

"Perhaps." Lord Worjaren prodded his middle finger toward Aridor's forehead. "We must free you, Acolyte, before they convert this success to greater victory. And they must be captured, these Life-friends. I feel the Cerendar hot about them."

"Yes, Lord. I was given a sign."

"Sign? I perceive signs enough to suit me in the Power focused here so unexpectedly. Now, come. With our joining I'll free you from the sleep-web; through you, I will send my own power against them. Your men await you outside in the street—use them. There is chance in physical might. I will be with you soon."

Aridor began to question, but the Lord's arm rose in its dismissive gesture and the Spell began.

V.

Feeling a hint of claustrophobia in Remis Sarsdarl's cramped quarters, Tashnark waited. For what, he wasn't sure.

A spindly black insect flew from the darkness into the orange flicker of the fire and landed on the ceiling directly above the main forge. It buzzed stridently several times, then fell silent. Tashnark watched its flight with interest, now that Remis had fallen into sleep again.

He felt edgy with frustration. Front door secured, enemy silenced, they had moved into the workshop where warmth and care might cradle the unconscious Remis until the magic damage the sorcerer had inflicted on her faded. What else could they do? Go to the Sumis-police? Arhl and he had discussed the possibility, but given that this attack might have been Family-inspired, Sumis could be involved. A healer? Her injuries were not serious, Arhl had insisted, and nor were they permanent.

"And how would you know?" Tashnark grumbled.

"I've seen this before," explained Arhl, with an air of annoying patience. "I can *feel* it. Her spirit is traumatized. Given rest, she will heal herself."

The workroom was a mess, littered with the chaos of uncaring search and unexpected combat. Three men down, one dead. Tashnark barely remembered killing him. In fact he could remember very little of the conflict, as though his mind, too, had been affected by the sorcerer's power. He wanted to regret the killing, but any guilt and sorrow he felt seemed curiously super-ficial. He fetched the sword he'd used, recalling an odd sensation of change centered around it—serpents and a powerful aegis—but it was ordinary now, machined blade, sweaty, leather-bound hilt, blood smeared on the dull metal. Nevertheless, until these strange events were clarified and resolved, he decided to hang onto it. He spent some time cleaning it.

Arhl flinted a fire. There was a small pot-bellied stove that was intended for domestic purposes—an encrusted relic attached by flues to the forge. It gave off erratic comfort. The building's wood-and-clay walls were poor at conserving the heat. "She needs warmth," he said.

"What do you think's really going on?" Tashnark stood by the stove to capture some of its ambience. "There's something very strange about all this."

Arhl shrugged. "The Families do not want her independent," he said. "Happens all the time."

There was more to it than that, but Tashnark found it impos-sible to talk of the other, weirder aspects. "I wish we could get some answers from this bastard," he said, prodding at the unconscious sorcerer. "Whose boots do you lick, shit-face?" he snarled, hoping to penetrate the man's coma.

"Can't hear you," Arhl commented. Tashnark slapped the bound man with a careless gesture and turned sharply.

"Why are *you* doing this, Arhl?" he growled. "A man's been killed and there's more power loosed here than I've seen in a while. We could be in big trouble. Yet you let yourself become entangled in a near-stranger's problems? Why?"

"I could ask the same question of you."

"But I asked you first."

Arhl considered, his eyes closing.

"Tell me," Tashnark said, only partially joking, "are you obsessed with this Remis? Have you been stalking her?"

Arhl's eyes opened sharply and Tashnark couldn't tell in that moment whether the emotion so evidently swirling in them was anger or fear.

Neither of them made any attempt to take the issue further. Tashnark could offer himself no solution, let alone attempting to give Arhl one. If one of them might be considered to have been stalking her, all indications pointed to him. Life had become absurd, that was all. He wished he could go home, back to normality, yet it was clear there would be no escape for him in that direction. He didn't even know what normality was any more. The dreams of Bellarroth? Were they normal?

"We shouldn't stay here," Arhl said suddenly.

"You think they'll attack us again?"

Arhl nodded once.

"What choice do we have?" Tashnark continued. "The woman needs rest, you said. At least we've got this sorcerer—he must be valuable to them, if they consider any man valuable. We can use it against them, if they turn up."

"They may not come in a way we expect."

The insect on the wall moved, and as though on cue Tashnark abandoned the conversation and followed the creature's progress. Its fine wings blurred once, carrying the steely-black body a hand-breadth to a gap between warping boards, where it hummed and folded its wings across its back. Then it walked around in a circle. The monotonous action weighed Tashnark's eyelids and sent him toward sleep. He felt his awareness of the room, of Arhl, of Remis...slipping away, struggled once, gave in to rest.

Shadow and light stabbed at him. He flung out his arm and felt the back of his hand scrape on something hard. The night was thicker and more textured than he remembered, and it smelt peculiar, like ancient uncorrupted skin. His fingers groped until he touched something recognizable. A sword. There were designs on it again, an interwoven amassment of serpents ensnaring the hilt in metal writhing. Growling lightly, he sat up. He could still see nothing, being shrouded in darkness, yet the movement seemed a visual thing, as though he were not so much acting as watching himself act.

"Wake!"

Wake? There was a voice somewhere, but in his confusion Tashnark couldn't locate its source.

"Wake! Come to me!"

"Is that you, Hanin?" As he said it he flinched at the name. It implied a knowledge and a history he only knew in his dreams. Was he dreaming now?

"Come to me!"

"Who do you want, for god's sake?"

The voice replied: *"I seek Bellarroth, who is my son."*

The darkness thickened suddenly, though as Tashnark could already see nothing, it was a subjective experience rather than an actual diminishing. Yet it made him fall back from himself. He was aware that the voice and the figure in the dark with its hand on the serpent-hilt spun away from him into an endless space. For an instant there was nothingness all about him, then oblivion came like a springing predator and he grabbed at normal sleep.

Once again, he dreamt of Bellarroth.

* * * * * * *

This time Bellarroth was with Hanin, climbing a mountain

toward its indefinite summit. Hanin was whole and fleshed now, though his gauntness reminded Bellarroth of bones. How that could be was irrelevant. Weirdness was the nature of this world.

They climbed for some time, talking little, but concentrating on the awkward ascent. It was very hot. Bellarroth demanded a stop, and at last Hanin agreed.

"There's no time to sit and dally idly," said the old man, tense and impatient, fidgeting while he waited. He took a canteen from Bellarroth and drank, then thrust back the hardened skin bag as though it were plagued. "Soon Lucishnor will come to feast upon Tammenallor's corpse," he stated, glancing at the sky.

"Is the Kharathahul dead then?"

"Not yet." Hanin's eyes shone with annoyance. "If it were so, we'd all be dead." He stood and paced around Bellarroth in a nervous ring, clenching and unclenching his hands. "After so long, and so much effort, to be thwarted by the Beast's stupid aggression. It was unlooked for. I tell you, son-Bellarroth, unless we reach our destination before Tammenallor dies, I fear we are all, even Tharenweyr itself, lost to hope."

"Tharenweyr? You mean the world you've talked about? The first?"

"Yes, my son—the real world from which this one was fragmented!"

Bellarroth huffed. "How is this so-called real world affected?"

"We are part of that world, son-Bellarroth, whether or not we seem to be. Its fate is bound to ours."

Bellarroth wanted to ask him about it, but Hanin stopped him with a gesture. "What we are doing conforms to none of your expectations, son-Bellarroth. The burst of Monster's blood which struck you down has done us a service inadvertently, for it enabled me to implant in your imagination images parallel to but more tolerable than the reality of our deeds. Truth can frustrate if it's too unfamiliar. Over the past years I've trained you well in mind and body—but there are limits. I must tread lightly lest your spirit revolt from the path."

Bellarroth gestured about him. "Then this is illusion, a false-hood? It must be, for I saw your body destroyed. I cut off your head."

Hanin gripped his clothes with thin, impatient fingers. "It is parallel. I am here, whole, having adopted the form you recognize. I am dead. Yet I am truly alive as well, as are you. All the dangers of this place are real, and triumphs as well." He released his hold. "This world is not stable. Nor is it consistent. It bends and twists and takes on forms that are more emotion than fact. Accept what each moment brings. Meanwhile we must reach the Heart of Tammenallor before It gives out on us. Be alert. The Monster's dying, but it's not yet easy prey."

Bellarroth grabbed at his sleeve, thoughts questing. The old man slapped his hand away. "We've been beyond Tammenallor's ken for a long time and hence spared the destruction attendant on Its wrath. In the past, damage to us has been unwittingly inflicted, an off-hand gesture. We are vermin on Tammenallor's Skin and often It scratches at an itch, as a man scratches at lice. But now It senses we are here—you and I, who have stolen knowledge from It since the first year of the Exile—coming to challenge It for the balance owed, and the right to escape this place. I've probed Its mysteries with my Art, I've sought out Its ways and struggled to maintain the life that Korrenea birthed, I've gained skill and lost patience. Now my part in this curse will end, and yours begin. There will be life or death." He managed a sort of crippled smile. "If this battle with Lucishnor doesn't kill the Monster too soon, then it may serve us to an easier passage. It may destroy us in the end, but in the meantime Tammenallor is distracted from more minute problems such as we."

He dragged Bellarroth up and gestured toward the foggy heights of the mountain. "We have far to go. Spiritual journeys are always the longest."

His emaciated form, so incongruously strong, bounded away from Bellarroth with a sweep of flowing blackness. Those robes were the ones he had always worn, a mark of his distinction, and they were made of the only real, woven fabric Bellarroth had *ever seen. Like the man himself they were strange, the heritage of life in another place...and the promise of escape. Bellarroth felt a touch of fear. Often he had cursed Tammenallor. Often he had struggled against the deprivations of their imprisonment. But it was all about to end, as Hanin had said. Beneath his feet the false, living world on which they had depended for—how long? He couldn't remember—was dying, slain by another fiercer cosmic Terror. Could they adjust to the transition?*

"Hurry!" Hanin cried. "Even in allegory there's need for haste." Bellarroth wondered at the old man's riddles and hastened up the slope.

They came to an open space, where hair-growth was sparse and only a few scattered hair-trees withered in the dry atmosphere. The light was dim and gray. A huge cave was gouged in the rough, warty mountain-side, dripping shadow about the worn ground before it. "This looks ominous," commented Hanin. Bellarroth shrugged, not knowing what the old man could mean. "Your sword, son-Bellarroth," ordered Hanin. "Take it in your hands and hold it vertical. It can light our way."

Bellarroth grasped the ornate serpent-hilt and drew the weapon from its sheath. "Where did this weapon come from, Hanin?" he asked, suddenly conscious of its uniqueness.

"It's a conjuring, son-Bellarroth," Hanin said. "I forged it long ago."

"You forged it? How?"

"In my mind.. How else?"

"In your mind?"

"It was necessary."

"It doesn't make sense."

Hanin frowned at him. "Seeking to find sense in this place will only kill you, son. We are outside reality, captured here by our own...my own....stupidity and guilt. It is our inner life that gives shape to this place in all its forms—and that shape is always mutable. It also connects us to the first world, to Tharenweyr. If we can fight our way through our own inner compulsions we can get back there. Perhaps. Now, be silent and hold up the sword!"

Bellarroth did so and the old man gestured at it, moving his old fingers in a flowing pattern and whispering odd words. As the Deep Summoning was completed, Bellarroth felt the sword-hilt throb as though with life. In a moment the blade was giving out a strange, colorless light that leaked from the symbols covering the blade. The light shed no shadows, falling out away from the metal sharply. "Lead us into Tammenallor's Heart," hissed Hanin, pushing Bellarroth toward the entrance.

Inside the darkness of the mountain, the sword-torch banished sightlessness in a sphere about ten paces wide. Beyond this light the shades ruled unhampered. Bellarroth made his way cautiously along the twistings and turnings, conscious only of the sword and of Hanin, who directed him in impatient tones to go this way or that, to forge ahead or to turn aside down barely perceived tunnels. The canny old man seemed to hold some esoteric knowledge that patterned their movement, as though he knew the way to Tammenallor's Heart. It was something that lay beyond possibility of knowing, at least for someone like Bellarroth.

"You were born in Tharenweyr, weren't you?" Bellarroth didn't break his stride in order to speak.

"Why do you ask?" said the old man. "You already know the answer."

"How did you come to be trapped here?"

Hanin said nothing for a time and Bellarroth was preparing to re-phrase the query. Hanin had never discussed this question, though he had often mentioned Tharenweyr itself. If this old man wasn't born on Tammenallor, then all pre-Exile knowledge must come from him. He would know.

"I have never encouraged much thought on this, son-Bellarroth," hissed the old man behind him. "You are bred with a spirit conscious of estrangement. But specifics...ah! they can foster despair."

He fell silent until Bellarroth thought he intended to say no more. The sound of their feet scraping on the floor of the cavern became so distinct that Bellarroth wondered whether Hanin had disappeared and left only his footsteps, moving inexorably behind him, disembodied in the gloom. He scowled, but then Hanin's voice made him jump. "There comes a time to face despair. I've shown you the moment of Exile, son-Bellarroth. Once I induced a vision in you and you saw the disaster as I did, so long ago. You thought it was a dream perhaps. Is your consciousness so weak that my efforts find no hold upon it?"

Bellarroth remembered, but he didn't understand. Again Hanin was ahead of him.

"We sought in those distant days—and back in Tharenweyr—to harness for ourselves the power of the Kharathahul, divine Monsters that were said to exist just the other side of what is real—and through them to control the true Power of the Cerendar, which is known as the Artifact of All-Power. It was an enterprise thick with folly, a dream of one who ruled in the land. Cormidthal, he was called. Legend warned us—the artifact is cursed, it said. No man may use it to any end, good or ill, save at great, overwhelming cost. The Cerendar was named the Bane of Life...yet it gave promise of Godhood. With it we thought to reach beyond the world and bind even the gods to our will. Foolish arrogance! The gods have an ironical humor. The Deepest Power of all grabbed us and made us vermin... vermin on Monsters of our own imagining. My guilt manifest as Tammenallor, supposedly the spirit of compliance, but in truth a Monster of Responsibility..... Bah!" His dismissal was so intense that Bellarroth could feel its pressure against his back. "Don't weary your mind in trying to understand this nonsense. It's pointless. Enough that I was thrown into this side-world—on to Tammenallor's shoulders—thrown here with Korrenea... and together we planned an end to the curse. You were born our child and for a while we lived in hope. Then, when I was bereft of Korrenea's companionship by the casual touch of Tammenallor's hand, I pushed my will to its limits, eager to expiate our sin, even alone. Now we're here, son-Bellarroth, and there's finality in our actions."

"You're my actual father?" said Bellarroth, stopping and turning to the old man in the gloaming of the sword.

"In all ways possible...and a few that aren't." Hanin slapped his shoulder and smiled at him sardonically from under his thick eyebrows. Then his face mellowed with sorrow. "Men do not listen to the true prophets, and I am a Man. If I'd listened then, your fate would have been vastly different."

"Listened to whom, father?"

"To a brave and wise prophet who defied Cormidthal's evil and paid for it cruelly." The old man coughed. "Farhassin was his name. Farhassin the Doomsayer. Known also as Garuthgonar. The Void. He predicted that our pride would bring a terrible end and it came upon us as he said. Too late now to heed his wisdom. Yet I remember much and in memory there is strength. Learn to remember." He looked seriously at Bellarroth, his brow tense with wrinkles. "He spoke to me, my son. Spoke to me alone."

"And what did he say?"

"More than he spoke, and much more than I gave credence to. Yet I remember. Should opportunity be given, he said, we must take it as a gift of Grace. Hanin, we will despair, you and I, often and alone. Lord Cormidthal promises that. But even when all is lost, I believe that the divine Errellinarth will not leave us totally abandoned. I scorned him self-righteously, but he went on. You mock me now, while you sweat with Cormidthal's fever. Yet later, Hanin, remember this: faith and knowledge allied may be a deeper magic than any power falsely sought. I remember his words well: Cormidthal brings disaster to Mikhalin...—Mikhalin was the name of our land—...and it will not be stopped. But death will not see an end to his evil. Remember that above all. The future will know his ambition and I fear a second folly may gain ultimate victory for the Dark Gods. I have seen it in the stone. We must stop him, Hanin. I remember those words, son-Bellarroth, and so must you."

"Who is this Cormidthal?"

"A madman—though we did not say so at the time. Then

he was a ruler in Mikhalin, a man of great strength and great ambition. We, some of us, saw him as our savior. In fact, he strove too hard, and in the end brought ruin to the world. You will meet him, son-Bellarroth...that I believe—but don't seek the meeting too hastily." The old man suddenly gestured for him to go on. "Quickly. I don't wish to maintain that light for any longer than I must. Nor have we come to feed your curiosity. Move on!"

Bellarroth stared, heart pounding, wondering at all the things he had learnt. Then he turned away and strode along the unknown passage, exuberant now. The edge this gave to his reflexes was timely, for he had barely heard the faint echo of his first steps die behind him, when something hideous was revealed in the effulgence of his sword. He gasped in shock, but in that instant the thing was gone. Bellarroth's flustered mind held a vague impression of teeth and eyes and horny armor, yet there was no sound in the gloom. "Hanin!" he whispered. "What was it?"

"Be ready!" the old man said. "Tammenallor seems to have found time and strength enough to turn on us."

Wind brushed across Bellarroth's skin and instinctively he thrust the sword further ahead. A silently-snarling maw burst into view, atop a large, heaving torso of skin-colored muscle. Bellarroth fell back, pushing Hanin against the wall. Sword-light flared from the creature's teeth, so close that Bellarroth had no time to adjust the focus of his eyes. He struck with the sword, causing shadow and light to dance strangely around the walls. He cried out....

...But the cavern was still.

Slowly Bellarroth lowered his arm. His eyes scanned the empty circle of light. His heart beat furiously. "Am I imagin—?" he began, when movement broke about him and a cat-like shape slammed into his shoulder, ripping razor-talons along the flesh of his fore-arm. His left hand snatched at the aggressor and gripped nothing. Again stillness followed the violence.

Blood trickled warmly toward the hilt of his sword. "So fast," *he gasped.*

The old man towered over him suddenly, his hand touching Bellarroth's wound. "You must act as fast," Hanin said in his ear.

A flicker of congealing darkness—Bellarroth leapt fiercely, screeching defiance. The light flowed over an amorphous tumor-thing, woven of writhing hair and animated liquid. Before it could adjust its attack, Bellarroth's blade slid into it, tearing it into a stream of floating debris. The thing flickered away as though it had never existed. "Tammenallor's minions are not untouchable," he grunted.

The cavern was silent once again. Hanin moved up behind him and whispered like a wind against his ear. "Nor are you, son-Bellarroth, nor are you."

* * * * * * *

Suddenly there was change, like a tidal force. Bellarroth's consciousness slipped aside, pushed by the current. The cavern fractured into separate images, then shattered and became darkness.

He felt uneasy, lost.

"Who am I?" he said.

"Tashnark," a voice replied—Hanin's voice. "You are Tashnark and you are under attack. Take care!"

Tashnark knew he was asleep and at once he was conscious that his sleep was full of voices—not the voice of his previous dreaming, which had been commanding, definite, lacking guile and conspiratorial veils, but other voices, soft and cunning. Garble was all he could make out, though occasionally words became clear, and at last he realized that what he was hearing was a spell-chant. He would have stiffened in preparation for self-defense, if he'd had command of his body. It, however, was sleeping peacefully. He tried to wake himself by willing some awareness of the floor beneath his rump, but there was no response.

"Who are you?" he asked at last of the vague shadow he sensed behind the texture of magical power. "What's this crap you're muttering?"

There was no answer, though he felt a distant awareness turn in his direction. A wave of force made him stumble. He struggled to regain his feet, misjudged the need, and fell heavily. He lay with his face hard upon darkness.

In that darkness shapes began to coagulate like curdles in a black milk. Leering, horrendous shapes. Faces of nightmare and disease. *Monsters*.... He wrenched himself away from the vision, feeling physical revulsion, and the darkness seemed to drip thickly from his lips like clinging slime. Coldness carried on a hard wind jabbed his skin as though with icy knives. He opened his eyes.

The world had become a nightmare.

There were bodies on the dirt about his feet, twisted, torn bodies, bent into strange contortions as though tossed from a great height. He recognized some of them with an oddly distant twinge of regret and fear: an old man from his hometown Zogran who had taught him many things and had been killed by a deforming illness; an infant, almost foetal, smeared with translucent gore—his still-born brother perhaps; Karlin, an elder sister by his father's first wife, who'd died in a riding accident; and his father, dead like the rest, held to the ground by a rough pole that skewered his chest. Eresteyin his mother, too, accusing him as her body crumbled to dust, her hand resting on the shattered brow of Ishwarin, as though on an holy icon. Nearby were newer corpses, freshly bloodied: Remis Sarsdarl, dark hair sprayed about her face, eyes dulled to opaque gray marbles; Arhl, his head crushed and broken, arms cracked like brittle bow-wood.

Tashnark cried out—perhaps it was a challenge—and from the silence that took over as his curse faded there grew a sustained roar, a screeching of almost-human timbre, but so cold Tashnark could scarcely credit it might come from a man. He crouched, expecting an attack, his fingers squeezing around the hilt of his sword. As he felt the sculptured metal his heart trembled, unnerved and disoriented. There were intertwined, ornamental serpents where none had been before and he could not, for a moment, remember what it meant.

Fiercely, he wrenched it from the scabbard and held the blade high. Light glimmered along its length like flaming quicksilver, running the etched designs and causing incandescent spots to dance before his eyes.

"What is this?" he cried.

A mute stillness smothered the sound almost at once. He lowered the alien weapon and glanced around, concerned to spy his enemy through the light-fog that surrounded him. At first he could see nothing. The air had turned cold, a chill biting at his face and making his eyes water. He choked down the growling in his throat, conscious of how conspicuous the sound was in the present noiseless calm. He waited, mesmerized by the deep quiet and the ruined bodies.

Suddenly a strident roar stabbed through his nerves and muscles. It came from no one direction. On an impulse he forced his eyes skywards, in time to see the jaws of a large flying monster emerging from the air. He flung himself aside and the creature, now whole, swung past him—a terrible shadowy mass, black and segmented, on thin, elongated wings that brushed the darkness as gently as the wind that ruffled his hair. It was about the length of a man and blackly metallic, its hide like armor, covered by tiny pricks that would rip his human flesh to ribbons should they rub against him. A claw on the end of one of its trailing legs clashed against his sword and he felt the monster's power wrench his shoulder. Then the creature was gone. Oddly, he recalled another fight, somewhere else, and blinked with the unrecognized memory. *He swung his sword and impaled something monstrous, something that spouted blood then shredded away into empty air.*

"You are Tashnark," a voice said, *"Take care!"*

He cleared his mind of Bellarroth.

And spun, sweeping his blade in hope of gutting the returning creature. But there was nothing to cut, except the wind and quietness.

The monster had landed on the plain a hundred paces from him, its compound eyes glowing darkly, as though currents of energy flowed beneath the faceted surface. Grasping jaws extended and withdrew in anticipation of attack. There were even multiple feelers twitching from beneath the joint where head-plate overlapped thorax. They looked wet and poisonous. What sort of miscreation was this?

The thing shuffled forward on its oddly jointed legs, its resting wings like a brilliant, translucent cloak across its back. Dust stirred, but the monster did not seem about to take flight. That, at any rate, was a blessing.

Instead it scurried at him so fast he scarcely had time to raise his guard. The dust-whirls rose thickly in clinging spirals and Tashnark choked, thrusting his sword at the black shadow. He missed, but the creature had missed him too. In the pause that followed, as it stopped and turned, Tashnark leapt at its back, jabbing downwards with the sword. Gritty air filled his vision; the insect's armor slid under his feet. Rows of spikes tore his breeches, would have mutilated his ankles but for the thick leather of his boots. His sword blade hit at a bad angle. It ricocheted off, throwing him hard to one side. He lost his balance and tumbled into the dust.

When he looked up, he couldn't see where the monster had hidden itself. Shadows crowded him, blurring outlines, hiding detail. But the tones of gray were cut by streaks and splatters of red, images of death, and his eyes focused on a man-figure that had risen among the other fragments. It was dark, solid, strong. Tashnark realized with a start that this newcomer stood clear and unobscured by fog, a discrepancy that the logic of reality denied. And he wore a familiar face.

Tashnark pushed himself up and stumbled forward. He grappled with the image like a drunken man, the world suddenly insecure. The figure was broad-shouldered, arms knotted with muscle, brown-skinned and rough-textured, black hair tied into three plaits, moustache unkempt, eyes red beneath heavy brows. Mockery hovered about his lips. Tashnark blinked, bewildered. It was a monstrous image of himself.

The figure stepped toward him with deliberate ease, lips moving voicelessly. Tashnark felt pain like a bruise in his head. Serpents were sprouting from the eyes of the figure; their hissing grew more hideously strident as each moment passed.

It reached toward him. Yellow liquid dripped from its finger-tips.

"Stay back!" Tashnark yelled.

The figure merely smiled.

"Take any shape you like, it won't gain you an edge," Tashnark said, pointing his sword. The figure's lips twitched.

"I have come to claim you." The voice was his own, distorted.

"Then you've wasted your time."

The figure gestured casually. "I am the monster that dwells inside you, my friend. I have no need to win you. I make you crude and thoughtless, I turn you to violence and denial, whatever you will. Do you want love, Tashnark? I am the one who keeps it from you. Can you accept that you are never more than a falsehood, doomed to ignorance of yourself and incapable of trust and innocence? Can you accept that there is monstrosity in your soul?"

"Shut up!"

"And if I don't? I can see you fear me. Deal with that fear now, in the way of all men. I'm unarmed, as you see."

Tashnark stepped back as the figure came nearer. The point of his blade turned to the specter's heart. Yet he couldn't strike. Instinctively he knew it would be a mistake. Here in this magical state symbols became psychic facts. What might happen in the real world if in this place he should slay his monstrous self? That might be an acknowledgement of the truth of this image, and such a confession could destroy him. He couldn't afford to doubt.

"I won't have anything to do with you. I'll ignore you. You're not real."

The figure laughed. Tashnark heard a rush behind him. A blow struck his shoulders from the rear and he fell into dust as it rose in a fury to blur the nightmare. The insect monster had returned and was upon him. He felt the sharp heaviness of its legs tumble across his thigh, and thrashed out with his only free hand, his left, in an instinctive shielding motion. It was a lucky move. His fist sank into saliva and loose skin. Though hard molar-like jaws were buried there so that he was bruised and cut, it saved him from a worse fate. The creature clicked and drew back. Then its wings outspread. Wind raised the dust into a blinding fog. The creature began to rise and as it did Tashnark felt its legs tighten around him. Spikes dug into his side. It was lifting him.

In a sudden panic Tashnark freed his sword-arm and struck through the cloud of dirt. He felt his blade jar and skid across the insect's armor. Then it hit something softer, cut into it. The monster's cry, more pained than he would have expected from so inconclusive a blow, shattered the silence and stung his ears. He thought he heard words forming in the screech: *"Hanin, serris!"* and another: *"Arin tel-ornthus!"* Then he was released. An instant later he hit the ground. He caught his breath and stood, straining his eyes through the murk for the next attack. One thing he now realized, though he should have known it all along: none of this—the dead bodies, the monster, the figure who had challenged him—none of it was real. It was, rather, an attack upon his mind. Its hold was tenuous—he could see that, for he was still alive, was gaining advantage—and somehow he'd threatened it. He must use this fact to break through and help the others. Maybe they were in even greater danger.

A dark insect-shadow appeared in the haze. Tashnark struck at it with all his strength and felt vibrations as the blade ground into the hard shell and sliced free into a more fleshy interior. Yellow ooze sprayed across his shoulder. There was no sound of pain, but the creature fell heavily into the dust, following the interrupted trajectory of its flight and dragging Tashnark after it. At that moment, as he stumbled and fell, a cold wind licked across the plain, smashing sand and air into a maelstrom of light and dark.

The current was powerful, as though hundreds of strong but rotting fingers were dragging at him, pulling him into the sinkhole created by the insect-creature's departure. Yet he knew he couldn't go there. To follow it into its own darkness would be his destruction.

The pressure mounted. It sucked at his flesh...or was it his mind? The distinction had been lost in this place. Frantically, he gouged his fingers into the earth and pulled himself in the opposite direction. Muscles across his shoulders and down his arms screamed at him in protest. But he couldn't hold against it. He felt his fingers slipping.

Then a hand—a healthy, muscular hand—reached through the air to him.

vi.

While he waited for Lord Worjaren Rehemon to act, memories came to Aridor—memories of the Vornarcan court, specifically that wonderful occasion when Eblamthezaik, the Dark God servant, deigned to bestow his blessing upon their endeavors. Aridor remembered the visitation clearly, and always would, but now the images seemed harsh and painful, as though viewed through a burning light.

A monstrous creature glared at him. The Ormsinir of Huedaik—Dark God servant. One of its two bird-like heads stretched out in a leisurely fashion. Its eyes contracted.

Lord Worjaren stepped forward.

"There is more to you than is common," the Being said quietly. "You have a nature we can use. But take care. You are our servant now, as always."

It dismissed him and Worjaren Rehemon returned to his place. Others followed, one by one begging the Godling's favor. The Godling acknowledged none as he had Lord Worjaren

Rehemon.

When Terissaron, lord of one of the surrounding slave-states, came forward and spoke his devotion, his demeanor was no different from that of the lords he followed. But his voice had barely finished echoing from the high walls when Eblamthezaik's words swept its last tones into oblivion. "This man stands condemned before us, a coward whose lies stain the sanctity of our presence. Even now he deals with the enemy."

"Master," Terissaron said, turning pale and trembling. "How can you believe this of so devoted a servant? Someone has defamed me."

"You defame yourself. To Eblamthezaik who reads treachery in your soul, your life is forfeit." The eyes of the Godling became more icy, as a scream tore from the throat of the wretched Lord. His shaking hands clutched at the air for an instant, finding no support, then he fell forward limply. So silent was the Hall that the thud of his collapse echoed like thunder over the heads of the gathering. "He shall be no more," the Godling said. Lord Terissaron's body began to distort, turning ugly and monstrous. His chest bulged as though the air had become a viscous fluid and refracted the light. Another face arose from it, a parody of Terissaron's intelligent features. It stretched out like a serpent, glaring at the people in the Hall.

"Praise be to Huedaik!" it hissed, in a voice forced from something that should never have spoken. The head retreated into Terissaron's body, and both it and its unnatural appendage crumbled to dust.

"We are merciful," the Godling's voice cracked through the silence. "Lord Terissaron feels no pain."

The memory was both horrific and glorious.

Freed by Lord Worjaren's attack, and sitting now in his coach, waiting upon the Lord's arrival, Aridor felt a moment of peace in the remembrance. But it did not last. A familiar awareness came into his mind, dragging new imagery from his sight-memory to form patterns according to its commanding will. Lord Worjaren Rehemon had activated the link that existed between them—the

Acolyte-bond of the Vornarcan aristocracy—and was making his way into Aridor's mind.

At once Aridor seemed to see the Lord before him, his robust, hard face, flushed as though with heat, forming from a swirl of foreign coloration in the night's bleakness. Once again, rain fell across the cinderblock street, though it did not touch Lord Worjaren's image. "I can barely sense them, Acolyte." The Lord's voice betrayed a restrained displeasure. "They have fled. But they must be found. You were close to them. Can you provide a key?"

A key?

He knew what the Master wanted. Something, some distinctive characteristic that might leave its mark upon the energy currents of the world, so that he could open a pathway to the ones he sought.

Aridor pictured his enemies in his inner Eye, like slowly clarifying landscapes in a morning fog.

First, the one he called the undead master—she was a spellbinder. Remis Sarsdarl was her name. He pictured the sharp contour of her nose, her thin lips, the rise of her cheekbones, her gray-green eyes. He wove his vision through her dark rolls of hair, stroked the fine texture of her light tan skin. He remembered the quality cloth she wore, noticed the jewellery around her neck, on her fingers. Jewellery? There might be something there.... No. He had read the magic in her when he subdued her, but it would be difficult to locate like this, in so large a city. No, they could not use her.

The other then? A mental picture of the male formed, a distant one, for Aridor had only seen him for a moment before his own power had betrayed him. Solid, strong, face dark and heavy, ruggedly unkempt. He recalled the man's eccentric hairstyle— and the special forms of his aura...that would be easier to find, but still like seeking a single fish in a vast ocean. Even to one who studied another's spirit in detail and with love there was an inherent difficulty in applying metaphysical search skills to human beings: they were so variable, so unpredictable in the way they thought and acted. Even tightly controlled currents of Deep Power would find it difficult to penetrate the chaos. No, there was little chance there and that chance so small as to become inconceivable in the short time and using the weak resources available to him. If he had time for major rituals then perhaps something could be done....

Wait. He pulled himself up with a start, remembering.... Yes, in the last instant of magical conflict, there had been a power-artifact present in the divination: some sort of weapon—he remembered its pattern clearly. Unlike men, a magical object had a fixed power-shape. It did not color according to ethereal moods; its nature was, however complex, finite. Familiarity was easier, location more definite. And this one's aura would be strong, enough to create waves visible to those who could see. However difficult such a task might be, it was a possibility not utterly futile. It might suffice.

He was about to direct his thoughts to Lord Worjaren, but there was no need. Worjaren Rehemon had been party to his musings all along.

"I fear, Lord," he said, "that the memory may be a false trail. My divination of these things would lack thoroughness."

"I am your senior, Aridor, by a greater number of years than you could guess. There is knowledge in me that the greatest wisemen of Zarth's Vornarcan Court barely conceive to exist anywhere in the world." Aridor held the fleeting impression of an ancient insanity momentarily on the edge of breaking out. "We will search, the two of us," the Lord whispered, "under a much older and more powerful clairvoyance," and without pause, words foreign even to Aridor's extensive esoteric learning began to sting the currents of Deep Power surrounding him into a lather of agitation. Vertigo wrenched his distant body. He thought they rose for a moment high above the ground, out of the coach, to the firmament, through it into unformed chaos. There was fire and fury, a high-waspish shrill—then they were speeding towards a point of magical discontinuity that filled his senses with sudden enlightenment. He knew where in the City the pattern was located, though part of him denied the knowledge and could not understand how the spell could have been worked. So fast. So exact.

Enough, Acolyte, that it has worked.

Aridor heard the voice and felt fear at the unknown, perhaps unknowable, powers his Lord was displaying. They'd been drawn toward the magic-pattern of the weapon in an instant. Once the Lord had known the object's inner form, experienced it in Aridor's memory, there had been only a moment of search. How was it possible? Aridor reached out and felt a profound relief as his fingers clutched the padded seat beside him.

Night-wind battered the coach, edging its vibrations up through his spine. His bones felt harsh and abrasive under the skin.

"Remain here, Aridor." The Lord's voice in his mind had a mellow reality more congenial than sensations stabbing at him through his body.

"Lord?"

"Stay and await my coming. I'm near and shall take them myself. A number of Thargonal's men are close on their trail, and I can use these and the men accompanying me now in the taking."

Thargonal was one of the Lords of Vesuula—indeed he was patriarch of one of the Ruling Families of the Merchant State. But he was also a Dark God devotee and in thrall to Lord Worjaren.

"I may need you too, Aridor," his Lord continued. "May need our bond—not for physical force, but the more subtle force of your spirit. Be open. Wait. The end is in sight."

Then Aridor was alone. He closed his eyes, wishing away his awareness of Lord Worjaren's power. It worried him, its illogic not of the magic systems he knew.

But perhaps the Lord's command of Deep Power was that of Eblamthezaik Himself. Aridor had seen Lord Worjaren Rehemon especially honored in the palace of Vornarca, when the Ormsinir had purged the Court of those considered unworthy and given to the survivors the task they were even now pursuing. It was not without precedent that special power might have come with the honoring.

An odd melancholy settled over Aridor. He sighed, wiping his hand across his forehead as though to smooth away some lingering crease.

vii.

The hand took Tashnark and dragged him back from the sinkhole. Tashnark didn't know whether he should resist it or not, but in the end he had little choice. It took him and the world changed.

Cold passed. Dust settled. For a heart's beat there was silence. Then Tashnark opened his eyes. He was sticky with sweat and something else...blood. He pushed himself up and through the dimness saw that he was back in Remis's workroom. The grate-fire was nearly dead, its embers shedding a vague red glow that gave ghostlike shape to objects in the room. He felt for his sword, gripped it—there were no serpent-designs now—and stood. His muscles felt strained and his head ached.

Urgently he glanced about the room. At his feet, disembow-eled, lay the corpse of a stranger and the stench of death tainted the air. The two wounded prisoners, who had been stashed in the corner of the room, were now dead, their throats cut—someone had decided they were more trouble than they were worth. The enemy wizard was gone.

Remis appeared before him, startling him. Her face was gaunt and strained.

"I don't know who you are," she said.

There was something wrong. He felt the wrongness, as though this place was not as real as it seemed.

"Was it you that dragged me back?" he asked.

The clash of weaponry carried to him out of the silence, galvanizing him into renewed action. It had come from the yard at the rear of the shop. Dark stains lay across the threshold—blood. Whose? He stepped over it, pushing aside an unhinged panel, and the damp night sprayed over him. A man was sprawled across the overgrown stone path that led down to the gate. Light glinted in splashes of blood around him. Tashnark didn't recognize him.

Nor did he recognize the figure that stepped out of the darkness shrouding the corpse. At first what he noticed about this one was a shirt decorated with alien symbols, and his bloodied sword, its blade catching at the light. He knew it wasn't Arhl and tensed, assuming a defensive stance.

"Please," the stranger said, stepping forward, "I'm here to help."

Lightning sizzled across the sky. In its flash, Tashnark saw a face. Youthful and serious, clean-shaven, with thick, well-defined lips. Hair, ratty with rain, hung limply about the neck. Eyes caught the light like a cat's—magic, perhaps, though if it was, it was magic of an ordinary, physical kind.

"We must get out of here," the man insisted. "Now!"

"Who are you?"

"I'm called Shaan." With a smooth movement, he wiped his sword blade clean against the cloth of his pants.

"Shaan? Do I know you?"

"I don't think so." He took another step closer.

Tashnark gestured a warning. "That's far enough."

The stranger held out his left hand in a placating gesture. "Please, we don't have time. We're too vulnerable here." The hand was muscular and reassuring. "Take it," he said.

Tashnark moved toward him, watching for signs of treachery. "It was you, wasn't it? You pulled me from that other place."

"Yes. Now you must take my hand again."

"Why?"

"Because you are still under threat. A false world forged by your enemy is all around you, tainting the world of the senses, leaking through it. I have helped you push it away, but the hold is tenuous."

"Why should I believe you?"

"Because you have no choice."

Close now, Tashnark stared into his eyes. The stranger didn't flinch. Tashnark saw no obvious guile in him, but couldn't allow himself to trust so easily. What sort of a name was 'Shaan' anyway? Insofar as it suggested the name of Vesuula's much-revered Guardian Deity, Shaa, was it supposed to lend him a spurious respectability?

"Why are you here?" he asked.

"I've been sent to help you."

"Help us against what?"

Shaan gestured in an expansive movement that swept casually over the City and the events of the recent past. "Haven't you sensed the powers at work here? This is no mortal conflict. Can't you feel the darkness?"

"Darkness?"

"The Rebels—the Dark God E'ashalsinir—turn their eyes on this place and this time. The air of all Rheateesha reeks of their plots."

For some reason he couldn't understand, Tashnark found himself unable to satirize this declaration. He wanted to scorn the notion, to deny reality to the Dark Gods—those distorted Raashyr made monstrous under the ancient influence of the creation deity Junsar's mistakes. But he couldn't. Instead he muttered, "Why?"

"That's the riddle that brings me here."

Wind howled through the workroom. At his feet Tashnark noticed a small mark crawling across the stones—the tiny insect he'd seen before the attack. As he watched it now, it looked up at him and its face was that of a man. It grinned at him. Tashnark frowned, and crushed the thing with his boot.

The garden and the walls behind him—through into Remis's house—trembled as though struck by some massive internal wind. They reared up, stretching into grotesque shapes, and then began to dissipate. Something new was leaking out of the gaps as the image thinned.

"What's happening?" he cried.

"Come with me!" cried Shaan, reaching for him.

This time, Tashnark grasped his hand.

viii.

The famed Wargrin-Othos of Koerpel-Na—the City's artistic precinct—was situated behind the large High Gate Market along Mummer's Avenue. A place of decorative stone, fancy metalwork, towers and artistry, popularly frequented, rich and beautiful. "An over-dressed whore," Tashnark had often remarked.

Now, in early morning darkness, it lay unnaturally emptied of patron and artist alike, its singers songless, its dancers still, its actors invisible.

The irregular wheels of Arhl's heavy wagon ground noisily on the stones of Mummer's Avenue and tossed unsettling echoes off the buildings they passed. The ornate buildings of the Wargrin-Othos—closed gaming houses on one side and warehouses on the other—towered over them like the cliffs of a wilderness pass. Arhl's soft growl urged the hesitant draught horses beneath the road-spanning Arch of Kentos. Tashnark heard him whisper to them, "There's nothing to fear, babies. Nothing to fear."

His eyes rested on the Arch, which was ornamented by weathered filigree and the cat-symbol of the ancient actors guild. Named for the area's most glorious thespian, the Arch formed a bridge from residential buildings on the right side to offices within the Wargrin-Othos itself. He let his eyes follow the structure up and over him as they passed beneath it. He thought he could see a small, dark blotch that might have been a window. Heavy raindrops fell on the cart from the smeared stonework, splattering with sudden energy, and one caught Tashnark on his forehead. Water sprayed into his eyes.

He blinked. For a moment the great theater district disappeared, replaced by a colorless fog. He blinked again and it returned. Above him, strange sculptured faces— gargoyles and stone gods—were wrenched into movement, turning to watch as they moved away.

"What the hell!" he muttered, trying to remember what had led up to this moment, but unable to recall the details.

Shaan gripped his shoulder in a firm clench. "You're still affected by the dream," he said.

"Dream?" Tashnark glanced around again. The familiar buildings looked grim and threatening. "This is the Wargrin-Othos. I know it."

"It's where our bodies are, but the sorcerer's power draws us away. At the moment he is distant, doesn't know exactly where we are. We skirted danger to reach Arhl's smithy, and have been ahead of the hunt ever since."

"I can't remember anything about it."

"What you remember doesn't matter. We must reach safety before the sorcerer can focus on us."

They were passing the open way where Tulid'bar Street— which led directly to the City's largest theater, the Tulid'bar Dome—intersected the Mummer's Avenue. Wind hummed between tall towers at the rear of an untidy forum. The noise was like a melody.

Tashnark glanced around as the wagon ground on past the Soydis and the Acoris Gaming Houses. Their adjacent façades were as impenetrable and as dark as the other buildings in the Wargrin-Othos, though Tashnark thought he caught a glimpse of candle-light in the upper storey of the Soydis House, and he wondered whether it lit the last strategies in some languishing card-game that had outlived the area's less obsessive occupations. There were definite, irregular light-washes spasmodically blanching the windows of a place further down the street—but that wasn't surprising. He recognized it. He had gone there himself several times, when his pocket had been full of idle change and his mind careless. It was the Sut-Siros brothel, palace of erotic and magical delights...its customers were commonly nocturnal creatures. Cold bit at his cheeks. He huffed it away, blowing warmth into his cupped hands.

Life was going on around them, oblivious to their dilemma.

Movement on the edge of his vision made him turn his head. A gray shadow scurried along the wooden façade of a darkened pub and leapt into an alcove. Tashnark kept his eyes on the place where it disappeared, and for a moment saw two spots of light that blinked at the wagon and then were gone. A cat? he wondered in amazement. He hadn't seen one of those for a long time. Perhaps it was a pet belonging to one of the Wargrin-Othos's foreign inhabitants. Or maybe just another omen.

Then Shaan yelled something he didn't quite catch, though its urgency was clear enough. Tashnark gripped his sword-hilt and converted the relaxed posture he had assumed into a nervous readiness. Remis, too, was alert and Arhl jerked the horses to a stop.

"Ahead, and on this road. They're approaching fast. And they're aware of us. I felt strong magic reaching this way, searching and driving them on. There's immense power with them—"

"The one who attacked me?" Remis's voice sounded weak with echoes.

"Not that one," Shaan replied, glancing into the night. "Far more potent...still a man, but unlike any man I've ever encountered."

"I don't like the sound of that." Tashnark turned toward Arhl. "Can you get us out of here?", surveying the road, knowing the nearest branch ahead was still a long way off.

"I'll have to turn about," grunted his friend, holding the horses with difficulty against their impatience to go on.

A gust of wind and its ensnared rain rolled over them and hissed for them to run. The distant perspective of the street was moving like a cloud of darkness—toward them? Perhaps. Something more substantial gave edge to the shadows.

"Too late!" The voice was Shaan's but there was a quality in it that transcended ordinary desperation as it might have arisen in Remis, Arhl, or Tashnark. Tashnark watched him leap from the back of the wagon, re-formed into a blur of agile motion. He heard the voice again. "Take cover! He summons power."

Tashnark scrambled desperately toward the rear of the cart. His knee scraped across a row of raised nail-heads in the battered wood. Ordinary pain turned his fear to fury. He drew his sword. Arhl had already abandoned his seat and Remis had dropped behind the back wheel. She muttered wizard-words.

No time, thought Tashnark.

He was about to grab Remis and say as much, but his forward-turned eye caught on a splinter of light beyond her in the unfocused distance, and when he tried to make sense of it, the spark stretched toward him like a breath of fire. It reached them in an instant, before he could cry out warning or alarm. A wall of incandescence and searing heat burst noiselessly only a few paces from where he crouched. The impact threw him backwards and he tumbled from the wagon, which shuddered and was dragged back. When he looked up, the light and heat had passed. From his prone position, through the wheels of the cart, he could see that one of the horses had been almost totally incinerated and the other lay dying in its companion's ashes. The smell of burnt flesh was overpowering.

He sprang up and glanced beyond the cart, past Remis, who was holding her head, stunned as much by the blast as by the abrupt disruption of her spell.

Wisps of dirty mist swirled around them as the wind fought back against the fire. Along the street human-shapes were taking form, whether magically or out of the darkness Tashnark couldn't tell. When he looked away from them, Shaan was beside him.

"Let's go," the youth whispered. "That was only a warning...a small thing. I can't fend it off indefinitely."

"A small thing!" Morbid terror spun terrible possibilities in Tashnark's mind.

"Just a tease."

"I don't think we've got much choice," came Arhl's voice from somewhere. Tashnark glanced around until he found him.

He was pointing back along the Mummer's Avenue, back into the darkness they had escaped. There were men there, caught on the thin edges of a distant street-lamp's pale aura.

Tashnark's throat rumbled. "Then we fight," he said.

ix.

Hanin's skeletal fingers swiped at his face, striking him hard. Bellarroth staggered. "What—?"

The moment contracted. As Shaan grabbed at his arm and gently restrained him, Tashnark snapped back out of the dream that was threatening to take him. The transition had come and gone in little more than a moment.

"No, Tashnark," said Shaan, his grip tight. "They're ordinary men, but enough to kill you."

Tashnark pulled himself loose, re-orienting himself, but he did not move toward the distant enemy. He let his eyes pick out the dim figures. There were about ten on foot and, in the more obscure background, a few riders. They were not in motion, but were clearly on the watch for any attempt that might be made to thwart their master's plan. Tashnark said: "What's to be done? Surrender?"

Nobody answered. Then Remis said: "I'm a spellbinder, but perhaps there's some magic I can adapt for combat—"

"Hear me!" A strong voice, emanating from the direction of the magic, filtered to them out of the night. Tashnark growled instinctively.

"I think we're about to be given our options."

"I won't suck up to Dark God scum," muttered Arhl.

Crouched in the shadows of the cart as far out of sight as possible, Remis had begun preparing a spell. It concerned her that her books and grimoires had been left behind. Memory would have to suffice. Combat gave little time for consultation, and fleetingly she wondered how her brethren in more offensive disciplines coped. Clumsy with fear, she began reworking the flexible structures of her *cerenil*, so that she could use it as center of a protective aegis, forming a barrier out of the Deep Power currents. Memory was a weak stay against failure.

"I have come on an errand already too long delayed," the voice said. As it spoke, the night air seemed to die away into stillness, as though frightened by the sound. When it continued, the words came from the air, from the road beneath their feet. *"Gentle handling and absence of leadership had thus far saved you, but now such leniency is abandoned. I have come. Submit or die. There will be no concessions."*

The street fell silent. Tashnark pushed himself up to see over the cart and strained his eyes through the gloom in an attempt to spy the speaker. But the dim shapes were unsatisfying. Where was Sumis when it was needed? Was it even possible for civil authorities to enter into this conflict?

Tashnark fingered his sword, scraping the point along the stones beneath the cart.

"What's in these buildings?" Arhl gestured tightly with his fist. His white skin was flushed red.

"Hostels and inns," said Tashnark. "That theater...." He pointed to the gilt ornamental façades of a building down the street on their left, "...backs onto an alley."

"We must go through it," said Arhl decisively.

"What? Break in?"

"The doors of these gaming rooms are strong, and a moment's delay will kill us."

Shaan, who hadn't seemed to be listening, pointed toward the right-hand side of the street. "One of those inns then...that one, older. Its portals look frail enough."

"But their wizard will burn us before we take half a pace—"

"Spells take time, even for him." Remis held up her *cerenil*. "I've bound a protection spell into the crystal. It's weak, but if we stay together it should keep most of his power off us...once, at least. I didn't have time for anything fancier."

"What can you do against *that*?"

But the echoing voice of their enemy curtailed Tashnark's

pessimism for the moment. *"There's been sufficient time for thought,"* it said. *"Come out now."* Silence, then: *"Don't force me to slay you."*

"Bluff!" said Remis. "He wants us alive. We can't give him what he wants if we're dead."

"He only needs one of us," Tashnark pointed out. "We'd better go now."

Remis spoke a word, a strange sound like a curse. Tashnark thought he felt the air thicken as though its currents had been bound tighter. This was the aegis, but it didn't give him confidence. "Come on," he yelled, standing in preparation for flight. Before they could move they heard the voice again, angry now and sharp with threat.

"I have no patience with folly."

His words were lost in sound like a blurring wind, and suddenly they were engulfed in flame. It writhed and hissed around them, white, red, scalding furiously at the air, ripping at Remis's aegis, sending sparks through onto their bodies to harmlessly die as floating bubbles die when they hit the ground. Remis staggered and Tashnark saw that her hands were bleeding.

"Run!" she croaked. "It won't hold."

Perhaps not, but for the time being, she had saved them. Now it was up to him. Tashnark lifted her bodily and leapt out away from cover. He loped with effortless strides toward the inn door, dark on the street's margin. The flames faded. Arhl and Shaan followed close behind.

For a heart's beat the street was silent and Remis held her breath, expecting fire to storm around them and death to come quickly. There was nothing left of her aegis, except blood that disrupted power had torn from her skin. Her pulses throbbed and pain prowled through her arms. Shaan whispered some hurried words but she didn't hear them. Only the wind-rush was audible, drowning the scrape of feet on the cobbles and Tashnark's hissing breath. Was there any spell-wording she could use, anything to reactivate the charm? No, fear had driven her studies away. Tashnark carried her on through those seconds, but when she heard an explosion behind them, the fear grew greater, drowning even the desire to remember. She glanced in the direction of the sound and for a moment, over Tashnark's arm, thought she saw smoke, flames and night surging around four vague, ghostlike figures on the other side of the road. Arrows were raining about the specters, but they simply ran on. *Who are they?* she wondered, but instinctively she knew. It was a reflection, the indistinct image of themselves.

And it was drawing the enemies' fire.

Shaan?

Then she was swept along and found herself dumped on the wooden threshold of an inn. A gold-tinted sign named it *The Red Pillow*. Its oak door was locked, barred by steel bolts, but Tashnark's shoulder tore them from the wood. From inside came a warm darkness that seemed to offer subtle comforts.

Remis glanced back at the street. The illusion had confounded their enemies only for a moment, though it had given time. A mounted man galloped toward them, shouting and waving a sword. The night was moving with antagonists. Remis was pushed through the doorway ahead of Arhl, and heard in her wake the dull thud of arrows pounding into the door-jamb and the outer wall. It was close. Shaan slammed the door shut.

"You people! What are you doing here?" They looked up the shadowy staircase to where an oil-lamp, newly lit, flickered uncertainly. There was an old man holding it, leaning on the balcony-rail and striking a defensive pose that failed to hide his apprehension. He seemed to be wearing a padded, silken night-gown. For a moment Tashnark wondered if he were some magical vision. "What do you mean, breaking the door like this? Have you lost your key?"

Someone said something in the gloom behind him and Tashnark realized that the glare of his lamp was obscuring other residents of the inn. He heard: "They've got weapons." "Robbery! Quick! Hide the jewels!" "What?"

Shaan held his hand to them pleadingly. "Go back to your rooms! If you value your lives, stay there."

"What do you mean by—?"

"It's the end of the world," Tashnark roared. "Hide!"

As though to confirm his prediction, a terrific jolt hit the front of the building and someone screamed. Plaster and wood-chip sprayed from the roof. "Come on!" Tashnark pulled at Shaan's coat. "Forget the clientele. Our necks are on the chopping-block, not theirs."

Remis followed them along the corridor toward the rear of the house. She was aware of Arhl's presence behind her, could hear his wheezing breath, rising and falling through the padding of feet on the boards. She pushed through a swinging door and into the kitchen. The air was thick with odors: heavy cheese, stews, a dozen different spices; Remis looked back along the hallway when she realized Arhl was not with her. He'd turned to face a group of men who had pursued them into the building.

"I'll hold them," he whispered to Remis, his hand tight around a short dagger-sword he'd collected from his forge-yard.

"Gut 'im!" yelled one of the men at the rear of the approaching group.

Remis grabbed at Arhl's shoulder. "Just scare them back. I need time. When I tell you, duck behind me!"

Before he could agree or disagree she had splintered a piece of wood from the wall and was smearing it with her drying blood. Words tumbled about in her mind. Just recently she'd read of a simple combative spell that utilized some of the principles of her spell-binding Art and joined them according to the principles of sympathetic magic. She'd read the words—but had never used them. If she could recall enough of them now, fabricating what was lost, perhaps she could be of use. She began the binding.

Arhl took a step toward their enemies, extending himself to his greatest height, and the men stopped, squinting at him in the gloom. "Out of the way, mountain-shit!" yelled the foremost. "They got frozen balls, Sarz. Gut 'im!" screamed another. The rest barked taunts and threats and came forward at last. But the hesitation had allowed Remis to complete the patched-up spell.

As Arhl made to take another step, she dug her fingers into his arm and, taking his cue, he leapt backwards instead, clearing the way for her. Remis tossed the wood-splinter and spoke the Goad-Spell that would release the stored power.

The attackers flinched, afraid of the words. But the wood fell harmlessly to the floor. "What?" hissed Arhl. The closest of the enemies laughed scornfully. "Not all your words sting, wizard. This'll cost you your head." He came forward. Remis cried out the words again, varying their inflexion. As the last sound died on her lips she sensed the Power rush up into her blood. It jumped, lashed out to the smears on the splinter. The corridor was suddenly filled with a roaring like wind. The man in front was thrown, screaming, clutching at his head, crashing against the others in a confusion of limbs and weapons. His bared flesh was pin-cushioned with tiny spears of wood. Most of the skin had been torn from his face.

"Quickly!" Remis said. Arhl and she backed into the kitchen and ran across the stone floor toward an external doorway. Pots hanging around the walls rattled slightly as though reacting to an external explosion. Beyond the kitchen there was an alley, a narrow space bounded by high brick walls and littered with heaps of refuse. Another alley ran off between the buildings. "Come on!" Tashnark yelled to her.

Images of an enemy face pierced by splinters flashed suddenly before her. It confused her and she paused to lean against the wall.

"Are you hurt?" Shaan asked her.

"It wasn't meant to be like this."

He nodded as though he understood. Remis was about to say more, but the sound of hurried movement interrupted her. Several figures came through the kitchen door, faces dark with the chase. Arhl pushed Remis away and would again have gone for their enemies had not Shaan sprung past him. "I will deal with these," he said curtly.

Arhl nodded and dragged Remis along the narrow alley. She lost sight of Shaan, but heard his opponents swear at him, the clash of blades, the fast shuffling of feet on stone and mud.

Beyond the line of pubs and hostels, they came upon an old stable yard, dark and cluttered, but allowing escape through to Canal Road and, hopefully to the roads behind Mallos House, offices of the Sumis police. Once there, Tashnark hoped, they would have eluded their enemies' net—or if not, they could in desperation seek refuge with the Sumis-Warden on night-duty. Perhaps their attackers would think twice about raiding an official building.

He thought of Remis and glanced back. She was there alongside Arhl, stumbling through the mess with a look of disdainful annoyance on her face and frowning half-heartedly, as though confused by the excitement. Well, why not? Which of them could possibly be expected to have their normal lives wrenched loose from secure moorings without some degree of confusion? Only Shaan seemed unflustered—and they weren't to know what was normal in his life. Tashnark strained his eyes to see back down the alley-way and identified Shaan there, battling several opponents. What was the fool doing?

"Tashnark!"

He focused on Remis, who was shouting wildly, and then followed the direction of her gesture. Two scenes impressed themselves upon him almost simultaneously, the one in close attendance to the other. At first he saw the back of a wooden stable, on one side a broken fence and a field of straw-like grass, catching at the night-air in wisps of faded light; through a gap in the posts, a dunnish mound, a beast sleeping in the pasture under the eves of the shed; shadowing walls still dripping dirty water; beyond these, Canal Road and the façades of adjacent houses. The sky had begun to surge again. Tashnark blinked at the suggestion of a human figure emerging from a veil of shadow near the stable, and suddenly, absurdly, the scene was gone. A memory, his mind cried, a wish imagined.

No escape. A tall stone wall.

He blinked again. There was no stable, no grass, no pasture, no visible sky. A stone wall extending from the rear of one inn across a space there only in memory. Memory. Remis gripped his arm, and he tightened his hold on his sword, knowing that confrontation had come. He felt the serpent shapes form on his sword's hilt without surprise.

No escape.

Shadows coalesced near the base of the wall. A man formed, tall, heavy in build, with robes like mist, dripping over him to form shadows about his feet. His eyes glowed as though they burned. He stepped forward, gesturing arrogantly. "What use in flight?" he said with gentle authority. Tashnark looked around, hoping for a way out. But ahead the alley, unexpectedly, ended in another wall, and behind him, just as strangely, the way they had come was now blocked.

"Magic!" he hissed.

"Lay aside your weapon." Tashnark's eyes went back to the stranger, forgetful of the walls, the alley-garbage, his allies.... His jaw tensed into a scowl. Fifteen or twenty paces, he calculated. Perhaps less.

"Aggression would be foolish!" the man said, a frown moving across his forehead and bending his sharp lips downward into wrinkles.

Tashnark took one step and the stranger raised his hand. Jewels flashed light into shadowy corners. His mouth opened but he said nothing, and a new look, a stretching of the skin around the eyes, almost like pain, urged Tashnark into action. A scatter of wind whipped the enemy sorcerer's robes. Tashnark shouted—something ancient or foul, he couldn't afterwards remember—and bounded wolf-like, his sword rising high for a death-stroke. He didn't expect to reach his enemy—only his own death seemed likely. The stranger's magic would repel his attack. His mind clouded and time stretched. *He faced the sorcerer, alone. He was no longer in the City at all, nor in the place of magic—but far distant, in some fiercer realm.*

* * * * * * *

His mind grappled desperately to find a point of stillness. Memory became foreign. For a moment he was both Tashnark and Bellarroth. Then the transition was over and Tashnark was forgotten.

He felt the sting of Hanin's skeletal fingers on his cheek and turned to stare a challenge into the wizard's opaque eyes. "Son-Bellarroth. The way is there. I bred into you the skills I lack, culled in your making from the soft tissues of Tammenallor's monstrous body. Use the knowledge, or your stupidity will doom us all."

Bellarroth suppressed his indignation, content to acknowledge the old man's wisdom, rather than his tone. "What should I do then?"

"Shut out sight. Move toward Tammenallor's heart without it. If danger threatens, I'll give you sign enough."

Bellarroth clenched his eyelids shut. He waited for some sense of direction to come upon him, breathing heavily in the sudden and disturbing silence.

There was a quaver in the skin beneath his feet and his eyes sprang open. "It's just your nerves," said Hanin.

Bellarroth nodded and obscured his sight with his free hand. He puzzled at the darkness for a while, seeking to pierce its secrets with an inner eye untricked by ill-shaped light. Only the presence of Hanin was strong enough to transcend his blindness. Then, when he was about to give it away, he thought he sensed a path on his right hand—where he remembered there had been a wall. Tentatively, wary of scraping his knuckles, he drew his hand across the roughly textured barrier. "It's useless," he cried.

Suddenly, before he could react, he was grabbed and spun by clutching hands. Hanin said, "Keep your eyes closed. Don't act from memory but by inspiration, without thought that you might tweak your nose on the wall." The spinning stopped and Bellarroth regained his balance, disoriented and flustered. He reached out with his mind and knew the path.

"This way!" he said and headed off carelessly, assuming that

Hanin would follow. He heard the old man's "Ah!" of triumph and smiled with pride at his success.

Then his foot caught on something and he lunged forward, opening his eyes in time to see the rising ground and to crash painfully onto his out-stretched elbow. His sword fell from his grip and its light disappeared like a fleeing wraith. Bellarroth cursed.

But it was not darkness that replaced the sword light. A steely gloom settled about him like ash.

"Up!" growled Hanin's voice and a boot jabbed at his thigh. "You seem to have succeeded, son-Bellarroth. Up, and meet our gaoler and host."

Befuddled, Bellarroth rose, grabbing instinctively for his sword. Its interwoven serpent hilt, knobbly under his grip, reassured him. Then his eyes searched the gloom ahead, latching at once onto the impossible figure there.

A throne, made of chiseled rock (impossible on this world of flesh) and inlaid with gems, rose before him to a height of some five men of his own size. Seated on the throne was Tammenallor Itself. The Beast was many times Bellarroth's size, but, even so, only a miniature replica of Its Great Self. How could they walk upon the Monster, yet confront It here in this cavern at the same time?

"Images," said Hanin, oddly distant. "We function in allegory, and face the Kharathahul's spirit in the form of Its body. Such is the magic we have woven."

"We?"

"Tammenallor and I."

"I don't understand."

Hanin did not reply. The dim light gave an illusion of instability, for the Monster's ugly head, squat, eyeless, with a wide, twisted mouth, was ringed by masses of serpents like hair, and this collar, squirming with movement, hid the solidity of the great creature's neck. The head looked as though it might slide away from the body and attack him, with no need to disturb the enthroned monarch.

"And so I must kill this thing?" Bellarroth asked, though it sounded absurd. The monster was watching them but did not react.

To Bellarroth's surprise, Hanin muttered a denial.

"Then why have we bothered to come here?"

Hanin grabbed him roughly, thrusting forward a gaunt hand to draw his attention. "How often do we have to go over it? Haven't I said before this that if Tammenallor dies, so must we? We live on Its shoulders, son-Bellarroth! Kill It? Of course you mustn't kill It." His voice softened. "And it's plain to see the monster's dying, without your interference." True, there were terrible wounds and burns on Tammenallor's gently swelling torso. The creature's eyes were filled with pain, and Its agony kept It rigid in Its seat. "We've come to fulfil a necessity. There are events culminating here that have been in preparation for centuries." Hanin shook his head. "But I fear we're too late. The monster is hard pressed by Its fate—and Its end will be ours as well."

One of Tammenallor's clawed limbs lifted slowly as though in gesture to them, but Bellarroth could read nothing except pain in the movement. He was silent, then pushed past the old man and strode toward the Kharathahul. Gray light played over him as he stared defiantly up at the monster's gnarled face.

"Tammenallor!" he exclaimed, "You're on the verge of death and can no longer raise effective horrors against me. I have met and defeated your minions. Have done with foolish and futile pride. Let us go."

The head's salivating lips parted and an inarticulate rumble echoed from between the jutting fangs.

In his own head Bellarroth heard: <You're too arrogant. Don't be foolish. No power will gain you what you want. Haven't you learnt anything?>

"Hanin?" said Bellarroth, though it didn't sound like Hanin. This voice was alien and vast, like something too big for him to hear properly. He turned, but something shifted in his mind and made him stagger. He looked past the old man to where a shape was darkening into solid presence. It was a tall, heavy-set figure—a human perhaps.... Bellarroth raised his sword and leapt toward the manifestation. There was a flash of fire that swept through the air toward him, a sharp, unfocused pain, and he was flung to the ground. His muscles writhed uncontrollably in a paroxysm that shook him like a physical force. Neither it nor the pain lessened for a moment that seemed to open up into a timeless space and Bellarroth felt himself falling toward dark-ness that must have been death.

"Hanin!" he cried. "Hanin!"

But Hanin was silent.

Power whipped around him, seeking a hold. It found none. "Hanin, my enemy!" the stranger cried.

* * * * * * *

Then he was Bellarroth and Tashnark.

* * * * * * *

And then he was only Tashnark again.

Confusion numbed him as the world returned and he might have stopped short had his momentum been less irresistible. As it was, his sword blade completed its stroke and cut deeply into the skull of the man before him.

But it was a different skull from the one toward which he had directed his blow.

He could not understand what had happened. There was an illusion in his memory of the sorcerer's face blurring, changing, thinning in a radiance of nearly imperceptible duration. Afterwards he stood silently beside the corpse and dropped his arm limply. His blade clattered on the stone. The walls were gone and wind blew across him, carrying the damp manure smell from the stable.

"I thought we were finished," said Remis behind him.

He said nothing. He was remembering the enemy's startled

cry and the look of terror and dismay on the thin, dark face that had replaced the first.

xi.

Santhid, a mercenary soldier in the pay of the foreign lord, leaned in against the sandstone wall as rain swept over him, watching Sire Aridor in his carriage. The bastard was in trouble this time. Captured. Made to look foolish. Made ineffectual. Ha! With a bit of luck, Lord Worjaren Rehemon, who was dangerous and unpredictable, would give him hell.

Santhid didn't like Sire Aridor, hated him in fact. His arrogance and scornful superiority was a mere reflection of Lord Worjaren's, but in an acolyte—in effect a mere slave—it was less tolerable. He was forever directing his scorn toward the likes of Santhid and Santhid did not consider himself a slave. A mercenary, an underling, yes—but *paid*. There should be more respect shown toward salaried workers than toward slaves. This *was* the city of commerce they were in, wasn't it?

He became aware that Aridor was calling him and considered pretending not to hear. But such overt disregard would gain him nothing except an enemy. Santhid didn't need enemies.

"Can I help you, sire?" he said humbly, approaching the carriage.

"I feel restless. Is there no news?" Aridor appeared strained, as though he hadn't slept for several nights.

"You'd know more than me, sire. I have no magic."

Aridor's dark eyes fixed on him, considering his answer.

"We must wait the Lord's pleasure, sire," Santhid added. "It's the slave's lot. To wait."

Aridor sighed, wiping his hand across his forehead as though to polish away some lingering crease. "Slave or freeman, no difference. Are you stupid enough to imagine there are choices in life?"

Santhid gave no answer, nor did the Chief Acolyte expect

one. Instead Aridor shifted himself toward the door of the coach and flung it open. "I'm tired of this carriage," he said. He stepped out and then turned toward Santhid, supporting himself on the open door. "All we can do is dream of freedom," he said.

At that moment, as the cadence of his words fell, he frowned, his mouth opening and his lips moving soundlessly. Santhid thought he saw Aridor's face waver uncertainly in the flicker of a light-trail that chose that instant to flare and then fade. The acolyte was washed by a fire-haze. Santhid blinked and when he looked again there was a different face, paler, more solid, hovering in the night.

"You!" he exclaimed.

Lord Worjaren Rehemon ignored his amazement and his impropriety and instead spoke the concluding words of his spell, sealing its magic from reversal. Santhid watched the Lord's eyes scan the carriage and the surrounding street, and feared to speak again, afraid he might annoy the Lord. But the grim noble moved away from him, over the damp cobbles to where a rider slouched next to his horse.

"You!" Lord Rehemon growled, all trace of disorientation lapsing into authority. "Take your beast and ride to the Mummer's Avenue. Seek whoever has survived. Fetch news of the enemy. They must not sink into hiding and be lost. Hurry!"

The man looked flustered, obviously confused by the Lord's sudden appearance. But he scrambled onto his horse. "And if they can't be found, my Lord?" he asked.

"They must be."

The man rode off. Worjaren Rehemon returned to the carriage, barely glancing at Santhid as he climbed in, and saying nothing. There was deep thought in his eyes, and an aura of pain about his face.

Suddenly he slammed the carriage door and banged on its roof. The roof-trap opened. "Sir?" said a voice from the gloom.

"Take me with speed to the Yucartel Chambers! I have urgent business."

"Yes, Lord."

The hatch slammed shut. As the carriage began to move, Santhid found the courage to ask the question that lingered in his mind. He leaned toward the still-open window, shuffling along with the moving carriage. "My Lord, what happened to your Acolyte, Sire Aridor?" he said in a voice that sounded pitifully frail even to himself. "One minute he was here...and then he was gone and you were there in his place. Where did he go?"

Lord Worjaren's colorless eyes scanned Santhid's face as though noticing him for the first time. "He plays his part," the Lord said.

Santhid stepped away from the carriage, watching as it disappeared into the night.

CHAPTER FOUR
DEALING WITH GODS

i.

Raashyr-Lord Shaa was numbered among the most powerful, and most revered, of Guardian deities. His temple in Vesuula was correspondingly built to be impressive. Silhouetted darkly against the lighter sky its marble-and-sandstone strength represented more than a haven.

The Temple dated from the very early times of pre-mercantile rule. Derthperrit, a noble of reputedly divine ancestry, had undertaken the construction, and his name still clung to it. Since then, with the growth of the City, the Temple had undergone much architectural change and ornamentation, and it remained a potent force in City affairs, at a time when Raashyr worship was generally in decline. After all, Raashyr-Lord Shaa was Guardian of the Deep Powers. Magic, as a tool and a weapon, could be denied by no one, even if the ontological nature of that magic could.

Remis, Tashnark, Arhl and Shaan approached the main gates of the Temple of Shaa-Derthperrit as the winds fell away across its towers of stone. This side of the Temple was a large dome, the walls high and straight, with tall, thin windows and a statue menagerie. Black minarets flanked the entrance. Doors of finely cast bronze stood at the top of a short, semi-circular flight of stone stairs. At that moment Tashnark saw no mercy in the Temple's vast, monolithic stillness and felt its disinterest aching in his bones. *There'll be no help for us here*, he thought.

Shaan struck forcibly upon the door. It resounded dully. A small window opened, lit by flickering candle-flame from inside. The wafting scent of some flowery perfume found its way into Tashnark's nostrils.

"What do you want at this hour?" The voice crept from the gloomy interior as though reluctant to enter the night's chill.

"Sanctuary," Remis croaked, sounding weary and hoarse.

"Sanctuary? From what?"

"Does it matter?" growled Tashnark.

"It does. I won't admit thieves in flight from their own misdeeds."

Tashnark thumped on the door—but Remis pulled at his coat before he could speak. "We're not criminals," she said.

The night porter grunted skeptically.

"Porter!" Shaan's voice was even. "Under constitutional law the Temple may grant Sanctuary to any who claim it, be their enemy within or without civil office."

"It's rarely given."

"Under Shaa's Law, however, you are honor-bound to give it."

Wind-blown leaves rustled around the edges of the stairs. The porter began to close the window. "I won't engage it legalistic or theological debate. Come back in the morning and you can speak to someone more patient."

Tashnark started forward furiously, but Shaan was quicker. He stepped in front of him and spoke strange words into the closing window. Remis drew a sudden intake of breath and froze in place. The suddenness of her reaction grabbed Tashnark's attention. A moment later the small portal opened. Silence became so oppressive even the winds seemed to drop away.

"What's wrong?" asked Tashnark, and Remis hushed him.

The night porter muttered something in magical garble. Shaan replied in the same. Then the small window closed—*so much for honor*, thought Tashnark—but almost immediately a bolt was drawn. The larger gate cracked open a hair's breadth.

Tashnark felt the strangeness of the moment; it was as though they'd gone into another dream-state. He was afraid to speak too loudly in case he broke the spell. "What's going on?" he whispered regardless.

"*Lasar'elis*! Shaan spoke the Command of Lasar'elis. I never thought I'd hear it used."

"What's Lasar'elis?"

Remis looked his way but he wasn't convinced she saw beyond her own thoughts. "Words of Annunciation," she said, apparently to the empty space between them, "for messengers... from the Gods."

"Cunning bastard."

"You don't understand." She was looking directly at him now, her gaze demanding. "No one would dare use those words deceitfully. *Varnis* follows—a Power-infused test of the speaker's truthfulness. To have spoken the *Lasar'elis* and to fail the test is a sin punishable, even in modern civil law, by death."

"Death? You're kidding? For pretending to be a god?"

"All initiates into Shaa's laws—all who know of the Command's mere existence—also know the restrictions it carries. And they would know the penalties of misuse, too. Deceit is not tolerated."

"Most of the bureaucrats in this City would be at a loss then."

The Temple doors ground fully open. They were three times Tashnark's height and looked thick and heavy—and as the porter alone was working them, the mechanism that moved the doors must have been finely constructed indeed. Shaan entered without hesitation. Beyond him a portly, dark-robed man bowed deferentially.

Though hesitant, Tashnark followed the others inside, hoping for some reassurance, but the interior of the Temple was huge and hollow and not very comforting. The perfume he'd noticed earlier was much stronger now, and it exacerbated his sense of doom rather than dispelling it. The weight of history and religion in the building's architecture oppressed him further. He barely reacted when the porter told them to remain in the echoing, columned vestibule and then rushed off in search of his superiors.

Remis shuffled from one side of the area to the other, occasionally whispering odd bits of information to Tashnark—information about Temple procedure and architectural nuance that meant nothing to him. He wasn't a tourist, for god's sake. The soft candlelight and weird shifting shadows made him even more impatient.

"Why are you telling me this?" he interrupted at last, looking at her as though either her mind or his had disintegrated.

"I thought you might be interested."

"Then you don't know me very well."

She stared at him, eyes dark and unreadable. "No, I don't," she said. "I don't know who you are or where you come from? I don't know why you were following me. I don't know why you helped me."

He wanted to give her an answer, but couldn't. Those reasons he was conscious of didn't convince even him.

"You needed help," he said. "That's all I knew about *you*. Isn't it enough?"

Was her gaze evaluating him with favor or suspicion? Tashnark couldn't tell.

"I haven't been given much reason to trust of late. I hope I won't be disappointed." Tashnark watched her for a moment as she moved away, but then, to avoid self-doubt, turned his suspicion toward Shaan. The man stood staring toward the altar, so silent and meditative that none of the others saw fit to ask anything of him. Arhl, too, was quiet and unnaturally still.

I don't like this, Tashnark thought. *Not this ancient mausoleum, not the overblown mysticism it brings with it, not this pretentious stranger it centers around.* He wanted to leave, yet one look at Remis' air of intense introversion, and he found he couldn't.

At last a priest approached and took them silently through the Temple spaces, deaf to Tashnark's aggressive questioning. The place was so gloomy Tashnark doubted he could find his own way back out. *That* worried him too. Made him feel lost. They followed the priest up a series of narrow wooden stairs, into small bare rooms where he told them to wait. Here the atmosphere was closer and its smell suggested damp vegetation. Shaan left with the priest, while the others said little to each other and dozed fitfully. When they talked, they steered clear of issues of trust, truthfulness and divine reverence.

Shaan returned alone, an hour later, looking exhausted. It was the weariness of age and it sat oddly on his youthful features. Tashnark found it curiously disturbing. "Where've you been?" he demanded, dragging his mind out of a thin stupor this place encouraged.

"I've been tested. They want answers."

"They're not alone. I could use some answers myself." As he spoke, Tashnark remembered the huge monster seated on Its rocky throne and felt the tremor of his sword pushing into the sorcerer's skull. "I'll rest a lot easier when I know what's going on. And why you appear from nowhere to save our skins."

"It's a long story."

"Telling us who the hell you are would be a good start."

"I shall.... I swear it. But you're tired, and the night's nearly over."

"*I'm* not tired—I'm confused and pissed off. Riddles give me a pain in places I'd rather use for sitting."

"You *will* have answers. You have my word."

"Good." He paused meaningfully. "Well, where do you come from then? All the religious guff that's being bandied about doesn't mean a thing to me. It explains nothing."

"It's the only thing that has a chance of explaining these events."

"Right."

Shaan sighed at the sarcasm. "Very well, if you want straightforward answers.... To get here I traveled southward, on foot, from a small province called Ke'raey-Eldis."

"That's some distance, though the place is definitely worth leaving."

Shaan gave him one of his flatly quizzical looks. "You know of it? I'm surprised."

"I've been around." Tashnark refrained from making reference to his father's expeditions beyond Rheateeshan borders—expeditions in search of dispossessed foreigners he could "recruit" into the slave trade.

Shaan nodded. "That was where my journey began, but where I'm *from* is less easy to explain."

"More riddles."

"No riddle I can answer. I have memories of childhood and growing up there, but they turned alien on me long ago and changed my history into that of someone else." He looked earnestly at Tashnark. "Are your own memories so definite?"

Tashnark was about to mock him, instantly aware of a succession of facts—familial facts: Sevthen, his father; his mother, Eresteyin, the children playing together roughly in southern Zogran when he was young. He recalled the pilgrimage to greener Vesuula, and his father's rejection of their native Nahallhan traditions, bludgeoned into a new conformity by the pressures of commerce and law. He was about to laugh aside the man's question, but like a half-seen enemy thought of his unnatural dreams howled at him and he clenched his fists in fury.

What was memory anyway? His own had been playing tricks on him well before his current nightmares began. Dream. Memory. Where were the lines drawn? Images of monstrosity came at night—but in the day too, when something, the movement of wind on grass, a word shouted in the street, the snake-totem that had drawn and repelled him from its place in the statue in Luris Square near the docks, when these things turned his mind inward. Then there were the recent flashes of another life, trees like serpents, and hideous figures that might have come from some hellish death-realm. What was illusion and what was real?

There was heat. He ran, near the end of his endurance, and saw a tangle of shapes in the stark glare. His mind clasped to that tangle and urged him on. Momentarily, as he drew near, the haze on his eyes cleared, showing him a thick mesh of smaller, vine-like serpents and fibrous strands like a cancer. In the midst of this, held and shredded by frantic, insensate fingers, lay a body, lifeless and torn, a corpse patchily shorn of its flesh. It was Hanin, dead but not dead. He felt despair, screamed out in protest....

Those memories were vivid enough to be real. "What do you know of me?" he said to Shaan, his voice subdued, as though to exclude the others, the enquiry genuine. Then he whispered even lower, "Who are you?"

Shaan reached out his right hand, strong but unblemished. No scar tissue, no calluses. He had the moves of an experienced swordsman, so how could his body fail to carry the marks of all that experience? His fingers held Tashnark's shoulder reassuringly. "In my home in Ke'raey-Eldis many years past, I learnt that I was more than who I thought I was, and the knowledge drove me out of the village in search of that person. *You are ours*, the Gods said. So I went and the search has led to this room. There are currents and eddies in the flow of destiny and I have been drawn here on one of them."

"What the hell does that mean?"

The man—Tashnark suddenly found himself unable to think of him as youthful, despite his appearance—smiled wryly. "All right, I'll be blunt." He tapped himself on the chest. "No mortal heart beats within this bosom, but one sent from immortal Shaa himself. I am indeed a Seed of the Gods—one of the *Saral-Raashyr*. Does this designation make it any clearer for you?"

For a moment the words made no sense. His posture, his claim—everything about him—seemed like a joke. This youthful stranger, a Saral? Mythical seed of the divine Guardians of the world? Mortal shadow of an immortal Raashyr? Tashnark's mind rejected it all, eager to avoid any understanding that would make his life more complex than it already was. He was too set in his ways to re-think his understanding of the nature of the world.

"*Saral-Raashyr?*" whispered Remis, who had moved closer

to listen. "So it's true?"

Shaan rubbed his forehead, as though to clean away some mark of infamy. "So I was told. If you see the touch of the Gods in me as a mere chance, a moment of doubt perhaps, then you see no more than I do—"

"Surely you know your own nature?"

"My nature seems more than my birth. There seems depth to my power I have yet to reach. I am caught up in a destiny that seems more than ordinary. It's all *seems*—a morass of *seeming*. I know what seems to be, but there is no substance to it. The Raashyr appeared to me and proclaimed me *Saral*, and so I would seem to be."

"There hasn't been a *Saral* in the world since legendary times," Remis commented.

Tashnark was aware of an unnatural stillness. Crisis lurked in it. Arhl was staring stonily into the fire, crouched before its tiny flames like a primitive totem, and chewing with thoughtful abstraction. He didn't appear to be listening—though Tashnark knew he was, without a doubt. Did Shaan's words make him recall the superstitions of his wilderness-youth, the fur-clad, white-skinned folk, memory of a twig cracking sharply in a crisp, alpine dawn, sending hunters like a shout along the valley floors? Returning over snowfields by an improvised trail to the crude tribal hall of his people and a fire warming battered hands? Had there been an itinerant sage there, uttering mysteries from distant lands and evoking in the young breast the passion for a greater life? What might Shaan be in Arhl's scheme of things?

Tashnark turned his gaze to Remis. She sat with her knees drawn up against her chest and engulfed in her arms. The folds of the cloak wrapped around her shoulders. She let her chin rest on her hands while she stared with fascination, no longer at Shaan, but at the stone of the floor in front of her. This person who claimed to be born of the Raashyr was plainly on her mind, however, and she was drawn to him. This fact infuriated Tashnark, deeply and irrationally. He ground his teeth together and wondered what beliefs Shaan's claims had confirmed for her, what he represented beyond his undoubted attraction as a man. At this moment Tashnark could barely conceive what it might feel like to be an adept of the Deep Power, had certainly never considered the implications of such magic beyond a pragmatic recognition of its usefulness and danger. The look on Remis's face spoke to him of ache, and that reaction bewildered him as much as the stranger who had inspired it. In the darkest parts of his soul, Tashnark wanted Remis to feel distanced by Shaan's posturing and lunatic claims. She mustn't feel drawn to him. He wanted to say so, aloud, but fought back the impulse.

It was Shaan who spoke at last. "Perhaps you are right and introductions, uncomplicated by riddle, are best made now, while the need is so hot in you. In stories we may find purpose. I, for one, shall tell you all I can."

He waited for confirmation and as no one moved Tashnark nodded in an expansive way, as though for the whole group.

And so Shaan began his tale, a history more ancient in beginning and more distant in end than any of them could have imagined. In later days the memory of that night was of low, reddish firelight playing about their faces, and Shaan's voice, drawing meanings out of the room surrounding them. Remembrance of the facts he spoke did not explain the feelings he evoked. For Tashnark those lay deeper, in some relationship of his own fate to that of the stranger, and as it was hidden from him, a riddle, he simply listened...and clenched his fists more tightly.

ii.

"If I tell you I was born and raised in the village of Carr-Rabin, a place deep within the terrain of Ke'raey-Eldis," Shaan said, "I will most likely tell you nothing. Little knowledge of those places exists in Vesuula. You, Tashnark, are the first person I've met here who had any awareness of it. Ke'raey-Eldis is just far enough distant to exclude it from attracting commercial interests and to keep it out of the standard histories. In my land ignorance is as deep. I once knew of the central lands of Rheateesha only vaguely, in songs and the tales of our few traders—and from the mouths of visiting slavers."

Tashnark caught what he interpreted as an ironic glance tossed in his direction.

"Carr-Rabin is a random scattering of hovels compared to Koerpel-Na, but its beginnings were heroic, rising as it did from the ashes of the destroyed continent, Mikhalin, further south. The wife of the Warrior Durras Dorth-sen, along with those of their people who survived the destruction of their former home, came to Ke'raey-Eldis to found a new colony—but only after centuries of survival in the wasteland created by Cormidthal's Great War. Dorth-sen was the Patriarch, and direct line of my family."

"So survivors of the Great War still live in that place?" Remis said.

"Descendents only. Dorth-Sen gave his life to enable the line to continue, allowing his Lady, carrying his child, to escape in a vast construct of magic bequeathed to them by the stone-worker, Farhassin. An opponent of the State's policies at the time of the Great War, Farhassin died so that a fragment might live, and too, I now believe, that fated conflict of a different and more extensive kind might reach its end."

Tashnark leaned away from the cold wall. "That's what legends are for, to lend glamour to mundane life. Doesn't make them true."

"It's no glamour. My own memory extends to the first years of settlement. I have lived a thousand years with the knowlededge."

"A thousand years?"

"My father was Dorth-sen himself, who found his people a way out of the wastelands."

Tashnark looked at him skeptically.

"Now you're telling us...what? That you're older than this city?"

"Please," said Shaan, raising his hand in a calming gesture, "your acceptance of these facts is irrelevant. Yet why should you find it so hard to believe? If I am Saral—a shadow of deity in the world—then I am already a miracle."

"I'm still waiting to be convinced of that. Identifying gods has never been one of my strong points."

Shaan smiled. "Let me tell you my history before you believe or disbelieve."

"I doubt it'll help, but I'm listening."

"As a youth, I would sometimes sleep in one of the rooms backing onto the temple, in anticipation of my duties. On one such occasion, I thought I heard the priest's low whisper calling me, and I went into the temple to find him. He was not there and I was returning to my room when I heard a voice raised in song.

"The singer was by the Altar of Shaa, kneeling with his arms spread to either side and head bowed. As I approached he sat upright and turned his darkened face to me.

"'Sir,' I whispered, 'what are you doing here at this late hour?'

"'Late indeed is the hour, Shaan,' he said. 'My name is not Shaan,' I replied, as I had another name then. He answered, 'I call you Shaan, for in this way are you spoken of in realms where the Guardians wait for the end to come. The Curse of Junsar is upon the world and you are called to duty.'"

Tashnark grumbled at the archaic pomposity of the words. Shaan's memory had already morphed into a religious morality tale. Remis nudged him, scowling for him to be silent.

"What?" he muttered.

"I was too bewildered to speak," Shaan continued, "but the stranger reached forward and though his fingers were not lain upon me I felt his touch on my face. 'We have longed for a sign, for Raashyr-Power within Tharenweyr dwindles and Guardianship is made null and worthless,' he said. 'Junsar's Curse hastens to its end. We need a sign that we too are not forgotten and that hope is not empty. The task I lay upon you is heavy and doom-laden but without it you are nothing and the Raashyr are without hope.'

"He told me then that he was a servant of Shaa and that I

was his Seed in the world. I thought him mad, of course, but he threw aside his dark robes and his face was revealed as my own, transformed by a glory I cannot describe—an otherworldliness that shone from within. Yet it was mine all the same."

Shaan paused, the light on him dim now as the fire in the grate hissed and spluttered. Tashnark glanced at his companions but their obvious credulity and awe made his own disbelief grow even stronger—this story of Shaan's had the form of legend, not of truth. "Saral!" he said, standing to ease a cramp in his leg. "You talk of being a Saral. But what the hell does that *really* mean?"

Remis protested. There was both annoyance and fear in her eyes. Tashnark huffed and turned away from her.

"I know why you might dismiss what I say," Shaan said. "Yet I swear the truth of this tale, a doom still unclear despite the passing of destined events. Accept my words, not to honor me—I am yet to earn any such—but so that we can understand what we have to do. All understanding paves the way to Junsar's healing."

Tashnark turned on him. "Okay, there's Junsar again! My theology is rather dodgy, but if I recall there was supposedly a Creation God named Junsar who failed to do what had to be done and trashed the world in the process. Right? A complete loser as a deity. Why would we want to follow in his footsteps?"

"To heal the faults that he began in the world's birth is surely more important than your pride and disdain."

"*My* pride and disdain? Seems to me it's always the Gods' pride and disdain that causes us grief. Why not deny the lot of them—all the interfering, useless deities? Reject the doctrines that pander to them and be free of the lot! Pain and anxiety is all they ever give us."

"Deny your hair grows and it will grow anyway. We live daily with Junsar's curse. What's the point in denying it?"

Tashnark turned back to the window. The others became distorted shadows reflected in the rough glass. Even so, he could see the shock on Remis' face.

"Forgive me," said Shaan, "but we are not talking of neighborly scandal nor the affairs of this petty state. Rather of the Greater World itself—Tharenweyr—and the strivings of its Powers. Would it help you to believe if I took you now to the priests who with simple spells could verify my claim according to Shastorenti lore? How about if I destroyed the Temple with a word? No, neither would convince you."

Tashnark shrugged. "At least destroying the temple might be amusing."

"It's your will I seek, Tashnark, not your mind. That will follow."

He placed his hand on Tashnark's shoulder. His voice lowered, and Tashnark sensed Shaan's next words were spoken to him alone. For the others, there was nothing; it was a moment from which they were excluded. "What you are is known, if not to those in this room, or to the Raashyr, then to the Powers that work deep in the world. You must accept yourself or life will wither in you." He turned away. Though Tashnark looked up, Shaan was already standing far across the room.

He breathed deeply, feeling a confusion that was almost pain.

"Even if we assume that you are what you say you are," he managed, "it doesn't explain why you're here, now, after a thousand years of procrastination."

Shaan rested his forehead on his palm for a moment. When he looked up, he seemed wearier. "It's *less* than a thousand years, as I've spent several centuries wandering the world. But I take your point." He shrugged. "Oracles were spoken to me as I knelt before Shaa's altar—oracles of destined heroes and terrible futures. It is why I left Ke'raey-Eldis, journeying over the world and watching empires come and go. Looking for signs. Why now? I don't know. It was said that events would focus around me—and so they appear to be doing."

"What did the oracles say?" Remis asked.

"Terrible predictions that left no room for denial. Shaan-Vaeyin, my divine birth-twin in the realms of the Raashyr, told me that events were drawing near to a point of Fatefulness, and the purpose of my being had now to be realized. Though the Raashyr cannot see the nature of the crisis, they perceive the currents in the world leading to it. And those currents are even now becoming a maelstrom of all-consuming ferocity." He paused, as though doubting his own words. "They believe the Cerendar artifact lies at the eye of the storm, for the oracles spoke of an object that fits its decsription that gives the tumult its fury."

"The Cerendar?" Remis spoke the word carefully, as though danger lurked among the syllables. "Then that's more than a legend too?"

"The Guardians fear it. What point would be in their fear if the Cerendar were only legend?"

Tashnark laughed. "Perhaps they're simply wrong. I'm not convinced they have any sort of a clue about anything."

"About some things they may be wrong, but this is a knowledge they have carried since before the advent of humanity."

"What do *we* know about it then?"

Remis turned to him. There was an intriguing warmth to her face, but one that did not belong to him. Tashnark allowed it to annoy him for a moment—if he hadn't known better he would attribute it to infatuation. He was disappointed. There was a romance to this Shaan that would speak directly to Remis' soul—but Remis was no impressionable schoolgirl. Shaan was a dream. A delusion. Perhaps even a madman. Surely she could see that. He wasn't grounded in the world the rest of them inhabited. He had the air of a slightly demented actor. His manner of speech alone betrayed him.

"This is my area of expertise," Remis said. "Magical artifacts. The Cerender is said to be the *ultimate* magical artifact."

Tashnark let his attention dwell on the gentle lines of her face, molded by fire-shadows and a frame of thick, dark-brown hair. For an instant light sparked off her deep azure pupils. He wanted to tell her he loved her—but of course he couldn't, even if it were true, and he felt no certainty that it was. He had no right to ask anything of her.

She looked at Tashnark earnestly as she spoke. "The Cerendar is mentioned in the sixtieth leaf of the Kaa Lists. These Lists were compiled by a great Gathering of scholars in the Age of Decline, when, it is said, the Raashyr urged humanity to establish laws against the weakening of magical practice."

Tashnark grunted.

"The sixtieth leaf is a listing of ancient Power-artifacts—basic reference for modern studies—and the Cerendar appears there. The object is supposed to be very old, lost now for...oh, many centuries certainly."

"What makes it so special?"

"Power. Massive power. It's believed to contain power beyond humanity's wildest dreams. *All* power, it's said. As far as I know its origins are completely lost. It's believed to be powerful enough to break the world apart."

"If it's so dangerous, why don't the Raashyr simply use their divine sight to find it, then lock it away somewhere inaccessible?"

"It's obscured from the eyes of the Raashyr, who normally see everything within the world," Shaan answered for her. "They cannot detect it and it has eluded them through all time—so much so that it's believed that the obscurity is deliberate. Perhaps it's too dangerous for even the Raashyr to control and the Greater God therefore keeps it hidden."

"Perhaps it doesn't exist at all," Tashnark commented wryly. "Rather like the Greater God himself."

"They believe it is hidden from them by their nature. They claim that it comes from *outside* the world and since even the Raashyr are *of* the world, they cannot see it using this world's deepest powers."

"Outside?"

"Beyond our reality."

"So knowing anything at all about it's impossible. Is that what you're saying?"

Remis took over the lecture again. "Not quite. We can know the artifact by its appearances in history and legend. For example, the Cerendar is recorded as being part of the Treasury of Orch-Lan Demon-skull, a monstrous chieftain of the Seventh Age. The Treasury was supposed to have been inherited by his lieutenant, when the leader was assassinated. The lieutenant disappeared afterwards, and the story goes that he tried to use the power of the Cerendar, but failed. Indeed, conventional belief says that all such attempts to activate the artifact's Power are doomed to failure. It seems the historian Shen-To of Othsinlintor interviewed one of Demon-skull's rebels, years later, as the fellow, confined to a madhouse, was breathing his last. He recorded the man's dying words as *All, and nothing.* So they say it can give everything, but only death awaits anyone proud enough to try and claim the prize."

"Very melodramatic," Tashnark scowled. "And this thing hasn't been sighted since?"

"Various histories claim it was discovered, many spurious no doubt. Rumors—"

"Surely the whole thing's a fiction. An Object of Ultimate Power? Every greedy sod in the world'd want to get their hands on something like that."

"The Raashyr believe it's real," said Shaan flatly, as though tired of making the same point. "They see great and fearful danger in it."

"But the thing can't be tamed," Tashnark insisted, "according to these tales. Why do so many search for it, even if it exists?"

"The desire for omnipotence," Shaan said quietly. "Grant that it's true, and ponder what desires it might spawn. Wealth, power, fame—the legends give these as the motives that move humanity to seek it out. Greed, as you say. Some ends have been commendable; but most arise from greed. None matter. They all finish the same. But people will dare the greatest of perils on hope only, no matter how futile."

"Some scholars believe that the end of each age is brought about by attempts to draw out the artifact's power," Remis interjected. Neither seemed to be talking to Tashnark now, only each other. *It's a tag-team match for know-alls*, he thought. *If only my brother were here. It could be a three-way contest.*

Shaan nodded. "Such destruction, all for hope! And there are beings mightier and more desirous than humanity. What result, should the Dark Gods gain Power without end?"

Dark Gods. Despite himself, Tashnark considered that and frowned. "Then where's this thing hiding? If our enemies tonight were from the Dark Gods, and in search of the Cerendar, they weren't particularly well informed. I hadn't heard of it before this moment."

"Would you know if you saw it?" asked Arhl. Hearing his friend's voice after his long silence startled Tashnark somewhat. He'd almost forgotten he was in the room.

"Suppose not. But that doesn't prove anything."

"It proves that you might have seen it without knowing it," said Remis. "It might be here, nearby. Anywhere."

"It is here most certainly." There was no doubt in Shaan's voice, only a deep resolution. "It's here and we're all involved."

"How do you know?"

"There are indications, signs of activity. Not much, to be sure, but signs enough."

"What signs?"

"Dreams and prophecies. Chance and coincidence. It is chance that has been guiding me. It led me to you. We are in special times when that which is hidden will be revealed. Haven't you felt it?"

"Maybe," Tashnark said, despite himself, "maybe I have." He wanted to mention his wild, impossible dreams then, wanted to draw them out in this company and find relief from some part of the burden. But, even as the words formed, something welled up in him—a physical sensation that tightened the muscles in his throat. Fear dragged at his heart, making it beat irregularly.

Then a voice in his head spoke: *<Not yet. There is too far to go. This trial is your own. They can't share it. Be patient and be strong.>*

He staggered against the wall, scraping one elbow on the painted stone, rubbing at his forehead with his other hand. No one noticed—except Shaan perhaps, and he didn't react.

"I've felt it," Remis said. She held out a dagger, the double-bladed one she'd taken from the corpse in the alley off Telfith's Street. "When I analyzed this dagger yesterday morning, there was something in its history I hadn't recognized till now. A light like a candle flame reflected through mist. It seemed to obsess the creature...Valarl—that was his name once."

"Once?"

"He was a necromancer, but he's been dead for...I don't know. Decades. And for all that time he's coveted a light, a light that in my visions he chased but never reached. It was shaped like the gleam of a candle flame, sparked into pointed arms as though seen through dust or misted glass, and bent in upon itself."

"I don't understand," Tashnark said, stating what he felt was the obvious.

"It's an ancient symbol." Remis suddenly strode to a desk on one side of the room. There was paper there and a pen. She dipped the nib into ink and drew. "This," she said and held it for him to see. "It's known as the *cerender* design. Which translates as 'Object of Light' in Goduulan, or 'The Gleam' according to recent semiotics."

Tashnark gestured sardonically with his large hands. "Hence the artifact's name? Which came first—the name or the object?"

Remis shrugged. "Who knows?" She pointed to the image she had drawn. Ink-hairs were spreading out in the coarse paper-fibre, blurring the lines, as though to hide the pattern. "It's common in magical ornamentation. It takes many forms." She scraped the pen across the paper again, drawing variants of her first doodle. "Some scholars see it as the oldest of all Deep Power designations—the Deepest of the Deep Powers. No one knows its real significance, though many have guessed. Spike mace, crab, fireball—the word 'star' crops up often."

"Star? What's a star?"

"A light in the night sky, the scholars think. A huge object of concentrated energy."

"Makes little sense to me. There's nothing in the sky except clouds. Day or night."

Remis shrugged. "What it means doesn't matter. The question is whether its appearance at this point in time is enough of a sign. An un-man, long dead, cursed with an obsession to chase a *star* in the dark?"

"You go from speculation to fact with the agility of a bullfrog."

"It is speculation, yes," Shaan said. "But that's all we have. Enough to hope that if it does exist, here and now, we get to it first."

"Is it? Is that hope so important?"

Shaan was silent for a moment. Then he said: "I have not told you everything."

"Really? Why am I not surprised?"

"It is another riddle, I'm afraid," Shaan went on. "One that demands any hope, no matter how desperate." He picked up Remis' rendering of the Cerendar and spoke while staring at it. "As I said, there has been prophecy in the Raashyr's homeland, and the end of that prophecy is blacker and more grim than I care to tell."

"But you're going to, right?"

"It has been foretold that the E'ashalsinir—the Dark Ones—will come battle-ready upon the world, riding out from the gates of their southern citadel, Nalim-Tar, and bringing with them the world's fated end. When? Not in some distant time, but soon—within a year, perhaps within a matter of days. I am sent, with many others, to find the beginnings of this event and to forestall it if I can. The Cerendar is the key. And we must hope that this day it has slipped through the Dark Gods' fingers and will be lost to them forever. Do you see now what you are part of?"

A sort of detached horror settled over Tashnark. Never mind that magic itself was indicative of higher universal forces—and forget that their civilization accepted in a thousand casually spoken words the reality of the Raashyr, hence their darker enemies. He had heard the litanies, though he took no interest in them. The marketplace was more immediate, its dealings and currents more tangible and amenable. One could grasp a beer glass and lift it high, and having done so could drain its contents and feel the warmth expanding in the belly. Beer had a more demanding voice than the call of belief—and the point of some scum's knife was the most compelling threat he'd ever had to face.

Then to be told that the E'ashalsinir, the distorted boogeymen of Darkness and Evil, were to come in force upon the world— and at any time now. No, he couldn't accept it. He'd grown up long ago and had no patience with fairytales.

Yet argue as he might, the signs were there. Much had been said, much conflict had been resolved and left unresolved, but in the end Shaan and what he stood for remained, and despite everything he had said and thought Tashnark knew that this foreigner could not be easily cast aside. He, like the others, though less willingly and in his own way, had felt something in the Saral's words.

More than that, he was aware of something moving in his own life—a force he knew nothing about and feared with all the passion in him.

What Shaan said could well be true. The monsters were getting restless.

But had the four of them stood at the heart of a gathering storm, and, all in ignorance, shattered the threads of doom? Had they come between fate and its end? Was the Cerendar lost once more, before it was found? Maybe, just maybe, it was over already.

"Have we saved the world then?" he said, hopefully.

"The salvation has only begun," Shaan replied. And Tashnark silently cursed him for the zeal in his manner.

iii.

A thin, boyish voice echoed through the halls like an ill wind, singing some wretched dirge full of lost love and misery.

Tashnark sat up on his bunk and growled his impatience. Except for the singer the temple was quiet and Tashnark resented being awakened by this low scoundrel's bawled-out melancholy. A night of struggle, a pre-dawn of near-death and bloodshed, and endless revelations and riddles—these cried out not for tunes to drag spirits further into gloom, but for some ballad to fill him with delirium and recollection of less fretful times. Why must love be forever lost? Tashnark wanted joy, not more misery.

He climbed out from the blankets and pulled on his boots. There was mud on them and one was torn. Legacy of the monster in his nightmare? No, he must have done the damage during their flight through the Wargrin-Othos. A vision couldn't tear his clothes. An illusion couldn't stain his pants with its foul, green blood. Almost immediately he dismissed the denial as ridiculous. How could he tell what the world was capable of?

The swish of a broom could be heard outside the door and as though in harmony with it the youth's voice began again:

> "O, bury my bones near a running stream,
> For there my tears will join
> The teaming waters of the earth
> And I shall no more dream."

Before the youth could continue the song, Tashnark flung open the door, growling like a bear with a hangover. "By my aunt's teeth—wherever the hell they are—I'll strip your bones now if you sing another note." Seeing Tashnark's unfriendly face suddenly appearing before him, the boy jumped back and dropped his broom. The words of his song were transformed into a gasp. "Give us a break, boy," Tasknark squinted at him through half-shut eyelids. "If you must sing, make it something more rousing."

The boy smiled nervously. Tashnark could guess what was going through his mind. No doubt the novice quarters were full of rumors—that these strangers had fled violence in the streets of the City and that one of them had whispered the *Lasar'elis* in the ear of the porter. The *Lasar'elis*—the Command of the Gods' Herald. Was it possible? Reverence would be making his brain all squishy.

"The songs I know tend to be sad or devotional, sir."

Tashnark grinned. He put his arm around the boy's shoulders and clicked his tongue thoughtfully. "Perhaps I can teach you another sort." His deep baritone, dry and cracked post-sleep, broke into the Temple silence with an off-key rendition of the famous tale of the Green Sty's drunken host and the merry maid he wanted to bed. Tashnark had barely got to the first salacious pun when he was interrupted.

"Tashnark!" Remis's voice made him release the boy and swallow the last notes of the verse he was mangling. "Where do you think you are? A brothel? Try to show some respect!" Memory of the anemic, overbearing governess his father had inflicted on him in his green years made Tashnark gulp back a belly laugh.

Remis glared at him, frowned doubtfully, then said to the boy, using the form of address appropriate to novices, "When are vespers, *litis*?"

"In an hour, when the light fades." The boy pointed down into the body of the temple. "This evening's will be in the Sar-Hadros chapel."

"Thank you." Remis glanced at Tashnark coldly, swiveled on her heel and strode off along the corridor. At the end of it she disappeared down the stairwell. Tashnark laughed uneasily.

He bent, picked up the novice's broom. "I think I've offended her religious scruples. Perhaps yours, too. I'm sorry." He offered the broom. "How was it she addressed you? *Litis*?"

The boy took the broom and nodded.

"My name's Danling, sir, Danling-Polarridal, till I rise in status. Then my family-name will become irrelevant. I will be of the family of Shaa. Just Caris-Danling, then—*Caris* meaning *Acolyte*."

Tashnark glanced around at the ornamental walls and watched

the faded light of evening shine on lead-glass windows at the far end. Something in the boy's words saddened him. "Perhaps you could show me around this place sometime, Danling?"

"I'd be honored, sir." Shyness stole into the boy's eyes. "I'd also like to learn more of how you came here than I'd learn from the masters."

Tashnark laughed. "Forbidden knowledge, eh?" He slapped the boy's shoulder roughly. "I promise to teach you a few juicy ditties to spice up dull company."

"Perhaps I'll have to consider what's appropriate."

"Correctness above all, eh?"

"I wouldn't wish to disgrace Lord Shaan."

Tashnark felt a surge of annoyance, his good humor vanishing. "*Lord* Shaan?"

"We are privileged, sir. We must respect the honor."

"The honor?"

"Yes, sir. His coming here glorifies our work."

Tashnark's voice was almost a growl. "Why do you lot trust him so easily?"

"The masters are children of Shaa by dedication. Why shouldn't they recognize one come from his bosom?"

"Come from Shaa's bosom? It's hardly a casual claim. The Gods aren't usually so generous with their darlings."

The boy shrugged. "I must go now, sir. I'll find you tomorrow."

He had closed to further discussion and Tashnark could see that nothing would be gained by pursuing the matter. He let him go and returned to the room he and Arhl had been given as a retreat. What was the answer? Shaan was a dilemma it was becoming more and more difficult to rationalize. How were the others coping? He thought of asking Arhl, but found him asleep in the bare room, and since he'd slept through two songs and Remis' scolding, it seemed unfair to wake him now.

At the window Tashnark peered between frosted panes out across the roof of a long, plain building—a kitchen or the acolyte dormitories. Its far limit was a stone's throw from the sea, and the ocean wash gave the silence here a pleasant fullness. Straight across the shingle roof, made luminescent by the glare of the Skywave's last bursts of radiance, there was another huge structure, the Faen-Hassur training college—and beyond that, the oval strangeness of the Hassur Libraries themselves. Weird and alien in the fading light, like great beasts nestling into sleep.

For a moment the image made him recall his dreams of Bellarroth. He needed to talk about them with someone—Remis perhaps. He thought that, maybe, he would *like* to talk to her. But he was afraid to attempt it.

He turned away, tired of squinting against the light. His gut rumbled and it made him wonder when the night meal was served in this place. Not, he'd guess, until after vespers.

A bell began ringing somewhere at the front of the temple. In response there was movement in the corridor and even Arhl stirred. Tashnark had always heard the bell-chant at roughly this time, from his home on Sarim-Way Road. *He* had never stirred in answer. "What's the bell?" Arhl's voice was groggy with sleep.

"Vespers, I expect."

"Would we be allowed to attend, do you think?" Arhl asked, as the chiming vibrations in the floor died away.

Tashnark shrugged.

"I will go. You?"

"I don't think so. I have no intention of becoming a pious bore at this stage of my life."

A sort of weary puzzlement settled over Arhl, so Tashnark explained what had happened earlier with the boy and Remis. He thought they'd have a good laugh together, but Arhl didn't find it funny. He huffed his disapproval and lectured Tashnark on maintaining due reverence. In him it was even less attractive than it had been in Remis.

iv.

The minor spaces of the Temple, bordering the main halls, were empty as Remis made her way through them toward the Sar-Hadros chapel. She knew the chapel to be off the Porch of Declaration, the center of the decagon that formed the common entrance to the Temple. Silence hung undisturbed around her, and moved like an undercurrent beneath the plainsong chants she could hear being sung in preparation for the evening rites. The chants themselves seemed a part of the building, as solid as the columns that supported the arching roofs, and as little prone to frivolity. In them she could hear the sound of humanity's highest aspirations, cleansed—at least in theory—of greed and hatred and selfish manipulation. Remis sighed. She had always loved this place.

Thoughtfully she walked past several galleries and around the edge of a domed chapel, pausing briefly to glance at the statue by the famed sculptor Kagranimis in its center. It was abstract and almost shapeless, a tangle of smooth flowing surfaces and twisting lines that somehow, mysteriously, drew a passive kind of Deep Power from the world around them and made it available to those meditating here. You could feel the force of it. When Kagranimis had shaped his original stone he had, according to tradition, failed himself to perceive the power it held; now Remis felt its strength. How could the sculptor have missed it? Perhaps decay was at the root. It was only when time had passed and the world had sunk further toward its fated end that humanity had realized the value of the mystic's stone-crafting. They needed aids in meditation as in magic. Now such art was highly prized in mortal attempts to replicate deeds once common and natural; but Kagranimis remained the master. His original works, few extant, were priceless.

Remis moved through the archway at the end of the Lower Porch corridor. The sweet scent of incense became stronger. She could see the Porch ahead, raised three steps above the level of the floor and constructed of light umber marble slabs delicately carved with scenes depicting power-users at work. Thin pathways twisted over the Porch so that the designs did not become worn under the feet of the many hundreds of priests who had walked to the central dais. There beneath the Porch's canopy of stone they had declaimed the seasonal rites since the temple was built. On the left of this structure was the Sar-Hadros chapel, this season dedicated to the vesper rituals. It seemed appropriate now, after the struggles they had been through and in the face of the threat that still existed, that she at least should attend the daily vespers, the rites in defiance of darkness.

There were several figures moving about behind the columns and rows of pillars that defined the Porch's environs. Remis watched them in the dim light that forced its way, like huge, thick-grained rivulets, through the tall, patterned windows. She tried to pick temple attendant from secular visitor. There were a number of the latter, and she trusted that the Temple-Governor had taken some measures to ensure that none of them were enemies. It would be disastrous to have to face opposition again, so soon, even in the heart of their new sanctuary. Since the early morning, as they had approached the temple in grim twilight, she had felt a burden of silent threat lift from her shoulders and had been content to surrender somewhat thoughtlessly to the temple's apparent security. Now she wondered how realistic the expectation of safety had been. Was there any escape?

Determined to push these unwelcome fears aside, since there was nothing to be done about them, she made her way out of the lower Corridor and to a spot behind the pillars along the Sar-Hadros Way. From there she could see both the priest and the participants within the chapel. At present there were only a few people in attendance, kneeling in postures of meditation. Remis joined them by kneeling where she was, and allowed her mind to empty itself of confusing and worrying thoughts.

Before she knew it she was aroused by a familiar trill played on a reed flute, and, glancing up, saw that a priest, whom she recognized as Corriman, had taken his place in the center of the

Porch and was composing himself for the beginning of the ceremony. A tall, red-skinned man with aquiline nose and firmly dimpled chin, Corriman had a distant look on his face that suggested a certain over-familiarity with the rite, as though its immediacy for him was fading with the years. Funny that Remis should catch that look at this moment after having attended rites here for so long—but now that it had come to mind she could see evidence of the attitude everywhere in the temple. How often she had come to this place, full of duty and virtue! For a long time she had equated it with the underlying worthiness of her magical studies, had found peace, meaning, safety here. It was good. Yet now she saw the air of careless assumption it had acquired over the years, a certain overfamiliarity.

On reflection it was no surprise. There was no pressure, no tangible conflict that could keep them earnest. She could only hope that the old, long-established ways would meet the new coming, perhaps the final challenge, with energy and faithfulness.

She heard heavy tread halting behind her and looked around. It was Arhl, followed by Tashnark. They both acknowledged her, the one with his usual shyness, the other casually. "He made me come," muttered Tasknark with a nod to Arhl. Remis smiled, hoping to forge some bond between them, despite her earlier annoyance. The way she'd reacted had been pompous and self-important. That she'd spoken in so matronly a fashion disappointed her as much as Tashnark's behavior had. She felt that they were bound together for the duration, however long that might be, and she didn't want any unnecessary tension making the bonding difficult.

"We can join you?" whispered Arhl. Remis nodded. He squatted next to her, balancing himself against the pillar. He mumbled some reverent words in a language she did not understand. Tashnark did not kneel but bent over and spoke softly in her ear: "Is it part of the ceremony, to prostrate ourselves?"

"It aids meditation."

He straightened. "I'll stand," he said.

"Don't fight it, Tashnark," she replied. "Just accept that we're part of something bigger now."

Tashnark gave a dismissive gesture. "I don't want to be part of anything—big or little."

"Perhaps you don't have a choice."

Tashnark's smirk was almost bitter. "Then it's worthless. If there's no choice, what we do is no more virtuous than...." He gazed around. "...these pillars. They hold up the ceiling, but they have no choice in the matter. So why should I respect them?"

Remis would have argued, but the flute played again, and she turned her attention to the approaching procession. There were about a dozen robed figures moving past the Porch and into the Sar-Hadros Corridor. They were led by Caris-Lorin— the designation *caris* indicating that Lorin was an acolyte of solid standing. Remis had never met her, for she had come to the temple only a short time before Remis' graduation. Stately and beautiful, she was lithe with the ease of Deep Power knowledge, her long hair reaching to her waist in an intricately woven braid. One day perhaps she would be a full priest. She seemed already to have the authority. Behind her came a group of acolytes and novices, allotted the task of responsorial chanters for this rite. Remis recognized some of them. The familiarity comforted her.

"What's this ceremony for again?" she heard Tashnark whisper. For a moment she watched a novice light incense candles and perfumed oil-lamps about the chapel. The mingling of scents was a heady perfume.

"It's performed, in different fashion, in every Raashyr temple throughout the world, each taking special measure against the dying of light. It's a special sort of spell, Tashnark, cast in support of life."

"Dusk's not a *real* threat."

"It's a propitious hour, that's all. Symbolic. You do understand symbolism, don't you?" She frowned, more at her own impatience than at his contrary attitude. She continued more forgivingly. "The rite makes use of the symbol of day's end to help us meditate on the world's ultimate fate and the moral responsibility it imposes on us. The Darkness it holds back isn't night."

The priest's voice, echoing on the high stone walls, interrupted her. *"I speak of a truth ancient in humanity. Consider, my people, the darkest night."*

Knowing the response, Remis joined with the gathered people in intoning the ritual answer: "We come, we come, and add the strength of our heart."

Caris-Lorin had reached the chapel-face. She stood silently before the stone-pattern decorating it, while the end of daylight hung like a satin curtain on the window. The chanters arrayed themselves about her, and for a moment there was silence. The flute players, two acolytes just outside the chapel, spun a melancholy turn into the temple stillness. Lorin raised her arms, and as her gold-embroidered sleeves flashed through the increasing gloom, the ritual began.

Celebrant: Grieve, my People, grieve with all that is.

Priest: In the wilderness Erellinarth met with Death, who spoke to him in these words: "Where thou art is Nothing, Erellinarth my vassal, and thou art became as the sands that shift in the tempest-wind and as tree without root." And Erellinarth cried out the Terrible Grieving, and Ur-Teth, the great God, always merciful, heard and forbad extinction. With a word Ur-Teth cocooned the fallen Sleeper so that he would not be lost forever.

Celebrant: Blessed be Ur-Teth, that grief comes to His ears.

Something moved at the edge of Remis' peripheral vision and despite her concentration on the ceremony she glanced around. Shadows hung thick among the soaring pillars and obscured the edges of the central space. A line of statuary in crevices across the top of the building—indistinct in the gloom—shifted uneasily as the light dimmed. She muttered the first words of a calming mantra.

Another peripheral twitch drew her attention—down, over to the left. Worshippers huddled there, but Remis doubted they were the cause of the disturbance. They were too still, too focused on the vesper.

Heart thudding, she stared beyond the crowd to congealing shadows that for a moment seemed to loom over them, spreading like a fogbank....

"Problem?" whispered Tashnark's voice, close to her ear. Startled, she spun to face him.

"What?"

"You seem anxious."

She glanced back toward the cloud of darkness. Only ordinary gloom clung to the walls now.

"It's nothing," she said. She tried to re-engage with the ceremony as the priest continued to intone its words. She found it difficult. Nervousness scratched in her muscles.

"Something's not right...," Tashnark commented suddenly. He was staring into the growing dark—first one way, then another. "You sensed it, didn't you?"

"There's nothing," Remis repeated, more out of hope than certainty.

A low, muscle-scratching groan reverberated through the stone beneath her knees. She jerked back on her haunches, forcing herself up. Individuals in the crowd glanced around. Had they felt it, too?

She noticed that Caris-Lorin's attention had been drawn away from the ceremony—she was looking up, left, out across the worshippers. Corriman, however, was intent on the ritual.

> Priest: Know that Erellinarth lies cradled below, and Tharenweyr is his cradle—world grown from a seed planted long ago. The vine bore fruit and the Creators—the Hiannel—were born to fashion the lands in

which Erellinarth would gain redemption. And one of
their number, Junsar-Hiannel, grew fearful of his task.
He doubted destiny's strength, and knew terror. "I will
build a fortress," he said, "where I will be safe," and so
he stole the Kartoranth, twin keystone of the World's
Far Boundary, and would pile stone upon stone upon
this deed and therein hide from terror. A great folly,
greater and more terrible end! For then was destiny
turned to fate, monsters born to walk where once life
would have been pure, all was given over to doom, and
the world was made ashen. Grieve, grieve, my People!

Remis gripped Tashnark's arm. All around them now the
shadows had massed into a distinct presence, threatening to
take on some monstrous shape. The darkness became increasingly dense as she stared and the low moan intensified in the
floor.

A deep voice yelled warning. More and more of the crowd
had sensed the threat. Some of them began to leave, clearly
disturbed, but the shadows were all around, thickening, blocking
their exit. They huddled together.

The edges of the building groaned.

"Dark power!" growled Tashnark. He grabbed for his sword,
but it wasn't there—he remembered that he didn't even carry
one. Within the city, no one but soldiers, guardsmen and robbers
did. The one he'd fought with during the evening before would
have found its way to the temple's armory by now.

"This can't be happening—" Remis began.

A huge spidery darkness swept up and across the high ceiling.
Wind from an opened door? The sudden dying of daylight
outside the windows? Neither explanation seemed possible.
Someone screamed. The crowd's fear became manifest as a
broken twittering counterpoint to the deep rumble in the floor.

Knots of worshippers broke up, shifting nervously, clutching
at each other.

"We've got to do something," Arhl hissed.

"I'll warn Corriman." Tashnark shook Remis loose and stepped in the priest's direction.

But Remis sensed something more—a strong, luminous power that was growing in the infinitesimal spaces between particles of darkness, reaching outward, drawn by the rhythm of the ceremony. Caris-Lorin was no longer distracted, but had re-focused on the ritual it was her duty to perform. She was working with Corriman now, singing her words into the night.

"No," Remis breathed at Tashnark. "Wait!"

He halted, perplexed.

Caris-Lorin's firm but mellow voice rose high across the temple in a complex litany. Nerves throughout Remis' body thrilled at the familiar majesty of the celebrant's singing. She knew the words, could understand the intricacy of the spell, but, glancing behind, saw a mixed expression of bewilderment and wonder on Tashnark's face. He felt the Power, too. Arhl was spellbound. Here was the strength they needed in order to face whatever dangers their new-found destiny might bring. Here were the names of all the world's hope, and in the names lay all the shattered fragments of life.

The interior darkness retreated.

The chanters, the priest and several Shastorenti among the people joined with Caris-Lorin in the spell-chant, as her words wove and swirled the air into a pattern of renewal and dedication. There was no physical light, only an intensity that was itself almost luminescent. It flooded the building, dispelling the fear the people had begun to feel. Remis felt that fear drain away, from herself and from those around her.

"What the hell was that?" Tashnark growled.

Remis gloried in the triumph, astonished in spite of herself at the intensity and fervor of the acolyte's celebration. Remis had rarely witnessed a vesper-ceremony so alive with Deep Power. The walls had become solider where once their strength had faded; the people moved toward true piety in an apotheosis of joy, and pushed aside darkness with the dedication of their will; now Corriman's stern face had lost its indifference and was almost aflame with zeal and urgency. She had no idea what had allowed the darkness to become so threatening. Had it been an attack from outside? Perhaps. But if so, it had had no effect. For a moment even the progress of dusk was reversed on the southward windows, and it appeared to Remis that the night was ablaze with premature dawn.

What had made the difference? What presence had turned the mundane ritual into something vital and alive?

A gift sent to them from the Raashyr.

Remis knew the name of the gift and let her own voice rise to spin a spell-thread into the ceremonial fabric of the Vesper; and while the song continued she knew no hint of despair, nor possibility that fate, and its Dark agents, might be victorious over their light. For a while, until silence fell again over the temple, she was safe and life unthreatened.

For a while, there was peace.

v.

A cold wind edged under the pub's main door. Grenard, a minor functionary from the Shaa-Derthperrit Temple in Koerpel-Na, felt the chill but was touched too by fetid warmth that soaked through the loose weave of his shirt. He wondered for a moment whether the warmth was related to the tall stranger approaching his table, as absurd as the notion seemed. The newcomer was cloaked and had an air of concentration about his face that made Grenard uneasy. Had he been discovered?

The aristocratic stranger sat down and stared into Grenard's eyes, in an instant stifling the protests forming on the temple-spy's lips. He touched his burning fingers to Grenard's fore-head and said in a low voice: "I am Worjaren Rehemon... Lord Worjaren Rehemon of Vornarca. You have seen me in this Home-seat—not here in this place, but entering the gates of Thargonal's Palace. You have also overheard some of Thargonal's guards talking to their beer and they have said that I, Worjaren Rehemon, have returned to the estate in a fury over the temple's actions. The guards talked of me in hateful and embittered terms." He smiled stiffly through his hard-lined lips. "Is this understood?" Grenard nodded. "Good. There is more. You have also heard rumors of planned coups within the High Council—and news of the Cerendar." He paused. "Do you have that name? *Cerendar.* It is the key to everything." Grenard muttered the word. "Very good. Tell your temple superiors that I have this artifact, this much-coveted Cerendar, that I have snatched it from the jaws of infinity by a quirk of fate. Tell them...you heard few details regarding the recovery of the artifact—only that it has something to do with an undead creature. You heard a guard say that Worjaren Rehemon will take the Cerendar to his masters within a month of this day. Is that clear? A month, and maybe sooner." Grenard nodded. "Ah, you are an apt pupil, my friend. Go then and report these findings to your priests."

Lord Worjaren watched the temple servant rise from his seat, gather his clothes against the wind, and move into the main road of Gihornter. He lifted the abandoned mug and drained its contents, then strode to the window. The walls of the palace were dripping with rain flung on them from the boiling clouds. In his rooms, Isal-Anul Thargonal, one of Vesuula's aristocratic leaders and Worjaren's host, would be rolling forgetfully with his pudgy mistress, making sport while his wife's absence freed him from marital restraint. Or he'd be issuing futile orders, mismanaging with a style all his own the properties and position that his father had bequeathed to him. Lord Worjaren Rehemon snorted, causing a nearby reveler to glance at him curiously. He scowled, and the man looked away.

A pub-wench walked by, and the sorcerer, his rank disguised under ordinary clothes, slapped her rear and said, "Have you Tenenian beer, girl?"

"Yes, sir," she replied, watching his hand furtively. "It's a rich brew, sir." She evaluated the wealth of his dress. Tenenian beer came from a mountainous region to the south renowned for the fertility of its vineyards; it was a fine liquor but inordinately expensive.

"So am I rich. Get me a bottle of it."

She nodded and moved away. Worjaren's mind followed her until she disappeared through a back door—she had a fine body, visibly sensual despite her loose clothing. He could easily desire it. Certainly she was beneath him in rank, but what did that matter? His rank had ceased to be of significance centuries ago.

Worjaren sat back at the table he had vacated earlier, thinking of the woman. Such dalliance was something he missed—the excitement of womanly flesh under his fingers and passion flaring in his groin. Long ago in Mikhalin he had had many women, and those as diverse as time and his ambitions had allowed. Since then, in this death-state he was in, there had been no such emotion in him—only a shell of memories concentrated around his desperate search for freedom. For too long he had suffered the burning of the monstrous Lucishnor's otherworldly fires, product of an impotent passion. He must be free—he must. Once again he would feel, not the scorching agony of living flame, but the cooler ground beneath his feet and air in his lungs and wind and rain and flesh touching his flesh. Once again there would be meaning in touch. That was all he desired. He no longer wanted to rule. He just wanted a place where he could rest, a place to seek love, a place where he could die as others died.

The key to these desires was the same Power that had banished him into his world of torment, an artifact cloaked in mysteries he was forced to grapple with. The Cerendar haunted and compelled him.

"Your beer, sir," said the wench, bending over him to place a silver decanter on the table. It was a deliberately provocative move. Worjaren reached out and ran his fingers down her neck into the exposed cleavage of her bosom. It should have aroused him, but instead it was like touching hot coals.

He leaned toward her so that his nose hung close to the skin at the base of her neck. It looked smooth and scented, and he wanted so much to catch a whiff of the sexuality exuding from her pores. But there was nothing, for smell was a sense that had left him.

"Sir?" she whispered.

"What is it?"

"There's a room at the back," she said. "I don't charge much and am considered good to be with."

"I'm sure you are." Worjaren dropped a coin between her breasts. "I'm sure you'd do your best. No doubt your flesh is willing and between your legs lies a haven of delights. But there's nowhere you can take me that I haven't already been, and all your skill could never quench the fire that burns me. You'd be seducing a phantom, for I simply wouldn't be there with you. I'm never where I appear to be, girl. Find some mortal to seduce."

She frowned resentfully and backed away. Worjaren watched her edge into the kitchens. He poured himself a dram of Tenenian beer. Its reputedly superior taste was no different to him than ordinary beer, however cheap. He might as well have been drinking pig's swill.

Wind blew a mist of rain along the front of the pub and, with dreary malice, the ancient Lord stared through it to the dark-stone palace walls. He longed for the action to begin, longed for some sign that freedom was possible. But his hope now lay in others.

The arrival of powerful enemies in Vesuula had changed his approach to finding the Cerendar. It was clear to him that the times were leading inexorably to a moment of confrontation. He had known that the Cerendar was destined to be at the center of conflict between the Raashyr and the E'ashalsinir—but he had hoped that such conflict would be further off, and that in the meantime he would be able to find the Cerendar and use it to free himself from exile and division. Now, time was contracting. The fated moment was upon him.

The discovery that temple spies were lurking about in Thargonal's home-seat gave him a clue. Clearly his own researches were stale. He no longer had the time to rely on them. Since the island Reyad, the trail had been dim and uncertain, a mish-mash of errors and failures. Surely these new enemies must be luckier than he had been. If they were as significant as they seemed, then that hope was not vain.

One of them in particular disturbed him—the one named Sevthen Ulart-Tashnark. In the last moments of his struggle with the dark Nahallhan on the streets of the Wargrin-Othos, he had felt the presence of something more than simple strength in the man. This Sevthen should have been beaten readily. He had seemed no more than an ordinary mortal, a man of resilience no doubt, but without special talent. Worjaren had assumed that this fight would be no different from other fights: brief struggle, easy victory.

But he was wrong. There was something in the man, a presence that knew Worjaren Rehemon and had vowed his defeat. Facing him had brought too unexpected a reversal, too fast a strike, for Worjaren to have read it clearly. He had had to back off, or the sword would have ploughed through his own head instead of his acolyte's. Ordinarily that would not have worried him—he could not be killed so easily. But there had been enough that was strange in this encounter to make him avoid risk. Worjaren had fled, but he had felt the touch of his enemy in the seconds before his spell had taken him away.

The only thing that seemed certain was that these people were special. They had to be searching for the Cerendar, and if so—thinking that it had been found by the Dark Gods—could they forbear to come to Gihornter to wrest it from him? No. They would come, secretively and in defiance of law; would risk accusation of treason to attack him before he could carry the artifact back to his Dark God masters. Violence would not deter them, if their fatefulness was real enough to be useful to him.

What did Worjaren Rehemon care for the parochial fool Sire Thargonal, or the other E'ashalsinir followers hidden under the aristocrat's roof? He didn't care for state laws. He had nothing but disdain for the Supreme Council and was content to let the temple and its allies succeed in the larger part of their plan. Only his own capture would be denied them, though he would let them think it possible for as long as he was able. In fact, he would help them in their invasion. He would guide them, give them the edge over Sire Thargonal's guards, lead them to the master of the House and deliver him into their hands. Let them have it all.

All he wanted was the Cerendar. His intuition told him that these fools, with whom he had for too long been tripping a measure, knew where it could be found—or at least had the capacity, the fatefulness, to find it. Perhaps they needed more information. Very well, he would let them have it. Thargonal knew the history of the search as well as any, and under the proper provocation would freely tell it to them. Perhaps they needed the undead heart that lay in his sanctuary under the Palace. They could have that, too. Lord Worjaren Rehemon took another mouthful of tasteless beer. Whatever it took for them to find the Cerendar artifact, he prayed they might gain it soon. A thousand years of torment had given him little enough patience to contain his eagerness. But when they took hold of the thing, once their fatefulness helped them to find it and draw it from its age-long obscurity, he would be there to snatch it away from them. Once he had it, neither the Raashyr nor the E'ashalsinir would be powerful enough to wrest it back into history before he had used it to free himself from his distant prison.

He stood and walked over to where the pub-wench was cleaning used glasses. Her softly curled dark hair swished about her shoulders as she moved, and her skin glistened in the lamp-light. She turned to him and frowned, but something in the stranger's eyes softened her resentment. Waving with her drying-cloth, she signaled to the solicitous tapster that she did not need his help.

Worjaren placed the silver decanter of expensive beer in her hand and dropped several more coins into its spout. "I insulted you," he said. "Forgive me. Fleshly pleasures are wasted on me."

"They're never wasted, sir."

"No?"

"No, sir. We all need love."

"Even if it's an illusion."

She smiled. "Some illusions are stronger than what's real."

He was silent for a moment, seeing the sensuous swell of her breasts as she breathed. Worjaren ran his hand through her hair. "I believe you," he said. "Come. See if you can make me forget."

vi.

The Temple Governor, Mir'gathel—a heavy-set woman with short gray hair and an air of refined patience—turned her eyes to the window of her study and stared across the roofs toward the darkened sea. Shaan had just finished telling her the story that Tashnark, Remis and Arhl had already heard. It was the night following their early morning arrival at the temple gates.

"A prophecy of doom," the Governor said. "There have been many."

"A certainty, unless we stop it," Shaan replied.

Mir'gathel fell silent. Remis watched, her heart aching. When the Governor spoke again her voice seemed thinner. "I have been Governor for seven years," she said without looking at them, one hand pulling at her hair as though to free it, "and all my life has passed in the service of the Gods. There have been times of ardent dedication, when zeal conquered all doubt and gave me the desire to fight directly in the name of the Raashyr. But more often are the times when weariness and mediocrity dulled me to the other, more youthful passions. I have watched the city at work and play, dancing with phantoms, and have been able to believe there's no reality in our rituals, no efficacy in our devotion. I've despaired.

"That's all over now. Doctrine has become real and I can touch truth with my spells, verifying it and fearing to admit what I know to be certain. I am afraid. Deeply afraid. What is it you bring to us?"

"I bring nothing, but am carried on a wave."

"It's a wave terrible to contemplate and what it threatens seems more terrible than I've ever imagined. The Dark Gods nag hard at our heels. They've fostered error and tried throughout our history to destroy us with it. But they've worked from far off, and we've been more concerned with human evils—greed and cruelty and injustice. Now, suddenly, the Dark Gods are on our doorstep and any error can bring an end to everything." She turned, face drawn. "I've grown feeble in this civilized state, where evil is institutionalized—so hedged in by law that common iniquity is all we ever seem to fight."

"It's the same evil," said Shaan. "Nothing changes. Evil is evil, big or small. We do our best moment by moment, and that is all that can be asked."

"It may not be enough."

"If we face up to what must be done, then it is always enough."

Mir'gathel smiled. "You have great confidence, my lord."

"I have more reason than most to be confident. Yet I know there are limits and that there is only so much that even the most powerful and fated of us can do. If we act with integrity, we still may fail, but we will have done what is expected of us."

Mir'gathel's eyes, strangely blear now, closed for a moment. Remis felt pity—for the Governor and for herself. "Shanis!" she whispered, the honored title indicating her devotion, "how can we help?"

"Tell me what I must do," Mir'gathel said. It was nearly a plea.

vii.

The next day began with a damp, depressing morning. Tashnark stared through wet runnels at the fractured scene beyond his window.

In the night he had dreamt—a real dream this time, not the metaphysical nightmare of Bellarroth. At first, even in his sleep, he had felt relief at this fact. But it hadn't lasted. In the dream there were ants, hundreds of them, and he was a corpse, prone near the dark entrance of a cave. Less than a corpse, just a few bones, it seemed—the forgotten scraps of some ogrous beast's dinner. The ants ate him, crawling through the sockets of his eyes. Though he must have been dead, the eating hurt him. He prayed that the marauders would tire of him and leave before they found something that was hidden within the bones— marrow, or the brain perhaps. But the ants kept on and he tried to call out, summoning any remnants of life in the shredded sinews along his jaw-line. "No!" the skull managed at last, "no desecration. Stay back." The ants, of course, were disturbed by the movement in his jaw-bone, though they were deaf to the words spoken. He felt the skull cry, but without tears, for its eyes were gone.

Then in his dream the shadows in the cave entrance— which itself was a frightening thing, like a giant maw—moved outward and became an ogre. The monster, his dinner-scraps violated, snarled in anger at the presumption of the ants. *I'm saved*, Tashnark thought in his dream. *The ogre will drive off the ants before they reach my soul.*

And indeed the ogre cursed the tiny insects vilely and swiped at them with its club. The skull and all it might have contained were crushed under the blow. All in all, Tashnark would have preferred to dream of Bellarroth.

I have no wish to be a hero, involved in important matters, Tashnark thought, as the rain trickled like tears down his reflection on the window-glass. *But what if that's what they'll make me be?*

viii.

News came from the City outside the temple as time passed. The events of that night had left their mark in many ways. Rumors flourished, rumors of thieving gangs and cult wars, but nothing was specific enough to dull the edge of the populace's unease. The citizens of the Wargrin-Othos district questioned Sumis—and were told of foreign pirates, now driven away or butchered. But the tale was unconvincing, and the scars of conflict were for a while burnt into the streets and buildings, visible for all to see.

Bodies were found—in and around a shop in the Street of Arlon's Rest, abandoned by its owner, who was missing, presumed dead. The contents of the shop had disappeared—in fact, they had been brought to the Temple of Shaa-Derthperrit, though this was known only to those within the temple. Sumis suggested that the owner was a foreigner and it was generally thought that he had been a victim of the attack. Temple Governor Mir'gathel, through her contacts, had arranged for official records of Remis' ownership to be obscured and replaced.

"That makes me feel even less real," Remis commented, trying to sound amused. "The City had pushed me into the margins before this. Now I don't even exist."

Languishing on a chair in one of the temple's sunnier rooms, feet up, bored, Tashnark gazed at the hard look that had settled on her features and was aware of an undercurrent of pain.

"Being invisible to the rulers of this place makes you *more* real," he commented idly.

When she didn't reply, he looked across at her. She seemed uncomfortably sad.

"What are you trained as again?" he asked. "Spellbinder?"

She nodded, regretfully.

"So what did you expect to happen once you'd graduated? The only independent spellbinders I know of are itinerants— and usually bad at what they do. The Houses want control of the rest."

Remis came over and sat by him, though she answered without making eye contact. "I know that now. Before, I don't think I'd even considered the issue. I was stupid."

"Why spellbinding?"

"I guess I just...drifted in that direction—I don't know why.

My father didn't approve, but my natural ability to draw on the Deep Powers was strong, so *that* determined where I was generally headed with my life. Within the magic arts, spellbinding seemed like a creative discipline. Being creative appealed to me."

"Creative?"

"Seeking out the material patterns of an object and enhancing them with a sculptured infusion of Deep Power. *Creating* something new within the old—changing it into an extended version of itself, full of potential." Tashnark was gratified to see the enthusiasm that infused her; it made her pain retreat and that's why he'd asked the question.

"I don't really understand the appeal," he said. "Seems like an indirect way of using magic. Better to take a more aggressive stance, to have more immediate control over the result. I have no *natural* ability myself, but if I did...."

She shook her head once, fiercely, making loose scraps of dark hair flutter over her forehead and cheeks. "No, no. That's not the point." Her green-gray eyes, sparkling now, held him prisoner. "It's not about control, it's about extension. Setting up conditions within an object that allow its nature to expand and influence aspects of reality—"

"We're talking love charms?" he interrupted cynically.

"At the lowest level, sure." She smiled. "I know spellbinding produces a lot of hack work...there's a demand for it. But many of history's most influential movements have centered around spellbound objects." She became thoughtful. "In a way the world itself could be seen as a vast magical artifact, spellbound by the Creators to achieve a pre-destined—or at least hoped-for—end."

"And is that what this Cerendar object is? Something spellbound."

Remis looked at him sharply. "An astute observation, Tashnark. If the stories about the Cerendar are true, though, no known spellbinder could have created it—it's far too powerful. No one has ever commanded that sort of power."

"What about one of the Creator Gods?"

The idea seemed to unsettle her. She suddenly withdrew from him—and Tashnark didn't like that. He preferred enthusiasm to thoughtful distance. And why should the possibility that the Cerendar was divinely spellbound be taken that seriously?

"Make me something," he said, to distract her.

For a moment she didn't answer, as though she hadn't heard. He repeated himself, louder.

"What?" she said.

"Make me something. A spellbound object."

She frowned. "Spellbinding takes a long time...a lot of study, effort—"

"Just something trivial." He fumbled in his pockets, but all he could find was a coin. He held it out. "What about this? Make it do something."

She looked at the coin, then up at his eyes. Tashnark found himself challenged and drawn by her stare. Moments stretched into minutes, or seemed to. He licked his lips, feeling his body fill with heat. Suddenly her attention had become discomfiting. He was about to glance away when she snatched the coin from his fingers.

"All right," she said. "But not here. Not now."

It was all he could do to nod dumbly.

* * * * * * *

On their second day in the temple a representative of the City Wardens turned up with a small military detachment to demand that "the bandits" be handed over immediately. Mir'gathel had explained that sanctuary in Raashyr temples was an established principle in civil law; and, after some appropriate blustering, the City Warden had departed. He had not been able to produce any official authority for the arrest.

"It was bluff," Governor Mir'gathel said. "Most likely, any real knowledge of what happened that night is being suppressed. It would not help our enemies to have their deeds publicly broadcast. They were the law-breakers."

Another body was identified as well, found in an alley behind the boardinghouse where much of the conflict had taken place. The dead man, his skull split, was a political ambassador from Dagest-Yanu, a neighboring state, who had been in Vesuula on a trade-negotiation visit. Kept secret, but discovered by the Temple's contacts, was the information that he had been staying in the Thargonal Family town of Gihornter, as Thargonal's guest.

"As I suspected, Dagest-Yanu is involved in this," Shaan said. "I've known for some time of the Thargonal Family's connections with that country and the Dark Gods they serve. Thargonal is a corrupt man. He will stop at nothing."

Tashnark grew afraid for his mother, whom their enemy may have known about and might use to get at them. He went to Mir'gathel in a lather to leave and get her to safety, but the Temple Governor had already anticipated the problem. She had sent warning to his mother, who had subsequently gone to stay with her ex-husband. The Governor gave Tashnark a note his mother had written. It said:

"I am well, son. Do not fear for me. Seek your path truly and the gods will not despise you. You have my uttermost love, always."

* * * * * * *

Misery provoked by his mother's message was at its most intense when Remis, aware of his mood, came up to him, touching his shoulder gently. "What's wrong?" she asked.

"Nothing." Then he shook his head. "Nothing new anyway. Call it indigestion."

"Can I help?"

Impulsively he hugged her, dragging her hard against his chest. After a moment she pushed away. He cursed himself. No doubt he'd been too forthright.

"Sorry," he said.

"I have a present for you." She held up a coin. "Something you asked for. I made it last night."

He took it, holding it as though it might explode. "What does it do?"

"It's what you wanted—a love charm."

He looked from the coin to Remis, sharply. "Really?"

"Sure. Why not?"

"So I can use this to...what? Make someone fall in love with me?"

Remis grinned. "It doesn't do the impossible." Tashnark growled and she slapped at his shoulder playfully. "Seriously, no use of Power, no matter how deep, can create or impose human emotions. The best anyone can do, whatever they claim, is to make a victim *act* as if he were in love. It wouldn't be real and it wouldn't last."

"Ah," he surveyed the coin yet again, "meaningless love. So this thing will get me laid, at the very least?"

Remis scowled, but visibly restrained herself from direct comment. "Compulsion spells are costly. This charm merely picks up on emotions you send its way and forms an image of your...." She hesitated. "...object of desire, just as if she were there in front of you."

Strange emotions, real enough for Tashnark's liking, settled on him like hunger.

"Try it," she said. "You have to hold the coin in your hand, hard, then think of the person you want. The magic I've put in the metal sets up a conduit through your flesh...from heart to mind. And, oh yes, it'll only work once...twice at most."

Tashnark considered the coin lying on his palm. He looked at Remis, his gaze intense. His fingers closed over the coin. "Maybe I'll save it for when I need it more."

Remis looked surprised at something in his tone. "I didn't mean for you to take the thing so seriously."

Tashnark thrust the coin into his pocket. "I'm nothing if not serious," he said. "Surely you've picked up on that already."

ix.

"Nothing! Nothing, you say!"

The Homeguard soldier, tired and nervous, baulked at Sire Thargonal's annoyance. He had ridden hard from the City and desired nothing more keenly than a hot tub and a mug of beer. Harsh words seemed too great an injustice. "They've been in the temple for seven days now, sire, and show no sign of stirring. As you say, sire, nothing has happened."

Isal-Anul Thargonal, Patriarch of the Commercial Family Thargonal, shook his head and turned away. He could not understand the tactics being employed by their enemies; could piece together little even of the plans of his friends. Since the fiasco in the Wargrin-Othos district and the death of Worjaren Rehemon's acolyte Aridor, Thargonal had heard nothing from Worjaren Rehemon beyond a curt command to have the temple watched. So he had watched, as closely as discretion and the cursed powers of the Raashyr-dogs would allow. Returning to Gihornter as a measure against discovery, he had then waited for news. Nothing. Always nothing.

No, not nothing. There had filtered to him information concerning a covert meeting called by the Derthperrit Temple governor. What it meant, Thargonal could not say. For a while it worried him that there may have been some plan in it to expose his conspiratorial activities to the Supreme Council, but none other than a representative of the fool Kharth'horun Family would be there. So it seemed unlikely. Golun-Alen, a Sumiswizard in his pay, stationed in the City, had assured him there was no sign Sire Thargonal's part in recent affairs could be known, let alone proven. The temple, he claimed, was making a gesture. A gesture! Thargonal grunted derisively and damned idealism to the seven hells.

Yet, to Thargonal's mind, the entire affair was as close to a complete disaster as he would care to get. One failure after another had plagued their efforts. Lord Worjaren Rehemon smelt disaster, of that Thargonal was certain. Why else would he disappear so thoroughly and leave no word?

Admittedly, such caprice was characteristic of the man, but in the present situation it was more capricious than usual. Thargonal wanted him here—to shoulder some of the burden of concern. What if something went wrong?

He slapped his hand on the side of the seat, causing his rings to clang against the metal-worked insert on its side. Let the Family owl shriek, he thought, and keep its eyes open.

X.

"You must be out of your mind!" exclaimed Arban, gesturing fiercely at the Temple Governor, Mir'gathel. This was the first time the senior priests had been called together to formally discuss the situation. Seven days had passed and only now, immediately after a rather stiff and uncomfortable meeting with the Kharth'horun Family—whose support was vital—had the Governor asked for the priests' input. At that earlier meeting the possibility of raiding the Thargonal estate had been suggested. No one had taken it seriously, until now.

Arban was a small, compact man, as gnarled as some of the gargoyles squatting on the Temple's towers. His arm was out-thrust and his forefinger scored the air pointedly. "I can under-stand how someone in your position might relish the chance to topple that aristocratic swine; and, sure, I can appreciate what temptation lurks in the mere hope of nabbing the foreign sorcerer—but I mean to say, it's all so flimsy!" Governor Mir'gathel nodded and would have spoken if Arban had not anticipated her and rushed on. "Criminally flimsy! There's barely a shred of evidence—nothing that would convict him in open court. Can't we gather some concrete evidence and then let the authorities act? We're not a police body."

Mir'gathel shook her head stolidly, causing her robes, which she wore for all interviews no matter how minor, to rustle gently.

Arban felt himself distracted from his argument. "You're aware, I dare say," said Mir'gathel, "just how much influence Thargonal has in Sumis? We would merely be opening ourselves to ridicule."

Arban huffed. "Ridicule? And this, this *treason* will save us from that, will it?"

Another of the priests, Corsinel, reached forward to Arban's shoulder as though to arrest a movement. "Arban," she said, "impropriety won't help."

Corsinel was a stern woman, her features angular and her hair tightly rolled across the top of her head. There was beauty there, but it was of a kind generally unnoticed by those who feared her.

"What?" stumbled Arban, taken aback. "Oh, yes. Shanis, forgive me!"

Mir'gathel waved the apology aside with a casual sweep of her fingers. "It's nothing, Arban," she said, running one hand through her close-cropped hair. "I expect disagreement. This is not something we can go into lightly. But I must point out, if I have to, that any attempt to gather evidence against Thargonal could have no result other than to alert him to us. There'd be no chance of exposing the sorcerer—and every possibility that the Dark Gods would take the Cerendar. Such a gain would put an end to more than the Temple's reputation. In all probability the world would be destroyed. At the moment they do not even suspect we know of Gihornter's role in this business."

"But the risk...." Arban ran his hand through his black hair, which was much longer than Mir'gathel's, with a gesture reminiscent of an actor's posturing. "The risk is too great. The only word we have that either the Cerendar or the sorcerer is at Gihornter is that of one man. Have you examined this Grenard? His story is so thin. I think, perhaps, that he has had the memories *imposed* upon him."

"Imposed?" queried Corsinel. "By whom?"

"I don't know. But it smells of a trap."

Mir'gathel, who was standing, hunched herself over the desk.

"Do you think I've made this decision without consideration and without concern, Arban? I have asked myself a thousand times, what is to be gained from such foolhardiness? There's only one answer for us. No risk is too great that is a blow against the Dark Ones."

"The Dark Ones!" said Arban cynically.

"Do you question that this is what we must primarily deal with?"

Arban's intense eyes, unintimidated, sparked with annoyance. "Of course not, shanis. I chant the creeds daily. But what word do we have that the E'ashalsinir are involved in these events in any special way?"

"Lord Shaan's!"

"Ah, the Saral. Now *he* is problematic, don't you think?" Arban strode across to Mir'gathel's crammed bookcases and slapped at the spines with the back of his hand. "Lord Shaan is impressive—that I don't deny. And his knowledge of lore is great. But these books tell me that no Saral has been born in Tharenweyr since Bran-kam in the previous age. He's been dead two thousand years!"

The old governor huffed disdainfully. "I thought this question at least was settled. You know as well as I do the limitations of all recorded histories. None can be comprehensive, least of all these ancient tomes whose backs you strike. The Saral has submitted successfully to the verification rites."

"The rites haven't been performed for lifetimes beyond counting. How can we be sure of them?"

"Yet his magic-aura bears the markings of the Raashyr."

"Yes." Arban flopped down into a chair and rubbed his hand over his head. Corsinel was staring silently at the floor looking like a statue of herself.

"We were in agreement on this point after the tests were completed," Mir'gathel pressed. "Why do you baulk at it now?"

She looked from Arban to Corsinel, then shifted her glance to the only other of her priests in attendance at the temple: Corriman. The tall lanky vesper-priest was standing back against the far wall, leaning on a window-ledge. He had said nothing during the course of the argument and had given no sign that he was even listening. "What do you say, Corriman?"

Corriman looked Mir'gathel in the eye. "My faith and my resolution are in tact, if that's what you mean," he said. He pushed himself away from the wall and strode toward the others, scratching at the bridge of his nose. "My concern for the Temple and its life has never been as acute as it is now. Yesterday as we chanted vespers I felt the urgency again.... I can't ignore it. The rite fills me with power and I can feel the pressure of darkness crowding toward some purpose just beyond our walls. The world is crying out for aid, could we only hear it. I believe Lord Shaan to be as he claims, Saral and true-born of Raashyr Shaa. I believe it because of the verification rites and because of the changes in spirit I have undergone since his coming. No, shanis, I am in agreement with you. If the Saral-Lord would sacrifice us to good ends, then I go willingly."

"Thank you, Corriman," Mir'gathel said. Then she turned to Corsinel. The lady was still staring at Corriman. "How do you feel about this, Corsinel?"

"Somewhat lost," she replied in a subdued tone. "I am not so constitutionally at ease with the idea of sacrifice. I enjoy our life here and, I suppose, fear to lose it."

"There is danger, but no certainty that we'll lose anything. We are not throwing away our temple life—merely fulfilling it."

"But there are such great risks, shanis."

"I know." Mir'gathel sat back into her chair. "And we have risked so little for so long." She looked back at Corsinel and her stare grew keen. "What is your opinion of Lord Shaan?"

Corsinel sighed. "My mind is conservative and I admit I have doubts. Yet I've felt the truth in the rites forcefully enough and my heart says that the Saral must not be denied. Were I wiser, perhaps, I would draw back and deny him. But Arban has often commented on my folly."

Good lord! thought Mir'gathel, *self-depreciation from Corsinel. What next?* Corsinel went on before the Governor could think of something to say. The words were dismissed quickly, as though Corsinel had detected their utterance as a threat. "Yet we mustn't allow folly to destroy us. We must be awake to necessity as well. I feel many reservations in this matter, despite the appeals of my heart."

Corriman shuffled into her line of vision. His sharply boned features seemed even more imposing than usual. "I too feel reservations, but I suppress them for the sake of duty. To fight the darkness has always been the basis of what we are doing here. If we abandon our responsibilities now in order to preserve the past, I fear the past will lose its meaning and end in spite of everything."

Mir'gathel nodded. "If we are here to fight darkness, yet take no action when the Gods speak to us with more directness than I have ever before known them to do, then we are worse than failures and we have lost more than our comfortable life."

There was silence. Governor Mir'gathel stood dismissively. "There is no time to pursue these arguments any further. I believe that I, and Lord Shaan, have your support, freely given. If not, then I fear I must command it."

They all recognized her authority and knew that the decision had now, for good or ill, been made. Mir'gathel would expect all subsequent discussion to take place in an atmosphere of loyalty. They knew this and accepted it.

"One of us must attend this raiding party," said Arban suddenly. "I would like to be the one."

The Temple Governor stared at him silently, delving for his motives.

"I'd be superfluous here," Arban continued. "Ill at ease and ill of temper. And of all of us, I'm the one with experience in battle." Once, long ago, Arban had fought with the army of a famous mercenary general. Mir'gathel could concede this point—she herself had never been at war.

"Very well, Arban," the Governor said. "Very well. You shall go."

"Thank you, *shanis*, for this confidence." The priest bowed and, with the others, made his way to the door.

xi.

"It amazes me," said Tashnark, after announcement of the Temple Governor's decision had been made. Once again they were in a small annex off the refectory—a place they often frequented during the unending wait, as the atmosphere was lighter there, more sunny and providing an illusion of normality. The temple itself could be oppressive. "Thargonal is a member of the Supreme Council. To invade his home-seat is an act of armed insurrection against the state. I'm surprised the Governor would even consider it."

Remis nodded quietly as she chewed on a crust of bread. "It's not political."

"Everything's political!"

"Call it what you like then!"

"How about *stupid*?"

Remis nudged him and smiled. "Now *you* amaze me, Tashnark. I thought you were the one most vocal in condemning the Council."

Tashnark huffed, snatching the bread from her fingers. "Sophistry doesn't change anything."

She stared at him mockingly. "Sophistry? I had no idea you'd been studying the art of speech-making?"

"I know sophistry when I hear it." He grinned. Then he added lightly, "Isn't it a small red bug that always tries to look bigger and redder than it really is?"

Remis laughed. "So you don't think it's necessary that we deal with Thargonal?"

"I don't know what's necessary any more." He took a bite of her bread. "Life's become rather too complicated and I can't understand the ends, let alone the means."

"Surely the end is obvious. Weren't you told? The Governor believes that the sorcerer, Worjaren Rehemon, is in residence in

Thargonal's home-seat and plotting political disruption within the City—"

"Thargonal and his clan are always plotting disruption. It's a family trait."

Remis gestured impatiently. "But this time there's a certain urgency to it—an urgency that concerns Shaan...and us. Mir'gathel has reason to believe that Worjaren Rehemon, who is known to be a representative of the Dark Gods, has found what he came here for—the Cerendar—and is about to return to his homeland with it. Disastrous, if it's true."

"And we're expected to commit treason in order to find out?"

"You baulk at treason in order to avert universal disaster?"

He shrugged in a careless gesture that was so intense it all but negated itself. He pushed his hands into his pockets, to stop himself from waving them at her, now that he'd finished off the bread. In one he felt the coin Remis had spellbound for him and began moving it around between his fingers. "I'm worried, that's all."

"Worried about what?"

"Worried about losing things...valuable things." He looked at her silently. "Things I've only just found." His gaze was challenging, and, finally, it was Remis who had to turn her eyes away. "It'll be all right," she said weakly.

"Nothing's certain...." Tashnark walked to the window and watched the twilight growing hazy, his hand still clutching at the coin. "...And how far will they expect us to go?"

"They who?"

He grinned, coming back to the table. "The small red bugs, of course!"

As he sat, Remis stood. She leaned over the table, pushing aside the slightly noxious herbal drinks that had been all they'd had to amuse themselves with since arriving at the temple. "I think you need something to take your mind off the bugs," she whispered.

Feeling her breath on his cheek, aware of the scent of her in such close proximity, he pulled away in surprise. His eyes studied the smooth skin of her neck. Remis noticed the direction of his glance.

"No, not that," she said. "Something you crave even more."

"Oh? Is there something I crave more?"

She flushed and turned away, only to reach beneath the table and retrieve a large leather bag Tashnark had assumed contained the sort of paraphernalia she needed to work her spells. Perhaps it did, but what she pulled from it now was a large bottle of Zejtolian liquor. She plonked it down in front of him along with a couple of glasses.

"Is that stuff even allowed in here?"

"Why not?"

"Well, you know, I assumed—"

"You assume too much." She made a gesture of enquiry. "Well, do you want some?"

He grinned. "Sure. You often drink Zejtola?"

"On and off."

She poured two rather large glasses of the translucent liquid and slid one toward him.

"Here's to insurrection," she declared, holding up the glass.

Tashnark followed suit. "Cheers," he said, and took a tentative sip. It wasn't something he could afford too often. The liquid was smooth and potent, higher in alcoholic content than he'd expected. Remis smiled at him, rather sardonically he thought, then swallowed the entire contents of her glass in one swig. She slammed down the glass, shook her head once as if to clear it, and stared into his eyes, challenging. A loose wisp of hair trailed down over her eyes.

"You surprise me," Tasknark said.

She shrugged, and muttered, "Your turn."

xii.

Shaan left the temple and did not return for two days. During this time Remis became increasingly aggitated and could barely restrain herself from using Power to seek his whereabouts. The others seemed intolerably phlegmatic and would not be drawn on the matter. Tashnark considered all attempts to work out what Shaan might be up to with open hostility. He became annoyed when Remis tried to talk about it and accused her of stupid adolescent sentimentality. She in turn became short-tempered and their emotions flared into arguments. Despite having known him so briefly and having met him under such suspicious circumstances, she felt strangely close to him—so these disagreements made her uneasy. One minute they'd be joking around together, the next minute one of them would suddenly be shouting at the other. Was it necessary? Those whom the Gods wanted together should at least disagree amicably. Surely that wasn't too much to ask.

"I think you're being a bit unreasonable about this," she said.

Tashnark snorted. "*I'm* being unreasonable? I'm the one who's been insisting we use *reason* rather than meekly surrendering to the wooly metaphysics you're all so good at pulling out of your asses. So who's being unreasonable?"

Despite Remis's determination not to react to his provocations, Tashnark's words made her angry. She turned away, clamping her mouth shut.

Tashnark went on. "If Shaan is a God—"

"A Saral is *not* a God," Remis snapped, turning sharply. "Saral are *from* the Gods!"

"Whatever. If he's one of them, he can look after himself. If he isn't, then he's been lying, manipulating us, and who cares what happens to the bugger?" Tashnark began sucking on a piece of toffee he'd produced from somewhere. The sound was irritating, so much so that Remis ground her teeth together to avoid saying as much—it would only seem petty. But the interminable slurping tested her patience. Finally, Tashnark stopped the noise long enough to add, "Either way, I'd rather we talked about something else."

Remis glowered. "Such as?"

He stared at her provocatively—serious or teasing, she

couldn't tell.

"Well?" she growled.

"Us?"

"What about us?"

This time he turned away, sucking at the toffee again—and kept going out the door of the refectory. "Forget it," he muttered as he went.

"Tashnark?" she called. "I can't stand it when we argue. And I can't afford to buy a bottle of Zejtola every time I want to smooth things over. We have to...."

If he heard, he didn't answer, and was gone before Remis could determine what else she'd been going to say. It felt wrong. She wished she knew what he wanted of her...she wished she knew what *exactly* she wanted of herself.

* * * * * * *

When the Saral did return, it was quietly and unannounced. Remis was walking through the main hall of the temple, on her way from the Supplication rites. In the grainy shadows of the side pillars, she saw a familiar figure kneeling before one of the altars. She hurried toward it, but then she noticed others.

"What news, Be'rin?" Shaan said.

Acolyte-Be'rin, a short woman lately returned from one of the Temple's daughter shrines, bowed slightly before she spoke. "Your instructions have been carried out, Lord Saral."

"Has there been trouble?"

"Yesterday there was an attempt by an outside force—a strong one—to influence some of our people. It would have been effective but for the protection you left us. The sorcerer certainly."

"What protection is this?" one of the others said. A woman and Remis did not recognize her. She must have come with Shaan, for there was no way she could have been simply over-looked. She was assured in her manner, unintimidated by her company or the temple. She was tall and rather wiry. Her features—what Remis could see of them—were handsome and assertive. Her hair was short and very dark and her clothes reflected the sophistication of her manner. They were expensive, but worn. There was a quality to the leather vest, silk shirt and pants that suggested a wanderer, and her boots, finely made though they once had been, were scratched and frayed by long use and many hard miles.

But two things about her drew Remis' attention more immediately even than her otherwise emphatic appearance. Across her back was hung a beautifully ornamented lute—of the Sumorle'en bardic school. Remis recognized the designs on it easily. The other thing, an odd contrast to this, was a black-metal battle-axe that was strapped to her left thigh. That weapon, which shared her side with a more orthodox sword, gave her a definite air of aggression.

Her companion was less demonstrative. He was lithe and strong and held himself well, his long, unkempt hair giving him a wild appearance. Like the woman he carried weapons—a sword and several sheathed daggers—and poking from the canvas bag tied to his back was the unmistakable neck of a lute. Probably he was an apprentice. A student of some kind usually accompanied Sumorle'en graduates on their travels.

"I wove a Protection throughout the temple when I left," Shaan was saying. "It was easily breached no doubt, but shattering it would have been enough to warn the temple defenses."

"So you are a Power-monger yourself, my Lord," the man said.

"An amateur only."

Remis moved towards them then, making sure to rustle her skirts to give them sufficient warning of her approach. Shaan looked around. "Ah, Remis," he said.

"I was beginning to wonder if you were coming back at all," she replied.

Shaan immediately indicated the two strangers, explaining that they were the main reason for his absence. It was fate's directive that they should play a part in events, he said, and he had been led to them.

"Led? How?" she asked.

He shrugged. "Call it intuition."

The woman he identified as Halul Gauth-Helonis and she was, as Remis had guessed, a singer and professional story-teller. In common with most of her ilk, she was a wanderer by inclination, though her Sumorle'en training suggested that she was a skilled warrior as well. She came from Votisphus, a large and historic city south of Vesuula, which explained her oddly modulated accent. She nodded to Remis and said, "Well met, sister. Lord Shaan has spoken of you. And I've seen you in my dreams."

"Dreams?"

"Sumorle'en graduates have a weakness for prophecy." She pointed to the man. "This is Mallorin-Sarcis. He's still in the Lower Order and under my tutelage."

"Pleased to meet you," said Remis. Mallorin simply nodded gloomily.

Halul nudged him with her elbow. "More enthusiasm, Mallorin. It's confirmation that we're at the start of a high adventure."

"That's what disturbs me," the apprentice replied. "Your adventures have a tendency to get dangerous."

"All the more to my liking. It's the stuff of great art."

Remis wondered what Tashnark would think of this pair.

xiii.

Actually, Tashnark was rather attracted to Halul at first, what with her flare and her songs. But the attraction was short lived. He soon found that her brash and self-centered exterior hid an equally brash and self-centered interior.

For a start she was verbose and pompous. Considering the other inhabitants of the temple, there was a certain absurdity to her egotism. She saw her arrival in their midst as a stroke of the most obvious good fortune that could come their way. Her extreme self-dramatisation and melodramatic manner grated on Tashnark's nerves—like the sound of an ill-tuned lute. It was different from Shaan's brand of self-caricature and in its way even more annoying. Conflict became inevitable and the opportunity for conflict was not slow in coming.

Halul's monologue had turned to the subject of combat skill, specifically swordsmanship, which in her, of course, had reached its height. She had given a blow-by-blow account of several major triumphs of her recent past, when she found herself challenging Tashnark to a sparring bout, confident in her ability to show the coarse Nahallhan a thing or two about real skill. Remis saw the way Tashnark's jaw-line tensed and felt a moment of concern.

"A sparring match?" Tashnark said.

"Why not? It'll pass the time," Halul replied. She guessed that Tashnark would be a surly and ferocious opponent, but she also knew that ill temper and ferocity did not win points against style and training.

"I'll need a sword," Tashnark said.

"No problem." She glanced at her apprentice. The man scowled but pulled a long blade from his baggage and tossed it to Tashnark. The Nahallhan caught it easily by the hilt and swung it around once or twice.

"So, do we fight?" Halul asked.

"Okay," Tashnark said casually. "If you insist."

"How will we decide the outcome?"

Tashnark bossed the tip of the sword with his thumb. "The best in battle is the one still standing at the end." His eyes rose to look at Halul from the shadow of his heavy brows.

The woman gestured impatiently. "This isn't a battle and we are not enemies."

"You make the rules then."

"Loss of sword or a body-touch. That'll be the signal to end it."

"Right."

Remis stepped between them. She grabbed Tashnark's arm. "This isn't a good idea. Someone might get hurt."

"Not I," said Halul smugly. "He may have a man's strength, but I have Sumorle'en training."

"He's not quite what he seems," Remis said.

Tashnark pushed her aside. "Oh, don't fuss. It'll be fine, just fine. I'm not going to kill anyone." His eyes locked onto Remis's and for a moment they smiled. He leaned in at her and whispered, "And don't be jealous. I never cross swords with women I intend to sleep with."

Remis released her hold, scowling.

They went to an area outside the temple and the singer-warrior spent several minutes flexing her muscles and her blade and moving through a series of well-executed turns and parries. There was textbook accuracy in her movements. Tashnark was impressed in spite of himself. Still, he made no such preparation, but stood limply scraping his sword in the dirt and grumbling impatiently.

"Can we get on with this?" he growled at last. "If a dance could win wars, the Wargrin-Othos would be a training ground for the Families' private armies."

Halul allowed him a forced smile. "I'm ready," she said, and bowed in courtly fashion.

At first her attack was governed by caution. Her blade spun a tight curve through the air, seeking a way past Tashnark's heavy defense. Her eyes, with a Sumorle'en's keen vision, sought to interpret Tashnark's intentions from signs on his face. But all she saw was a plodding wall of resistance—no trace of quickness or cunning, and no knowledge of feigns in his glance. Gaining confidence, she made a sham pass toward Tashnark's right-hand side, then turned her blade quickly to the left and jabbed home the point. To her surprise, the Nahallhan's blade was there before her and knocked her thrust aside easily.

With intense concentration, Halul rained a volley of cuts toward several diverse quarters of her opponent's guard. Tashnark parried them all, sweeping his sword cleanly back and forth, allowing nothing to provoke him.

What's he doing? Halul thought. *Won't he ever attack, or is he just waiting for me to tire? That's no way to win a trick.*

She drove at Tashnark fiercely, swinging, lunging, cutting with all her skill. The other backed off a step or two, moving at incredible speed and with amazing anticipation. An ambiguous smile wavered over his lips. It filled Halul with fury. But she forced herself to remain calm in the face of Tashnark's provocations—an obvious attempt to draw careless anger from her. It mustn't happen, she thought. Skill must win here.

What she didn't see was that beneath Tashnark's patronizing smirk was a more honest admiration. He had begun defensively, to draw out Halul's abilities and to gauge her strengths. What he quickly realized was that she was very good. Much better than him. When Halul's blows began storming his defenses and his blade whistled around him like some deadly insect, he'd known instinctively that he couldn't win like this. Soon enough, Halul would worry open a gap and he'd lose. For a moment Tashnark forgot his plans and just fought without design. Before long, he felt his timing begin to slip and a twinge of desperation entered his strokes.

As the fight progressed Halul began to taste success and it spurred her into a paroxysm of energy. Her blows and thrusts edged ever more speedily around Tashnark's clumsy blocking action. In her mind, she was already celebrating victory.

Suddenly Tashnark felt his desperation reach a point where it fused with something else—a power outside both himself and the world. For a moment, time slowed. He saw Halul execute a dexterous movement and her blade bore toward a point below his defense. His consciousness moved sideways.

The hilt of his sword squirmed under his fingers and he knew it had changed.

Bellarroth was there, like a phantom, but this time Tashnark didn't move over into that alternate being.

Instead they joined.

Power ripped through his arms.

Halul felt the change as it happened, though she did not understand what it was. Her eyes caught a tightening of Tashnark's face and a widening of pupils that in her experience normally signaled attack.

At the same time Tashnark's outline blurred. It was only a momentary thing, but in that moment she thought there were two people there. One was Tashnark, broad and muscular, of middle height. The other was a red-haired, ragged male of enormous size. The two shapes wavered and coalesced. Halul shook her head to clear what she interpreted as dizziness. Tashnark clarified again. Dismissing the moment, Halul took an opening that suddenly appeared before her. It should have given her a winning swipe.

Instead Tashnark's sword moved at dazzling speed toward her own blade and slammed against it near the hilt. Her wrist, despite experience with such jarring blows, was jerked painfully. That alone would not have beaten her, but the blow was a mere prelude and was followed by an assault that took her completely by surprise. Such blows rained on her sword that she thought either it or her arm must break. Fatalism stole over her, evoked by the impossible speed and strength that Tashnark was displaying. Then, before she could grasp the significance of that in her mind, the sword-grip was thrust from her hand and the sword spun away out of reach. She looked from her empty, aching fingers to the Nahallhan, who was standing breathing heavily with his sword-arm dangling at his side. His eyes could not see her.

"Tashnark?" she queried.

He dropped out of his trance and frowned. "What?"

"You won," Halul said. "The basis of Sumorle'en lore is recognizing what is hidden and yet still I judge by appearances. Must I always be a student?"

Tashnark shook his head. "You nearly had me and you knew it. There's something of a cheat in this victory. I had help."

"Help?" queried Remis, coming forward now that the combat had ceased. "What do you mean you had help?"

For a second Tashnark looked confused. Then he lifted the sword. "This," he said. "It's a good sword."

"Tolerably good," Halul said, grinning wryly.

xiv.

The incident faded quickly, almost deliberately, in Tashnark's mind. After a few hours he could not be sure what had happened. All he recalled was the flurry of combat, and the help he'd received from his alter ego had disappeared from his memory. It left him restless.

He tried to learn a rollicking ballad or two from Halul; but the singer didn't seem to know any that she was willing to share, and all she would render for Tashnark was a dreary, historical saga of interminable length. What stimulation he gained from watching her lithe, intense movements and the sharp sexuality of her face could sustain his interest only so long. Eventually, he left her to it and went wandering in the temple grounds by himself. It was while he was there that he came upon a slightly built, wizard-robed figure sitting on a post overlooking the sea. From experience Tashnark knew that it was a fine place to sit when one was in the mood to think sombre thoughts. He went over and took a place by the stranger. If he was here, within temple grounds during this time of crisis, he had obviously gained the Governor's imprimatur—Tashnark was curious to know how he fit in the scheme of things. After all, that was the order of the day, wasn't it? How they all fit—in the scheme of things? "Not the best weather for taking in the view," he said.

The stranger turned light amber eyes in Tashnark's direction. He was bearded beneath his hood—short, reddish-tinged clumps uncharacteristic of Shastorenti fashion. His hair was curly. He replied slowly, "Depends what you want to see."

Tashnark nodded and, wiping grime off his hands, offered the man a greeting. "I'm Tashnark," he said.

The stranger returned his handshake. "I can forgive most

things. My name's Raaneon Sar-Pelledol." He smiled. "I've heard of you, Tashnark. Barely respectable, but interesting."

"News travels too freely in this place. But your source was mistaken. I'm not at all *barely* respectable. In fact I'm not respectable at all."

"I was being politic. The gossip was quite thorough."

"I suppose you're stupid enough to believe everything you hear?"

"I'm notoriously naive."

Tashnark grinned. "Were you trained here with the rest of the bunch then?"

Raaneon raised his eyebrows under his cowl. "Wizards aren't trained, they're educated. It's a complex process of physical and moral adjustment. Haven't you had the lecture?"

"I think I was sick that day. But you haven't answered my question."

"I was educated in the Votisphus Academy, hundreds of miles away—their entry standards are lower." He laughed to himself, then saw that Tashnark had joined in. "We're getting personal rather quickly, aren't we?"

"I feel out of place here," Tashnark said. "You look like you might feel the same."

The wizard's acknowledgment was slightly guarded.

They talked in a desultory fashion for some time after that. Raaneon seemed unsure of himself, though there was no guile in him that Tashnark could detect. They had things in common—interest in foreign beer, memories of a certain flop-house down near the harbor front in Votisphus, a somewhat pessimistic turn of mind—and in ways that would not have been approved by the temple watchdogs they analyzed Halul's sexual appeal, touching on others of their company in passing. Tashnark become uncomfortable when their occasionally lewd evaluations dragged in Remis, and quickly terminated the discussion.

Nevertheless he liked this Raaneon and felt strangely eased by his presence. As a result, his curiosity grew. "Since I've already violated social etiquette by asking about your past, may

I go even further?"

Raaneon shrugged. "Abandon propriety, my friend. Life's too short."

"Are you planning to be involved in the Gihornter business?"

A breeze whipped off the sea and sprayed them with icy droplets. Raaneon swept his hands through his hair, pushing back the cowl. His eyes wandered to the rocky foreshore where ocean currents and wind were breaking waves apart into flecks of foam and spray. "I worked for Thargonal the Corpulent once," he said.

"Really?"

"Oh yes. I was in his house-guard for over a year. I bought my way out in the end."

"Does Shaan know about this?"

"Of course. That's why I'm a part of it, I guess." He squirmed off the fence-post and strode to the edge of the cliff. "I've been close to Thargonal's plans and I know what he'd be capable of doing to gain influence. Now he's dallying with this Worjaren Rehemon from Vornarca. There was talk of the sorcerer before I got out. Sorcery's foul, Tashnark. Not so much because of what it does directly, though that can be bad enough. The problem is, it's a perversion of the Deep Powers, drawing on distortion."

"I don't understand that. What do you mean distortion?"

"Sorcery feeds off the *drontagis*—the *Monster* principle. According to accepted theory, the world's full of tension created by the struggle between Form and Chaos. Sorcery uses that tension. It corrupts, distorts the natural world, no matter what end is sought in using it. If Worjaren Rehemon's in our state I'd do anything to see him driven out. Working for Thargonal gave me an awareness of the man's potential, given the right allies."

Tashnark scowled. "I feel less safe than ever."

"Safe? I'm not sure I've ever felt safe. Perhaps safety's not the point."

Waves slashed on the rocks below them as though aware of their voices.

CHAPTER FIVE
SEDITION IN GIHORNTER

i.

He knew nothing of Time, or darkness, or thought. There was only pain, and there was no end to it. A gnawing, craving, lustful pain, like sexual yearning, infinitely heightened, had he memory of life. It galvanized him into taut agony, convulsed him without movement, stung him with flame-like flails—as though he burnt without being consumed and without relief. He would have screamed if he had voice. But voices are the province of the living.

Then the intensity fell away, like bindings that were suddenly gone. He could see, desire, move. He stood.

For a moment he ignored the burning image that hovered in the alley darkness, saw instead the woman before him. She held the thing that had caused him pain—the dagger; had taken it away and drawn his mind back from its prison; stood now without moving, unafraid. He would have struck out again in that direction, and leapt after the Fire for which he yearned, but something made him pause. He knew this woman, felt in her the call of common blood. He had spoken to her, though the memory was dim.

His mind formed words. *I am Valarl*. But they would not sound, and so were lost. He gestured wildly and, succumbing to the fever inside him, snatched at the hovering gleam of light. It spun away down the alley, out into a wider street, and he followed it.

It led him far across the darkened city—along open ways, through narrower roads, dark between towering hills of stone and wood, across grass which dampened his feet unnoticed, and beside stone wet with dew and black with foulness. He followed it by the moving oiliness of a river, over a bridge he could no more name than think of as a bridge, past buildings lit by orange flickering, and men who challenged him until he roared soundlessly and scattered them from his path.

At last, some time later, the gleam led him down a narrow stairway and he smashed through a closed door into a candle-lit room. There were two men. One was small and slight—he could be ignored. The other was a fattish, wide-eyed shadow, his features obscured by the glare of the jagged-armed image he held. The fat man cried out in dismay, but did not release the gleam, even as Valarl—who no longer knew his own name—came toward him.

"You're dead!" the man yelled. "I was rid of you."

Valarl grabbed at the gleam, felt his hand grip the fat man's wrist, held it with an emotion that was not quite joy. The gleam did not fly away from him this time. It was there, solid, no longer merely an image. But the fat man would not give it up. Valarl pushed at him and the man staggered back—but the gleam remained there on his hand. He was sobbing.

"The wristlet, Zeth'han. It wants the wristlet. Give it up!" the other man said.

But Valarl did not hesitate. He twisted violently on the wrist and snapped it between his two hands, ripping away a trail of blood and flesh. The fat man screamed, pain and fear mingled into despair, and then fell, jerking and thrashing in a semi-conscious hysteria. The gleam fell to the floor and Valarl snatched it up. He roared a wordless exclamation of triumph. Nothing else mattered. The cries of the fat man, who pawed at his handless arm, sobbing and insane; the horror of the thin man, expressed in a fearful scramble away from the blood and the violence; the sounds of others coming, drawn by the noise:

these things no longer concerned him.

He had it. It was his. Now he must follow the trail home, to where he could sleep, to the tomb from which he had come and the oblivion it promised. He did not know that it could not give him rest, that the curse was not so easily appeased. No, so long as his dumb spirit lay encased in this dead flesh, so long as the Cerendar exerted its power upon him, then the pain and desire would tear at him. All he knew was that he must go, follow the trail back to its source. And more. He wanted to be one with the gleam, the spark that transcended the world, to consume it as its existence consumed his freedom. He wanted it within him, to take the place of the life that was stunted in his breast.

Crying out without a sound, he raced into the streets, back the way he had come, back to Telfith's Street, back through roads and houses and buildings, back past frightened men and women and children, into Hassur and out of it, back to the place where the handless man sobbed and died, back to a house owned by a man named Sorn-De'an, who had unknowingly bought the gleam from a seller on the Docks, only to have it stolen—though again he had not known it—by Zeth'han and his friend; through Koerpel-Na Valarl raced, like a Fury seeking impossible escape from its own lashes; back through the gleam's recent history. Back he went to Lazul, where the gleam had lain for some time, owned by a man named Wefer, who had found it in a vault in Apophis. He returned to Koerpel-Na, racing the passion that made him weep in tearless frenzy. To those who saw him pass he seemed a spirit or demon, speeding with superhuman determination toward some appointed victim, careless of the furore he left in his passing. To those who got in his way he was Death itself, and if they escaped with their lives it was because he only wanted them out of his path, so that he could follow the trail of the Cerendar, back through its past. Twice Sumis tracked him down—twice he eluded them, not by guile but through the violence of his passage. Afterwards, but for bruises and cracked bones, they might have thought him a nightmare, and were glad of it when news of his wanderings ceased and he disappeared from sight. The last report came from the docks near the mouth of the river Tak'han, where he broke the back of an over-zealous watchman. There was no other news.

Now, surrounded by water, he swam toward his distant retreat, the gleam nestled within his empty heart-cavity but giving him no comfort. He thrashed forward, infinitely obsessed, lost to time and hungry men, seeking impossible rest in ground that had long rejected him.

Far away, the island Reyad was silent, touched by evening.

Waiting for the world to end.

ii.

When they finally left the protection of the temple—surreptitiously, of course— Tashnark made sure he traveled with his new friend, Raaneon. For a while they managed to mitigate each other's fears by talking about them in a blackly exaggerated manner—they would be torn limb from limb, their hearts would be consumed by demons, the world would end and they would drink themselves silly while it did. But in light of what they knew, their darkest speculations sounded all too likely and the exaggerations began to turn sour.

Instead, Raaneon gave Tashnark a run-down on the Thargonal estate's household structure, characterizing it as a second-rate tragi-comedy. His mocking account of an occasion when the Sire arrived at a House meeting drunk and naked made Tashnark guffaw loudly. Arban ordered the pair of them to be silent, as though they were schoolboys.

At the edge of the district border, the group split up and Tashnark was disappointed to find Raaneon assigned a different route. "Afterwards," he said, "we'll meet at the Refectory and swap tales—suitably fictionalized, of course."

Raaneon shrugged. "Not all fiction ends well," he grumbled, before waving casually and disappearing into the mist.

* * * * * * *

Gihornter was like a dark stain on the pastureland, hard against the night horizon that rose in a gentle gradient toward larger hills behind it.

The road was becoming damp now. Though there had been no downpour, the constant drizzle was enough to create puddles. This same damp, cast across the gray township, had driven people from the streets and there were few to notice their approach. Tashnark saw only two inhabitants—one a laborer returning slightly inebriated from the town, the other a derelict, huddled in defiance of weather under a crude shelter formed of branches and old cloth. He was far off the road in a paddock and Tashnark noticed him by the dim glow of an oil lamp. He rode over to check him out. A ratty-haired face, like a tribal totem, appeared from the shadows, startled by the looming form of the horse.

"Be off with you, boy," it yelled. "I ain't hurtin' no one and I ain't got nothin' to be robbed of."

"Don't worry, old man," said Tashnark. "I was just wondering why you were out here on a night like this."

The face huffed and, as it withdrew, muttered. "Tryin' to live, is all!"

For a few moments Tashnark watched the flickering light and the shadows behind the hutch-frame. Then he yelled: "Can you tell me, is there likely to be much going on in the town?"

Wind-howl was his only reply until the internal shadow emerged again. "Pub'll be open, but the Owl's the only one does much lurkin' after nightfall. Predator, ya know—slayer in the dark."

Tashnark rode back to the others, and relayed the fellow's warning of a "slayer in the dark". Remis laughed.

"The Owl is the Thargonal Family emblem, Tashnark. I guess the guard keeps the townsfolk under a curfew. It's fairly common in home-seats."

Gihornter's surroundings were partly industrial—a large

tannery and pasturage feeding animal-herds destined for the slaughterhouse—but much of its outlook was a patchwork of small farms and clusters of residential housing. To the north-west there were mines. The Thargonal Family owned a large cross-section of this sparsely utilized land, of course, for Gihornter was its home-seat.

The town was constructed on lines similar to those of other home-seats in the Vesuulan state districts, built around an ancient family homestead and developed over many genera-tions. Through its center ran the traditionally named Keat-Rewi—on one side of which were the massed adjoining houses of the lower classes and workers, and on the other side the patri-archal buildings: the palace, the homeguard barracks and the stables.

The town was walled, not in modern fashion—a free-standing enclosure—but in the manner of the old war-state cities, the walls being part of the structure of the home-seat's internal buildings. Huge gates had once been able to seal the inhabitants effectively within its walls, but the way into and from the home-seat was free now. Only in time of national crisis or other well-defined extremities was it permitted under the Ko'erpel Charter—an historical agreement between the Koerpel-Na aristocracy and the independent temples that defined the legal workings of the State—that the home-seat be closed to external traffic.

They rode to within sight of the gate-arch, though they kept themselves hidden from any watchers on the walls. There, on a track behind a row of mainly empty tenements, they huddled in the wet waiting for some prearranged signal. Acolyte Be'rin rode off into the night to meet others in a forested patch near the Lesser Gate. There was some obscure reason for this, some-thing of Shaan's contrivance, though Tashnark made no attempt to fathom it. Shaan would be with those others, on the east side.

What had bothered Tashnark most about the journey from Koerpel-Na was that it had given him too much time to think. Smuggled out of the temple in a cart beneath sacks and canvas, he could too easily remember that he did not understand what was happening within himself, could reflect on the warrior from his dreams, Bellarroth, and the monstrous landscape clarifying there day by day. He let the thoughts come for a while, but speculation got him nowhere, and eventually he resorted to complaints or old tunes to keep more difficult matters from his head.

Now that they'd arrived, delay encouraged him to fret. Restless, he made his way on foot down an alley to a gap from which the home-seat walls could be seen. He crouched behind a leafless, twiggy bush. A lamp-light moved across the battlements on the right of the gate-tower, misted by the wind and rain. Guards, no doubt. There was a dim smudge in the top tower-window, too, indicating a stationary watch. Beyond both of these, and the walls, the town was obscured for half its length, becoming visible on the northern side where the agglomerated mass of stone-roofed housing appeared on the rising slopes.

Tashnark noted the home-seat's relative smallness. More like a fortress than a town and hence more readily defended. The embellished towers and tiered balconies of the Thargonal palace looked impenetrable. The Thargonal house-guard would certainly outnumber the raiding party, despite a handful of soldiers donated by the aristocrat Kharth'horun, who unofficially supported the temple for various idealistic reasons of his own. *Political advantage, most likely*, Tashnark thought.

A noise behind him broke his reverie. He rolled away, grabbing at his sword. But it was only Halul moving like some phantom out of the darkness and rain. "Do you make a practice of sneaking around?" he said turning back to the home-seat indifferently. Halul squatted next to him, her axe scraping on the stones. *Why does she encumber herself with it?* Tashnark wondered. Such axes were neither subtle, nor particularly flexible at close quarters. There were better choices of weaponry for someone like Halul.

"Is there much movement?" the woman said.

"Wind and a few guards."

They watched silently, for perhaps a minute or two, both

stubbornly confirming the observation. It was Halul who succumbed to the challenge to speak. "Perhaps they bed down early in Thargonal's household. That'd be to our advantage." Tashnark said nothing, doubting the possibility. "The place is certainly quiet for this hour. I don't like it." The night hissed in the bushes and along the alley. "There's a guard of fifty men." Tashnark looked at her aghast. "Thargonal's there too, of course, and his younger daughter. His wife's off visiting. There are six or seven house-servants, and at least four who couldn't be identified—Power-workers, and foreigners, I guess. And the Vornarcan Lord, Worjaren Rehemon, naturally. Without confirmation of that we'd still be in the city."

"Have you counted the mice in Sire Thargonal's cellar yet?"

Halul smiled tightly. "Only the rats."

Tashnark laughed briefly then frowned. "What in the holy name of Ur-Teth is the Saral's plan?"

"Haven't you been told? I thought you were his confidante." Tashnark shrugged. "Apparently it's some contrivance of his that's holding things up," Halul said. "Some special magic. He wants to throw confusion into the household, dull their faculties—and avoid bloodshed."

"Is there any hope of that?"

"Who can say? The priest Arban seems doubtful, but if we simply push our way in, who knows how sprightly the guards'll organize themselves to block us off."

They fell silent again, pessimism mulling about in Tashnark's mind. He glanced surreptitiously at Halul, whose profile was attractive enough to take his mind off the absurdity of this enterprise for a moment. High cheekbones. Sensual lips. The leather vest she wore emphasized her small, firm breasts, as did her posture, which was always thrusting forward. *Don't go there*, Tashnark thought. *She's trouble. Besides...what about—?* He didn't finish the thought, instead turning his attention back toward the palace. Wind whistling between the buildings sounded like a lament to him, as though he were still hearing a lyric the Sumorle'en's apprentice had been singing earlier:

"...a leaf afraid of Autumn
That hangs on the winter's breath,
I softly wait to greet anon
The hardness of the earth...."

"Why are you here, Halul?" he said suddenly.

The woman licked her lips and turned her face askew of his, so that she wasn't looking in his eyes. Her profile was sharp and uncompromising. "The Saral fetched me. I was waiting for him."

"You've met before?"

"Never. But I'd been warned he was coming."

"Warned?"

Silence. Halul stood and began to move away. "We'd better get back," she said, "I think the signal's been given."

"Wait a minute!" growled Tashnark, annoyed by her evasion. But her back was to him and she was striding between the dark houses through the rain.

Nice ass....

He cursed and followed.

iii.

A sort of non-committal fatalism was the state toward which Tashnark aspired. In this condition he wouldn't feel the bitterness nor would he seek to deny the follies of the human heart. He would accept whatever came—the good and the bad, the wise and the foolish, the beautiful and the ugly—displaying equanimity both elegant and divine. Nothing would make him fret. Nothing would mean that much. Meaning, he often felt, was a vastly overrated concept.

Once, as a child, a passing greed had caused his groping fingers to brush aside one of his mother's most treasured statuettes and it had shattered fatally on the stone floor. He had cried over it, but no amount of tears could draw the shards back together again, and no regrets, however profound, could reverse the mulish irrevocability of time's progress. How, he reasoned, could meaning be sought, when the slightest chance provoked unending sufferings that were without redemption?

Yet disinterest escaped him. He cried without shame. Pain ached his spirit. Too often he railed against his father, state politicians, life. Just when he thought he had achieved indifference he would commit some act of stupidity and feel disgust, or would succumb to a course of action without any assurance that his motives were other than altruistic. When any of these things happened, he'd sigh inwardly over his failed aspirations, and abandon them to oblivion.

As they approached the Owl-Gate of Gihornter, Tashnark was sighing with every step his horse took on the worn cobblestones of the Keat-Rewi. Any excitement he might have felt at the prospect of adventure had had too much time in which to dissipate, and all he now felt was the stark idealistic foolishness of it all. To thwart Thargonal's plotting by capturing a sorcerer so powerful he daunted even the god-like Shaan? To retrieve a legendary object so potent it could destroy the world? What right had they to think they could succeed in either ambition?

Rain and a deepening chill had doused Tashnark's internal fire. The brazen glint of the Thargonal Owl, hanging on the arch of the town gate, struck him as ominous and threatening. Grimly, he slumped in his saddle, beneath an encompassing cloak, hiding his sword as their priestly leader Arban demanded and waiting for the Watch's challenge. When it came he started stupidly as though he'd been awakened from a drifting sleep. It took a great deal of willpower for him to refrain from drawing his sword.

He glanced toward Remis. As though she sensed his gaze, she turned in his direction at that instant and smiled reassurance. He acknowledged her, strangely comforted by the moment.

They pulled their mounts to a halt under the shadow of the town's walls and waited like weary travelers too worn out to look up. Wind swept rain into the narrow shelter under the arch.

It was Arban who answered the call from the watchtower. "We seek shelter," he yelled, throwing back the hood of his cloak so that spattering rain formed a mist about his bald head.

The guardsman above leaned over the parapet and grumbled. "Who are you?"

"Merchants from central Ko'erpel-Na," Arban shouted. "Three of us at least, and the others servants and family. Have you an inn open in this town to keep the rain off our heads?"

"Merchants of what House, man?" The voice was dutiful in its boredom. "This is the Thargonal home-seat."

"No threat to the family to be sure. We're from outside the state originally, and too small to concern the lord."

Wind fractured the guardsman's reply.

"...inn, man...but you'll find no room there, I reckon. There's a bunch of players in residence, little pleasure this night'll give 'em."

"Perhaps a stall."

A heavy fall of rain suddenly flung large droplets over the tower-area. The guard frowned. "I don't give a damn. Go to the inn. I'll send the marshal to see you when he gets back."

Arban waved. "Much thanks!"

"Just make sure you give us no trouble. A night like this puts everyone in a bad mood." The guard gestured them through impatiently and turned away to his warmer cell before they could move.

"Quickly," whispered Arban and rode through the gate toward the dark form of Argin-Thargonal's statue—an ancestor of the present patriarch renowned as a monster-slayer. The others followed, Tashnark glancing nervously up toward the tower. The watch would be blind so long as he remained in his room: that would give them time to meet the others, perhaps a spare moment to move into the palace grounds before they were seen to be acting abnormally. Time would be precious and he prayed that whatever alarm system the watch might utilize would work inefficiently in this wretched damp.

Again he looked for Remis but could not see her. Where had

she gone?

He glanced toward his right. The palace sprawled there, secure behind its walls and ornate metal gates. There were one or two lamplights visible in galleries along the front, but mostly the large building seemed unoccupied. What that meant he could not guess. Perhaps it was a trap. "It's too quiet," he said to Halul, who had appeared beside him.

The woman seemed oddly solemn. "There's something wrong," she muttered, scratching at her earlobe. "They say there's a sorcerer in the palace, but I can't feel his presence there."

Tashnark looked at her sharply. "Can't *feel* his presence? What do you mean by that?"

"Nothing. Forget it," she said.

Across the market-square, where abandoned produce stands and booths for display of merchandise created an artificial forest of darker shadows in the otherwise open space, they saw a figure waving and rode toward it. Shaan's clean-shaven face formed out of the grayness. He nodded to Arban and Tashnark, but turned his attention to Remis, who had reappeared from somewhere and now slid down from her dripping mount. Tashnark glanced intently around the market-square and noted the silent presence of several of the aristocrat Kharth'horun's men—or so he presumed—and various other less recognizable phantoms. He wondered fleetingly where they had secreted Raaneon, his pessimistic wizard friend. Perhaps with Kharth'horun's commander, Helloris, at the back door?

Then he noticed a form moving quickly behind a line of stationary wagons at the base of the watchtower. He wondered who it could be. "Shaan?" he whispered, moving his mount toward the Saral and leaning down. "Is that one of ours?" Shaan glanced in the direction indicated.

"No," he said.

Tashnark leapt off his horse and ran across the damp stones. But several of the temple's mercenaries had seen the man and were closer. One moved after him and the shadow saw he was spotted and began to run. His voice came through the wind: "Help! Bandits!"

Tashnark swore. He was about to urge himself to greater effort, when the running figure suddenly jerked in mid-stride and fell as though he'd been tripped. Tashnark drew his sword and hurried to the spot. The figure was lying face down on the stones, groaning. There was an arrow protruding from the small of his back. He twisted around as Tashnark knelt beside him, his face, the face of a boy, contorted with pain and terror. Tashnark clenched his teeth. The boy, a mere adolescent, tried to speak, but blood welling into his throat choked off the sound. "Don't try," Tashnark whispered. "Lie still."

The boy nodded and Tashnark turned away, knowing the signs of death. Anger welled in him. To bring the youth down with a shaft had been unnecessary, barbarous....

Something struck the stones at his feet and bounced away. For a moment he felt disoriented, unable to locate the source of fire. He ducked behind a cart. Vague movement trembled across the square. A horse roared dully, and several voices cried out, one saying, "Beyond the corner, man!"

Intuitively Tashnark glanced up toward the watchtower's parapet. Against the firelight he could see the guardsman staring down toward them. Tashnark stood, searching for direction.

At that moment there was a flash of fire in the dark, followed by a dull, explosive crack. The guardsman on the tower twisted out of sight behind the stonework. Tashnark ran toward the first movement he saw. It turned out to be the priest. "What's happened?" he said.

"Trouble. I dealt with it." Arban pointed to the dying boy. "Who was that?"

Tashnark shrugged. "No one." He glowered darkly. "Who shot at him?"

Arban rubbed stubby fingers across his deeply etched forehead. "Who can say? One of theirs, I think. They must have been as confused as us. Went for the movement."

"Theirs?" Tashnark said. *It's madness,* he thought. He looked at Arban seriously. "Then our plan is blown," he said.

The priest shrugged. "Contracted rather. We must go in at once."

As though part of the wind itself, Shaan came out from the dark. "There was a patrol about. By chance, one of them was watching us in the city and must have recognized us. I saw him there, three days ago. Now he's dead, may his spirit find peace. Sir," the Saral, strangely innocent in his haste, gripped Arban with urgent intensity, "relay to all our Power-workers to begin the spell I've taught them. I will provide the focus. It's urgent."

Arban nodded and began spell-casting at once. "Guard us," said the Saral to Tashnark, "we need five minutes," and closed his eyes. Wind gushed fiercely across the square, causing the stalls to rattle and whistle. Tashnark growled. Guard them? If that was what they wanted, why must they place themselves here in the open?

Arhl came up to him while he waited, watching the anticipatory movements of Kharth'horun's soldiers. He held a crossbow and exuded a hint of metal oil. "It's close," he said. "There's no time to stand around."

"I know, I know. Whatever they're up to, it'd better be damned cunning. Where's the Sumorle'en and her journeyman got to?"

Arhl shrugged.

The delay seemed endless while they huddled there, expecting some fevered alarm at any moment. The palace grounds were less than one hundred paces from where they stood, the gate watch was killed, the home-seat crowded around them like a waiting predator; yet they remained in the public square, exposed for anyone to see, throwing caution to the night-winds for the hope of some untested enchantment. What surprised Tashnark was not his participation in the madness, but his patience in doing so. He should have been fuming against the stupidity of it, but something was calming him, easing the doubt within his spirit. He could not name it yet, but it felt, though new to him, paradoxically familiar. He found his attention wandering too often toward Remis, who was there near the Saral, still and contemplative with the rest.

The wait seemed endless, but when their tarrying was inter-rupted at last—by distant boot scraping and a light moving within the palace—Tashnark suddenly realized that little time had elapsed. No more than a minute or two. He looked at Arhl. "That's it," he muttered.

"He wants longer?"

"Yes."

The large blacksmith began re-loading his crossbow. With his thumb he twisted the spanner that set the cock. Tashnark snorted and drew his sword. Across the market, half a dozen soldiers, one or two with powerful crossbows, were running for position behind shrubs scattered piecemeal on the grass before the palace walls. Others were carrying longbows, and were squatting ready to fire. Behind, as obscure movement on the roofs of the village-housing, Tashnark thought he could detect other watchers—townsfolk probably, disturbed by the strange activity in the precincts of the palace.

A temple soldier came running up to them, his face flushed. There was a dark stain on his sleeve and sprayed across his jerkin. "There's someone approaching the gates," he said. "We must attack."

"We can't...until they've finished." Tashnark indicated Shaan and the others. "Hold off if you can."

"Hold off? The only strategy we have lies in surprise. What foolishness keeps us back?"

"His," said Tashnark, pointing at the seemingly comatose Shaan.

The man breathed out an impatient sigh. "Stupidity!" he muttered. Tashnark leveled his sword at the gate of the palace. Even from here the barrier's ornate strength was obvious. "Do you think there's been a general alarm given?"

The soldier paused then shook his head once. "No. There's too little sign of it."

"So we stretch our luck a bit further."

He nodded, though with obvious reluctance. At that moment,

on the top of the wall, a hand-held lamp splashed its light through the rain like a bon-fire. Several of Kharth'horun's bowmen loosed arrows at the man holding the lamp, but they missed. The man ducked down, then his voice could be heard. "Here! It's me ya fools. Are ya drunk?"

Silence.

"Is this some kind of joke?" the voice said. The man's head appeared. "That is you, Samish, ain't it? Samish?" He disappeared again and the light moved off rapidly.

"There'll be alarm enough now," whispered the soldier. "Why didn't the fool archers hit him?"

Through the wind that whipped suddenly about them, driving coldness into their skin, they heard bells ringing a dull clamor. At that moment the Saral's eyes opened and the wizards moved, Remis among them. Staring into Shaan's face, Tashnark caught a trace of unexpected puzzlement. "What's the matter?" he whispered.

Shaan shook his head. Water dripped from his lashes and the ratty locks of his wet hair. "I don't know." His green eyes fixed on Tashnark. "We were stronger than we should have been. A presence.... I can't account for it."

"But it's done?"

"Yes. Though I don't like it!"

"Aren't you ever content to leave riddles alone? What've you done?"

Shaan made no answer, not to him at least. He turned to all there. "There should be minimal resistance. Only those active at the height of the spell will remain awake. It won't last, but at least we might avoid some killing."

An officer of the temple guard ran toward the palace, shouting for his men to group there. The wizards and the others followed, raising a susurration from their movement, as the wind blew their clothes and their feet padded over grass and along the cobbled entrance way. Wind-roar hid any noise from within the palace walls. "Gate's barred," yelled one of the men.

Tashnark pushed his way forward anyway.

* * * * * * *

Arban gestured everyone back and, before his intention had become clear, he was calling out the words of a spell, weaving his hands through the wind and rain in a delicate dance. There was beauty and grace to his ritual, Remis thought, as she sensed the magic build. A spark of blue light jumped from his aura. With a violence that shattered the delicacy of the spell, the metal and wood of the gate tore apart. They all cringed. She saw Tashnark stumble backward in response to the concussion, winded but safe.

"Go!" cried the priest.

Glancing at him, Remis noted the strain in his movement now and wondered at the cost of that powerful blast. But she had no opportunity to consider it for long. In the distance, despite the wind, the sound sprang up of men shouting; the clash of blades and the shriek of crossbow bolts mingled with the cries, and she knew that the other raiding party—led by Kharth'horun's Helloris—had breached the gate into the stable-yards, and that once they had entered they had met resistance. Then someone was pushing on her shoulder, hissing for her to move, and she followed after them over the blackened ruins of the smashed gate.

The first thing she saw when she entered the palace was a body, brokenly slumped on the elegant base of a pillar. The body was bloodied, its back torn where a sword-blade had skewered it from a front-on thrust. There was still a twitch of movement in the limbs.

"Many more'll die," Arhl said, pulling at her sleeve. "Let's not be among them."

They ran up the stairs of the palace entrance and a wounded man was lying there; Remis recognized him as one of Kharth'horun's men. A spear protruded from his belly and he looked at Remis with weeping eyes. His blood was spilled across the floor. "Burn me," he whispered, his voice a mere rattle.

Blanching, a cold horror growing in her chest, Remis knelt

beside him. Behind her, further inside the building, the sounds of combat gave a broken rhythm to the lieutenant's breath. "I couldn't," she said, steeling herself to examine his wound.

"You must have pity. I'm dead and...would not...have my corpse...left...left for them to desecrate...." His mouth stopped, remaining open, and the life in his eyes departed. Remis stood back.

"I'll do it," said Arban, beginning the simple spell.

Remis turned away, but she felt the heat of the burning on her back.

iv.

As she scaled the highest level of the tenements, Halul recalled the words of an old song.

> "What shadow's that o'er yonder?" said the soldier
>   riding past,
> "Why, 'tis only rabbits fleein'," the Stranger answered
>   then.
>
> "What moves among the dyin' trees?" the youth
>   atrembling asked.
> "'Tis only foxes seekin' out their burrows in the glen!"
>
> "What is it worries now my mount?" the soldier's face
>   was gray;
> "The silent cry of rabbits slain," he heard the Stranger
>   say.
>
> "And why, sir, dost my breath come hard?" The
>   Stranger looked away,
> And the youth was found adying in the dawning.

She felt as unsettled and as distressed by omens as the soldier in the ballad and yet questioned neither her part in this venture, nor her impulsive pursuit of an intuition across the rooftops.

It was all a matter of calling. She knew that the Powers had chosen her to carry the secret burden of this task, so how could she deny the duties of that bondage? Up until a few days previously she had been bending under the weight of inaction, verging on denial of her importance, because nothing of more than incidental significance had come her way. There had been no clarification of her destiny, for...how long was it?...five, perhaps six years. Then the Saral, like a ghostly visitation come in response to her prayers, told her of great deeds and a dark possibility and she had followed him without pause, certain of her role. There was a great deed somewhere in history for her, and so she must seek it out and forge it into shape before the ultimate darkness fell. Only in this way could she serve.

She was like the hero of Rothan's Lay:

"Sword chisels glory from rock-miser Time,
While my song beats out the rhythm of its blows."

Something caught Halul's eye further along the roof, an incongruent hump on the edge near a buttress. It moved—a human shape—and not Mallorin, for he was circling around the other side of the residential mass, seeking entrance to it from the road there. Halul gripped the leather-embossed handle of Gard-Pardel, as her axe was named—*Opener of the Way*—and flung mental feelers towards the figure crouching against the lighter night-sky. Nothing.

She released her concentration and the axe and moved silently to the figure's side. It was a young boy, and as she saw this, Halul heard as well what she had not heard through the night's noises: a low weeping. Below, she could see the home-seat's market square, dotted with the dark shadows that were her comrades. There seemed little activity. The earlier skirmish had dwindled to quietness. The palace remained still but for one lamp-warden walking the outer chambers.

"Boy," said Halul, in her most soothing voice. The figure scrambled up and away from her, fear struggling with the grief and exhaustion in his face.

"Boy, what's wrong with you? I won't hurt you."

"Don't kill me, please."

"Why are you afraid? Do you deserve death?"

"No, Lady, I've done nothing."

"Then I won't kill you. What's the matter, boy?"

The lad breathed heavily, his gasps rough in the wind. "They killed him. They killed my brother."

"Who did?"

"They did," he said, pointing. "Brigands or somethin'. We was carryin' ale to the Watch when we sees them hidin' in the square. Others come and Doron, he says, 'I'm gonna get to the Watch, he ain't seen 'em in his cubby-hold!' and he tries to sneak behind, though I wouldn't. But...but they saw him, now he's there with an arrow in his back...." He choked and more tears came. "I got scared and ran—"

"Boy, boy," Halul leaned down to his level, "cry for your brother, but cry at home. If he's dead, he can't feel hurt any more, and if he's not you can't do anything till the trouble's past. Tell your father, come back when the fighting's done, but here you could be in danger."

"You one of the brigands?"

"I came with them, yes, but we're not brigands."

"You killed him."

"Go home, boy. We mean you no harm." As she spoke there was a violent explosion in the vicinity of the palace. Looking down she saw the gate fiery and broken, and the 'brigands' running through the breach. The boy pulled away from her and scampered across the damp stone.

Halul let him go, glancing once toward the struggle in the palace forecourt. Then she moved silently across the tiered roofs toward the center of the housing block. Somewhere here she had detected a Dark presence, though it had been faint and unreal.

She hoped she'd find the sorcerer, for unless she did she'd later feel that she had deserted her companions for nothing when a skilled arm was needed; and should they die there, she'd find it hard to forgive herself for abandoning them.

Glancing along the entombing overhang of a large structure to a stairway leading down to lower levels, she allowed an innate caution to slow her feet. The air was thick, not only with mist, but with smoke as well, for there was a conglomeration of chimney outlets here. Noises echoed from below, running, perhaps shouting—the sounds of a population disturbed in the night. There were smells, too, domestic smells and the faint acrid stench of refuse. What insensitivities could allow people to make their homes in this fashion, stacked irregularly one on top of the other, hearing, smelling, touching each neighbor without choice or freedom? Halul couldn't understand why they tolerated it. She had always been a wanderer, fixed to nowhere, needing only what she could carry.

She moved to the stairway and its darkness, curling her fingers around the axe-handle to will its powers to reach out. The presence was there! She concentrated her efforts in an attempt to locate the source of the evil taint that impinged on her expanded awareness. A throbbing, almost a pain, drew her downward. One step...two...into shadow and unlit gloom. Her eyes widened, gathering light in that place, her senses feeling for direction. The powers of Gard-Pardel flowed out like waves upon the surge of her perception, and sought their prey. There was an almost animalistic lust in the axe as it searched for the Dark God presence.

Halul's feet descended more steps, some strewn with garbage. Here and there well-holes gave a profounder depth to the shadows and changed the timbre of the passageway. Halul pressed on. The presence of a Darkness deeper than the night clarified in her weapon's eagerness, until the pressure moved her steps to an unconscious rhythm and all hesitancy was lost. The stairs became a corridor, with doors on either side. Someone passed her, several boys swore at her as she pushed them aside, a woman struck at her with a long loaf of bread. She ignored them all, maneuvering past patches of light and shadow cast by randomly placed lamps and open doors. The passion of her axe grew. Breathing heavily, she drew it from the thongs that held it to her waist and swung it over her shoulder. The blade struck and gouged a runnel in the plaster wall.

"He's here!" Her strained, inhuman voice whispered in the gloom. Gard-Pardel cried its delight inaudibly.

The corridor opened into a damp courtyard. Another stairway led to a yet lower level. The axe dragged her along a straight hall that ended in a terrace, roofless under the sky. Wind flung rain on her. There were people here, gathered in whispering groups to catch sight of the disturbance in the palace. Halul heard a voice say: "Perhaps one o' the Lord's devils is gettin' out of control."

Halul ran past them and they stared at the strange madwoman with the raised battle-axe, watching her but making no move to stop her. Perhaps they thought her the demon loosed. Halul was sure now that the sorcerer was travelling, whether fleeing or in ignorance Halul could not tell. But she was getting closer.

Then she saw a tall, cloaked figure at the top of an external stair that led down to the street. The axe shrieked and, as though somehow aware of the cry, the sorcerer spun around to face her. "What foolishness is this?" he said.

Halul took no notice of his imperious frown, nor of the ritualistic movement of his hands. Instead she bore down on the Dark Lord, bloodlust and insanity swamping her instincts. *Alive*, her free mind was shouting, *we want him alive*; but the Axe knew no compromise and sought only vengeance. It lunged out at the sorcerer whose soul it could read, hating him, denying him life. Halul too saw the spirit of her victim take form in her awareness and, more sane than the Axe, understood its strangeness. There was the expected distortion, inner form twisted into a parody of life and Eternal Being, but more, a jungle of horrors on which the *drontagis* E'ashalsinir Death hung like a fungus on a tree. And beyond that opened out an ageless emptiness, space devoid of being, endless and without comfort; power grasped and violently ill-used; lives, not only of men and beasts and plants, but of lands and times as well, all wasted and barren; and a fire, an eternal, non-consuming fire, power revenged in a holocaust of terror. The fire had taken shape as a gigantic monster, so large she could not take it in. Halul recoiled in shock.

"Back!" cried the sorcerer, or whatever he might truly have been. "No one is free to see into my soul."

His gaunt hand, like a death-paw, struck at Halul and fire appeared. Halul's body jolted and was flung away, while flame thrashed at Gard-Pardel's blade. Clouds, like smoke from the burning, palled Halul's sight. The axe swung wildly and its momentum threw Halul into unconscious darkness.

When she awoke, her mind was a maelstrom of ill-under-stood imagery. The sorcerer was gone and Halul was lying in the street. Like her, Gard-Pardel was in pain, but in the Axe the pain was an insatiable hunger. Groaning, Halul rose to her feet, and, finding herself unsteady, leaned against the rough brick wall.

She closed her eyes and called the mind-form of her apprentice before her. "Comrade!" she whispered. "I'm here. Hurry!"

Mallorin came and found her still shaken and weak. Her face was red and tender, as though it had been swept by fire, and in her eyes lingered a touch of something—some dark emotion that Mallorin had never seen there before. "What's happened?"

Halul shook her head gently, in doubt and denial. "I don't know," she said. "Something I don't understand." She gripped Mallorin's arm, hooked Gard-Pardel in its thong, and glanced down the street where it followed the hill toward Thargonal's Palace. "How goes the raid?"

"It's quiet there, mistress."

Halul frowned. "We must find the others quickly. The Saral must be told what I've encountered here."

"What is it, mistress?"

There was silence. Halul grinned sardonically, her teeth ghostly in the shadows. "The beginning of something terrible," she said.

Mallorin knew better than to ask her more while the fey mood was upon her.

V.

The night was steel and sudden brawls, sword-blades catching firelight and flinging it crying through the blur of movement. It was a hubbub of raised voices followed by low shuffles and boot-pounding. Another attack, bodies thrust aside, cursing, running on through halls of almost obscene extravagance. Then a roar, the wind-rush of a crossbow bolt, arrows where upper galleries gave a vantage point for snipers. Then a lull and the Saral indicating the next phase of their seemingly aimless chase.

There were fewer to attack them than Tashnark had expected. Perhaps the wizards' spell had caught many at rest and, though they would be roused by the tumult, perhaps it was enough that the ones affected had been delayed. Perhaps it had cheated the homeguard of drilled spontaneity in the face of alarums. Whatever the case, speed—their hurried and furious drive into the Thargonal sanctuary—had so far given them an edge. Few homeguard soldiers stood in their way; and those that had, unsure of the numbers they faced, gave way before them. In such confusion it was easy for the homeguardians to think that a full-scale assault had taken the whole palace and that the Family defenses had collapsed. Soon enough they would take thought, and rally under some competent officer, but by then, if all went well, it would be too late and the invaders, having gained their objectives, would have fled.

Those objectives seemed obscure and futile to Tashnark. He watched for attack, fought and ran. He worried about Remis, but lost sight of her and had to trust that she would be all right. Shaan and Arban led. He could see no pattern to their movements and soon came to believe that whoever of importance may initially have been there, they were in the vicinity no longer.

Of course, cult leaders of such a kind would have safeguarded their presence. Probably a plan of escape had been fashioned for contingencies and now it had been implemented. Probably they were long gone by whatever devious or deviant means they had at their disposal, and this raid—and its deaths—were in vain. Certainly, up to now, it was only soldiers the invaders had fought.

Shaan stopped and was studying their surroundings intently. His brow was furrowed. "Down," he said to Arban, "the trail leads down. Yet I can see no way from here."

"Cellars?" suggested someone.

One of Kharth'horun's men pushed his way into the conference. "No, not if they went down from hereabouts. I've seen the floorplans of the palace. The cellar goes off the kitchens back yonder. The only other marked underground rooms are two cells beneath the homeguard barracks and the crypt under the southern wall. We're near neither."

"Are you sure they fled downwards?" Tashnark said to Shaan.

"Yes," he replied curtly. "And from here."

The room they were in was a library, with huge lead-light windows that in daytime would have shed colored mists across the thick carpets and lavish furniture. It was high-ceilinged, and an upper gallery provided access to innumerable volumes stacked in book-shelves taller that several men one on top of the other. *Probably passed down over generations*, thought Tashnark, *and little added to by the current Patriarch, I reckon.* There were also alcoves about the walls, containing statues and large oil-paintings of Thargonal ancestors. Tashnark noticed the one of Argin slaying his customary monster. It was half obscured by a carefully placed potted tree.

"A library's a traditional place for secret-panels," he said, "and whatever the records say, I can't believe that the Thargonals have never seen fit to construct passageways giving access to their bank vaults beyond the walls. It's not natural. How old are the plans anyway?"

"Two hundred years, at least," said Arban.

Tashnark grunted. "So I'd say there are unmarked tunnels beneath the place, and the current devotee of illegal worship would want space to hide the evidence." An idea had come into his head just now and he pursued it with melodramatic vigor. He gestured knowingly. "And what would be the least suspected place for a demon-lover to conceal the entrance to his private lair?"

Arban scowled. "We have no time for games," he said.

Tashnark pointed to the portrait of Argin-Thargonal. "Behind a picture commemorating the glories of a demon-slayer. Where else?"

Shaan rushed to the alcove and the others followed. Remis re-appeared from behind Tashnark, frowned at him and said: "Do you have to act like a fool?" Tashnark molded his face into a mask of mocking innocence.

"Yes. It's here," Shaan was saying. It took a little time for them to discover the hidden mechanism, and for several of the men to crank the pulleys to raise Argin's portrait. The chains moved silently, well-used, and exposed a tunnel-well. There was a ladder leading down into an oily gloom.

The soldier climbed down first, despite Shaan's protests. With no time for argument, the others followed quickly. Someone whispered a command for silence and comments died away, leaving a darkness filled with scraping sounds and the clank of weapons on the walls. The descent seemed long. Lifting each foot and reaching down for the next rung, balancing, gripping. Remis, below him, growled at Tashnark when he stepped on her fingers. He snarled a brief reply.

But the exchange and the climb, as well as the darkness, were abruptly cut by a violent concussion and a blaze of light. A voice cried out warning and smoke and shards of splintered wood sparked trails in the air about them. Tashnark gripped the ladder tightly, gasping as breath was forced out of his lungs by the blast below. The noise was deafening. He let it flow around him like an ocean current. Then it subsided into quietness again.

"Remis?" he whispered, suddenly afraid.

"I'm all right."

He breathed out.

Further below, Tashnark could see the scars of embers glowing. They lent no clarity to the darkness between.

But whispered voices soon revealed that casualties were few. Arhl had several splinters in his leg, Arban was bleeding, the Saral had escaped altogether. The leading soldier had suffered most, for Shaan had delayed the man's descent only moments before the base of the shaft had erupted into a power-inferno, and the blast had stripped the skin from his legs. He was bleeding and groaning, lying in the embers. Shaan dropped down beside him and Arban, who had trained in basic neurological spells at one time, eased the man's pain.

It was obvious that the spell that had caused the trouble had been a departing shot, flung at them as those responsible fled from the room. Otherwise they would have been attacked again. Certainly the soldier would have been incinerated. Later, back at the temple, he confided to Tashnark his belief that the Gods had preserved him, perhaps for some higher purpose. How else could his escape from the power-blast be explained? "I was exposed to their direct line of fire," he said, almost proudly. "I saw the fire-wave flow about me, the Saral-Lord pulled me up, but not beyond the blast."

"You were held by Shaan?"

"Yes. The power wrapped around me, yet I live." He winked. "A miracle. The Gods must have helped me."

Tashnark, of course, felt he could pinpoint the source of aid more closely than that. But he said nothing. He could understand why Shaan might want no praise.

At the time, entombed beneath the floors of an enemy palace, there was no leisure for praise or religious zeal. They cared for wounds hurriedly, and sped in pursuit of the Dark acolytes. The bottom of the shaft led to a landing and a short staircase, the foot of which opened onto a low-roofed hall. Several arched doorways offered possible paths. Some of the wounded man's comrades carried him, such encumbrance further lessening the group's coherence, but they could not wait. Most of the group would follow Shaan along a dark, narrow way; the remainder must come as their path led them. Ambiguity of direction divided the party yet further and a hasty rendezvous was organized beyond the home-seat walls. Then they moved, splitting away into the oil-lit gloom. Tashnark's curiosity was pricked by an exit they chose to ignore. It was behind the entrance stairs, leading back beneath the palace, and hence gave little assurance of escape. Yet it bore checking, and something—he might call it an *intuition* had the word more meaning for him—something urged him to seek there.

"I'll look," he said to Shaan. "You go on."

The Saral nodded, glancing ahead eagerly, barely listening. Remis gripped Tashnark's arm. "Be careful," she said.

He grinned. "You're worried about me?"

"Of course I am—I worry about *everyone*."

"Come with me then," he suggested. "We can do this together."

She shook her head, glancing toward Shaan. "He needs me more...he'll need every scrap of Deep Power—"

"Fine!" Anger threatened to rush from the center of Tashnark's chest and he made a conscious effort to force it back. *Stupid*, he muttered, as Shaan and Remis and the others disappeared along the corridor. What did it matter? He had his own path to tread. He turned to take it, and found the young novice Danling waiting for him.

"What d'you think—?" he began.

"I'll go with you," Danling declared. "Just in case."

In case of what? Tashnark wondered. Danling was only a boy, and Tashnark had seen too many boys injured. He would have preferred to go alone. But Danling insisted and there was no time to argue. Delay made them vulnerable.

"Come on then!" he growled.

A corridor was behind the doorway, unlit and ominous. They walked along it for some way, and their tread was circumspect. Both were wary of the gloom and the hollow warmth of the place. It was a way frequently used, that much was clear, for the stone floor was smooth and the corners free of web. Occasionally they heard noises, but distance made them meaningless. "We should go back," Danling muttered. "It's too far. We must be well beneath the other side of the palace now."

Tashnark grunted. "We'll go on a little more."

A dim yellow light appeared ahead, flickering like candle-flame. Tashnark pointed it out to Danling. "See, it's not empty."

"We could've come through to the dungeons by this time."

"We'll see."

They continued until a door with a barred window in it formed before them. But it, was no dungeon beyond the bars. Tashnark felt a tremor pass through his muscles. He looked at the boy, but the other was unaffected.

"It's some sort of shrine," Danling whispered and began murmuring the words of a protective invocation. Tashnark peered through the window, gripping tightly on the hilt of his sword, and studied the sanctuary inside. Obscene *drontagis* images. Ornate candelabra supporting dull-flamed waxen spirals. Totems of an alien kind. Along one wall a large carved relief of a hideous creature—a tall, multi-headed bird, serpentine in its extremities. Tashnark recognized it. An image of Dread Huedaik, E'ashalsinir-Lord, high among the ranks of Rebel Command.

"Dark Acolyte lair," he murmured. The room seemed deserted, so he pushed on the door. It opened and they entered, attack-ready.

"Dare you come here?"

The voice jerked them around—Tashnark with sword raised, Danling simply surprised. Fear made him weak.

"I said, dare you enter the sanctuary?"

The voice was that of a heavily built man cloaked in trembling flickers of light and the folds of a thick robe. This garment was quilted and elegantly patterned. His fingers were spread as though holding some invisible object in the air.

"What I dare depends on what's to be found," Tashnark

snapped.

"Don't bandy words with me, fool!"

By some insight, Tashnark held his sword vertically before him. "Are you Worjaren Rehemon?"

"Worjaren Rehemon? Ha! A chimera. Do you know what the words mean, fool? *A highland mist.* If you seek mist, go to the mountains."

"Who bandies words now?"

The shadow's fingers tightened their grip. "I quibble, and I quibble with your life."

Were they sparks that spat in the gloom and teasing candle-glow?

"No!" cried Danling. Before Tashnark could stop him, the boy had leapt to intervene. Magic flared up around him, blazing fire and power off the polished contours of the statues. But the enemy's spell was too well advanced. A roaring wind tore across the chamber and tossed Danling aside like a marionette of paper. The boy's body slammed against the sanctuary wall, spitting blood as though crushed inside. It crumpled lifeless to the stone floor. Tashnark too was hit, but he only staggered, slightly stunned, for Danling had taken the brunt. His sword rang like a temple-bell. His flesh stretched and ached, and his sword, still held before him, became incandescent, as though absorbing the waves of Deep Power. He willed his arm to twist the sword, his legs to move toward the sorcerer, his mind to cry out in rage at Danling's death.

Power stripped his consciousness from him—slowly, endlessly, like sandstone worn by wind. He forced his mind awake, but the room disappeared *and he was striding through a strange land, where the sky was scarlet and the trees like giant serpents snatching for the sky. He struck at an image that leapt at him from the haze, he screamed fury and an alien word, he felt his sword become a mass of twisted metal asps.*

"Hanin!" he cried. A serpent-tree, black against the sky, came toward him, mouth open and flashing fangs like swords. He struck, bloodless, struck again, again, gouging at the crea-

ture.

Then the nightmare ceased and Tashnark awoke. Tears were running down his cheeks. The magic had dispersed. Before him, its head severed, arms hacked and bloody, lay a corpse. He staggered back, denying it, ignorant of it. "No," he muttered.

He sank to the floor and whimpered as a child might whose homely security was threatened by mysterious adult concerns. He closed his eyes tightly against the world. Time passed.

Many heartbeats later he opened his eyes again. An image of bones weeping in a marsh had begun to haunt the darkness behind his eyelids, and he suddenly decided that it was not for him to turn to bone here in a sanctuary-tomb beneath Thargonal's palace. There was something he had to do; many things...Remis. She trusted him—he thought that perhaps he loved her.

He stood up and went to Danling. "I didn't want you to come," he whispered, though the boy was beyond hearing. Tashnark shivered, and looked at his sword. It was bloody, and the hilt was a mass of metal serpents. He wiped off the gore on a wallhanging behind the power-circle of the sanctuary, then slashed at the curtain in fury, tearing it from its anchorage on the ceiling.

He went back to the body of the sorcerer. It was lifeless and still unfamiliar. Despite its severed head, it was clearly not the same person as had cried out at him on the night they had fled to the temple. Not the same. A Power, but not the one he had come for. The Mist was still elusive.

Angry and bewildered, Tashnark stepped over the sprawling corpse to investigate an alcove that had, until now, remained unnoticed. It was from this niche, shrouded by curtains, that the sorcerer must have come. Desire for its secrets displaced in Tashnark the rancor boiling ineffectually within him. He slashed the curtains aside with his sword. The small space revealed contained a heavy incense perfume, books and parchments, and a low table. On the table there was a small jewellery chest, plain but suggestive enough. Perhaps something of value to the sorcerer, hence to his enemies. Tashnark reached out and flipped back the lid, gasped at what he saw and involuntarily retreated from it.

A heart. Human. Not a dead and bloodless thing, desiccated by age, but alive and throbbing, like some blind sea-creature breathing desperately on a tidal rock. His mind spun, furiously connecting images and memories. He might have grown angrier, might have cursed that the oppressive array of mysteries had in this way been added to—but his mind turned away from these emotions, and he immediately saw another possibility. He lifted his sword and with its tip slammed the lid shut. This was no new riddle, but part of an answer to an old one. First an undead creature: a living corpse, its chest empty. Now, an undying heart, divorced from its natural seat but still beating. It couldn't be a coincidence. This thing had to be the heart of the creature Remis had met in the alley off Telfith's Street—and he had been brought here to claim it. Yes, *brought*. It had been inevitable, despite his skepticism of such statements made by others. He had been *brought* here and would take the living heart to one who was supposed to be the descendant of the corpse to which it belonged. What would Remis think of that, he wondered? What would the result of that meeting be?

Quickly he sheathed his sword and placed the jewellery box under one arm. He imagined he could feel the palpitations of the object inside it. Then he went to the dead Danling, and, sorrow swelling up in him, hoisted the boy's corpse across his shoulder. He would not leave him here, in a sanctuary of evil powers, nor indeed anywhere in Thargonal's dung-heap.

Snarling once at the body of the sorcerer and again at Huedaik's image, he left the place and ran back down the corridor after the others.

vi.

Part of the palace was burning. A pall of smoke gathered

above its roof. In front of Raaneon one of his comrades, a temple soldier he'd spoken to only moments before, cried out and staggered, his shoulder turned to blood and torn flesh.

"Oh shit," Raaneon whispered to the wall near him, "I don't want to be here." The wall didn't offer any alternatives, so he ducked down a corridor, crouched, and conjured a spell. The space behind him, where the metallic twang of a crossbow being released had come from, erupted into splinters of wood and stone. "So much for bloodless raids," he mumbled.

It would have been some comfort had he arranged to have Tashnark by his side. Their acquaintance was only brief, but in that short time it had become apparent to Raaneon that the Nahallhan was a major player in the fate they were all blindly pursuing—as well as being an excellent fighter and a witty companion. For Raaneon he, rather than Saral Lord Shaan, radiated safety. Having him there would have dulled the edge of Raaneon's fear.

Still, it was pointless wishing. He was alone in Thargonal's palace and he had a job to do. Best simply to do it.

When all was quiet again, he jumped up and ran the length of the hall. He seemed to be alone, though he could hear distant fighting. From the noise, there was no way to tell who was winning and who was getting their ass kicked.

He sighed, wondering what to do next. A door leading off the hallway creaked open. He flattened himself out of sight to see who it was and whether or not it'd be a reasonable thing to fight them. Raaneon had no intention of getting into futile struggles.

The head that emerged was a woman's. Her hair was gathered into a bun and her lips were lightly painted. She was wearing a servant's dress. "It seems clear," she whispered to someone inside the room.

A child's voice replied and though the words were not distinguishable, Raaneon could tell they were spoken by a girl. Thargonal's daughter?

He stepped out of hiding. The woman, a matron to the child, saw his harassed glare and the short, thin-bladed sword in his hand, and she screamed. She tried to duck back into the room, but Raaneon was faster. He flung the door open. The girl, Issen-el-Thargonal, scrambled behind her governess' skirts while the woman glared at Raaneon defiantly. "Get out!" she screamed. "Get out or I'll shoot you."

The wizard noticed then that she was holding a small, loaded crossbow. He also noticed that it had not been properly wound.

"Please," he said in a helpful tone, "I'm not after the child, your lives or even your honor. I just want directions." He gestured nervously. "How do I find the exit?" As he spoke he had another thought—remarkable, considering the circumstances—and added, "and Lord Thargonal's whereabouts."

"I'll tell you nothing." The woman's voice bristled with hysteria. "You're brigands and I don't trust you."

Raaneon frowned. "I haven't got time for this. Tell me or I'll take the girl instead of her father."

The matron's eyes flared. She raised the bow and jerked at the release trigger. Raaneon flinched. But, as he'd expected, nothing happened. He jumped forward and yanked the weapon from her fingers. She shrieked and gashed his face with the fingernails of her other hand. "Where is he?" Raaneon growled in his most threatening tone. "Is he asleep?" The woman shook her head. "Somewhere on this level?" Raaneon raised his voice a touch. She nodded mutely, glancing to her right.

"His private rooms?"

"South wing," she managed.

Raaneon turned to leave, but at the door he chanced to look back. The woman and her small charge were staring at him as though he were some incomprehensible monster. He felt sympathy for them.

"Stay in here," he said gently, "and lock the door. It'll all blow over soon and we've no intention of taking over the place. We're after your master's Dark God friends, that's all. So stay calm and out of the path of stray arrows, and you'll be fine." He slammed the door behind him. "Poor girl," he muttered. "To have such a father."

Thargonal's private rooms were easy enough to find. They were in an isolated part of the house and lavishly furnished. Raaneon thought it showed abysmal taste. The clamber of distant struggle was dim and barely audible, and he hoped Thargonal, were he here, had failed to notice. Perhaps he'd been indolent when their spell was cast, and was still asleep under its effect. What did surprise him was the lack of guards. Did it mean that the Housemaster was not in his rooms? He sighed again. That'd be typical. All this struggle to find the man's whereabouts... useless. His trust in the nurse...wasted.

He went through a small library, a solarium where the Sire used to eat meals when in attendance there, and a reception room. Suggestively, the solarium table was covered with plates and the remains of a half-eaten meal. There were several empty wine bottles. One thing was clear. Two people had dined this evening and from the setting the atmosphere had not been business-like. He began to understand why there were no guards around. Thargonal had wanted to be alone with his guest. Raaneon grinned knowingly. It was a good sign and suggested that Sire Thargonal and his concubine were embowered within.

The reception room, however, was not devoid of life. On a couch an old man lay sleeping. Raaneon went up to him and shook him awake. The fellow was startled and the fear in his eyes was of his master. He'd been discovered snoozing at his post. "What? What?" he burbled.

Raaneon frowned. "Fool!" he said. "Do you presume to flaunt your master's instructions this way? I might have been his wife or one of his daughters. Where'd you be then?"

"Sir, I —"

"Sir, nothing, idiot. Go, before I decide to report your negligence. The Sire's left through the solarium. He didn't see you asleep. Go on, or I'll report you."

Too confused to think, the ageing servant gathered his arthritic limbs and hobbled, mumbling incoherent apologies and appeals, out toward the door. There he first heard the distant clamor of battle. He looked back at Raaneon, suspicious. The wizard showed his sword and gestured fiercely for him to go. The old man stood unmoving for a moment, his face a mask of frowning wrinkles. Then with startling speed he darted into the solarium—which adjoined the reception room—and along the short passage toward his master's chamber door. "Sire," he yelled loudly, and bashed on the door, "you're under attack. Sire!"

Raaneon reached him quickly and threw him back. "Run!" he said, threatening the man with his sword. The servant got back on his feet and in a moment was gone. The wizard heard him shouting for help further along the upper landing.

Raaneon turned his attention to the door. It was locked, of course. Gritting his teeth, and hoping there was nothing more deadly than a knife or two in the chamber beyond, he raised his boot and kicked. Several blows later the doorjamb split and he broke the way open with his shoulder.

Inside, the room was half-lit by an ornate freestanding oil lamp. There was a large, canopied bed and clothes strewn everywhere. The air stank of sex. A woman sat on the end of the bed, reaching off it with one leg, as though caught in the act of escaping. It was a noticeably shapely leg. Her dark hair was tousled, stuck to her forehead in patches by smears of perspiration. She looked up at him with intensity, showing little fear, and dragged a blanket over her naked flesh. It did not cover her breasts.

Raaneon walked cautiously toward her, finding it difficult to look her in the eye. His attention kept wandering. "Where is he?" the wizard muttered. She seemed to be alone in the chamber, but that, of course, was unlikely.

"Who?" Her voice was studiedly sensual. "I was asleep. You woke me."

Raaneon frowned, swallowing nervously. "Thargonal," he said and felt stupid for having answered. Of course she knew who.

The woman shrugged. Her shoulders were smooth and invited caress. "He's not here," she whispered. "I'm alone." She let the blanket drop and then yawned, stretching out her arms. Her firm body glistened in the lamplight and a stab of tension passed through Raaneon as his pulses quickened.

But the moment passed. By some accident he looked at her eyes and they weren't focused on him. They seemed to be watching something behind him. He spun around and Thargonal was there, naked, gripping a large vase in his hands and preparing to attack him with it. Raaneon grinned at him and raised his sword. "Put that down, sire," he hissed, "or you'll lose your manhood."

The aristocrat glanced down involuntarily at his dangling penis and threw the vase aside. A flush colored his skin, visible even in the dim light. "Who are you?" he growled. His arms, far too flabby and unexercised to be effective weapons, trembled as he clenched his fists. Ordinarily he might have taken on this foolish young man, but right now his nakedness made him feel vulnerable.

"Your wife's avenger," Raaneon answered, smiling pleasantly. "Now put on your pants and boots. And don't try anything. I'm quite good with this thing and not inclined to show mercy."

Thargonal shrugged darkly, but did as he was told. When he was finished, Raaneon tied his hands behind his back and pushed him toward the broken door. The sounds of struggle were clear now. "You won't get out of here," Thargonal said, trying to regain some dignity.

Raaneon grinned. "My friends control the palace now." Hopefully there was some truth to this claim.

Movement behind him made him glance around, afraid of attack. But it was the woman. She was standing with the blanket wrapped around her, her eyes passively watching them leave. Raaneon was about to continue on his way when she shrugged self-consciously, and said, "He owns my husband. He owns me."

Raaneon turned back to Thargonal, jabbing him lightly with the tip of his sword. The aristocrat swore. "At the moment," the wizard said, pushing Thargonal into the passageway, "he owns no one."

Raaneon and his prisoner went out into the palace and headed for the exit. In time, to Raaneon's relief, they met up with some of Kharth'horun's soldiers, and he relinquished the aristocrat to their care. They were none too gentle with him, but Raaneon was indifferent.

The signal for retreat was given. Less than twenty minutes had passed since the attack began.

vii.

Memory chose the oddest times to toss up images of the past.

Remis ran, almost oblivious to the present circumstances, along corridors beneath the Thargonal Palace, and remembered a time years past. Master Salisith en-Tormis, her tutor then, was a middle-aged conjuror whose most notable characteristic, to his fatuous students at least, was a bent jaw-line that set his face into a permanent grimace. His voice was sibilant.

Student-Remis had been moping about for some weeks at the time of the memory, afraid of her training. On some days she felt threatened by the ludicrous presumption of it all and was seriously thinking of leaving the school to take up a less demanding occupation. She had no idea what alternative might be open to her.

In her memory she was sitting beneath a rocky overhang below a coastal cliff off the school grounds. The day's heat was intense, stealing as glare into her shadowy retreat. Her melancholy defied the brilliance of the sea. Master Tormis had hobbled down the carved steps from the cliff above and sat on a rock at the base.

"What's bothering you, Remis?"

"I was seeking some peace; that's all, sir," she responded *without enthusiasm.*

"I know you," he went on, *"and I can understand what's frightening you. But don't run from it."* She remained obsti-*nately silent.* *"I've known it,"* the old teacher gestured back*

toward the Faen-Hassur building. *"They all have, I'd guess, though few have the honesty to say so. Too many rest their self-image on a certainty of vision that the wisest of sages would be reluctant to admit to. They survive, even knowing the fears."*

"I'm not them."

"You're stronger. That's why you might feel it more. Remis, I'm an old man, imperfect in body and long since resigned to an anonymous existence whose greatest significance might be to retain life until it departs me. Magic is a curse and a blessing, like life. Yet we pursue both. To deny them is to embrace the Darkness. Listen to me now. You'll get over this melancholy—it's nothing; the spirit's natural response to a failing world. You'll survive and forget it. Forget me. And neither forgetfulness will matter. Then one day you'll be baffled and distressed. You'll know turmoil greater than this childish doubt, though in truth they're the same doubt, the same distress—as are all doubts. Never mind that. It's constant. You'll know more terror than this, perhaps ultimate terror. At that time, recall this sand, the glare, my twisted jaw and breathy stammering. They're real too, certainties despite the terrors. Don't be too afraid, not now or then. You'll find friends, lovers, perhaps enemies. Your past will fill up, like a fish net, with the squirming realities that crowd around the passage of your life. They're all real. You are real, Power is real. If you fail now against this doubt, how will you fare under more serious provocation?"

How could he have known? Few get mixed up with fate so intently as this, to battle beside a Saral-Lord in a Ruling House home-seat, finding more mysteries than a mundane life should have in it and seeing men killed in honor of those shadows. The glare from the heavens, as on that day in memory, may have illuminated the shelter where she crouched, but it also made her squint. How could she see anything through the death and violence? Why had her life become so unnatural?

And yet she remembered Master Salisith en-Tormis' words, *they are the same doubt, the same distress*, and she wondered: wasn't the beggar, scraping through garbage in an effort to live, as concerned with the mysteries as herself?

So she ran, Arhl beside her, Shaan and Arban ahead, others—soldiers, anonymous people, Be'rin perhaps—moving like phantoms behind in the darkness. Some ahead. Shouting reports. Guiding. She heard weapons clang on the walls. Several times she glanced back, hoping to see Tashnark—but, no, he wasn't there. Would he be able to catch up with them again? It worried her; she should have paid more attention when he decided to go his own way, should have talked him out of it, or gone with him. What real help was she here, where the only useful magic was hard and combative?

She heard the shriek of crossbow bolts, but she never knew where they hit in relation to their flight. Shaan, the Saral-Lord, intense and implacable, directed them, knowing, even where branching would lead them astray, that the ones they sought went *this* way, not *that*. "They split up here," he would say. "Some went to the right. Forget them. There is no Power there."

Arban asked if he felt the presence of the sorcerer ahead. He frowned. "I don't know. I thought.... No, now I'm unsure. Perhaps we've been fooled."

So the Saral-Lord had doubts, even in the midst of the task he was born for. Remis didn't know whether or not to take comfort in the revelation. On all levels there was mystery.

Once they came to a corner and would have turned into it if Shaan hadn't cried out. They pulled back as a wave of misused Deep Power tore at the adjacent wall. "Such force, destructive, negative," Arban whispered. "If this isn't the sorcerer it's one close to him in strength."

"An acolyte merely," Shaan said. "We've lost the other, I think."

Yet they ran in pursuit, wondering where they were being led, and to what end. The end was soon apparent. Like an anti-climax, the corridor became less of a construction and more of a cavern, until finally it narrowed and was a natural tunnel, thin, winding through a hillside. Its dirt floor was cuffed, the walls unlit. They stumbled along, feeling the sides of the tunnel as the rock-shelves drew together. The roof became lower and lower. Then they were crawling, squirming through a tight gap, breathing damp and earthy closeness, their hands and knees dragging over rock and sand. Shaan went on ahead, concerned that when they emerged they would be vulnerable to ambush; but the diffused gloom of night soon leaked into the thicker dark they were in and they crawled out onto a hillside safely, without being menaced. The cave entrance had been well hidden by rocks and bush, now thrown aside, and beyond a slight rise of ground textured by the roots of spindly trees, they were afforded a clear view of the land.

They were outside the home-seat, some distance beyond the walls. A small stream, filled by recent rains, wound its way out of the overlapping hills and into bushy distance. There was no sign of homestead or road, but in the shadows at the bottom of the slope there was identifiable movement. "Down there," someone yelled, "by the stream."

The ones they were pursuing were fossicking in the scrub. There appeared to be seven, perhaps eight, of them. Some were looking in the direction of the hidden cave-entrance, bows drawn, crossbows primed. A Power-blast cracked the silence, but it had no noticeable effect. Others were dragging something onto the water. A boat. Preparations had indeed been made for escape and escape they would, on the rushing stream's current.

Several of Kharth'horun's men jumped from cover and threw themselves down the slope. Crossbow bolts thudded into tree trucks, the soil at their feet, men's flesh. Then a distant voice: "Stay back...stay...want no trouble...will kill...." The wind, still moist and strong out of the threshold of the cave, broke his words and obscured the enemies' activity. "We must get down there," whispered Arban.

They jumped forward, sliding, leaping down a dim trail; Arban conjured a fire-globe that exploded on the stream just beyond the enemy boat. The sorcerer's acolyte replied in similar vein and Power ripped across the trees, burning the air blue for an instant. Several of them were sent tripping by the blast, but none were injured. An arrow downed one of their soldiers.

Yet even as she stumbled across the sloping hillside, Remis knew that escape was impossible for these men below them. They were not outnumbered and they might still have time to board the small boat and be carried away; but, no. That was not what gave her conviction. It was not the strategic facts, nothing definite. Remis watched magic-fire spark a blaze above the Saral-Lord, then fade away, leaving Shaan unharmed. No, it was not even the enemy's lack of real power against whatever it was that Shaan represented. It was simply a perception of fate, the terrible fate that dogged her tracks, Shaan's, Tashnark's. At the moment, that fate was carrying all before them. Would it, she wondered, ever desert them, or, turning against them, drive them headlong into death? And did even that matter, in the mystery that was finding an incarnation here about them?

The skirmish became a disjointed thing in her mind, a series of actions without meaning or sense. It was all unclear, like a dream, or broken images in the water that swept through her memories of the affair. She remembered Shaan, lithe and eager, dancing forward like some woodland animus, sword sweeping aside arrows that sought to bring him down. A man, an empty face without name, challenged the Saral-Lord and was cast from him as easily as the arrow-shafts, and doing as little damage. He cried out, split apart in a splash of blood, and disappeared into the stream. She saw in memory the boat escaping from them, impossibly far. A soldier rose on the water to shoot at them and an arrow from Arhl's bow knocked him over the bulwarks. There were cries of pain, surprise, glee. She recalled them, too. And Arban's drone, a magical commentary, underscoring each meaningless noise. The water near the escaping boat suddenly reared up like a fist and the gunwale smashed apart, men falling into the stream. The wind gathered up the flailing shadows, spinning them into the night. "They're escaping," someone yelled, perhaps herself. She stumbled into the water, following the others, feeling the cold stream turn the dirt in her boots to mud. Her cloak tangled about her.

Another memory of Shaan, like some river-god now, splashing toward the upturned boat.

And a man, a stranger, looming from the stream like some solid dawn mist. Hands upheld, flexing, bent staves of Deep Power gathering desperate attack from the air.

The water began to burn, staining the night with streaks of blue discoloration. Flames hardened, becoming a vision of horror, a demonic fury with eyes like death. Remis saw it, saw as well its lust for the Saral's life. Her mind a blank, she sought frantically for words to cast defense across the water. Nothing came. "Shaan!" she cried and, lifting a stone from the creek bed beneath her feet, she threw it furiously in a futile effort to warn him. It skimmed the swirling waves, penetrated the blue-fire demon and erupted like a power-charged ball. The sorcerer's acolyte screamed, a sound of terrible despair, and for a moment stumbled toward the Saral, his clothes and skin burning into blue swirls. Shaan raised his sword and thrust it into the man's chest. He slumped back into the water and was carried away by the currents, surrounded by a spreading red stain.

It should have been the finish. Remis staggered and collapsed, aware of the power-drain in her spirit; but a hand caught at her and lifted her up. Arhl. Across the stream the remnant of the enemy force—one, they would later learn, an E'ashalsinir priest from outside Vesuula—had reached the opposite shore and would certainly escape. No one was near enough to stop them. Remis watched the dark, benighted figures scrambling up the embankment, and was filled with absurd disappointment, as though this escape damned the entire raid. Stupid, hysteric tears blurred her eyes. "They'll get away!" she whispered.

"Yes," said Arhl blandly.

But then there was someone on the top of the embankment, a tall armored figure, like an avenger, rising to block the path of the escaping men. He met the first of them, a homeguard officer, and struck him down with one blow. His sword glistened light-trails in the sky. "Surrender!" he roared, "or die!"

Remis, far from him and certainly not the subject of his

address, felt an irrational urge to submit to him. It passed and she saw that the skirmish was over. The enemy had succumbed. Confused, she looked at Arhl, but there were no answers in his puzzled glance.

"Mystery and Fate," she whispered, and the stream growled around her waist as unruly as her own memory.

viii.

The wind should have been cold against Lord Worjaren's skin but instead it burnt. He slumped in his seating harnesses and let the horse carry him on undirected. Everything he touched was turning sour. Failed plans, missed opportunities. Mistakes. Now *all* his acolytes were dead.

Lord Worjaren Rehemon closed his eyes and remembered other mistakes, made that night over two thousand years ago, when he'd held the Cerendar in his hands.

"Your worship," said the messenger, "the northern stronghold, Harlorn, the Verib Hill...Elegris as well. They're all gone."

"They say the mountains are boiling," commented a servant.

"You must do something, worship, or we are dead."

Dead! If only that had been true!

In his imagination he saw the Cerendar on its silver plinth, central dais of the Cormidthalin War-vault, aglow like a multi-hued fireball, and surrounded by his Council. He heard the chanting, felt their power joined to touch the ancient substance and to activate the artifact.

It hadn't worked. There had come neither freedom nor death! Not for him.

Only error.

And endless fire.

The Cerendar had thrown him out of reality and onto the back of a fiery monster—Lucishnor, the burning Kharathahul. He was there now, surrounded by flame, even while he was *here*, among mounting failures.

Angered, he snarled at the driving wind, pushing forward onto the throbbing neck of the beast. Up until recently he had been confident, supremely confident, that he would regain the Cerendar, then free himself from the monstrous bondage. Confident in his power, he had used, manipulated, lied, usurped...seeking through the world for evidence of the hated and desired object. For a thousand years he had not doubted.

But now. Now when it is within his grasp again, it slips away, plans crumble, despised allies fail him, he fails himself. Suddenly there are forces challenging him: an undead spirit, Life-serving wizards, the bastard son of a slaver whose arm is the first strength raised with effect against him for as long as he can recall. And there is recognition in him for this bastard, this Tashnark. They have never before met, but he knows him, knows him.

Fated spirits....

And the woman warrior with the black axe, who had driven him out of Thargonal's home-seat. What was she? What part did she play in all this?

He had never been subjected to so much opposition, not since he had found a way to project himself back into the world from outside, albeit as an illusion. What was happening to his plans? They could not be allowed to fail. Not fail. There was madness in failure. Hopelessness. No, he must not fail.

The horse reared and stumbled on the rocky mud. Worjaren cleared his mind to steady the beast and in doing so banished his doubts.

The Fated ones had the heart of the undead creature now; they had the fat fool Thargonal and the hollow clatter of his knowledge. With or without his acolytes Worjaren Rehemon would follow them until they found that for which he sought. His quest, and theirs, would end. He would take the Cerendar, take it decisively. He could get new allies. Allies were nothing— mere weaponry, like the daggers in his belt, the words of weak, Shastorenti spells. Use them, sacrifice them. Play Dark God against Raashyr. Games of politics and religion. It was all nothing.

For him there was but one loyalty, one imperative.

Cerendar.

Power.

Freedom.

CHAPTER SIX
SEA-CHANGE

i.

Zeth'han was dying.

For a moment pain was overwhelming. He couldn't see the torn stump of his wrist, nor his friend's convulsive sickness, nor the glee of the monster that had re-appeared to inflict this torment upon him. He knew only tears and pain. He thrashed against the floor while blood sprayed out of him and dotted even the most distant walls.

Then, with a jerk, his awareness of the pain faded. His eyes, filled with tears, focused on the flickering candle on the room's side-table. Beams of refracted light stabbed toward the walls and burnt the blood-splatters away.

Time slowed and his mind filled with memories.

* * * * * * *

Reyad was safe from personal agony for Zeth'han. As the penal colony's Overlord, his quick, cold temper and pudgy body terrorized both his subordinates and the convicts in their care.

These were degraded men. They had committed crimes back in Vesuula for which transportation rather than death had been deemed the best alternative—and they were neither influential nor imaginative enough to have escaped that judgement. Under the watch of guards embittered by self-imposed exile, these unfortunates worked the stony, semi-fertile ground, coaxing only the most noxious of weeds into life. They knew no hope and in most cases believed their lives irrevocably chained to the place. In a society bounded by influence how could one escape who was totally without friends and abandoned even by the gods?

One of these men came to Zeth'han with a proposition. The man's name was Theor-Wal and he was a bankrupt Vesuulan trader. He told Zeth'han tales of a buried crypt, a fragment of which he discovered as he worked a rock-strewn field some days before. He had managed to keep the discovery secret from the guards and from his fellow convicts, he said—but now he needed help. He couldn't excavate the tomb alone and observed.

"What do you hope to gain by bringing this business to me?" said Zeth'han.

"Your indulgence, sir...and your promise that should anything valuable be found we'll share the reward and I be permitted to buy my freedom."

Zeth'han was in an indulgent mood that day and his frustration with the tedium of life on a penal island was on the surface of his mind. He supposed that an ancient crypt here on Reyad might contain treasures. He knew too that should this Theor-Wal find anything, it did not necessarily have to be shared.

Consequently Zeth'han assigned Theor-Wal to the position of Honor-Warden and allocated him several men to help with the digging. Normal work-crews were diverted from the area under some pretext of urgent farm-maintenance, and Theor-Wal and his men began the tedious job of archeological excavation on the buried tomb.

Then one day, nearly a month after the enterprise began, Theor-Wal's work-crew failed to return to the main camp at nightfall and the matter was reported.

"There's talk they'd uncovered the main door, sir," said an informant.

Zeth'han snarled his displeasure, filled with sudden suspicion, and ordered some of the wardens to go to the excavation site to investigate. If Theor-Wal had been working some deception, he would pay dearly—now, rather than later, and his death would be more lingering than Zeth'han had originally planned for him. Faithlessness in others made Overlord Zeth'han Orstel very angry.

The guards returned with their report. They had found what remained of Theor-Wal's work-crew in the newly opened tomb—the door had been broken, smashed aside...there were stone coffins in the place, some scattered gold...and blood. One of the men had been battered to death, another was unconscious halfway up the stair-well.

"Six men altogether were assigned to the detail! What of them?" he demanded.

"Gone, sir. No sign at all."

"And what of Theor-Wal?"

"Broken neck or something, sir. He was clutching an old dagger."

"Dagger?"

"Yes, sir—fancy, double-bladed piece. Couldn't get it out of his grip."

The conclusion was obvious. Theor-Wal had found something all right, something precious enough to cause a mutiny among the men. There had been a squabble, one was killed...another injured...Theor-Wal knocked aside when he tried to stop them.

"I want the other men found," screamed Overseer Zeth'han in a black rage, "and I want them now!"

The convict found unconscious on the mausoleum stairs was questioned. The man spoke of a corpse and a knife that Theor-Wal removed from the corpse's chest. "And the body rose from death then," he said, his voice trembling and his breathing becoming deep, "and, sir, it struck at Theor-Wal and killed Kranid, who stood near to 'm...and the men tried to escape, I tried to escape, sir, but the thing was there...violent, strong, it was...and it knocked 'em aside...I can't remember anything else, sir...only that—"

"A fog to blind me." Zeth'han rose, his belly heaving. "What sort of fool do you take me for? A dagger and a witless tale to draw my mind from the truth. I'll know why you tell me these lies." He had the man tortured, despite his obvious terror, but the convict's strength failed him and he died before the story had changed.

"Find me the others!" the Overlord cried.

And while his men scoured the island, Zeth'han visited the mausoleum alone, having forbidden further search there. He lusted after imagined treasures now. The extreme events had whetted his imagination...there seemed a real hope of wealth and freedom. But he found little in the tomb...a few small caches of burial-gold in the coffins, a piece of ancient metal-working or two...found little until his eye was caught by a glint in shadows on the wall above the empty coffin. A quaint metallic shape was gloomily defined by stray light from the lantern he carried, a shape hidden in a niche in the stone-relief. The lid of the empty coffin had partly obscured it. He reached up and removed a small square box, slightly bigger than his fist and covered in arcane symbols he couldn't read. The lid came loose when he gouged it with a pick. He looked aside.

Instinctively he threw the box away from him, squealing out a distressed yowl. Echoes danced around the stone walls...dust swirled through the lantern-light...and Zeth'han backed away, his attention held by the impossible thing that spilt from the shattered box. It moved slowly, pulsing in the dirt. A heart. A living, human heart.

Zeth'han remembered the ravings of the man he had questioned to death, and an image of undead violence broke the paralysis that had held him from running. He fled from the tomb. That afternoon he sealed the mausoleum doorway and buried the unnatural heart under the tomb's ancient rubble. At least he felt himself safe from the thing in the tomb—though the heart beat steadily in his dreams.

In the days that followed, Zeth'han determined to take the treasures from the mausoleum—what there was of them—and leave Reyad and its soulless exile. Of the three men who had disappeared, search parties discovered the body of one at the base of a shallow incline, where he had fallen and broken his back. Another corpse washed up on the rocks off the northern headland—a bloated, half-eaten monstrosity. The last was never found. So Zeth'han, even less at peace with the penal colony than he had been before these events, gathered together what he could and prepared for resignation.

Of all the artifacts that came from the mausoleum, it was the strange, ritual dagger that filled him with most hope. Magic was valuable and he believed the dagger to be imbued by some element of the Deep Power. Inscriptions Theor-Wal had found on the outside of the crypt connected the tomb with the Valarl family, and though Zeth'han knew nothing of this aristocratic line, he anticipated that record of it, and its treasures, would be uncovered somewhere. So when the regular Corporation supply boat arrived, he resigned to the ship's captain and handed command to his immediate inferior. The ship gave him and his wife free passage to the larger island chain Cantalcis, where the Vesuulan government's regional representative offi- cially dismissed him. Severance pay, the accumulated savings of enforced frugality on Reyad, and the hidden proceeds of his plunder of the Valarl mausoleum, made Zeth'han and his wife temporarily unconcerned for the future. His wife, a determined woman named Torenis, had long regretted their stay on Reyad and the ignominy of Zeth'han's position as Penal Overlord. She was from Vesuula and longed to return there, so that, when her husband found nothing informative about the dagger in the meagre libraries of Cantalcis and began to look elsewhere, she welcomed his sudden decision to travel to the vaster reposito- ries of Vesuula.

In due course, Zeth'han and his wife reached the merchant state. Zeth'han tried to ascertain the value of the knife, and refused to believe it when told that its Deep Power-infusion was too minimal to raise its worth to the level to which his imagina- tion had elevated it. He rejected several reasonable offers to buy the weapon, remaining determined in his conviction that the dagger was part of a valuable mystery.

Torenis scorned him as he walked from each dealer's shop, still clutching the ornate hilt with its double blades. "This is absurd!" she screamed. "What are we to do? Starve while you dance to the tune of these stupid daydreams?" Zeth'han cringed from her, uncertain and afraid, haunted in his dreams by a beating heart and Theor-Wal's twisted body. "It's worth much more than that," he whispered, stroking the engraved runes. "They all want to rob me." Torenis laughed and called him a contemptible fool. She had grown to hate him more for his stubbornness than she had already hated him for his failure.

As the months passed, Zeth'han's life grew heavy and sluggish with poverty. He gained and lost several jobs. He also lost a great deal of weight. He took to drink with what money he could find and his wife took a lover.

One night, bolstered in courage by ale and a sense of injustice, he went to the home of Dom-Sizhab, a merchant whom he knew to be Torenis' lover. Dom-Sizhab ordered him off the premises and, when he refused, tried to remove him by force. Zeth'han resisted and in the ensuing struggle stabbed Dom-Sizhab with the dagger, which he always carried with him. The wound was minor, but Zeth'han was arrested, and his victim remained determined that he should suffer the full penalty of the Law.

In gaol Zeth'han met Sinash the Thin-boned (as he rather quaintly called himself), a thief. These two became friends and Sinash offered Zeth'han a thieving partnership.

A few days later Sinash was released. Torenis persuaded Dom-Sizhab to go lightly on Zeth'han and the latter was guaranteed freedom on payment of a heavy fine. Zeth'han of course had no money—but Sinash unexpectedly appeared at the prison with the ransom. Zeth'han was grateful. "I'm ready to join you, thief," he said.

Sinash slapped his shoulder. "When Fate bites at your heels," he mumbled in his dark, philosophical manner, "there's no recourse but to bite back."

Zeth'han moved his few belongings to the other side of the

City, where he shared a slum tenement with the thief. Several nights later, they robbed a warehouse, taking several rolls of expensive textiles. For a while they lived on the proceeds of this and other minor robberies. Zeth'han was beginning to enjoy himself again. He was getting fatter.

Then one night the two thieves were prowling some well-to-do streets near Cartel Street above the University grounds. It was a quiet, unhurried evening with few citizens abroad to harry the thieves' surveillance. Zeth'han clutched his dagger nervously.

"What's the matter with you?" Sinash said, watching his friend's strange manner and hearing his breathing quicken.

Zeth'han said nothing. Images flashed unbidden in his mind. Images of Reyad and of Theor-Wal's murder.

Violence and bloodshed, an intense, glowing object like a candle-gleam, a man with burning eyes.

Something pulled his attention toward a large, white-stone house.

It was an omen.

"I think we should try this place," he said.

"Why?" asked Sinash.

"Intuition."

Being a man greatly influenced by impulse, Sinash decided to go along with him. They climbed the front wall and once inside the house found some money, a few artifacts made of gold and silver, and a small box of jewellery. Among the items that Zeth'han claimed as his share was a small, intricately designed trinket, a metallic wristlet of exquisite fineness, which Zeth'han saw and immediately demanded without discussion. It was not their way to make such demands. Sinash let him have the thing, but the intensity of Zeth'han's passion provoked suspicion. He wondered whether Zeth'han was working some sort of cheat. Later he was somewhat placated when Zeth'han did not attempt to sell the wristlet. He assumed it had simply captured his friend's fancy. He understood such impulses.

The other proceeds of this robbery proved valuable enough

to take their minds off the unusual aspects of the affair. Suddenly quite wealthy, and much given to proud self-confidence, Zeth'han came once again to regret the injustices of his recent past. He remembered in particular his wife's desertion of him, and so he praised the dagger, firstly that it had wounded the scum Dom-Sizhab, and secondly that it was to himself a talisman of good fortune. In a pub by the Docks, named The Night Binge, *he drank enthusiastically to the dagger and its as-yet undefined magic. Drunkenly he determined to return to Dom-Sizhab so that the dagger might fulfil its desire—to cut out the polluted hearts of Torenis and her lover.*

As he walked through the streets on this errand, he became aware of a strange figure running at him, silently roaring and waving its arms in grasping fury. It was like something in a nightmare. Zeth'han bolted, thinking himself pursued by a madman.

He ran into an alley, hoping to lose his pursuer. But the alley was a cul-de-sac.

He turned and the shadow engulfed him.

* * * * * * *

Back in a blood-splattered room in Vesuula, the anaesthesia of the memories broke suddenly and pain flooded through Zeth'han's body. He screamed out an animal roar.

"Zeth'han!" yelled Sinash, "Zeth'han! Can you hear me?"

But Zeth'han could hear nothing.

ii.

When Tashnark caught up with the fleeing group some considerable distance outside the tunnels beneath Thargonal's home-seat, it didn't take him long to find Remis.

"You're uninjured," he muttered as he approached, his presence drawing her glance.

"Seems so." She smiled a welcome, which was gratifying, though it didn't last. Instead, what caught her attention was Danling's limp body.

"Oh god!" she moaned. "What happened?"

Tashnark explained, while she stood still before him, eyes closed, her hand holding the boy's. Perhaps she was seeking some hint of life in him—Tashnark didn't understand, but he let her do it, knowing she'd find nothing. The corpse was growing cold and stiff. Even to a layman it was obvious that whatever spark the boy's flesh had once held, it was gone now, gone for good. Then the Temple hierarchy came to take charge of him and Tashnark turned away, keeping Danling out of their reach. "I'll carry him," he growled over his shoulder. "He was my responsibility, he died in my charge. This is my burden."

The priests protested and Tashnark snapped back at them, but Remis intervened before it came to blows.

"I can understand how you feel." She grabbed Tashnark's arms and made him concentrate on what she was saying. "But they know the rites, Tashnark, and can bear him as he would have wanted. He was devout. Give him to them."

"They didn't own him—not yet."

"Please," she said, her voice low and soothing. "It's important. Trust me."

He looked into her eyes and felt the determination and sincerity in them. Reluctantly he handed over the body. Then he stood silently, bereft, watching the impromptu funeral procession move off with the boy's corpse. None of it seemed right.

"It's how it must be, Tashnark," Remis said. "You're not to blame."

"Oh?" he replied, barely seeing her. "I'm not so sure."

* * * * * * *

From their meeting at the pre-arranged rendezvous, where horses were made available, to the coast where the ship was waiting, was a ride of some two hours. The ragtag army from the Temple of Shaa-Derthperrit made it there without difficulty or incident. Luck, if such could be said to function in human life, was with them in this—everyone arrived at the rendezvous outside of Gihornter and those missing could be accounted for, sadly, as dead. Three soldiers of Kharth'horun's homeguard, two of the mercenaries, a wizard recruited by the temple. Danling, of course. And Caris-Be'rin, whose command over the Deep Powers had not been enough to save her from a stray crossbow bolt. These were their dead. Eight.

Hopefully, such loss would be balanced against what they'd achieved, despite the fact the sorcerer had eluded their net. They had captured Thargonal, the stocky, unctuous aristocrat, and had eliminated several prominent Dark God acolytes in the process. Moreover, the Gihornter home-seat was no longer available as a Dark God crèche and enemy functioning was hindered; at least, so it was hoped. Was the loss of life—theirs and that of the Thargonal guards—justified by such ends? Tashnark doubted it, and if he thought about it too closely, was angered by the suggestion that there was any validity in a balance sheet that saw life as a tradable commodity. He hadn't lived in the City of Commerce long enough—even if for most of his life—to be seduced into that argument. Comfort shouldn't come so easily.

Strangely enough, perhaps, Shaan said nothing about the death of either Danling or the others, not to Tashnark at least— nothing to comfort, nothing to express his own regret. It was almost as though these events were of little consequence to him. Nor did Shaan take any part in the priests' ritual mourning. The fact of the Saral-Lord's apparent indifference sat in Tashnark's chest like an undigested lump during their ride. It turned his sorrow to resentment.

"He doesn't care," he hissed to Remis at one point.

"Who?" she replied, drawn out of her own reveries.

"Him!" Tashnark gestured toward Shaan, who was some way ahead of them.

"How can you say that? Of course he cares. That's why he's here."

Tashnark huffed. "He's here on the Gods' business, that's all. How can anyone think that any end justifies these deaths?"

Troubled, Remis turned away and fell silent.

Yet in the quest for justification, was there comfort to be gained from the fact that they had salvaged the heart of the undead creature? With it any hope the sorcerer might have had of controlling the mystery it represented was lost to the Dark Gods. Potentially millions—all life—had been saved. Shaan saw this as a priceless treasure, worth any sacrifice. "This heart may be the key to our search," he declared. Tashnark was doubtful, but that surprised no one, least of all himself.

So they rode to the coast, a direct route, previously mapped for speed. A temple-owned ship lay at anchor, hidden in a cove, ready for them to board her. It was the fifth hour before dawn when the ship weighed anchor to seek refuge at sea.

* * * * * * *

In Gihornter, confusion was so prevalent little was organized for some time. Briyalt-Sarnir, Thargonal's Guard-commander—who had escaped both death and capture—rallied his men with a sort of languid efficiency, but refrained from notifying government authorities of the attack until such time as Thargonal should confirm the desirability of this action. The Sire had a strict sense of propriety in these matters and Sarnir was loathe to do anything to incur his wrath. He knew, as did many others in the palace, that Thargonal used his Family estate for purposes at best frowned upon by other members of the Ruling Families, and was wont to tread lightly in unusual circumstances, lest he expose the Sire's illegitimate activities to official scrutiny. Most of Thargonal's 'guests' had either fled or been killed, so far as Sarnir could work out—he knew of the existence of a contingency plan to empty the palace rapidly should it become necessary. Apparently this plan had been realized despite the confusion, and indeed many of the some-what inflated homeguard—too large by accepted Council standards—had disappeared with the more prestigious alien visitors. So there seemed little need for undue embarrassment. Yet still he sought authority, and this hesitation served merely to ensure the attackers' safe escape, though Sarnir had not intended it should. He did send out a scouting party, but in the night and somewhat confused they missed the trail.

At last it became apparent to Sarnir that Lord Thargonal himself had been abducted. The Sire's personal lackey, an ageing fool, confirmed this with a tale of suspect derring-do and personal bravery. Sarnir knew the time for indecision had passed. He sent a messenger to the nearest Sumis office in neighboring Tarigath town and officially made announcement of the raid.

This was about five minutes after the Saral and his people had boarded the temple ship. Two hours later a large squadron of Sumis troopers arrived in Gihornter.

The home-seat was placed under temporary Council-law and an investigation begun. Sarnir cooperated to the limits of his duty to Thargonal, but was adroit enough to steer the Sumis officers away from his Lord's secret tunnels. Statements were collected from several of the peasants who had watched the attack from their rooftops, one a boy whose brother had been killed. The home guard was also questioned but none could put a name to the aggressors. Yes, there had been magic; yes, they were powerful; we were desperately outnumbered. There must have been hundreds of them. And weapons—yes, they were well armed. Commander Theyin-Darlis of the Council force smiled at the obvious exaggerations, for they suited his purposes well. He had been bribed by unnamed sources to obscure the truth, and such inflation of events served this end without incriminating invention of his own.

Other evidence was meagre. None of the attackers had been taken alive. The dead were either incinerated or without identifying marks. The only hope was that some of the bodies might be recognized, but this didn't happen at the time and after that, Theyin-Darlis would see to it that the opportunity was minimized. The bodies would be quickly and mercilessly disposed of—publicly mutilated and burnt as an object lesson to rebels and to still public concern—and in the process their usefulness in identifying the attackers would be eliminated. The investigation would be a failure in that truth would be obscured. Theyin-Darlis would write a report in which he would state his belief that the attackers were pirates who had pillaged the home-seat and taken Thargonal either as ransom, or for some revenge motive arising out of dealings the Sire might have had with the said brigands (though the naming of such transactions was of course outside Theyin-Darlis' personal authority). One way or another the Commander sought to undercut suspicion of internal political sabotage.

One hour after the arrival of the Sumis squadron in the home-seat, indications were found of the path of the attackers' flight. Judicious questioning of local farmers and early morning workers allowed Sumis to track the 'pirates' to the coast near the village of Orshaf, where they had apparently rendezvoused with their ship. It was now the sixth hour. A rider was dispatched to Koerpel-Na to notify the State Naval Guard.

iii.

The strange armored warrior who had appeared out of nowhere like a legendary hero called himself Rondan-El-Therill. A silver-gray cat accompanied him, a cat whose eyes were vivid green and who answered to the name *Shadow*. It was a remarkable animal, not simply in being a cat. More than most animals, it showed a keen awareness of the humans with whom it had contact, especially Rondan-El-Therill. It had been with him for some thirty years, the warrior said, and had been bred in the legendary city Zhornn itself, where the Merilan cult was believed to have originated. It was, of course, a greater wonder that the warrior—who had materialized so dramatically to block the enemy's escape—had himself come from that legendary place, and was an apostle of the Merilan Precepts.

"Yes, I adhere to the Precepts and the rigors of Raashyr-Lord Therill's eternal Decree," the Merilan warrior said, after mutual greetings had been made on the leeside of the skirmish. "It's on his task that I journey, and under his guidance."

Later, when Tashnark caught up with events, Rondan-El-Therill came as something of a shock to him—he hadn't thought there to be room for yet-another stereotypical hero-type in this business. He said as much to Remis and she suggested it was clear that 'this business' was extensive in its implications and might need as many heroes as they could find. Tashnark didn't like the idea at all. He had hoped, albeit naively, that an end was in sight.

During the fearful ride through the last hours of night to a meeting with the sea, there was little opportunity—or will—for talk. Even Valarl's heart, secreted in Tashnark's saddle-gear, was left in abeyance for the moment. Each remained locked in lonely pondering or thoughtlessness, limp in the wake of stress and combat and death.

Rondan-El-Therill joined them as naturally as if he had been all the time expected. The Saral welcomed him, allowing his part without a hint of query, and indeed they rode for much of the way together like comrades reunited. Tashnark found the Merilan-warrior easier to accept than, say, Halul, for reasons hard to articulate. Perhaps it was an air of inevitability in the manner of his coming. Or the fact he looked so much the part. Everything about him—his manner, his armor and habili-ments—was a cliché of romantic legend. This man might have stepped out of "The Tale of the Welcome Knight" or "A Song of Ancient Glories," both well-known expressions of Merilan precept lore. Stepped out and declared himself an incarnation of the fabled Gnossel-En-Therill, the first Merilan Warrior. If he had he would have been believed, in this company and in these circumstances. Twenty days ago Tashnark would have thought him merely absurd; now he was ready to tolerate his claim, even if under an assumption of general agnosticism. At the moment the world was squirming with miracles.

Oddly, though, Tashnark found it difficult to hold an image of Rondan-El-Therill in his memory when the man wasn't present in the flesh. He didn't recall that the Merilan warrior was particularly nondescript—in fact, he thought the man's appearance to be startling. Yet there was a chameleon quality about him that made him hard to bring to mind. He was tall—or at least gave an impression of stature. He was dark-skinned—or he was pale, like Arhl. Though perhaps neither. His face was...Tashnark couldn't recall and had to be looking at him to give him any sort of presence. It was very strange.

The Merilan-warrior, in fact, said very little about himself, even in answer to direct questions. He did not avoid answers but was not inclined to go beyond their letter, nor was he free with unsolicited insights. Tashnark waited for them, like the others, but nothing came, nothing much at least.

"Zhornn? It is as great as the legends say, yes," he would declare. Or "I was guided by the lore of Therill. I can offer no greater illumination."

Once Arhl asked him how, *exactly*, he had found them. Had he known what he was looking for? Did he have any idea what they were doing?

His face was sternly pensive for the time it took his cat to rise from its position behind him and leap to Rondan-El-Therill's shoulder. He looked the animal in the eye and it slipped down between its master's crotch and the front of the saddle.

"Shadow knows my will," he said, "though the necessity may be more than he can rationalise. So too I know Therill's will, though I hear no word and know no reason."

"Giving in to vagaries," growled Tashnark. "I don't have that sort of faith."

Overall, however, no one asked much of the Merilan-warrior. They were not yet at ease with him, not yet bold enough to show their curiosity. That and the natural aloofness of legend protected him for a time from the company's questions. Mostly he rode apart from them, in conference with Shaan.

Tashnark spied Raaneon's curly red hair through the crowd. He called him over and they spent an enjoyable hour or so elaborating each other's tales into major epics. Later Halul joined them and described her meeting with the sorcerer among the residential hill-houses of Gihornter. Her account left Tashnark unsatisfied. The trouble was, she left some details vague, while she described others with an intimacy of detail it seemed impossible she could know. And her descriptions were full of lumpy poetic metaphysics.

"What do you mean he wasn't exactly human?" he interrupted.

"There was a fire in him, an ageless fire from another world."

"In him? How would you know what was in him? And what other worlds are there?"

Halul frowned. "Don't bully me, Nahallhan. I'm no liar, and no fool. I offer the information to you as I offered it to Lord Shaan."

"You've spoken to Shaan? What did he have to say about it?" Raaneon leaned forward expectantly.

"He accepted its truth, if that's what you mean. And without question."

"The gods are notoriously gullible," muttered Tashnark.

"He had no comment?" Raaneon persisted.

This time Halul attended to his question with less aggression. "Comment? Yes. The Saral said it was as he feared. There's a secret to this adventure that transcends even the expectations of the world's eternal enemies."

"What in hell did he mean by that?" Tashnark gazed out across the night, imagining for a moment he could see to the end of the world. But of course there was only obscurity.

"I think he hardly knows himself."

Raaneon nodded sagely, as though this conversation made sense, scratching at his short-cropped beard and looking thoughtful. Then he said: "I wish things were...clearer."

"Of one thing the Lord Saral did seem certain," Halul continued. "He's convinced the sorcerer *intended* us to attack

Gihornter, that he fooled everyone, magically perhaps, to think him in the palace and in possession of the Cerendar."

"Fooled everyone? Why should he sacrifice his allies?"

"If we knew why, we'd know a lot."

Tashnark snorted. "Sounds like bullshit to me. The great Shaan is trying to make everything into a mystery, that's all. Suits his purpose."

They fell silent, listening to the roar of the wash and the boards groaning around them. After a while Raaneon said, "Mind you, he doesn't have to try too hard." Tashnark only grunted.

Later still, after several rounds of repetitious analysis, Halul was nudged into song by the sight of the Merilan warrior's cat. Unaccompanied by its master, but with a disturbing sense of purpose, it strolled to the bow and crouched on some accessible rigging, staring back toward the coast.

"Now what's that thing up to?" Tashnark muttered, and Halul's pleasant contralto replied:

> "A watcher of dark winds, it sits
> Unheeding false alarms;
> The nations are seduced to ruin
> The children seek false charms.
> And the Watcher like an ancient stone
> Awaits its lonely death
> Knowing only hopelessness,
> Abandoned without breath.
> 'O weep, Kor-her'anaris!
> Your children are not there;
> I scent the death of thousands
> In the dying of the air.'
> But the Watcher sits unmoving,
> Devoid of spite or scorn—
> Will awaken yet its people
> To the pride of ancient Zhornn."

Tashnark scowled at her. She grinned her toothy smile. "The beginning of a Zhornnis ballad-cycle," she said. "It seems relevant."

"What's it mean?"

"Legend has it that the center of Zhornn is the ruins of a city so old that the most archaic of records cannot say when it flourished. No one knows its name, so the Lore says, although some believe that the Merilan High Priest passes knowledge of that place to his successor every twenty years. It is said a disaster overtook the nameless city, but prior to its coming there was warning given, and in response one set to watch for signs of the end. The city's fate was sealed even before the Watcher could see the danger—and now, though appearing to men as rubble, the Watcher stands before the old gate road that once led into the city. It is said this Watcher has the power to awaken the timelessly ancient rulers of the city when it sees fate has been fulfilled. When that might be, no one knows."

"What of Zhornn? And the Therill cult? Where do they come in?" asked Raaneon.

"Zhornn was supposed to have been built around the ancient city by Therill himself as a bulwark against its loss. The Merilan Discipline was established at this time, presumably as a means of protecting the city. Little is known of Zhornn and the Merilan, for they're close-lipped on these matters. Even its whereabouts is obscure, though many believe it to be in Hebor." Hebor was a landmass far to the east, across the sea—there was little love lost between Vesuula and Hebor, and diplomatic relations between the two countries tended to run hot and cold.

"You say the Merilan Warriors are part of a defensive structure. Why do they wander about then, as I know they do?" Tashnark interjected.

"Raashyr Therill, Upholder of the Good, claims to be interested in the morality of the whole world, Tashnark, so we might ask why in the first place he developed enough of a concern for the 'nameless' city to seek to preserve it?" Raaneon looked to the woman.

Halul shrugged. "How can I answer either question? The precepts aren't for the uninitiated."

"Perhaps," said Raaneon, squinting thoughtfully into the sky, "perhaps part of the survival of Zhornn's kingdom is dependent on the general righteousness of the world. Goodness brings its own reward. A more universal form of sympathetic magic."

"Perhaps," frowned Halul, "but it sounds more like art than truth."

Raaneon smiled. "Perhaps we could ask Rondan-El-Therill, since fate has conveniently dropped a rare Merilan in our laps. Straight from the cat's mouth, as it were."

Tashnark shook his head and his braided hair swung in the salt-wind. "It all gives me a headache," he hissed. "I've never known so much confusion—and I'm one of the most confused people I've ever met."

"It's always been there," said Raaneon.

"But up to now it's kept itself to itself. I'd rather it stayed a recluse, and let me get my bewilderment from a beer bottle. Much more enjoyable."

They joked for a while around the subject of alcohol's ability to illuminate or obscure secrets and the night thinned into dawning. At last a sailor came to summon them to join the expedition's leaders. Raaneon and Halul went, but Tashnark was in no mood for godly murmuring or righteousness. The others could give him a summation of the priest Arban's harangue at some later date and in a more succinct and digestible form. They disappeared below and left him alone on the rear deck with the Zhornnis cat. It looked at him as though conscious of his attention, and whisked its tail lazily. The ship lurched, but the cat didn't move.

"What secrets are in your head, I wonder?" Tashnark muttered, walking toward the animal. It meowed and, as he reached out to touch it, leapt to the deck. Tashnark watched it as it sauntered away from him. Once it glanced back as if uncertain or curious. Then it darted away. "Superior bastard!" Tashnark growled.

Mallorin appeared soon after, though he didn't notice Tashnark. He settled himself at the rear of the ship and began to strum.

One thing about him struck Tashnark as irritating: his dismal choice of song. He was as Danling had been in that. Choice of song always cannily appropriate and always, if not depressing, then at least unsettling. This rhapsodic pessimism he did not have of his mistress Halul; it was his own specialty. The mistress tended more to the heroic.

> My comrades all, from battle hale,
> *Sing far-lay-da and chiralee.*
> Let's follow now the blowing gale!
> *The waves rove on the sea.*
>
> We set out brave and falter not,
> *Sing far-lay-da and chiralee.*
> Bound as with a silken knot.
> *The waves rove on the sea.*
>
> Sailors, turn your skills to sail,
> *Sing far-lay-da and chiralee.*
> That we may strive and never fail.
> *The waves rove on the sea.*
>
> Behold the mist! Our visions die!
> *Sing far-lay-da and chiralee.*
> The cursed wind calls, a storm is nigh!
> *The waves rove on the sea.*
>
> May not our tossing ship sink down?
> *Sing far-lay-da and chiralee.*
> And would not then my comrades drown?
> *The waves rove on the sea.*

So sing, and never speak our fear!
Sing far-lay-da and chiralee.
Not waves, but men, are strangers here.
The waves rove on the sea.

Tashnark muttered under his breath, looking through the soft light of morning at the choppy waters of A'hekmuth Harbor. Far distant, dimmed by mist, lay the more southerly shores of the Parun-Naron district; closer and to the north the large island Keb'thorn-Ellin—an offshore base for Family warships—threatened them silently. Everywhere, between land and their ship, water. Water that might raise up waves against them. Tashnark frowned. For all his voyaging in company with his father's slavers he had never made friends with the sea. Their relationship, a cool tolerance at best, had never changed. Mallorin's song didn't help much.

He staggered across to the hatch and climbed down shakily. Nodding to the men in the galley, he lowered himself into a corner and determined to brood for a while. There was no beer on board, not drop enough to give a teetotaler a hangover, so melancholy was the only retreat left open. The aftermath of conflict and sorrow was always characterized by thirst, and with nothing available, what recourse was there but to mope?

In private answer to Mallorin's ditty, Tashnark whispered gruffly:

> "'I'll face the sea, I'll see the face
> Of drowned men deep below.
> I'll beat it hence,' The knight did crow,
> And struck it with his mace."

He screwed up his face and then shook his head sadly. "Awful," he muttered. Turning to the man closest to him he pronounced: "Poetry is an abomination, especially when sober." The man, one of Kharth'horun's soldiers, sighed as though with the deepest recognition of the truth of this maxim, and then sank down beside Tashnark. There was a flask secreted in his cloak. He winked. "Rum?"

Tashnark recognized a kindred spirit at once.

iv.

Morning light was a salty crust on the port window. The sea murmured beyond the cabin like an undercurrent of voices, and Sire Thargonal, hearing its whispers, scowled his displeasure. *Damn Worjaren Rehemon to Hell's most noxious pit*, he thought. *This is his fault, all of it.* Lord Thargonal hated the sea. He never traveled on his own ships, and even intended that when he died, he should forego a proper water burial. Better to be interred in the ground, and ride with the land's slower movement to ultimate doom.

Not that, at the moment, he had much choice. The thought chilled him. These fanatics—what would they, what must they do with him? The choices were few. They had him and would no doubt kill him. Why else bother to attack Gihornter against all the codes of Vesuulan law?

He rubbed his forehead with his ice-cold palm. Fear was not a pleasant emotion. Where was Worjaren Rehemon when he was needed?

"My lord Thargonal," said the youthful man who had all along been treated with incongruous reverence by the others, including his elders, and was looking at him now expectantly. Thargonal had seen the same look on the face of his guard-dogs before they ripped an intruder to shreds. Inwardly the aristocrat cringed—an unfortunate observation at best. Outwardly he cast a glance of studied haughtiness in the rebel's direction. "Do I know you, boy?"

"I thought your spies might have said something. They hounded us for long enough."

"Spies? What do you mean? I have no spies. Surely you're mistaken. I'm a banker. What do I need with spies?"

"From what I hear you practice devilry as well as banking," interjected a thin woman with dark hair closely cropped and wearing a man's garb. She was carrying a rather nasty-looking axe and, by the gods, a lute! *A singing assassin? Music while you die?* The incongruity urged the aristocrat to glance at the other occupants of the small cabin. There were seven, besides himself: an ominous number—too many to bargain with and far too few to hide among. Especially as he seemed to be the main attraction. He felt a futile surge of anger well up in him again, its object vague. Was it best to curse Worjaren Rehemon for deserting him, himself for being so unprepared, or the rebels who had had the effrontery to accost him in his own sacrosanct home-seat? Why must he suffer this indignity? Everything had been going so well, and should have continued so, to his eventual political benefit. But now....

He glowered meaningfully at his tormenters. There were several Deep Power-workers: a young female, quite attractive in a non-provocative sort of way, and a red-haired male, the miscreant who had captured him in the palace. Minor practitioners only. There was also one who was much older than both these—a male, and possibly a priest of the temple. He was not dressed in ecclesiastical robes, but that meant nothing. They hadn't exactly been attending a synod.

"Give me a name," he ordered the youthful leader, "so that I'll know how to curse your infamy."

The man smiled in quiet amusement. "You may call me Worarberli-arn-Arber Ecad Eldis-Seracis nom Dar-Sen."

Thargonal pushed upward, carried by fury. "How dare you mock me with this vomit! I'm a Supreme-Lord of the Vesuulan Free-State and deserve more respect!"

"Deserve?" spluttered the female Power-worker. "How can you dare—?"

"I dare because I am Sire Thargonal of home-seat Gihornter, one of the Twelve of Merchant rule. I have the dues of law behind me. While you...you...rabble! You have only dishonor and lies to shield you from the gods' anger."

"The gods wouldn't deign to crush you under foot, Thargonal," said the woman with the axe.

The Lord laughed bitterly. "They've spat on me though, to hand me over to filth such as you. But don't talk to me of what the gods might do. You must be godless to violate the sacred laws of our state like this."

"Godless?" smirked the female wizard. "I don't think so." She gestured at the leader. "Shaan can tell you what the gods think. He knows them well."

Raashenti, Thargonal thought. Aridor had speculated on the possibility of special Powers come from the Raashyr. *O spare me! Surely it isn't true*. He pulled himself together quickly, latching onto the name used.

"Shaan?" he said. "So the god has a shorter name after all. It's auspicious...and suspicious as well. Am I supposed to think that Raashyr-Shaa Himself honors us with his presence?"

In the following silence his sarcastic manner turned to nervousness. Inwardly, Sire Thargonal felt an irrational stab of panic scratch across his heart. *Madmen! Madmen or worse! They believe it possible*.

There had to be a way out. Had to be. He didn't want to die, certainly not at the whim of religious zealots. There were fewer things harder to bribe than those who *believed*. Lord Worjaren's chief Acolyte had been the same. *A believer*. He had had a vision of Darkness and it had kept him tied to ideals, blind to the greater demands of expedience. These kidnappers, they would have a different vision, less accessible perhaps, but as demanding. There had to be a way out.

"Master Shaan," he forced himself to say, "if I may call you by your truncated name. I offer you my good will. Free me and I won't identify you or your friends to Sumis or the Council. I have other enemies, I'll be believed—"

"No, you won't identify us," said the man calmly, "but don't think us stupid enough to fear your bluster or find faith in your word."

Thargonal scowled. "So you plan to slay me?"

"Perhaps. It's not less than your treachery deserves."

"Treachery?" Again aristocratic wrath rose in the Vesuulan lord. "You're the traitors, not me."

"You ally yourself with alien sorcerers," said the older of the wizards, "you rob the people, you murder, steal, and plot against your peers."

"There's no proof. It's all lies."

The one they called Shaan made an irritated hiss. "We don't need proof. We've seen all we need to see to convict you in our hearts. But there *is* proof, and you couldn't afford even the attention that mere accusation would bring you, your politics are based so extensively on a delicate balance of influence. Perhaps, free, you could hand us over to the law—but would you really wish us to speak of what we have learned?"

Retaining a careless frown on his face, Thargonal thought: *They'd be at my throat like predators to blood-scent, my mercantile confederates, my peers. Wagulnak seeks the slightest excuse to cast me down and many wait for elevation.* Gamin-orm Wagulnak, head of the most powerful Family in Vesuula, was high-lord of the Supreme Council. He considered the Thargonal Family to be a second-rate lineage, and resented what eminence the clan had managed to achieve through its commercial prowess.

Thargonal didn't show his thoughts. "Against threat to the security of their position, my peers would side with a reptile. Do you think such precedent as you've set can ever be tolerated?"

"Indeed so," the leader replied, without apparent concern, "but you, as soon as might be appropriate, would follow us into disgrace."

Thargonal huffed. He thought, *Damn it! Where's Worjaren Rehemon?* "This jostling with threats wearies me. Just tell me what it is you want and have done with it."

"We want information. Tell us about your plotting, my lord, tell us why your people have shown undue interest in the spell-binder Remis-Sarsdarl, tell us what you know of the Cerendar. It is said that the Cerendar has come to Vesuula; what do you know of it? Why is it so coveted?" He paused, then held up a small box. "And tell us what you know of this?" He opened the lid and positioned the interior so that Thargonal could see into it. For a moment the aristocrat leaned over the box cautiously, unable to define the unexpected shape. Then he recoiled. There was surprise and disgust in his voice.

"What trick is this?" he cried. "A heart?"

"A heart."

"It's still living!"

"Yes."

"What should I know of such things? I'm no necromancer."

The youth slammed the lid shut and put the box aside. "Clearly you weren't fully in Worjaren Rehemon's confidence. This heart came from a chapel beneath your palace."

"Beneath my—?" Thargonal's attention turned inward for a moment, seeking to rationalize these new facts. What had Worjaren Rehemon been up to? And why had he concealed the true state of their affairs from him?

He pulled himself together. "You keep on about this Worjaren Rehemon," he sneered. "Yet I don't know anyone of this name."

"Sire Thargonal," the leader said in measured tones, "you should answer truthfully or I might lose patience. I can assure you that if I choose, I could make you tell us everything without omission, but the process would not be pleasant and it can have destructive side-effects."

Thargonal believed it, too. He cleared his throat nervously, but tried to maintain a modicum of disinterest.

"You know Worjaren Rehemon," the leader continued, "a sorcerer under whatever name you choose. Tell us of him."

Thargonal stared at the youth silently, while his mind fumbled about for some reply. "You'll be found," he said feebly.

Shaan struck furiously on the cabin wall, so that the aristocrat felt the blow's vibrations against the soles of his feet. "Not before you become something more useless than horse-meat." His eyes blazed momentarily.

Frightened, but relieved by this display of anger, Thargonal forced himself to smile. He fashioned it on his lips with all the contempt and insolence that a lifetime of state politics had refined in him. "Again I assure you," he said sardonically, "I'm a simple banker. I have friends whose lives are their own and who may or may not be in league with devils. But I myself...why, I know nothing of sorcery, or plots, or this mysterious Worjaren Rehemon."

The woman with the black battle-axe stepped between Shaan and Thargonal, her brow wrinkled. She held up her hand to the leader and looked at Thargonal with an understanding smile. "Sire Thargonal," she said in a Votisphan accent, "there is something I think you might consider while you toy with disaster and the thinning tolerance of my comrades here."

"Oh? Some gem of bardic comfort?"

She smiled. "Simply a thought, comforting perhaps, but not bardic. It occurs to me that it couldn't be loyalty that keeps you reticent. That would be out of character. So, what then? Perhaps you hope that Worjaren Rehemon will come?"

"If I knew him, perhaps I would."

"He's abandoned you to us, Thargonal. I met him in the home-seat, tried to kill him and failed. Shaan believes he not only let us attack your palace, but encouraged it, perhaps hoping that the sacrifice would help him achieve his objective, through us. Do you think him capable of such treachery?"

Thargonal did, of course, and the suggestion, once made, took form as a strong possibility—almost a certainty—in his mind. Where had Worjaren Rehemon been all those days while Thargonal waited? Skulking, plotting, keeping himself out of danger. The aristocrat frowned. It was a telling argument. Perhaps it was time that he worked for his own survival. "You'll guarantee my safety?" he said to Shaan. "Will you give me your oath that I'll be freed?"

"I swear it."

He nodded, pursing his lips in clerkly thoughtfulness. "Very well," he said. After all, survival—personal and political—was the basic urge in men's hearts, and in the end beyond morality.

V.

"Begin with Worjaren Rehemon, my lord," said Shaan, settling into a chair. "What is this sorcerer?"

Thargonal smiled with covert meaning. "He comes upon me with little warning, demands all my loyalty, then abandons me to humiliation. I should've told him to get out of my sight then. I've often wanted to deal with him as decisively as you do."

"But you didn't?"

"Are you mad? He's too powerful. Silent and morose. Keeping his true intentions to himself and his acolytes. But volatile, and dangerous when moved." The aristocrat looked hopefully at Shaan. "Your people slew his chief acolyte. Have you disposed of the other two, perhaps?"

"Yes."

"Oh, good." He looked pleased. "They were low-born. Dagorn is a warren of those who lack breeding."

"So Worjaren Rehemon came from the Dagorn Shires."

Thargonal nodded. "Insisted on calling the place Dagest-Yanu. King Zarth the simp demands respect for his kingdom."

"Why did Worjaren Rehemon come here? And when? Please, Thargonal," Shaan sighed wearily, "spare us your invective."

Thargonal contracted his brow into a mass of grooves. "Allow me this at least. You and Worjaren Rehemon have left me little else." He stared at the porthole and rubbed his chin. "Where was I? Ah, yes. Worjaren Rehemon. The Great One came, my friend, on a quest. You know that, of course. His master—not Zarth, but the god Himself—had honored him with this duty—"

"God?"

"Huedaik," he snarled, forming the barred sign of respect with his arms. "May the Eyes of Indifference save me from his notice!" He smiled knowingly. "Perhaps news of happenings in Vornarca haven't reached you—they've kept a tight rein on it certainly."

"What happenings?"

"A purge. They say the Ormsinir of Huedaik—the Dark God's personal servant, made from his own flesh—came to King Zarth's court and slew those in whom he detected treachery. Killed them with a glance and caused their bodies to distort, to take on hideous shapes, before crumbling to dust. To be sure, such unnatural death galvanized the righteous into action. The Ormsinir spoke of the Cerendar artifact. The Dark Gods smelt its presence, the creature said—and inflicted the faithful with a quest."

"Gaining this Cerendar was the aim of the quest?"

"The Great Work for which he was born, said Aridor. Worjaren Rehemon, you must understand, said very little, and that always concise. He never explained himself directly. It seems he's one of King Zarth's most prestigious lords. No doubt kissed his ass regularly when in Court."

"What evidence did he have that the Cerendar was here in Vesuula?"

Thargonal laughed. "Evidence? How should I know? He told me there'd been a sign. Perhaps some monstrous rodent pissed in his boot." The Sire shrugged. "Oh, mind you, there were other plans as well. A trickle of Dark God missionaries have been passing through Vesuula for generations and Worjaren Rehemon was to consolidate the Work. I'm convinced now his promises were humbug."

"Promises?"

"I was to lead a political infiltration. Amusing, don't you think?" Thargonal stood and walked carelessly to the porthole. "I can't say I regret the loss too greatly. When I gain rightful power here, I won't share it with some insane interloper." He turned back to them, his face full of mock seriousness. "I trace my line from the first Governor of the area, you know— Kar-Herdron of Elfindorl."

Shaan motioned him to return to his seat. "Can we talk of Worjaren Rehemon?"

"You grow impatient with my quaint ramblings. I beg your pardon. I don't function well under threat."

"Tolerably well, Thargonal," Halul said.

The aristocrat bowed sarcastically, in theatrical style.

"Enough!" Shaan's voice was hard and firm. Thargonal felt a discomforting energy in the man's tone that reverberated deep in his bones. He frowned and sat down. He rubbed his forehead, letting his palm linger on his temple. His pudgy fingers shook. "Worjaren Rehemon came several years ago," he continued. "There were rumors of a purge within the Dagorn court, as I said; it would have coincided with Worjaren Rehemon's departure from there. I don't know what that means, if not what he claims. At any rate he came, decreed Vesuula a Yanuran mandate and ordered my cooperation. I gave it. I'm no fool, as you can see by my willingness to help you now.

"But you mustn't think he spent all his time in our fair State. No. He left his Acolytes behind him like a trail of turds and disappeared northwards. He went to Bors and Cantalcis—that I know. But why is a mystery. Following some lead, I would guess, but who can say? *He* certainly didn't. *Our* time was spent overturning bureaucratic rocks and raking the slums—all useless, so far as I could see. Keeping our ear to the ground, Aridor said.

"When Worjaren Rehemon returned, he was excited about something; I could tell by the way his nostrils flared, though the rest of him was as sombre as ever." Thargonal laughed to himself. "There were hints of a secret...now I think of it, perhaps that box was behind it. I think I may have seen it...." He shrugged. "Be that as it may, we were launched on a search for someone called Zeth'han—strange I remember the name. As far as I could gather he'd migrated here from Cantalcis and Worjaren Rehemon thought him important."

"Did you find him?"

"Alas, no. My...agents...tracked down a registration certificate with his name on it. That's all. And his citizenship award."

"What was it he'd declared?"

"I don't remember. By the gods! Am I a Hassur clerk? These are all petty details, handled by others, and long ago. I'm a

Warden of the State and have more pressing business at hand."

"Such as you were engaged in tonight?" interrupted Raaneon, who until then had said nothing.

The aristocrat nodded with a sardonic twist of the mouth. "Exactly. It requires the closest attention."

Shaan dismissed the comment. "Is there more?"

"Oh yes. There's always more. Worjaren Rehemon, you see, my friend, had a genius for acquiring names, appellations for us to hunt and pick over like vermin. Having exhausted *Zeth'han* as a diversion, we next were given *Wefer*. I think this was Aridor's idea, the fool. Hope sprung from a hunch. I scorned it all, of course, but the worst of it is he may have been right. When we found this Wefer, Worjaren Rehemon persuaded him to talk and he claimed to have owned this Cerendar thing, and knew where it was."

"Where's Wefer now?"

"Dead. We found a hole his size, and he's safely tucked up in it.... Oh, please, don't glare at me as though I was responsible. It was Worjaren Rehemon. His magic has a way of tearing the mind apart." He raised his eyebrows to the rebel's leader. "You were saying something similar about your own abilities earlier. Well, Worjaren Rehemon has fewer scruples."

Shaan stared at the taunting man before him for a moment, but no sign of his thoughts showed on his face. Thargonal's leer faded.

"What happened to this knowledge then?" His interrogator's voice was almost a whisper. "Tell me something useful, my lord, before I regret our bargain."

"Wefer claimed that the Cerendar was in a bank vault, in Kelnel. Worjaren Rehemon sent his men after it—but, if it'd once been there, it was already gone. There'd been a robbery— the overseer and Head Guard were missing."

"Were they found?"

"One was. He was dead. The other vanished with whatever Wefer had secreted in the bank stronghold. It's most regrettable—but what could be expected of such a place? Standards are dropping. If Wefer had used one of *my* banks nothing would have been lost."

"Except his life, of course," said Raaneon.

The aristocrat honored him with a glance, but did not reply. "We searched for many days," he continued, "and found nothing."

The room went silent, so much so that Thargonal glanced around nervously. The ship tilted. Then Shaan said in the same low voice, "You're lying, my lord. Your mind cries out with the falsehood."

"Lying? How dare you, sir!"

"Lying!" The man's tone hardened. "I'm only interested in truth."

Thargonal sighed. "You have style, my friend, that I'll grant you. You read me well. Yes, I am lying. Not, you understand, to dupe you. No. I duped Worjaren Rehemon, you see, and *that* is a dangerous occupation."

"How?"

"It was simple. I sent a man to Kelnal before Aridor got there, and had Wefer's treasures from the vault under secret Council orders. The overseer and Guard were very cooperative and easily framed afterwards."

"So you obtained the Cerendar?"

"It's very embarrassing, my friend. Treachery is one thing, but to be inflicted with treason compounded is another. My man ran off with the treasure, planning, so far as I could gather, to escape over these very waters with it. I traced him to the City, though Worjaren Rehemon knew nothing of it. My man was robbed on the docks while he waited for passage; some petty thief escaped with the key to ultimate Power—and knew nothing about it! Ha! Don't you love such ironic justice? The robbers robbed by robbers. I fully believe the legends that the Cerendar is cursed. We had it all but in our grasp then at once it was gone again, as securely lost as the gods might wish. Let me assure you, before you ask, it did not reappear. It was gone, like a will-o-the-wisp, leaving us floundering in darkness." He grinned at the woman. "You see, minstrel, I too have a poetic turn."

"Are you sure it was the Cerendar?" asked Remis.

"Sure? How can I be sure? I saw nothing, obtained nothing. Worjaren Rehemon remained equivocal, the issue forgotten. Me?" He laughed. "I don't even know what this Cerendar looks like."

"The search ended then."

"The search as it related to Wefer, yes. Not otherwise. Aridor sniffed out new trails, one being this Remis you mentioned. I remember he was full of the quiet and supercilious self-denigration that used to make me despise him so intensely. He'd found the woman...to whom he'd been led by the hand of Junsar itself, he said. Ha! He was full of such religious guff, and positively dyspeptic with fate's blessings. He was blessed at last with what he wanted all along—"

"What had the woman to do with this?" asked Remis, curious to know how she'd been dragged into these plots.

Thargonal shrugged carelessly. "I'm of the opinion that it was all horseshit—a fabrication to hide the realities from me, put me off the scent. Aridor claimed—I got none of this from Worjaren Rehemon—that there was some sort of phantom stalking the City, a thing interested in or somehow connected to the Cerendar. He had me arrange for aides to scour public records—I don't know what became of the scouring, so save your questions—but apparently Aridor was up to something. He said this Remis—on the surface a mere low-grade spellbinder—was the creature's master.

"I don't know if it's true. Nor do I care." He slumped in his chair. "I've said enough. What more can I tell you? We shadowed Aridor's suspect—my men did—and tried to take her. Surely you know the rest. Aridor made mistakes, you fought him, he died." Thargonal gestured with his hand. "I'm finished. My part of the bargain is honored. Am I free?"

"One last question," said Shaan. "Why does Worjaren Rehemon want the Cerendar at all? What does he intend?"

"They say it has Ultimate Power," Thargonal tapped on the chair absently. "Surely you know this? And isn't it the thirst for Power that drives us all? I seek Power; I'm talking to you now because I wish to retain it. You too deal in Power." He indicated Remis, then Shaan. "Wizards and gods, sorcerers and demons. Power-mongers one and all. Don't sneer at me or my ambitions and think yourself superior in righteousness or more selfless in cause. It's all the same in the end and fate will rework the issue as it sees fit. If there's superiority it lies in this: you have me at a loss, holding your righteous Power to my pragmatic throat like a razor. There's no other morality more compelling than this."

For a moment there was silence.

"Well, have I said enough?" The arrogance in Thargonal's voice was little more than tiredness.

"For now."

Thargonal's eyes turned on Shaan. "For now? What do you mean?" he demanded, standing. "You promised to free me."

Shaan gripped his arm and forced him to sit.

"I have little sympathy for you, Thargonal," he said in a voice that brooked no argument, leaning close in toward the Sire. "Without men such as you, the real destroyers have no means of spreading their evil. Society, unaided, would be too strong to succumb. You are the vehicle they use, yet as such you are no more guilty than a common thug. You toy with forces you don't understand and you play games of politics when what is at stake is Life itself. But it does not mean I will coldly butcher you. In battle men die, but there is an absurd ethic to killing that does not allow such execution as you rightly deserve. I will leave time to settle the account. I promised you freedom—so you will be freed when our work is over."

"When your work is over. What does that mean?"

"It means I don't trust you not to interfere—and at the moment we need as little extraneous interference as possible."

Complaint came naturally to Thargonal's throat, but he didn't dare utter it. "Where are we going then?" he said weakly.

The man turned away from him, real contempt obvious in

his manner.

vi.

"So what happens now?" Tashnark did not look at Remis as he spoke, but watched Koerpel-Na grow clearer in the distance above the Harbor's gray-green waves.

"What do you mean?"

"You know."

Remis was silent. Finally Tashnark turned to her and saw her distress. "What do *you* plan to do?" she said before he could speak.

He shrugged. "What are the choices?"

Cool wind swept around them and a gull flew low over the ship's prow. "Shaan thinks he can locate Valarl using the heart you discovered in Gihornter."

"Why? Worjaren Rehemon had it and he apparently couldn't find the creature."

"Worjaren Rehemon didn't have me."

"You?"

"I'm Valarl's descendent. That's how he spoke to me. Blood-links are very strong."

"Descendent?" He stared at her for a moment, saying nothing, though Remis felt it was not her he was seeing. "Remarkable," he added, after a while. "How long have you known?"

"Valarl told me himself when he first summoned me, though I didn't fully accept it or understand the implications until later. Hassur records confirmed it."

Tashnark looked back across the Harbor. It was an ordinary, mid-month scene. Ships moved about busily, ensuring that the *Spirit* was nicely inconspicuous among them.

"So you're still stuck in this—" he waved his hand carelessly. "This passion play."

"Yes."

"I was flirting with the hope that we could get out—get back to normal." He glanced at her. "Talk."

"When we find Valarl, we'll have to go after him. Shaan believes he'll lead us to the Cerendar—and the artifact must be located."

Tashnark didn't dispute this point. He simply nodded, aware of converging forces. *Fragments*, he thought, *fitting jaggedly together*. But to form what?

It reminded him of a verse and, before he could question where it had come from, he recited it:

> "Fragments of a broken land
> Linger unrequited
> In patterns of destruction.
> But time is not slighted
> And nothing lost."

"What's that?" said Remis.

"I don't know. It just came to mind." How much more of the pattern was he not seeing?

"I have to continue with this," Remis said. Tashnark felt her touch his arm. His gut tightened.

"I know."

"What about you?"

His mind swept upward in a disorienting surge that carried him far away. He remembered Bellarroth and Hanin...and other, unresolved feelings he could not abandon. Remis knew nothing of these—and he could say nothing.

"Are you all right, Tashnark?"

"I guess so."

"You haven't answered my question."

He touched her face gently. "You haven't been listening," he said.

vii.

Somewhere beneath her awareness—which ploughed through endless plains of greenish sea—Remis first questioned the extent of her strength. She was tired, but it was a fatigue of the spirit, not the proper weariness of limb that her movement through the waves should have brought. Why didn't her arms ache? How was it that when night fell and early winter winds splintered the waves into icy shivers she felt no chill, no intolerable coldness in her bones and on her skin? There was nothing except this perception of sea—and an inner torment that drove her on. What had brought her here?

A hand touched her forehead. She started and blinked and the sea was suddenly gone, its motion replaced by sounds alone—and a more distant swaying. Blue eyes looked down at her in a familiar face so welcome that it made her heart throb painfully and tears well in her eyes.

"Shaan?" she said the name as though it was an evocation. Perspective shifted about her like the tumbling crests of wind-tossed ocean-plains. "Have you found him?"

Shaan nodded, his hair about his face in a wind-blown halo. "Valarl's corpse has been sighted, distant but clear. There's no need to drain your strength any further."

"How long have I been under?"

"The spell was cast three days ago. That night, when it was clear that the one we sought was at sea off the western coast of Vesuula, the Temple ship *Spirit* was set on course to seek him out. It's now early dawn and we sail northward through the straits of the Coral Fringe."

Remis said nothing. Three days had gone from her while she maintained divinatory contact with Valarl, three days of spiritual draining. Little wonder she was tired.

"You must rest now," Shaan's voice seemed like a healing whisper, and his hand reached out to touch her once again.

Remis pushed herself up, though weariness flooded her head

and forced her back onto the couch.

"You must." Arban's hunched frame and polished scalp loomed over her and obscured her vision of Shaan.

"No," she said again, with less conviction this time. "I'll miss Valarl. He's my blood and now that we're about to confront him, I can't sleep the moment away. Once, he greeted me as kin. Surely he'll answer to me again?"

Arban huffed. "This is undeath we're dealing with. Forget logic. Even if he honored you then, this time he could kill you. Don't try to find consistency in the dead." He gripped her arm. "You must sleep, or you'll be no help to anyone, least of all yourself. Sleep, I demand it. I'll weave you a spell of Quiet and wake you before we tackle the creature."

"Promise?"

"I'll make sure of it," said Tashnark, who had been sitting unnoticed by the couch. Relieved, Remis let wakefulness gently drift into slumber.

From somewhere she could feel the disembodied beating of Valarl's heart. It was in rough counterpoint to her own heart's slow rhythm.

viii.

Spirit was a small caravel, and space for human cargo was limited. Its hull, filled now with ballast, could carry some sixty tons in cargo, but its aft cabin and a couple of cramped stores beneath it were the only rooms intended for use by passengers. The crew slept where they could; Tashnark had claimed a pleasant spot near the main hatch. High on the top of the deck's curve and shadowed by the hatch-cover, he managed to remain dry and comfortable when asleep. At other times he strode about the deck or sat below in the cargo hold. Occasionally he sipped beer from several casks he'd managed to hide there.

The crew was a pleasant enough lot. In the main they had a healthy reverence for the priests and hence Tashnark, and though this sometimes resulted in a simpering meekness it gave him a lever in his search for privilege. They were also rather superstitious, and when he was in a good mood this seemed to Tashnark rather quaint. He was familiar with seamen, from voyages in his father's ships, but those men had been rougher, more barbaric in their beliefs. The crew of the *Spirit* followed omens and placated gods of a more delicate kind, softened by temple dogmas.

One spoke to Tashnark of himself on their second day at sea, some fifteen miles off the Sessenth Peninsula beyond the entrance to the bay. The waters spread before them like a restless savanna, the land behind already lost in a gray wall of mist. The wind was bustling, colored by the possibility of storm. Fine spray rained upon them continually, shattered off the *Spirit*'s bulwarks as it sped west.

The sailor was middle-aged and blotchy in complexion, as though continual exposure to the sea had caused his skin pigments to fade. His hair, similarly, was falling in clumps. He'd been standing intractably at the tiller for some hour or so when Tashnark climbed down the access-ladder to join him. It was like being in a pit. Directional codes, placed on the mizzen by the navigator, gave the fellow the ship's desired bearing, but the unnatural confinement, aggravated by their current rough going, made Tashnark feel uneasy. "I suppose you've sailed these waters quite a lot?" he said.

The sailor looked at him dully. "It's the major shipping route out of port, 'cepting southward."

Tashnark nodded.

"Shipped to Meresarn once—fifteen years ago," the sailor went on, obviously glad of company. Though he talked and listened freely, Tashnark noticed that his eyes kept harking back to the navigator's rod. "You're from there?"

Tashnark frowned. "Not any more. Once. A long time ago, that's all." Then he added, touching his braids, "Sometimes I like the old traditions."

"If they've got meaning...." The sailor let one hand slide off the tiller and scratched his beard with it. "I been on ships most of my days, merchant navy for a good deal. Now hire m'self out to the temples along the Kelish coast—private businesses. The Families won't have me. Refused work on a slave-ship belongin' to Gormath, insulted the captain who was a cousin or somethin'. But there's a tradition in me own kin 'bout slaves—grandsire was one. Can't abide it."

Tashnark thought he'd better change the subject. "You like working for Derthperrit?"

"It's unexcitin' but they're good people as you'd rightly be knowin'. The old governor's a saint."

Unseen, Tashnark rolled his eyes skeptically.

"I reckon them Raashyr'll show themselves one day and there'll be plenty'll be sorry for deeds misdone and honor misgiven." The sailor touched an icon that dangled at his neck. "I give due to Raashyr-Lord Cuuluth when the times of obligation come round, touchin' the cap to Isarl, Queen o' Ships—for good measure, you understand. I never been done wrong." Isarl was one of the new breed of deities; her status as Raashyr was questionable.

"Most sailors I've known stick with the Caluthim temple—a puppet of the State, I know. But I've dealt with their High Priest, and he can work miracle enough with his Family ties."

The sailor hissed and spat on the already-awash deck boards. "Monster-shit. He helped me out o' my job with no Power but boot-lickin'. No. When the ropes strain and the shrouds is torn to rags in unseasonable weather I know where to look. The water flows out of the North and is bless'd by Lord Cuuluth on its way, and there's no losing that blessin' till it touches the Dead Seas, and Horkdis fouls it with his spewin's." Horkdis was a colloquial name for Gaharlgeth, supreme among the Dark God E'ashalsinir—Tashnark was amused by the disrespect its use here implied.

"And you suppose Cuuluth hears you over the storm?"

"I dunno. Reckon he might. Leastways he has ears to hear, in his own seas, but when you're shippin' far from the City there's no way Caluthim can hear. His ears are in Family pockets."

Tashnark laughed. "Well put."

The sailor frowned. "I'm a sea-dog, but no fool."

"No," said Tashnark, "no fool."

* * * * * * *

One day, toward midday, the ship hit foul weather. It was hard going for several hours and they were blown off course by a sudden change of wind. As a result, the next morning found them little further advanced on their journey. The ship had lain at anchor for an hour or two during the night, giving the crew a chance to rest, but dawn saw them quickly on their way. Then the wind turned so that they flew ahead of it and they made excellent time for most of the day, the third out of port. Tashnark was seconded to steady the tiller—a task requiring strength in the fierce tail wind—and so his mind was kept well away from thought of the nausea the tossing waves had provoked in his stomach.

It was in the night that a reading of the Power-flow told the pilot they were bearing north-west. The watch sighted white-water ahead and they realized how dangerously close they had come to the Oul-Jus, a seventy-mile spear of islands and coral reefs that jutted into the strait and had scuttled many ships in the past. The crew worked feverishly to reset the sails; the *Spirit* turned safely and skirted along the side of the reefs. Charts of the area were extremely accurate and kept them away from dangerous shoals.

When Tashnark was tossed out of sleep next morning the jagged turbulence at the tip of the Oul-Jus was clear some three miles to the port side. He stood for a time watching it and tracing cloud break-up in the dawning sky. Occasionally sea birds appeared and wheeled about the ship. The rigging creaked and throbbed in gentle strain, and waves rushed past the hull with deep whispers. The air was thick with brine. It was very peaceful. Arhl joined him and later Raaneon, and they talked spasmodically of the night's disturbances. At about the third hour—Tashnark heard the hour-chime sounding through the wind rush—Raaneon went off to fetch water and some bread to settle their stomachs. While he was gone the Watch cried out a sighting and all eyes were turned ahead of the prow.

The day was fair and the air calm. The stormy drizzle of the previous days had dissipated somewhat and distance-haze had withdrawn several miles. A mildness was in the air, tinged by enough hint of grayness to remind them that the weather might turn bad at any time. Tashnark could see some miles ahead, but from his low elevation it was insufficient to give him a view of the sighting.

Far to the northwest he could see the blue, shredded outlines of the Krith islands and beyond that the less solid massiveness of the isle Sildan, spread like some enormous whale across the distance. For a moment he wondered if it was these that had drawn the Watch's call.

Grumpy with sleeplessness, Arban appeared from the aft cabin in crumpled robes. "What do you see?" he shouted to the Watch, who hung like a limp standard from the crossbeam of the forward mast.

"A single moving wake, sir!" He threw his words down at them like a challenge. "The seeing-spell has revealed it."

Arban was apparently convinced, for he turned without acknowledging Tashnark's presence and lurched back to the cabin.

"I guess that means we've caught up with Valarl's ship," Tashnark said to Raaneon.

"There's no ship ahead." Raaneon had been working his own spells. Now he ran his hand over his red beard as though preening and handed Tashnark a lump of toffee. "Whatever it is, it's too small."

"No ship?" Tashnark gripped onto the rail with one hand, guided the toffee into his mouth with the other, and stared intently into the distance. In a few moments, seeing nothing, he said: "If there's no ship, how's he got this far?"

Raaneon smiled cheekily. "I would've thought that was obvious."

An incredulous grimace distorted Tashnark's face. "Swimming? That thing must have been going for...I don't know...ten days or thereabouts. Zeth'han—poor beggar—had his hand removed weeks ago and according to Remis, Valarl would have headed off soon after...." They had been given news of Zeth'han and his fate on their brief stop-off at the temple's wharf.

"Exactly. Many days at sea and only halfway through the Straits. Too slow for a ship."

"But swimming? Nothing's that strong."

Arhl shrugged. "Nothing that lives."

The wizard bit at his toffee and then spoke slurringly, his mouth full. "Yes. And Valarl is cursed. Few physical limitations to stop him."

Tashnark was silent, in contemplation of this absurdity. "I don't believe it," he growled at last. Raaneon, who felt that a creature so absolutely determined was one no sane man should consider hindering, wished he could share Tashnark's doubt. Unfortunately his studies had taught him the possibility of such a thing, and he was left with no comfort.

"Should be some tussle to get him on board," mumbled Tashnark, and Raaneon regretted hearing it.

The *Spirit* ploughed on through the dull green water, the eyes of its crew seeking ahead for visible sign of the creature sighted magically by the Watch. The Krith group of islands solidified as the strait narrowed. On the starboard, perhaps twenty-five miles off, the cliffs of the Karon district gathered in gray-brown mist-clouds as though covered in a dim veil. At last, perhaps an hour later, as interest waned and many began to declare the Watch's spell faulty, someone yelled: "There it is!" Tashnark felt himself tense. He stared earnestly into the distance, the sea alight now with the Skywave's risen fire.

"I can't see anything."

Halul, who was leaning on the bulwark near him discussing

something bardic with her apprentice, pointed past his shoulder across the sea. "It's there. Just a smudge."

"I see it now. Incredible! Skaath knows I wouldn't have believed it." Tashnark squinted at the dim shadow ahead that broke the water's surface-glare, his mind trying to make sense of the vision. Faintly, he began to distinguish its form. Halul sang:

> "The man will never rightly be,
> Who lives upon the briny sea;
> Except it pass that fish are found
> That walk upon the solid ground."

"Your lyrics grow worse," said Tashnark.

A dull sigh escaped the Sumorle'en's lips. "A children's rhyme, friend. Not mine."

"You perpetuate the misery."

Slowly the *Spirit* drew closer and closer to the tireless figure in the sea. It was using a sort of floundering breaststroke, Tashnark saw—but what it lacked in grace, it gained in strength. Each thrash of its glazed, sinewy limbs moved it a body-length through the waves. There was no sign of fatigue in its movements. Lines of observers watched the strangely alien creature with fascination as it swam, oblivious to their approach, toward the obscured distance. Each wondered at it, unnerved and filled with growing apprehension. No danger as yet, but something about it—its inexorability—suggested that danger was close.

The crew took in the shrouds and moved one sail against their forward rush. The ship slowed gradually as they caught up with Valarl, until finally they were moving parallel with it, and at its speed.

Tashnark gazed across at the creature, watched the water-surface as its limbs broke through it, saw the corpse-like pallor of its hardened muscles and flesh, the expressionless face, gaunt and hard, with eyes like burnt-out coals. Tashnark's hand touched the cold hilt of his sword. It was smooth and familiar.

The creature was careless of the ship's presence. It swam on, and there was no indication that it had even seen them.

"Unnatural," muttered a sailor, over Tashnark's shoulder. Tashnark nodded and wondered where the limits of the natural lay.

ix.

"Remis, wake up."

For a moment it was not clear whether she was being shaken physically or whether the voice was merely having that effect on her head. Remis blinked twice, then opened her eyes.

"I thought you'd gone for good," said Tashnark.

Remis listened for a dozen beats to the throbbing in her temples. It would grow into a headache as soon as she moved.

"We've caught up with Valarl," Tashnark said with an evasive smile.

"How long have I been asleep?"

"Barely an hour."

Remis groaned and put her hand over her forehead. "It feels like it." She sat up. A sharp pain stabbed behind her eyes. Tashnark gave her a mug of cold tea to relieve the tension there.

When she felt better, they went outside onto the main deck where Valarl's capture was being organized. Most of the crew had gathered along the side of the ship and were looking port side—pointing, laughing, frowning grimly. The more superstitious were patently unnerved by the creature in the water. Others were merely fascinated. Remis and Tashnark went over to Shaan, Arhl and Halul who were standing by the bulwark. The fresh sea-tainted breeze made Remis dizzy as she too stared toward the swimming apparition moving parallel to their own path.

"Death, a thousand years in passing," she commented, as much to herself as to those about her.

Shaan lay his hand upon her shoulder. "The undead mirror

Raashyr immortality," he said, his voice so low that it was meant only for her. "In them death is suspended at the point where life departs the body, so they retain death's pain and loss, but never its rest. A most terrible immortality, without knowledge of life. It's a cruel and unforgiving curse. We must feel pity for this Valarl, no matter what his crime. He has lived too long with this obsession."

"Obsession?"

"It's clearly a thing of restless urgency, seeking, though perhaps without hope, for peace."

Remis looked to the creature in the sea, no longer quite a man, and watched with swelling compassion the tight, compulsive twisting of its pale body as each stroke dragged it forward. "Can we help him?" she asked.

"Perhaps," said Shaan, "if our pity proves greater than his curse."

* * * * * * *

Urged by the ship's mate to action, because he feared the freshening wind would make it impossible for them to maintain their current snail's pace movement beside the creature, Arban organized for a net to be brought from the hold and suspended off the rigging. This was lowered into the water to ensnare the swimming corpse.

As Valarl entered its mesh the crew pulled the ropes and drew it from the sea like a haul of fish, their muscles straining under the unnatural weight. The creature seemed heavier than a man, laden, like their ship's hull, with the accretions of time. But at last they pulled the dripping figure above the surface, water running off its pallid skin like runnels of pale blood, and the wind swung it over into collision with the ship's side. One moment it hung limply, as though uncertain how its environment had changed; the next, as it went out of sight against the inward-bend of the hull, the ropes of the fishing net jerked in the sailors' fingers. Several of them yelled in pain—they'd been holding the rope loosely, and its running fibers burned their fingers.

"Hold onto it, blast you!" shouted someone. Then for an instant the net swung back into view, and the creature was thrashing in furious gyrations, tearing at the wire-entwined threads with convulsing fingers. It seemed to be screaming—but, eerily, Remis could hear no sound.

"It won't hold."

The net came apart suddenly. Like a rock the creature fell into the sea and disappeared under the surface. Several of the sailors cursed. Then there was silence.

Everyone waited, eyes searching the diminishing turbulence of the water for sign of the creature's re-emergence. A gull squawked high above from its perch in the rigging and the wind tossed the sound like a distant scream. "Where's it gone?" asked Tashnark, unnerved yet again.

Remis said nothing. After a few more moments someone else, Raaneon perhaps, muttered. "I assume it doesn't have to breathe."

Then the ship shuddered beneath their feet. Everyone froze in a weird tableau of expectation. When the *Spirit* shuddered again, the impact was accompanied by a splintering thud that echoed up through the boards.

It was Halul who voiced their thoughts. Her long features were stern. "Is it smashing the hull beneath the waterline?"

Tashnark glanced at Remis, who was staring wide-eyed at Shaan, as though he must inevitably be the one to save them.

Immediately several of the sailors ran to work the pumps, and one or two others, on their own initiative, leapt down the hatchway. "Stay away from it!" Arban shouted. Then, softer, he swore a priestly oath, hunching tiredly into himself.

"The thing'll sink us," Raaneon murmured to the wind. "Hell of a way to flounder."

Shaan began moving toward the hatch as another blow reverberated in the planking. He drew his sword. "Brother Werrinlit," he said to the harried pilot, "it seems we must grapple with Valarl more directly. You must be ready to mend whatever damage it's caused and with haste."

"We'll be gettin' the dredges goin', sire, don't you worry." Werrinlit's balding pate bowed at the Saral.

Shaan went on. "Remis, perhaps now we need your kinship with Valarl to calm his fury. Miris...." To Arban: "Fetch spells to bind his limbs."

"And I," spoke Rondan-el-Therrill, who had until now maintained a distance from the rest, watching the abortive struggle from a position on the poop deck where he had stood as unmoving as a statue. He came forward. "I'm skilled in battle and my blade is powerful. No common weapon can cut through enchanted flesh. You may need its magic."

Tashnark had been growing steadily impatient with the talk, and could see only the sinking of the *Spirit* as a consequence. "We've no proof even a magical blade will stop it," he said, flinging aside his cloak and unbuckling scabbard and leather bindings. "Yet there's one weapon left that we know for sure can threaten the thing."

Remis pulled the ritual-dagger from her breeches in response. "You mean—"

"Yes! That's the one," said Tashnark. "It held the creature immobile before you removed it. Maybe it can do it again." He snatched the dagger from her fingers and turned toward the bulwark before anyone could stop him. Pausing briefly to grab the free end of a mooring rope, which he looped into his belt, he said: "Go by all means and wait for Valarl to break in through the planks. I'll meet it on the other side." With that he leapt over the edge and into the water.

"Tashnark, no!" yelled Remis, but he was gone.

No one said anything for a moment then Raaneon muttered, "He *can* swim, right?"

As he struck the chill water and felt it churn around him in a stream of bubbles, Tashnark suddenly wondered what the hell had possessed him. He supposed, as he thrashed his arms against the water to push himself back to the surface, it had seemed reasonable in the instant before he leapt. Brave deeds always seem reasonable when you're in a reckless mood— that was their horror. Logical consideration and retrospective thought dulled their sheen somewhat.

More disturbing to him was the possibility that he'd acted simply because Remis and the others had automatically looked to Shaan to help them—and some childish impulse in himself had wanted to undermine the Saral-Lord's pre-eminence. Jealousy, pure and simple.

Either way, now he was irrevocably committed to being the hero.

He broke the surface and flung water from his eyes. *Stupidity*, he thought, seeing the huge abraded hull of the *Spirit* moving stolidly away from him. *The ship's faster than me!* His mind whirled desperately. He knew he couldn't match it swimming, however sluggish its movement. *Rope!* Feverishly he flung his hand beneath the water, grabbing at the mooring rope he'd stuffed into his belt. It was nearly played out. His fingers numb with cold, he tied the rope about his waist and braced himself. As the rope's limit was reached it tightened suddenly and dragged him through the churning side-wake. He gasped and was choked on a mouthful of water.

Above him, when he wasn't tumbling headlong, he could see figures gathered along the deck, staring down at him fixedly. One of them would be Remis. He tried to wave a sign of reas- surance.

Suddenly he realized that he didn't have the dagger in either of his hands. It came as a shock. For a moment he was afraid he'd dropped it and that it was drifting now through deepening waters, heading for an inaccessible resting-place on the sea floor. But then he felt it tucked in his belt. He must have put it there sometime in his tumbling fall.

All right. Here he was in the sea, his impetuosity dampened in chill water. Rope tethering him to a small caravel that was, at this very moment, threatened with scuttling. And somewhere on the ship's bottom an undead creature, bent on its destruction. *Well*, he thought, *I might as well try to do something, before it's too late.*

He spat out a mouthful of water, as he gripped the mooring-rope and dragged himself along. The barnacled hull of the ship drew nearer and he could hear the thudding caused by the undead creature somewhere along its extent. He took one hand off the rope and touched the planks. They were rough with dried pitch and sea-life. He'd rip himself to shreds if he tried to crawl along it.

Uncertainly, he glanced across the hull, searching for some handhold. What he saw was a rusty metal rung bolted to the wood. Grinning absently, he let go of the rope and grabbed at the rung, feeling its flaking layers of rust scrape on his palm. But it held. He huffed in relief. So far so good. The wood groaned under his touch as Valarl, somewhere below, clawed at the ship. *It must break through soon.* The hull was thick and crusted, and the creature's strength minimized by water resistance, but once Valarl found a split, he'd be able to tear the planks away with relative ease.

Taking a deep breath, Tashnark ducked beneath the turbulent rush of water along the side of the *Spirit*. Visibility was poor. He was in the ship's shadow and the movement of the currents continually forced his eyes shut. With effort he could just make out another rung, in line with the one he held and an arm-length further toward the keel. It was as he'd hoped. There would be a number of such holds along the bottom of the ship, intended for use in repairs made at sea. Where they hadn't fallen off or corroded away, he could use them to reach Valarl.

Tashnark resurfaced and caught his breath as best he could.

It wasn't easy. Half of what he breathed seemed to be spray. And already his muscles ached. The strain and exertion was taking rapid toll of his endurance.

He gasped an old Nahallhan oath, one that was typically half a curse, and dragged as much air into himself as his lungs could handle. Immediately he thrust beneath the surface, using his feet, which were protected by his boots, to gain purchase on the jagged surface. Currents snatched at him like the fingers of demons, frantic to spin him away into the wake of the ship.

Light here was scarce and patchy, the dark water blurring everything into greenish shadow. Tashnark's eyes stung in protest as he scanned the descending curve of the hull. His chest began aching to release the foul air and take a gulp of fresh, but he thrust forward to the next rung, and then the next. He could last only a little longer, he knew.

Then to his left, further toward the prow, something darker than the swirling shadow-eddies moved against the direction of the currents. Simultaneously, Tashnark heard a dull pounding carried to his ears on the roaring water. Valarl.

But his lungs were stretched as far as they would go. Orientating himself quickly to the dark shape of the creature, he pushed himself back the way he had come, desperate for the surface. When he reached it, he spluttered and gasped for several moments, emptying his lungs and refilling them compulsively. Then he noticed that something had changed. The rush of water past the ship had slowed still further, easing the effort needed to maintain his grip. The *Spirit*'s remaining sails must have been furled, or reset to bring her to a halt. Forward movement was sluggish now. Tashnark glanced up at the heads just visible over the bulwark and shouted: "The slower the better. I've found Valarl and can get to him."

A voice, possibly Raaneon's, replied: "We've started to take in water."

Another, Remis's, said: "Be careful!"

He took a breath and plunged down quickly. It was easier now he knew where he was going and now that the current was less insistent; and he reached his previous position with lungs still strong with air. A sort of cockle-weed floated in the water all about him, swimming past in undulating ribbons. He hadn't noticed it before. Flailing out his arms to brush some of it aside, he located Valarl and tried to judge the angle of his own attack. Even as he did so and took the dagger from his belt, the creature was scratching its fingers along the barnacle-encrusted hull, causing the sea to churn in through an opening gap. Its back was toward Tashnark.

He pushed himself off from his handhold and swam toward the creature. There was enough movement in the ship, and the water beneath it, to make the maneuver difficult, and his boots and pants made it no easier. But he thrust his arms fiercely and the power this gave moved him steadily along.

As he drew toward Valarl, the creature seemed to sense his presence—or more likely, the presence of the dagger. It turned about, snarling, kicking its legs smoothly to maintain its position. For an instant its black eyes and gaunt skeletal features were clear through the greenish film, then it lunged at Tashnark, clawing with manic fury. There was little control in this action. Tashnark pushed himself aside and grabbed at the creature's neck, hoping to swing across its back before it could snare him. Muscles in his diaphragm began to shudder, anxious for air. He forced the pain aside. A touch of dizziness passed furtively over his mind.

His hand slid on the hard, water-smooth surface of Valarl's skin. *No, I'll lose the chance*. Water like a shield came between them. The creature turned, gripping his left arm. Pain flared as it squeezed. He hardened his muscles against the hold. Another hand moved, crashing on his face. He thrashed out with his free hand and the knife grazed the creature's thigh. It cried out. Soundlessly. *Weed on his face*. His grip loosened and he was pushed away. He jabbed at the creature's chest, his lungs screaming, a cloud filling his mind. The dagger struck, sank into Valarl's stomach, and instantly the creature was motionless, twisted into peace.

Desperate now, despite this success, Tashnark steeled himself against his weakness and held onto Valarl's corpse, afraid it would sink out of reach. Quickly, he untied the mooring-rope from his own waist and secured it around the thing's chest, held from slipping off by its arms. As a fog drifted over him, he paddled for the surface. With a violent surge he burst free of the pressure.

He emerged into a red light. Blue lightning cracked overhead.

He started to sink again but something gripped him, holding him unconscious. His mind blurred as his thoughts shifted and changed.

"Stay awake!"

It was Hanin. He—Bellarroth—recognized the voice.

The water became fire.

Through the burning glare Bellarroth saw that the air was thickening, forming into a man-like shape. The figure was tall and regal, though pain governed the crippled way he held his body. Nevertheless his demeanor was threatening. Bellarroth raised his sword and leapt toward the manifestation. Fire flared, sweeping through the sickly atmosphere toward him; a sharp, unfocused pain scorched the inside of his head, and he was flung to the ground.

Lying flat on the roughly textured skin, groaning helplessly, Bellarroth forced his eyes to re-focus upward. Hanin had not moved. Though darkness blurred the lights of his face, his sorrow was obvious.

Bellarroth tried to push himself upright, but couldn't.

<Time contracts,> said an internal voice, like an echo in his skull, whispering to him as though from deep within the living ground on which he rested. <Be alert to treachery and wait for my power to take you.>

Who is that? Hanin?

<No one so human—but another victim of this curse, certainly. I am driven by powers too great to resist and the time has come for them to be fulfilled.

No one human? What's that supposed to mean?

<It means what it means.>

Bellarroth grunted skeptically. Who are you? Give me a straight answer. Conundrums make my head ache.

No reply was forthcoming. But movement caught his attention. Bellarroth succeeded in gaining his feet this time; he looked around, aware of the monstrous Tammenallor on Its huge throne. The Beast sat impassively watching them.

"Bad time you pick to haunt my dreams, Cormidthal," Hanin said.

The man-figure had clarified now and Bellarroth saw his face. Its lines were stony and angular and the eyes burned as though they formed a thin shield holding in check the heart of a furnace. An aura of flame around him, shifting in and out of focus, turned the air red.

So this was Cormidthal, ruler of the legendary Mikhalin, of whom Hanin had spoken often. Once this man had brought ruin to that southern empire and perhaps to the world—Bellarroth had long been conscious of a guilt that could not be unraveled from memory of him. The guilt was Hanin's. The memory was Hanin's.

Yet I've seen him, *Bellarroth thought.* I know him.

* * * * * * *

Tashnark's soul was wrenched. Memory swept through the back streets of Koerpel-Na, gathering fire and confrontation. His sword descended.

Then the image broke.

"As always, Hanin," the stranger replied. "Did you think me dead?"

"I hoped it only."

The man smiled. "So old and still bitter. You forget that I too have suffered exile. I have lived on a Kharathahul's back like you and a worse life it gives than this one you have led. I've suffered in fire, Hanin—fire and endless pain."

"On Lucishnor?"

"Yes, on the Fire-Demon. Can you imagine my torment? I suffer it even now."

"How can you?"

"I am there still."

Bellarroth was steadier on his feet by this time and approached the two men. Cormidthal, as Hanin had named him, raised his hand in warning.

"Stay back, son-Bellarroth." Hanin's eyes did not leave Cormidthal's face, though Bellarroth seemed to feel them on him.

"So," said the other, as Bellarroth obeyed, "further proof of your happy lot. I, Hanin, have spent the years alone. Who came here with you?"

"Korrenea. Long dead."

"Korrenea. I remember her. A plain woman, but as I see, plainly worth the effort." He turned to Bellarroth. "You cannot attack me, boy. You haven't the Power. Don't get me wrong. Death would be a blessing, but it is a blessing I am denied. My curse is stronger than your sword." He tapped his chest. "This body you see here is merely a projection—solid enough it is true, but secondary nevertheless. I am here and on Lucishnor as well. You would have to fight me in both places, with the strength of a god, if you'd fight me at all." He dismissed Bellarroth with a wave of the hand. "But we won't talk of impossibilities."

"What will we talk about then?" said Hanin.

"Past loyalties and new alliances."

Hanin snorted. "I'm older now, too old to re-live the stupidities of youth. I've been given a long time to contemplate your evil and my own folly. Our life together in Mikhalin is too long past."

"I'm after a more practical alliance."

"As you claimed it was then. We all followed you, Cormidthal—all the fools and the ignorant. We took part in your Rites, convinced that you'd found an answer to the riddle of the Cerendar, a way to use it in our benefit. You conjured its

Power for us in words, but the deed merely condemned us to exile—and Tharenweyr, no doubt, to chaos."

"You've grown eloquent, Hanin."

"I'd rather you said wise."

Cormidthal sneered. "A small wisdom, which cannot see the one route to freedom."

Suddenly he wove his hands in an intricate pattern and the air became hotter. Bellarroth staggered away from him, propelled by the intensity of the heat.

"Cormidthal," said Hanin, though he made no move to interfere, "you played with Power once and it brought despair. Don't meddle with this, too."

"I have nothing to lose."

Now the heat was a tangible presence, a flaming mass that drifted toward solidity. Cormidthal screeched, "Lucishnor al-Enith serrabis dom!" The shape clarified.

Bellarroth saw Tammenallor shift on Its throne, Its pained features facing outward, as though staring eyelessly at a shape burning out of the darkness.

<The time has come. Welcome, brother.>

The voice in Bellarroth's head was filled with joy and sorrow both. He knew the voice wasn't speaking to him.

<Time for what?> he said nevertheless.

<Time for resurrection to begin.>

The fire had taken on a shape now. It was Lucishnor, present like Tammenallor in a diminutive form, but aflame with barely suppressed power.

<Tammenallor, it begins,> said another voice in Bellarroth's head.

<Yes, we will be re-united.>

<Guilt will join with lust, the will for recompense with the power of desire.>

<Yet there are deeds that must be done.>

<And lives to be retrieved.>

The Monsters faced each other across fire and blue lightning.

"With the Kharathahul together, there is power enough to

free us," Cormidthal was saying, apparently unaware of the voices. "Join me, Hanin, and we can subdue the Power to serve our ends."

Bellarroth's concentration was directed inward.

<Go back, Bellarroth,> the echoing voice said, <Go back to the first world. The way must be prepared.>

<What am I supposed to do?>

<You will know—and you will return to me, for the Cerendar binds us to our fate, and there is no escape. Time is bent here, twisted and endlessly spiraling in upon itself.>

Bellarroth felt his grip on the words and the place slipping away.

Fire became sea. There was sky above and the dream faded into reality.

Again, he was Tashnark.

xi.

It seemed that he lay on his back for a long time, breathing heavily. He drifted away from the *Spirit*, careless for a moment of both the ship and its fate. Time passed while the blueness of the sky calmed him.

Then he heard voices. They whispered to him of impossible things, efforts past hope of success, heroism of legendary stature. He ignored them all. But one was insistent. It called his name and he knew it was Remis. He looked toward the sound. His hand reached into his pocket and gripped the coin she'd enchanted into a love charm, though he did not activate it. There was no need to bring her illusion to life, not yet, for she was there, in front of him.

The *Spirit* was several hundred feet away, wandering further as sea currents and winds dragged it slowly northward. "Tashnark," came the spellbinder's voice, "are you alive?"

"Ask Arban, or the Saral. They're the philosophers."

Remis turned to say something to the others, and warily

Tashnark abandoned his indolent drift, swimming with his awkward style back toward the ship. When he reached it at last, they threw him a rope; but he was too fatigued to climb it, and they finally had to haul him on board. Remis hugged him despite the fact he was wet, and weedy, and sour of temper.

The corpse of Valarl, still now but as unnatural as ever, lay protrate upon the deck, its sightless eyes staring at the rising Skywave. *But was it sightless?* Tashnark wondered. The Saral knelt over it.

"So it all ends."

Arban, gnomic beside Shaan, looked up and shrugged crookedly: "Perhaps. But there is no sign of the Cerendar artifact. What demons plague that thing that it evades us even now?" He stood and stepped toward Tashnark. "By chance, did you see it, or anything like it, while you fought the creature? Think hard!"

At that moment the Watch, perched high on the unrigged mainmast, yelled a sighting and all eyes were directed southward off the stern. There was a ship plainly visible in a patch of sky brass-rubbed across the distance. From the set of its sails it was a large one. "Merchant ship?" Raaneon was looking out across the waves.

"Possibly," answered Arban.

"There are no regular galleys due now," said Werrinlit with the authority of an experienced captain. "The Families might be about though. They follow their own whim."

Tashnark nodded. "Schedules are nothing. My father ignored them. Likely as not, this ship is innocent."

"Perhaps."

"I don't think so." Halul was staring out over the sea, one hand on her axe, her sharp face tense. "I've several times felt an uneasiness in my heart but now there's a focus for it. Whatever that ship's business, it's carrying someone with a spirit distorted by Dark God corruption."

Shaan nodded. "I expected it. Captain Werrinlit, I suggest your crew set the sails and put us on a hasty course away from this ship. The sorcerer has found us."

xii.

That it intended to catch them, the carrack quickly made clear. It dogged their wake insistently, drawing nearer as the *Spirit*'s crew worked to set the sails.

"I recognize the ship, sir," whispered helmsman Bresal-Engil to Tashnark, as the latter strained on the mainstay. "I worked her once when I was not in exile. She's the *Derargarth*, sir, belongin' to the Thargonal clan. The name means 'Sea Predator'."

"Thargonal! Pig's blood!" Tashnark's surprise and annoyance was such that he nearly released the rope. Hadn't they warned the treacherous son-of-an-ass about retaliation? He handed the seaman the ropes. "Take this, friend. You've brought intriguing news."

He found Shaan and Remis in the poop-deck cabin. Arhl was there too, tying cord about Valarl's corpse in cunning barbarian knots. Tashnark noted with a smirk that some person of delicacy had draped a blanket over the undead's nakedness. The dagger was, of course, still stuck in its stomach, and so unlike flesh was its skin that it looked for all the world like a ship's figurehead waiting to be fitted to the prow.

"That ship is Thargonal's," he declared and was annoyed when the Saral responded with a nod.

"We can hardly blame Thargonal for that, can we?" Shaan pointed toward the part of the ship where the sire was presently being held. "This is the sorcerer Worjaren Rehemon's work."

"Can't we get Thargonal to send him a message?"

Shaan stood and went over to a seaman's map spread out on the table. "It would do no good. Worjaren Rehemon does not obey Thargonal."

"He'll turn us into outlaws."

"Worjaren Rehemon won't report us to Sumis or the Supreme Council—he wants what he thinks we have. It is for this he sacrificed Sire Thargonal in the first place. He has no interest in politics."

"I hope you're right. I'd like to go back to Koerpel-Na when this is over."

The map Shaan had spread before him was of the Ar'chithin Isles, the group defining the western extremity of the Ut'Santh-Norrid Straits. These islands covered an area some 150 miles square and had been well charted as a guide to ships using the strait on their route northward to Apophis or beyond. The largest of the islands, Avaletol, so far as Tashnark could recall, was populated by several sizeable communities of foresters and fishermen, and boasted as well a number of less lucrative mines. These industries were controlled from Koerpel-Na. The other three large islands—Sororon, Sildan and Elegis—covered a considerable area but could only have supported small fishing communities. Innumerable coral islands and reefs were marked everywhere, both Oul-Jus, which they had already passed, and Krith, now on their port side, clearly designated by ornate lettering. Altogether, the effect was one of maze-like confusion.

Shaan indicated their present course, parallel to the Krith. "It's plainly the intention of our enemy to catch us at sea—or at least to prevent our return to the City. Miris-Arban feels that this is no official action or else it'd be a naval vessel tracking us. Rather it seems an example of the Familial piracy that often occurs on the fringes of the law. He feels a return to the City would be our safest policy in so far as our enemy seems reluctant to draw general attention to himself. In taking us at sea, he would remain hidden from Sumis and Family scrutiny.

"But we'd surely be taken. The straits are relatively narrow and to turn about in this weather would put us at a disadvantage. The carrack is not so far behind that we could afford delay. To go about, the pilot also feels, would be to give ourselves to them. So we must flee ahead." He pointed then to the coast of Vesuula on his map. "Here there is a hope of refuge perhaps. Weas'nul, a minor port town. We could make it there if need be—yet I'm sure our enemy wouldn't hesitate to turn the local authorities on to us. It's a long way from Koerpel-Na, and Family crimes can be easily hidden."

"True enough. So what does that leave us?"

"The necessity of flirting with lesser dangers."

Shaan scored his finger along the map, stretching a line that ran in toward the most northerly of the Krith islands, wove between reefs and shoals, turned across the face of Sororon and proceeded, through a jumble of hazards, toward the west coast of Avaletol.

"This course puts us at risk, but it may work in our favor. The *Spirit* is small and maneuverable. If the weather remains calm, we may find we've gone where our enemy's vessel would founder. Thus we can pick our way through to a point below Oul-Jus and outrun the carrack back to Koerpel-Na. It's a longer and more taxing journey than was originally planned, but there are stores enough to last us."

Tashnark drew attention to himself by clearing his throat. "It's a fool's plan. We'll be the ones lost, keel torn apart on a misjudged passage. Better to fight."

"Anything's better than that." Remis touched his arm. "You fight well, Tashnark, perhaps enjoy it—but I don't know, and nor do others here. Most of the crew are true seamen, not a soldier amongst them. Can we afford the fight, Tashnark? Think what's at stake."

Tashnark's mind grappled with the problem, but the debate was already won. A confrontation with this Worjaren Rehemon, whoever he might be, was absurdly part of his memory, though the outcome was vague. Of course it was foolish—Worjaren Rehemon was powerful, more so than all of them perhaps. But it would happen. The ancient name *Cormidthal* trailed across Tashnark's thoughts. One day, and one day soon, he would have to fight this phantom. He knew it, though he did not know why.

"It may be best," he said, "Or it may not. I can't say. But I've known several men who've challenged the Reefs looking for a shortcut through to Avaletol. Luck alone saved their lives."

Shaan acknowledged his doubts. "Yet there are paths of safety for smaller ships. The fishermen ply their trade easily enough—"

"This is no trawler."

"No, but if need be we can lower sail and use sounding poles to thread the narrows."

"And what thinks our boatswain and pilot?"

"They have your doubts, but see greater necessity. It can be done."

Tashnark grunted. He looked at Remis, who eyed him sarcastically. "If you seek my blessing, then you can have it," he said finally. "Consensus must be maintained." He pointed at Valarl. "Does our dead friend have a say, too?"

Remis kicked him in the ankle.

xiii.

"Do you regret coming with us?" Remis asked Arhl as they stood on the poop deck watching both the distant carrack and the approaching mass of jagged islands. The day had grown dimmer, though it was only the fifth or sixth hour. Huge banks of cloud were gathering in the southeast. The wind had picked up, a worry now they were nearing the reefs.

Remis went on absently when the wide-shouldered mountain-man offered no reply. "I mean, our acquaintance has brought you wounds and struggle and constant harassment. This last death-threat doesn't seem unusual."

"I regret nothing," said Arhl. "I was directed to come."

"Directed? What do you mean?"

Clearly he had no intention of explaining further. He turned back toward the *Spirit*'s pale-flecked wake. "My wounds are near to healed now—I'm barely aware of them. Such injuries are easy ignored."

Remis mumbled some polite acknowledgement. Arhl's half-smile grew. "How often can one work side by side with a god's son?"

"I thought you'd want to go back to your forge. Business will be falling off."

Arhl stared into the distance. "I won't be going back. Not yet."

"I think I understand."

"Do you? I hope so. I want you to understand. And I want you to understand too that I feel as much a part of this struggle, this mystery, as you do, Remis. I may not be related to Valarl, and I may not be Raashenti, or in any way fated like these others, but I am still part of it.... I can't leave till it's all over, and maybe not then...and death? What of that? It's natural enough in men. This danger we're in is nothing, because our deaths will come when they will, in season or out, whether we struggle with demons or stay cozy in our beds. Makes no difference."

"A brave philosophy!"

"Is it?" Arhl said whimsically. "It feels...mundane."

xiv.

The wind was gradually turning against them. It had swung around several points and, though it still carried them speedily across the waters of Ut'Santh-Norrid, it threatened to play havoc with the sails' current setting. Waves were choppy about the hull.

Raaneon had climbed down into the hold to examine damage caused by the undead creature's bashing. It wasn't that he distrusted the work of the crew's caulker—on the contrary, he'd thought the fellow most competent and well versed in his trade. Raaneon simply wanted to *see* the finished job to satisfy his own feelings of unease.

Among the water-barrels and stones, the wizard came upon something hunched in the shadows—a crouching figure that seemed to be in distress. There were occasional moans, gasping snatches of breath, and, as he continued to listen, a smattering of words. These were barely audible, mere inarticulate mutterings, but occasionally they became recognizable and could be heard as speech. Still Raaneon could not understand them. What was it? A foreign tongue perhaps? Or some sorcerous spell-sending?

Taken aback by the thought, he stepped away, grabbing at his sword. He found nothing, however, and remembered he'd abandoned the thing much earlier. In his haste he knocked against a pile of small casks, overbalancing the lot. They tumbled about him in a thunderous avalanche.

The crouching figure was up in an instant. Raaneon found he had a dagger-blade resting against his throat before the last cask struck the deck and long before he had a chance to focus on his opponent. Luckily, it was only Halul. Her sharp eyes studied him. "Those casks shouldn't have been loose," he muttered. "I wonder why they weren't tied down?"

Halul's eyes looked red and savage—and yet, perhaps it was just the residue of surprise, for her lips formed their characteristic grin, and the knife-blade was withdrawn from the wizard's neck. "You were a dead man then, magician," the woman said, sheathing her dagger. Raaneon noticed that Halul's left hand was gripped tightly about the handle of the black-metal axe. Odd, since she had this weapon already in hand, that she'd instinctively defended herself with a dagger she'd had to unsheath.

"I thought you were a spy." Raaneon laughed as carelessly as he could. "Muttering in the dark like a bewitched toad! What in Hell were you doing?"

Halul turned away, leaning over to draw her lute to herself. She let her axe drop to her side, firm on its leather strap. Raaneon tried to examine it, but Halul's motion and the gloom hid everything except its blackness from him.

"So happens I was composing a song," Halul said, with badly feigned sheepishness. "Would you like to hear it so far?"

"A song?"

"Yes. It concerns the Saral and his battle with the Dark Acolytes."

Raaneon frowned, despite himself. "In what tongue?"

"Lesser Goduulan, of course."

"Really? It didn't sound like Lesser Goduulan to me?"

A touch of annoyance, a transient frown, soured the Halul's

reply. "You misheard!" she said, outwardly polite, "or perhaps I was thinking aloud in the Sumorle'en-Wording. What does it matter?"

She pushed past Raaneon, heading down the ship toward the hatch door. Raaneon frowned and scratched absently at his beard. In a moment Halul had climbed the access-ladder and her footsteps sounded on the deck above. They were stern and definite. Sighing, Raaneon decided he must have offended some artistic scruple or dared to over-hear some esoteric bardic matter, and continued on his way to the ballast-area.

XV.

Arhl Mogarni remained squatting beside Valarl's corpse after the others left to see to the sailing of the ship. He was feeling tired, it was true—a weariness that he found disturbing and wished would pass. But it didn't, no matter how often he rested, and it distracted him perpetually as he sought in his clumsy fashion to grasp the threads of this duty. It was the ghost of his mother that had led him here and Lord Shaan who had given the random events meaning. Yet he continued not because of them, but because of Remis.

In the short time he had known her he had come to care for her deeply. Not in the way of a man desiring a woman. No. That was too *ordinary*. At first, when he had worked for her at his forge, he had felt attracted in that way, it is true—but such a fancy had been a passing thing. It bore no fruit, not in him nor in Remis. Then, as now, he had known it was not desire that had drawn them together—rather, it was something more obscure and more mysterious, something he had not understood at that time. When his mother came to him on the night these events began, however, she had provided a clue—and her words had bound their fates together with a knot so intricate and so tight there was no escape from it. As he had told Remis, he did not regret the bondage. He had come to respect her all the more, to care for her as a friend. He had seen her take vast responsibility upon herself without complaint and without self-aggrandisement. He had seen her integrity and great inner strength.

Of the others, apart from the Saral-Lord, he thought little. The temple priests he honored for what they were, Tashnark he accepted as a mystery, a dark and worrying one. Rough, full of civilized folly, powerful—he was a being outside Arhl's understanding and as such, comrade only as circumstance allowed. Their acquaintance beyond that was nothing. The wizard Raaneon Sar-Pelledol and Halul the Singer: these were passing company. No more.

He stretched his arms and looked toward Valarl. *"Can you stay with him for a time?"* the Saral-Lord had asked, and Arhl had nodded. If the godling wished it, he must succumb. He had never been one to begrudge the gods their due.

Suddenly he jerked into alertness as the cabin door opened. He heard the breezes beyond the walls rushing into the ship's sails and smelt brine. The swell was rising.

A sleek, gray shape padded in through the opening door, its green eyes watching him suspiciously. It was followed by the large figure of its master. "Ah," said Rondan-El-Therill, seeing Arhl squatting there, "I feared the corpse had been left unattended."

"I'm here all right," Arhl replied.

"So I see." The Merilan warrior moved over to Valarl and stood staring down at the corpse. There was silence but for the ship's creaking and sounds of sea and wind. The cat seated itself at a distance from Arhl and began to clean its fur with aloof disinterest. Arhl's eyes flicked from the animal to the man—in his mind they were indistinguishable. This Rondan-El-Therill and his cat were as elusive as the wind that came to swell the ship's sails.

"They all believe the answer lies here in the unrotting corpse," said Rondan-El-Therill thoughtfully, "and still it resists them." His eyes, green like his cat's, turned to Arhl. "You are of the Sohas tribes of Wysumbria?" he asked, though it was more like a statement.

Arhl nodded. "And you are Merilan?"

Rondan smiled. "Do you have anything of the Gift?" he asked.

Arhl looked at him sharply.

"I know that some of your people see things that others are blind to, know things that others do not know. Are you one such?"

Arhl sighed—he never talked of the Gift, held silent by tribal mores and by fear, yet this Merilan warrior seemed to give him license to speak about it. "On occasion. But it's a withered skill—weak, patchy and unpredictable."

"Nevertheless, it brought you here, didn't it?"

Arhl nodded.

The cat suddenly stopped its grooming and prowled to Arhl's side. It sniffed him tentatively without touching him. When Arhl raised his hand to it, it arched its back to be stroked. He obliged.

"Why are you so lonely, Arhl Mogarni?" The Merilan warrior said suddenly and Arhl looked up, startled. Yet he saw no point in denying these words.

"I am *man-alone*," he replied simply, giving the ritual word from his own people's tongue.

Rondan-El-Therill squatted as Arhl was, and returned his gaze to the corpse. "I too. Zhornn was ever a desolate home."

"My tribe were wanderers, hunters in uninhabited lands. Now they are dead—and no foresight saved them."

"Yet you have looked for them in many places, lately the Merchant City?"

Arhl nodded, recognizing the truth of the new idea as it was spoken.

"I too have wished for a spiritual resting place, my friend. But the world is old and restless. Moments are oases, but the winds leave them dry. We fulfil what we are."

Arhl closed his eyes, afraid of these words that so well defined him. "And there's no hope?" he asked anxiously. The cat purred against his arm.

"There is always hope." Rondan-El-Therill reached over and laid his right palm on Arhl's wrinkled brow. Arhl felt a weight depart from him and strength, impermanent but restful, infuse him and ease his sorrows. He looked at the Merilan warrior in wonder.

"I can heal," Rondan-El-Therill said, "though there are many pains beyond my power. Would you abandon this quest, Arhl Mogarni, if you knew it would be your last struggle?"

Arhl frowned. "Last?"

"You may never return to Vesuula, or indeed the lands of humanity."

Arhl looked into his eyes but there was neither terror nor sorrow. "I wouldn't," he said.

Rondan-El-Therill said nothing more about it but turned his eyes to the corpse yet again. "And I cannot offer either rest or cure to this one. His fate was written long ago and his pain is that of the world. Even the Gods are helpless in the face of it. Yet his presence offers some hope—"

"What do you mean?"

Rondan-El-Therill turned back to Arhl, reached out and took his hand. He held it between his own hard palms. They were strangely cold. "I—or rather this cat that is no cat—am powerful beyond imagination, yet we cannot touch the thing that created us, for fear that it will destroy both us and the world." For a moment, Arhl closed his eyes, unable to focus for long on the face of this strange man. "Yet fate takes many forms, using as its vessel...*a vast and powerful array of motives and histories.*"

Suddenly the man's voice had changed. No longer deep and commanding, it had become feminine and familiar. The muscled flesh of the hands that held Arhl's was soft now, though still cold. Arhl opened his eyes. He met a dark female gaze.

"Mother?"

She smiled gently. *"You have come far, son. Though there is a greater distance still to go."*

Arhl tried to pull away, but she would not let him.

"What is it this time?" he managed.

"Do one thing for me, Arhl." She looked at the undead creature, lying immobile under the control of its talisman, and the
action forced Arhl to do likewise. *"Take your knife—and cut
into this creature's chest."*

"But it's already dead."

"Do it for me." Her hands released him. *"Not to kill it, for
you are not able to do that. Only to lay its secrets bare. If you
cut where its heart should be, the flesh will give way."*

Why he did so, Arhl had no idea. Was it the habit of obedience, or was it simple necessity? For whatever reason, he
reached for his knife, eased it out of the scabbard on his belt, cut
into Valarl's naked chest. Dry skin, retreating from his blade,
rolled back across the cavity from which Valarl's heart had been
taken.

There, surrounded by desiccated flesh, something metallic
glittered under the cabin's fractured light. It was smaller than his
palm, stony and jagged along its edges, as though broken from
something larger. Yet the design carved in relief upon it was
unmistakable in shape. The air around it seemed to shimmer.

Arhl lifted the object free with his long, trembling fingers.
The corpse shivered as he did so. "Is this it?" he said. It seemed
like an anticlimax.

Then the world shuddered. An intense vibration struck every
part of Arhl's body, a tremor that swept through him and concentrated within his bones. He might have fallen; he couldn't tell
for sure.

*Instead he was floating in an endless space. The ship, the sea
beyond it, distant land, even the firmament that always swirled
above them—all had disappeared. Tharenweyr itself was gone.
Vast emptiness—a vista such as he could never have imagined—stretched out before him, and the incredible distance was
dotted with brilliant shards of light that pinpricked the darkness, many gathered into concentrated masses like huge clouds.
Between them and retreating into impossible distance was more
space, more darkness, more points of light. Millions of points of
light. Billions. Uncountable numbers of them. Arhl hung there,*

knowing this was a dream, but unable to understand what it meant.

After what might have been seconds or days, he became aware of presence, the pressure of something tugging at him, and glanced around, his movement spinning the lights into trails of fire. A gigantic ball, perfectly spherical and bigger than anything he'd ever seen, spun slowly beneath him. It was covered in masses of roiling cloud. Between them, he could see that the surface of the globe was covered in vast seas and landmasses that clung to its contours, disappearing out of sight around the sphere's curve. Was this a world, he wondered? A world like Tharenweyr? Yet how could that be? His world, the only world he'd ever known, was a cocoon, holding the creatures that inhabited it safe within its encompassing firmament. This thing, this impossible object floating in empty space—how could it exist? How could anything live on a world so exposed to emptiness?

Beyond it was a larger concentration of light—not a point of light like all the others that dotted the darkness, but a glow as large as a gold coin that threw an intense luminosity out across the distance between it and the sphere turning at his feet. He knew then that all the points of light were like this one, just further away. It was only distance that made them small. The new, bigger light would, nearer yet, be even more massive than the impossible inside-out world over which he hung. Everywhere, the openness and size of this place he was in was so great as to make thinking of it impossible.

Then he was sweeping past the spherical world, past it and out toward the disk of light beyond. It grew bigger and bigger, until it was no longer a flat circle of light, but a gigantic seething ball of fire, with flames bursting out from its surface like the tentacles of a huge, continually morphing monster.

Overwhelmed, he felt his mind beginning to shut down as the flames swelled and surrounded him completely. Their glow obliterated vision and the dream itself was engulfed.

The ship, the cabin, beyond the windows the sea and the

comforting, closed-in sky of Tharenweyr returned. Arhl stared at the object glowing fiercely in his hand, still burning with alien fire.

Then the fire bled away and the object became dull and life-less once more.

"The quest for the Cerendar is ended," said Rondan-El-Therill. He stood behind Arhl, his voice firm and real. "What did you see?"

"I— I don't know," said Arhl, standing shakily. "Perhaps it was the end."

"The end. Yes, the end. But of what, do you think?"

Arhl shivered, steadying himself against a chair. "What of this?" He held out his hand, the Cerendar nestled in his palm.

Rondan-El-Therill stepped back. "That is not for me to say." Arhl fancied that, for a moment, the Merilan warrior had become transparent, fading like an afterthought in proximity to the Cerendar. No, how could that be? He was still there, though further away now.

"Is it over?"

"For some. For the rest, nothing is resolved."

"Nothing?"

The Merilan warrior nodded in acknowledgment then was gone. Arhl hadn't seen him leave. Thoughtless, the Sohas tribesman-in-exile sank into a chair, his heart pounding, his hand clutching the ancient artifact. Emotion surged between exultation and fear.

It was some time later before he realized that Rondan-El-Therill's cat was lying curled in his lap. And later still before either moved.

xvi.

By the seventh hour *Spirit* was close enough to the Krith shoals to cause attention to be given to subtler maneuvers in its sailing. The ship was slowed and sailors took positions at various points along the deck to relay direct instruction to the man on the tiller.

All around them the gray-green sea was broken and white-flecked and to portside a small island, totally barren, threatened them with its jagged approach. The *Spirit* moved through a narrow passage between this isle and a coral bank, clearing both by some 200 feet and scaring sea birds into a squawking fury. Behind them the *Derargarth* had turned away and was running a parallel course half a mile or so beyond the reef-edge, waiting for them to change direction away from the deadly maze.

The sailor lashed to the bowsprit, fingers clenched about a sounding line, shouted standard clearance. There was another man on the forward mast who did likewise. "If we make it through Krith in a westerly direction there's open water for some twenty-five miles," Arban was saying. Shaan gazed toward a misty landmass to the northeast.

"And then?" Tashnark sat on the deck with his back resting on the bulwark. The only water he could see was a thin smear washing around his feet. That was how he liked it.

"Then we can thread our way between the major islands of Sororon and Sildan—and if it's getting dark, find harbor on Avaletol. Or we can turn south and chance another run."

Tashnark grunted but did not comment. At that moment he was aware of the approaching figure of Arhl, who had just emerged from the cabin. There was a purposeful sureness about his stride and demeanor that made Tashnark curious, as he hadn't seen it before in his friend.

"Lord Saral," Arhl said, bowing his head to Shaan. The Saral-Lord turned without comment, as though expecting this visit. "I have been with Rondan-El-Therill," Arhl went on, "and listened to what he said. Guided by him, I searched Valarl's corpse."

"And did you find what we have been seeking?"

"Yes," he said calmly.

"What's that you say?" Arban's robes rose about him in a flurry as he leapt forward.

Slowly, and without slight to the priest, the pale So-has blacksmith held the object out to Shaan. The Saral took it from his fingers. He studied it, but showed no sign of being affected by it in any way.

"Where was it?" Tashnark got up for a closer look.

"In its heart cavity," Arhl replied.

"The heart-cavity? No wonder we couldn't find it. The cunning devil must have pulled the artifact from Zeth'han's wristlet and thrust it into his chest. I was sure his flesh was uncut."

"So it was, but my knife did the job."

Tashnark frowned, not understanding any of this. It was an unexciting artifact, now that he saw it, not the kind of object that might inspire savagery and flush the Dark Gods out of hiding. Hardly seemed worth the trouble. Little bigger than a Vesuulan gold coin and with much less of an appearance of value, it lay solidly on the Saral's palm without hint of power or ancient significance. Its colors were dull and tarnished, and though the line-work within the design was intricate and fine, its basic element—the gleam with its circle and radiating arms—lacked potency.

What was it supposed to be? Tashnark wondered. It reminded him of a type of sea crab he had once seen off the Erdugal coast.

"Is it the real thing?" he asked.

"It *is* the Cerendar," Halul spoke from beside him. Tashnark looked at her and the inevitable Mallorin coldly. The damned singer had been sneaking about again, like an alley cat on the prowl! "For a time I thought it couldn't be—but it is, and the legend has come to us." She reached out to touch the artifact, but Mallorin stopped her.

"Mistress, no!" Halul frowned at him then let her hand drop.

"It gives off no power-emanation at all," Shaan was saying.

"So it is written." The Sumorle'en, her voice becoming ponderous, sang:

> "Where Power reigns no sign is,
> Where Might exults, no spell can say,

Where Cerendar lies, no Eye may judge."

"It seems like nothing," Arban said.
Shaan made no comment.

xvii.

The *Spirit* pursued its path safely through the treacherous seas, though not without difficulty. Submerged coral, often barely sighted, eccentric currents that would snatch at the ship and pull it toward dangerous shoals, sandbanks oddly raised to scrape at the keel, winds spun into furious eddies by the scattered islands—these things threatened them all the way.

Once they were nearly snared by a drift of thick seaweed. It turned the water around them unctuous and clogged the rudder, necessitating a cold swim for one of the crew. Another time, inadvertently wedged into a narrowing passage between banks, they reefed the sails and poled the ship through to clear water. The swell on occasion drove them against the rock or sand, but no damage was caused to the hull.

The crew became edgy. Hours went by, and dark clouds gathered in the south. Tashnark stood at the stern as they passed the lee side of a rocky spire rising almost unheralded from the surging waters, and searched the misty distance for sign of the enemy ship *Derargarth*. There was nothing except broken sea and the dark patches of island-rock.

Toward the ninth hour he saw something smooth and serpent-like slide in silent undulations through the shallow pools surrounding a small outcrop on their starboard side. It was a sea snake, no doubt, armored in shiny metal-green scales—but its size was staggering. About as thick as his own torso, and, where visible, as long as the ship, it was as monstrous a thing as he'd want to meet. No one else seemed to notice it, so Tashnark kept quiet. But the sight, suggestive as it was, unnerved him; he had heard many ancient tales of ships taken by monstrous creatures from the depths. He'd never seen one before. Why was this here now?

From the Krith reefs they moved into a clear expanse designated Charinon on their maps. A stiff opposing breeze made its crossing a long and tedious one and it was the twelfth hour before they reached the southerly side of the island Sororon. Again they were forced to negotiate a network of dangerous channels. The sky was completely overcast now. Twilight would come quickly and night itself was only a few hours off. The captain was concerned that darkness would catch them still among the reefs, but there was little choice. They could not safely drop anchor where they were—not, at any rate, with a storm threatening to break sometime during the night—and so they went on, determined to reach safe harbor on Avaletol. As it happened, the going was not as difficult as expected. With admirable dexterity the navigator found them a path and the channels proved less indistinct than expected. Even the swell seemed cooperative now.

As darkness grew like moss in the air, Tashnark squinted through it at Sororon. The huge island was some thirty miles wide here at its southern end. It curved away from them behind smaller, more fractured islets that stood like sentinels or the statues of ancient, inhuman gods. Sororon's cliffs were themselves an awesome sight, even from Tashnark's position some three miles from their base. White foam and heaving swells marked their entire length, and above them, the land was bristly with gorse and spindled trees as it rose high and then fell away out of sight. At this distance and in the closing gloom Tashnark could see little detail, but those cliffs and the hill-summit behind them seemed to him infertile and wild.

Clouds rushed northward over the top of the island. Wind blew the shrouds suddenly and they flapped until the crew righted them. The *Spirit* rocked violently and Tashnark felt spray soak his back. Impressions came and went, but his mind was suddenly elsewhere. The thickened mist turned reddish and the sea solidified into something more substantial.

It was not ground.

Two men stood off to his left: he knew them.

Hanin and Cormidthal.

And to his right, facing each other, monstrous creatures so huge he thought they must sink beneath the waves.

<No, Bellarroth,> he said, *<I won't give way to you. I'll stay who I am.>*

<Who are you?>

<Me?>

<Yes, you.>

He couldn't speak. A weight like an anchor stone dragged on his mind.

<Well, who are you?>

<I...I...am...you.>

The weight disappeared.

Bellarroth looked up again, his mind clearing of the alien voice.

He stepped toward Hanin.

"Why is he here?" he said, indicating Cormidthal.

The stranger raised his hand, forcing Hanin to remain silent. Then he answered the question himself. "To free you both. I have already manipulated Lucishnor's spirit and the manipulation has brought the Beasts into conflict. And I have formed this image of myself so that we can speak together, face-to-face."

"Image?"

"Image, yes. A corporeal projection. I am bound by the curse to Lucishnor's burning flesh and cannot leave it—but Power can do many things. Where the reality of freedom is denied, still there may be illusion."

"What Power, Cormidthal?" Hanin said. "Your Power did not always extend this far."

"The power of the Monster, Hanin—what else? The Kharathahul are pure spirit-energy and in that fact is the key to everything. Fate has bound us—but perhaps the bonds can be used to thwart fate. Would Junsar resent such arrogance, do you think?"

"You babble empty rhetoric."

"As foolish as ever, Hanin. I remember you were always the least imaginative of my Circle."

"Yet you would pursue folly till you dropped, in hope of gain."

"It's a wizardly trait—the pursuit of folly."

"And you've squeezed truth from that saying many times."

Cormidthal's face was a calm mask that barely hid his annoyance. Bellarroth could see he didn't wish to follow that route yet.

"Hanin, listen to me," Cormidthal said. "I've spent my time on Lucishnor researching the ways of Deep Power within the Monster and it has brought me this far toward escape. This body is an artifice—little more than that—yet it acts and provokes reaction. It may not be true, but what is truth to someone like me. The reality is that I am forever on Lucishnor, burning in its flames, and I cannot care for truth that denies me my life in the first world."

He paused. Bellarroth could see the Monsters standing impassively. What are they waiting for? he thought uneasily.

"With the Power of our two monsters joined, Hanin, I shall do more than create an artifice here. I shall take the illusion to Tharenweyr itself."

The ground seemed to heave suddenly, and Bellarroth stumbled. Like running dye, the images around him bled into a thick, dark mist.

Then there was water surrounding him.

* * * * * * *

He was on a ship.

Tashnark shook his head and tried to think—before the world became dominant and blanched the dream in his memory. It was important that he remember.

"Sir, you're in the way!"

When he turned, Tashnark was surprised to find that the

crew was in turmoil.

"What's up?" he asked the sailor, but the man did not have to answer. The air mass to the south of them, where the Sildan islands stood like sea-chained giants, was dark with mists and surging clouds. Pillars of rain miles high caught the last residue of light and formed massive moving curtains. The water boiled and foamed, flung into waves of spray or mountains as tall as the *Spirit*'s masts. While he watched, Tashnark saw the storm expand eastward toward the Charinon Sea, and the islands on its edge were lashed into obscurity by the furious winds. Avaletol itself, a dark line stretching all the way along the western horizon, was much closer now and could have provided harbor against this storm. But there would be no reaching it tonight. The storm was bearing north and by the look of its winds nothing would be able to force passage against it. Avaletol, like a huge vanquished galley, sank into a shroud of black weather and disappeared from sight.

Tashnark found Shaan and the others huddled in conference at the stern. They looked puzzled, worried—Captain Werrinlit, who might be expected to understand best the consequences of this sea-tempest, was agitated to the point of hysteria. Tashnark heard him cry: "Order what you will, the task's mine. I say to you we'll be swamped in an instant, broke in pieces. Already the foresail's torn.... No, my lords, Avaletol is hopeless. I'm for turning the ship north. Our only chance is to run with the storm. I've seen 'em less fierce than this cause ships to flounder, and there's no other course. None. North it is, if you leave me breath to give orders."

He turned on his heel and stalked off down the ladder from the poop deck, bumping against Tashnark as he went. His eyes glanced at Tashnark insanely. "You'll needs man the tiller with Engil," he shouted, "and keep her steady." Then he was gone down the ship's waist.

Tashnark raised his eyebrows. "Man the tiller?" he said, approaching the others. A series of choppy waves smashed against the hull and he staggered. In that instant the wind increased. There was a splintery, groaning crack and a voice called "The arm! It's gone." The ship tilted violently and ocean washed the deck.

"Where in Hell did these winds come from?" he shouted to Remis who had grabbed him to avoid being tossed over the edge. A jagged bolt of lightning split the sky above them and the air cracked with thunder. For a moment their senses were stunned.

"Been unsettled for days!" Remis replied at last.

"Unsettled?" Tashnark shook his head. "Insane is more like it!"

Wind howled and the sea appeared to jump skyward in increasingly successful attempts to take flight. There was chaos on deck. Men rushed about through drenching walls of mingled rain and sea, grappling at tackle, lashing down and reefing in the sails, shouting inaudible comments. At times the deck was so awash that Tashnark could not believe the crew remained safe on deck after the wave had passed; but if any were drowned, nothing was said then, and later, they were not in a position to know.

A huge trough sucked the *Spirit* into its depths and hung a mountain of water above them. It looked like they'd be swamped. But the crew managed to crest the waves without causing the ship to broach to, and they raced on northward then, praying they would miss Sororon, which so lately Tashnark had watched on their starboard side as it slid by them. Now, smothered in darkness and rain, they couldn't see its rugged cliffs, nor, under the gale, hear the sound of the sea pounding on its rocks.

Tashnark joined Bresal-Engil on the tiller and together, guided by a crewman who watched each wave to give due warning, they fought to keep the *Spirit* straight. The captain had stripped the ship down to bare poles and she scudded before the wind, so that any mistake on their part could easily result in a fatal roll that would sink the ship and drown them. Tashnark was forced to exert all his strength, guided by Engil's experience as helmsman, yet he found time to wonder idly what the

Saral and his Deep-Power mates were doing while *he* broke his back in struggle for their lives. Conjuring their magics against nature's huger will? It seemed pointless.

Once again, his mind took a moment to worry about Remis's safety.

Then the sky flared into cracks of brilliance and thunder screamed as though the air was in pain from it. Water lashed across Tashnark's shoulders and poured in like a flood through the tiller-port, almost washing away his grip. A crewman, assigned to bale shipped water, began to work feverishly with his bucket.

How will it end? Tashnark wondered. Apparently they had missed Sororon, but if the storm held up they would eventually reach the huge reefs that spanned the gap between that island and Avaletol at its northern end. No amount of divine supplication would save them from being torn apart on the sunken snares there.

"Be lettin' up," whispered Engil suddenly.

"What?" Tashnark turned his attention to the wind above them and the pressure the sea was exerting on the tiller. "You sure?"

"Aye."

"So quickly?"

Engil nodded, his hair plastered on his face in ratty strips. He looked balder and older than ever. "It happens."

Soon it was obvious enough that the experienced mariner was right. Even Tashnark's untrained senses could read the storm's weakening. Still the ship pitched and rolled, still water and wind in a chaotic mixture tumbled about them, and drove them on; but it was lessened. Either the storm was dying, or they were reaching its edges.

Tashnark abandoned the tiller to Engil and climbed back onto the deck. Wind nearly tossed him from his feet. He steadied himself on the slippery boards and then glanced ahead into the dark waves of driving rain.

"Damn the Gods!"

Drenched cliffs squirming with a thousand cataracts loomed out of the mists and waves on the starboard side, barely two dozen ship-lengths away. The *Spirit*, slowed now but still helpless in the swell, rushed past them with hardly a glance, though many of her crew stood wide-eyed with horror, staring at the obscure rocks and fierce eddies. Werrinlit came rushing onto the poop-deck, frantic with haste. He leaned over the edge of the tiller-hole without speaking to Tashnark. "Engil, ease her to portside," he shouted. "There's rocks, damn it, and Sororon's cliffs!"

"Sororon!" Tashnark repeated to himself.

"Yes. Sororon." Werrinlit sidled up to him and together they stared into the obscurity and the turmoil. Lightning sparked the clouds into brief fire and for a moment, despite rain and the gloom of night, they could see Sororon so near it made them gasp. The cliffs were falling away into lower stretches of broken coastline, but returned in a huge, bay-like arc. The arc bent ahead of them, still several miles away, and formed a rocky, jagged promontory. In that instant of clarity it was obvious that the *Spirit* would never be able to swing wide of the bay's reaches.

Werrinlit gripped Tashnark's arm as darkness and rain collapsed over them like some monstrous judgement. Neither spoke. The moments flew by, but they didn't move. Both were staring into the gloom. After a moment more, Tashnark heard the captain mutter "Spark, damn you, spark!"

Obediently, lightning shattered the darkness. This time they saw the arms of the bay clearly. The island, stretching into rain-clouded gloom, seemed all around them.

Werrinlit plunged away from Tashnark as though pursued by demons, and began issuing orders to his frightened men. Like a drowned toad, Arban scrambled across the deck, questioning the captain's fury. Shaan and the others also emerged from the poop-cabin, but there seemed little purpose in their arrival. Spontaneously, Tashnark had felt a surge of hope; but what hope was there? Captain Werrinlit was preparing them all to abandon ship, and even Shaan, Saral-Lord kin of Raashyr Shaa, could not will away Sororon's storm-shrouded bulk.

Light raced in freakish patterns across the low-slung clouds, dancing with the winds. Fleetingly Tashnark saw Sororon appear as an irregular, patchwork darkness—close now, too close. The ship was turning, seeking a tangential course away from the island, but broken white in the sea suggested coastal shelves and outcrops of rock. There was little chance—none, he thought—of missing them. A strange annoyance made him frown. He felt no fear. It was frustration that filled his heart and mind, frustration that caused him to grip the handle of his scabbarded sword—he'd taken to wearing it once the enemy ship was sighted—and curse Junsar for the fate that seemed inevitable. This end he could not govern, could not deny. And Worjaren Rehemon, safe on the *Gerargarth* somewhere beyond the Archithin Reefs, would survive them, never knowing that Tashnark had desired to face him and accuse him of...of what? He didn't know. Worst of all, Tashnark would die never knowing, and with the question of Bellarroth and what he was unresolved.

Then suddenly the activity across the deck took on a more purposeful appearance. Shaan, who had been gazing intently into the gloom as though it didn't hinder his sight at all, turned to Arban, spoke some quick instruction then bounded toward the companionway. The Power-workers—Remis, Raaneon and another whose name he'd forgotten, one of the crew—huddled together in an action distinctly reminiscent of spell-preparation. Perhaps they were going to turn the ship? Or still the storm? *Could they do either of those things?* Tashnark wondered.

"Quickly!" Shaan leaned close to his ear in order to be heard without mistake over the wind's continued roaring. His breath smelt of aniseed. "Take the tiller and see if you can turn *Spirit* starboard!"

"Starboard? Toward the island?"

"I have read the water channels and there's beaching there we might survive. Go quickly."

Hope, after all! Tashnark threw himself back against the wind and leapt into the helmsman's hole. "Starboard!" he yelled to Engil, who, blinded to sight of the island and its rocks, did not question this instruction. While he tugged the sea-slimed wood Tashnark thought of his own prompt obedience to the Saral's word. With a little more experience, he could become a worthy disciple.

A grinding crunch sounded from below them and the ship lurched sideward. *The reef*, Tashnark thought, subduing a stab of terror, but there in the Hole he could see nothing. Seawater poured over him and the tiller pulled against his grip. He struggled to keep it steady, the effort sending his mind blank. Shaan appeared above them gesturing for more turn, and Tashnark and the sailor fought to oblige him.

For a time—mere heartbeats in length but vast in its quiet anticipation—they waited for the onset of disaster.

Then the ship shuddered under their feet. The tiller was wrenched out of their hands, Tashnark receiving a painful blow to his side. Scrambling madly for a grip, they sought to draw it straight, but the rudder had jumped its gudgeons and was lost in the surging waters that swept over them. Tashnark was thrown down, coughing the sea from his mouth, grasped at Engil but could not reach him. He felt something heavy fall across his legs. The ship was rocked sharply. Harsh, wood-tear cries drowned out the sound of the wind and water for a moment, and the grinding lingered as the keel was scraped along the island's offshore rocks. Tashnark tried to regain his feet but the deck was at too great an angle and movement threw him sliding into more water and more painful blows. He cursed, shaking wood splinters away. Then the ship jolted violently, flinging him forward again. The stern seemed to lift, hang still for an instant, and with a final roar settle into shuddering stillness.

Tashnark waited for more blows, but none came. Movement, except for a slight shifting caused by waves breaking on the hull, had ceased.

For good or for ill, they were beached.

And, at least for the time being, alive.

CHAPTER SEVEN
CORMIDTHAL

i.

From the forecastle of the *Gerargarth* Lord Worjaren Rehemon watched the tempest he had helped spawn. It both pleased and annoyed him. The fury of it was a spectacular expression of his own agony and frustration—but mere fury was surely a sign of impotence and a thing he had always shunned. It pleased him that his command of the Deep Power, reacting with the stresses already alive in the air above the Archithlin Isles, should cause such extensive fury. But he knew he'd lost of control of it. It was all he could do to prevent the storm from ensnaring his own vessel; reason suggested that his enemies, caught in its midst, must surely have perished. And that fact, despite everything, was to be regretted.

Regretted? Yes, for they had the Cerendar, upon which his own salvation rested. And if now they were drowned in the sea, then the artifact itself must have sunk with them. He would find it eventually, no mistaking that—water was no deterrent to a man who could not die and whose body was far away and wracked by endless fire-pain. No. The sea would not hold the Cerendar from him forever. Stuck in a crevasse, eaten by a sea monster, buried in slime—whatever tricks fate might play to thwart him of his prize, he would find it nevertheless. But it would take time. And though he had time in abundance, Time to him was a torment and a judgement. Time was what he sought to deny. It was to be regretted if now he must take his search to the ocean-floor.

But he hoped the need would not arise. If all were as it should be, then his enemies would prove more cunning than to be beaten by an ill-tempered sea. His enemies would survive the storm, if his intuitions were true—survive to give him the key to freedom.

"Lord," whispered a lackey deferentially, cringing up to him like a whipped dog. Lord Worjaren scowled, hating the fool. All his chosen acolytes gone, butchered, he was left with fools and was forced to deal with them as best he could.

"What is it?"

"Lord, the Spell-Watch reports that the caravel has run aground on that isle there." The man pointed ahead and off port-side. "In a bay with a coral mouth."

"Ah. Then they have not drowned themselves."

"No, sire. It was a good beach-grounding. But they won't be sailing off in a hurry."

Worjaren Rehemon smiled inwardly, though his stony features remained rigid. He had not asked more of his adversaries than they could deliver. He flicked his forearm toward the bridge. "The storm abates. We'll go in after them, on oar if need be. Tell the captain."

"Aye, sire." The man scampered away.

The evening's darkness closed in around Worjaren. He spoke a sentence formed of ancient words and for a moment was still. He remembered his task, he remembered his need, he remembered the failures that had plagued him. Again he felt his acolyte, Aridor, die under the blade whose wielder had sparked memories he abhorred. He remembered the hatred of his contemporary, Hanin, stone-worker of Su-Laseth in Mikhalin, and recalled the anger he had felt when Hanin, and his spawn Bellarroth, had defied him on the monster Tammenallor. He looked out into the darkness.

"So you would fight me yet," he said in a low voice. "You have found a way back into reality and wish to challenge me.

Let's see who is stronger. We are both aliens here, Bellarroth Hanin-son."

He took an intricate metal shape from his robes and held it before his lips.

"*Skaaroth-helis bar hend-so'thaz.*" He spoke the words like the curse they were. "*Com-zarb arc'hin ord poran-harnis. Harnis, harnis.*"

In the blackened sky above, the clouds began to gather and swirl—and a gateway opened for Terror.

ii.

Tashnark crawled up from the corner of the tiller-hole and helped Engil onto the deck. The helmsman seemed to have sprained his ankle and was in considerable pain. "It's not perfect," Engil muttered in reply to Tashnark's complaints, "but it's better'n drownin'."

The *Spirit*'s deck was listing slightly but had somehow managed to settle in an upright position that allowed walking on its planks. There were crewmen everywhere, seeking friends, harnessing equipment, thanking whatever deity they choose to give credit to—doing the things sailors did after a miraculous escape from death. Tashnark noticed several lamps being lit, flaring awkwardly into hazy life. Of the storm there was barely a sign. Wind still scurried across the decks and waves pounded on the hull, but neither were particularly intimidating compared to the giants that had driven them ashore only moments earlier. The sea was almost calm. The storm itself had swept on and could be seen far across the island, visible as a spectral light that skirted along the bottom of the clouds. Above the ship there was even sign of clear sky; it was lighter now, the darkness becoming normal twilight.

Apparently Shaan's tactic had worked. Though the keel of the ship was irreparably torn, he had beached them on a gravel spit and the water that churned around the ship's hull appeared to be little more than shoulder-deep. On either side and before them a sandy crescent shed pale light under the gloom, defined by the white-foam crests of a shore-break. Beyond these, stunted dune vegetation was visible as dark markings on the sand. Distant mountains were silhouetted when lightning yellowed the sky. Tashnark wondered how pleasant a place this island would prove to be.

Engil seemed to read his mind. "Old volcanic isle, this. Used to be mines on the eastern shore—but not now, I reckon."

"Anyone live here?"

"Fishermen perhaps. Us for the duration."

Tashnark helped the crippled seaman down along the main deck and handed him over to the ship's tender-of-bruised-flesh—a thin, nervous woman with bulging eyes that seemed permanently astonished. Then he sought out the others. They were gathered at the prow, sheltered from the weather by the raised bulwarks that supported the bowsprit. They were obviously exhausted. Tashnark wondered what they'd been up to. "Well, that was fun, wasn't it," he commented lightly.

"Fun?" Arban pushed himself to his feet. "*You* may have had fun, but *we* have struggled against well-nigh inevitable death."

"Have *we*?" Tashnark parodied the priest's scowling intensity. "Well, these bruises on my ass aren't altogether the result of sitting on it."

Was that a repressed smile on Remis' face?

Arban huffed, furrowed his eyebrows and headed off along the deck. He muttered something about finding Lord Shaan. Tashnark watched him cynically and was about to say something when he felt the air carry a new disturbance to him. The sudden awareness was heavy, like a huge pressure pushing down on him, and he staggered under the assault. Noise screamed in his ears. *Harnis. Harnis.*

Then there was pain stabbing through his muscles like a fine needle—though it was not pain, but an empathic awareness of another's pain.

Serpent-trees sway against a red sky. A monstrous being

casts a burning shadow over his face.

"Who is this man, Hanin?"

"One who can free you."

<Beware, Bellarroth. Beware.>

"Tashnark? Are you all right?" Remis grabbed his arm.

"I felt something. It was...." He was about to say that it was Worjaren Rehemon and that he'd felt the sorcerer's magic surge around them. But he was suddenly conscious that the others hadn't felt it, and he clamped his mouth shut.

"What?"

"I don't know," he said. To give some logic to his outburst, he added, "The tiller broke. Fell across my leg."

Remis frowned. "Then have it seen to. You'll be needed now, Tashnark. Don't lame yourself."

Tashnark nodded dumbly, his mind elsewhere. How he knew, he couldn't guess, but he was sure the sorcerer was nearby and calling on the Deep Powers. But what sort of magic was it that *he* sensed yet was hidden from the likes of Arban. Perhaps even from the Saral-Lord. Was it Worjaren Rehemon's presence that activated the dream inside him?

The crew began conveying stores to the beach. Shaan turned up, looking worn and troubled—but he said nothing, though Remis tried to give him the opportunity to confide in her. It disappointed her that he was so reticent, that he encouraged aloofness in himself by withholding his confidence. Perhaps, she reasoned, he felt there was no time to be wasted in self-revelation.

Tashnark went to help the crew as they unloaded the hold. All the while he kept alert for sign of trouble. When he could, he let his eyes scan the sea and probe into the darkness within Sororon—but there was nothing to feed his fear. He listened to the voices of the crew, caught above the wind and the rasping waters, listened to the seabirds that flapped overhead, calling to each other or to the night. He could sometimes hear squawks echoing out of the island's scrub and he wondered what beasts were there. But nothing alerted him to danger. Not yet.

When danger came, he was lowering a keg of fresh water over the side of the ship, helping a seaman balance it in a small canoe they were using to carry the stores to the beach. A rope was tied to the keg and Tashnark gripped it hard, edging it seaward. At first he didn't notice the anxiety swelling in him; his muscles strained to keep the load steady. But when the sailor failed to guide the keg properly and Tashnark heard it splashed by waves, he growled a curse and looked down. What he saw was the fear on the man's face.

Tashnark tossed the ropes aside and abandoned the keg to the sea. He glanced around. In that moment, as his eyes went to the sky, he heard a high, keening roar that caused the hackles to rise on the back of his neck. At the same time he saw that the darkness above was swirling like a great vortex and that somewhere within it wind, mist and fire had conspired to take on a hideous shape. A bat-like monstrosity swooped into existence and spat fire across the swaying mast-tops. While Tashnark followed its movement, the thing dropped seaward, turning the water to steam where it touched. A huge, knotted claw reached out to rake at a sailor standing in its shadow, and it tore the wretch into offal that stained the sea with spreading darkness. Then the demon rose again and turned back toward the *Spirit*, twisting tentacles erupting from its underbelly like a monstrous octopus trying to escape from its gut.

It was no simple monster, Tashnark could see that at once. There was a grim intensity in its eyes that chilled him beyond anything he had ever known. This was not merely Death, it was Distortion—the sort of evil that Raaneon had tried to make him understand. He could feel it now, and with understanding came emotion. He watched it in terror and fascination both.

The demon seemed so solid that its flight was a preposterously unnatural thing, yet its outline waxed and waned in the darkness as though the night was a mist that thickened and thinned alternately, obscuring the demon's shape, then clearing away in a moment. Three beaked heads on stalk-like necks twisted about with a gracelessness that didn't hinder its movements at all—and a fourth head, he saw, sprouted from its tail. Or was it another neck and the head its front? Certainly this one was different from the others. Though he only had a moment to absorb details, he thought the head was human—a man's twisted face, scowling impossibly, continually turning to fix the world with its glance.

A claw rasped along the bulwark toward the prow, gripped, then pushed the monster into air again. Where it touched, a smoldering stain was branded into the wood.

The thing moved fast. Its flailing tentacles grabbed another sailor, wrenched him from the deck, and and tossed his body into the sea. Then it was gone again, caught up in darkness.

The sky flared red.

For a moment Tashnark saw flames spreading out from the demon, taking on the shape of a larger Beast. The flames rushed together.

Lucishnor.

The word made him stagger. *Spirit* tilted.

Thrown off-balance, Tashnark jerked from the dream almost as it was forming. He grabbed at the bulwark with one hand, to steady himself. With his other hand he drew out his sword. The hilt had become a squirming mass of serpents.

<*"This is unfair. I have no choice."*>

<*There can only be choice when time is free. Until then, you are as fate has made you.*>

Tashnark forced the voice into silence. The demon hovered above the deck, holding a human torso as though for their inspection.

One of the sailors leapt at the demon, swearing and wielding a grapple-pike. He pushed restraining hands aside, scrambled close, and thrust the pike's metal tip into the monster's flesh. The crude weapon entered the creature's dark skin, hung there for a moment while the man screamed in pain, then fell with a clang to the deck. The demon seemed untouched. It slashed silently at the sailor who had attacked it and the man was swept overboard wreathed in flame.

With that, Tashnark drew back. Perhaps, in this case, it would be prudent to moderate action with caution. A creature impervious to a pike thrust through its gut was unlikely to worry about swords.

<*It is indifferent to all physical attacks.*> The voice inside his head came as no surprise. <*It may be wounded by magic, but vanquished only by the spirit.*>

<*"Who are you?"*>

<*A friend.*>

<*"A friend? Really? Well, I interact best with friends over a beer. You don't have a bottle on you, by any chance? I could use a drop or two right now."*>

And then the demon spoke—and other voices were forgotten.

Ugly, ill-sounding syllables dripped like slime from its mouth—a low gargle of sound that swelled and faded like the swaying of the ocean about them. Tashnark might have assumed these to be some kind of animal growl, except that they seemed so coherent, and at times formed words he could recognize.

Then its heads moved backwards and forwards, as though unsure where power and influence was situated, and said in an unnerving multiple voice: "Cerendar. Cerendar. Give to me, or you will be torn and ended."

For a moment after the words faded, no one moved or spoke. There was an unreality to the situation that defied action. Wind drove darkness about the creature and obscured it.

Shaan walked slowly forward, halting several paces from where the demon dripped blood and flame onto the deck. His unyielding stature thrilled even Tashnark, a strength and determination that showed in his posture, the set of his eyes, the motion of his arms. He drew his sword and it sparked a reflection of light as though catching fire hidden in the sky. "Understand, creature, that I am Shaan, Saral-Lord and Seed of the Raashyr, and it is I who hold the artifact you seek—not these others. Know also that your master shall not have it of me, and you I command to return to the pits of Hell."

The demon did not move, but began a muttering chant. "Hell," it sang, "Hell. It is not my home. Other...I am Other. Made of fire, but not fire of Hell's furnace." It snapped at Shaan with one of its beaked heads. Remis shouted a warning, but Shaan raised his sword and something in the blade kept the creature back. "Your swords do not bite," the demon howled, "not bite me."

"No sword forged of mortal steel perhaps." Shaan's voice had an edge, elusive, that suggested he was working some power to hold the creature at bay. "This weapon is older even than your master and has been touched by Raashyr-fire."

"And this," came another voice, typically melodramatic, "this blade carries a truth you might not find harmless, demon. Dare you risk your existence against its edge?" Rondan-El-Therill stood firmly across from Shaan, impressive in his glinting mail, which caught the fire of the demon and transformed it into beauty.

Again the demon began singing, but this time the words remained barely comprehensible. They were obscene, corrupt, and gave out an aura of meaning like a stench. The creature rose higher into the air, slowly—then with a burst of speed it circled about the ship, sending everyone scrambling for cover. One figure remained still, and, despite his own selfish fears, Tashnark spared it a moment of concern. The priest Arban.

He was spell casting. Eyes turned skyward, arms weaving patterns in the air, lips forming the esoteric sentences that raised and defined the Deep Power he was drawing upon, he stood for a moment isolated on the deck, and his foolish vulnerability made Tashnark stiffen. Perhaps Arban had fought demons with his magic before. Perhaps he had subdued them. But, as Tashnark knew, this one was no ordinary demon, and Arban's spells could only annoy it.

Raaneon had also seen what Arban was doing, and he was closer than Tashnark. He leapt to the priest's side and tried to drag him away. The priest dismissed him with a magical stroke and Raaneon crashed across the deck.

And the demon, made conscious of this simple magic worked against it, appeared over the poop-deck overhang, running fire along its edges. Shaan rushed to intercept its movement, but he was too late. Arban was lifted away, dripping a trail of sparks like glowing ash from a fire-brand, hit the bulwark with a loud thud and collapsed across the planks. Half his body was torn away.

Rage swelled in Tashnark's chest. His mind screamed its fury and despair. *Arban!* he cried, *Arban, you fool!*

<*The priest is gone.*>

<"It's not right! He wasn't part of this.">

<*All are part of this—and at the worst, all will die. This world was not made for justice.*>

<"No? What was it made for then?">

The ship disintegrated around him as his emotions tore at its stability with more anger than the storm they had lately escaped. <"What do you want from me?">

Fire rose like a forest of serpents.

<"I'm sick of all this damn chaos—all the dreams and mind-shit. Tell me what the hell you want or leave me alone!">

Time and space fractured.

* * * * * * *

Once again the perceptions were Bellarroth's.

Cormidthal's eyes closed briefly as though they sought to block out some pain. Then they opened, fiery with impatience.

"Your Power and your insight, Hanin—that is what I want of you. I am seeking for the Cerendar in Tharenweyr, but it eludes me and your eyes could often see in the profoundest darkness. I need you, I know that."

"You need me?"

"Haven't you worked it out? The Kharathahul Monsters are the broken parts of Power, the Deep Power drawn by our own Spirits externalized into gaolers. If we control that Power, perhaps this illusion can find the Cerendar in Tharenweyr and we can revoke the curse—even turn it to our original purpose."

"Revoke it?"

"The Cerendar bound us to this Fate; the Cerendar might unbind us. And perhaps unwittingly, by focusing our inner strength into these creatures of the spirit, the Cerendar has given us the means to conquest. I am part way there. Give me the Cerendar and my new Power will subdue it forever."

"Madness!"

Cormidthal's eyes flared and he towered up in fury. "Don't always snap at my heels like a dog, Hanin! I'm not asking for friendship or admiration. Surely you want freedom?"

"What I want is perhaps not possible. But the dilemma you have created is something I can't ignore. Long ago you sought ultimate power to pursue your career of conquest. The search ended in disaster. Now, you suggest that we continue the folly. I say, no. Rather exile than a continuation of your sin."

"This time the aim is freedom, Hanin—not slavery."

"It never ends so simply."

An intimation of something sinister moved in Bellarroth. Cormidthal pointed at Hanin. "You followed me then, Hanin, not through love, but because of my strength—"

"I honored your greatness once."

"You submitted to my power. I am more powerful now— condemned and rewarded by the Cerendar for my presumption. I don't intend to stop just because you have no vision."

As he spoke, Bellarroth acted. He leapt forward, swinging his blade sideways across Cormidthal's arms. The sword should have sheared through flesh and bone, but instead his muscles baulked, tightening stiffly as though turned to steel.

But it was his own teacher who had stopped his lunge.

Cormidthal smiled. "You've grown powerful, Hanin."

Hanin's colorless eyes turned to Bellarroth. "Save action for the time of action." When he gestured, the grip on Bellarroth disappeared.

Save action for the time of action? Bellarroth thought. What was the old man up to?

Hanin turned back to Cormidthal. "Perhaps you can do all that you say, Cormidthal. Perhaps you can force my loyalty.

There is always doubt in everything, and even the inevitable is a bond-slave to chance. The Cerendar is lost and must stay lost. I will never help you to seek it out again, and again be accessory to Apocalypse."

Something became entangled in Hanin's words, other dim thoughts that were heavy and alien in Bellarroth's mind. Neither Hanin nor Cormidthal seemed to notice them.

"All my time on this Monster I have feared that your mischief was not ended. I'd hoped, of course, hoped to make what stumbling block I could, to hinder your way...."

The argument continued, but Bellarroth had ceased to listen. Echoes began to reverberate in his head, growing into the familiar voice of Tammenallor.

<The time of the first ending is here, Bellarroth. I'm sending you to another place.>

<"You're sending me? What do you mean?">

<It has all been planned. You will grow there and the curse will be resolved. You'll ride the spatial currents and once again return. But in the meantime you must be alert.>

<"Who am I, Tammenallor?">

<You are yourself—and you are nothing. A dream of hope.>

<"So what am I supposed to do? How can I act on statements as meaningless as that?">

<Wait. And look for me. Until time is freed the Cerendar holds us all to its purpose.>

<"Can't you explain it? Can't you speak clearly for once?">

<Soon you will return here—at the right time, when the fragments converge. That which was broken will re-unite, though time and space can never be the same again.>

<"And it'll all be well?">

<All will be as it must be.>

<"Darkness will lose?">

<There is no loss. The universe allows nothing to be lost.>
The echo died.

Bellarroth looked around at Tammenallor, monstrous on Its throne, and Lucishnor flaming beside It. As he did, a tremor *shook the ground. The Tammenallor-Monster was rising to Its full height, torn wings spread into a black aurora. The air thickened.*

"Now's the time, Hanin," Cormidthal said.

"Too late, Cormidthal. You're too late. I'm already dead, and even you can't kill a dead man."

A hand of magical force reached out at the old man. His shape seemed to flicker. The ground heaved and split. Gray-blue light became incandescent with spinning green trails of brilliance, all emanating from Tammenallor.

Hanin was gone.

"What's this?" Cormidthal seemed to notice Tammenallor's movement for the first time.

The Monster was glowing, changing. For a moment Bellarroth thought he saw it as a lithe, cat-like shadow.

Then the power of the transformation flung him away. He blinked.

* * * * * * *

"Eresteyin, my wife. It's over."

"The child, Sevthen? What has become of the child?"

"It lives. It lives."

"I thought I felt it die."

"Against all expectation, it lives. A boy. The midwife pronounced it stillborn—but despite all, it lives. Can you hear it crying, Eresteyin?"

"Yes, I hear him."

"He must have a name."

"Tashnark. Call him Tashnark."

"Tashnark—'unexpected visitor'. It's a worthy name. Tashnark it shall be."

A cry burst from Tashnark's lungs, as the strange memory fractured into new forms. He staggered, almost collapsing.

What was going on? Something seemed to have reached culmination, a point of convergence and incipient action, and tension was alive through every part of him. He felt his sword-hilt. *Serpents!*

Tashnark tried to think, tried to gather images and information into some kind of coherent knowledge. But his raging emotions kept shredding the thoughts into nonsense. Then he saw Arban's body, the demon and the other struggling figures. His emotions focused into rage. He moved forward.

"No, Tashnark. Don't be stupid!"

He might have pushed this person he barely knew aside, but another emotion suddenly diluted the rage. Instead he looked at the one who had come between him and the demon. He looked at her and he knew her.

"You can't hurt it," Remis said. "You have nothing but anger and anger has no edge against a demon, not one like that. It was spawned in fury. It *feeds* on it."

Tashnark knew she was right. His power had not been made to fight this monster—but to turn on another.

Another—far away, outside what he knew was real. Waiting for confrontation.

Time and space bending upon themselves.

He looked past Remis to where Shaan and Rondan-El-Therill dodged the creature's sweeping claws and spears of flame, and sought to thrust their weapons' blades into some vital nexus of its monstrous life. Who else was there? A lithe figure moved about smoothly, in its hands a black-bladed axe. Was this what Halul had been waiting for? Tashnark frowned at the odd thought.

"It's not susceptible to ordinary force, Tashnark. Don't let useless anger destroy you."

He looked into Remis' eyes, thinking: *Why is she doing this? Where is her fury, her indignation?* She had been closer to the slain priest, her heart had grown soft over Shaan, fighting near to death even now. Why wasn't she urging Tashnark to join the slaughter? How was she so self-controlled? Could she stand back and do nothing?

"Arban died—" he whispered.

"And others, too. It's wrong. It's terrible. But we need you, Tashnark. *I* need you. Help me get to the other ship. Hope of stopping this lies there, I'm sure of it!"

Other ship?

He glanced off the *Spirit*'s portside, out across the dark sea. Silhouetted against the lighter sky was a large galley, lights in its cabins and on its masts reflected hazily over the fracturing ocean-surface. Oars sprayed out into the water like fins and forced the ship on as it cleared the reefs there. Tashnark growled in his throat. *Cormidthal*!

<*Bellarroth! Now is the time.*>

<*"I'm not Bellarroth. Stop talking to me as though I am!"*>

He sensed anger.

<*Bellarroth or Tashnark! Why do you quibble over names when the time of destined purpose has come? Your friends will die, the world will end, unless you face him now.*>

<*"How can I face him? He's too powerful."*>

<*Victory is not your concern.*>

Tashnark's hand went to his sword-hilt. The entwined metal serpents shifted under his fingers and he cried out as the asps entered his hand and tangled with his sinews. No escape from this fate.

<*"It's not fair. I haven't been given a choice."*>

<*Every path has been chosen. Nothing happens that wasn't willed.*>

<*"But whose will?"*>

<*Your own, of course.*>

Frustration boiled through his body—painful, aching. Then as suddenly it drained away and into the empty spaces it left behind came a sense of vast, incomprehensible necessity.

<*"How can I face him alone?"*> he groaned.

<*Who said you'd be alone?*>

Damn it! Tashnark calculated quickly. The *Gerargarth* was about a mile or so distant and coming steadily closer. It had to anchor far from them or break its keel on the rocky beach. Its deeper draught would keep it away.

Behind barely formed plans the distorted crowing of the demon mingled with the grunts and cries of its attackers, and glancingly Tashnark appraised the battle. He knew that, like Cormidthal, this demon could not be killed. It too was an illusion, a corporeal projection sent from the far side of reality.

Somehow, it was up to him. That was the way everything pointed, that was what the voice suggested. Up to him. He had to do what was necessary and what had been planned for him to do since the days of the Great War. But who had done the planning? It didn't matter. Quickly he retreated to the edge of the ship, intending to slip down into the canoe they'd been using to ferry stores to the beach. But he'd forgotten Remis. She grabbed his arm as he climbed over the bulwark. "What are you doing?" He looked at her blankly. "Where are you going?"

"Stay here!" he said. "There's something I've got to do."

"I'm coming."

"The hell you are." Tashnark shrugged her hand away. Over her shoulder he could see Shaan striking a blow at the demon, nicking it with his sword-tip and spraying fiery blood like a burning net over the deck. The demon roared, lashed out and the Saral stumbled, cuffed across the forehead.

"I must," Remis said, her voice desperate. "I can't do anything here except watch while they die."

Shaan regained his balance and dodged a more killing blow.

"You can't do anything there either." Anger, of more general origin but directed now at Remis, made Tashnark's voice fierce. "This is no College-fancy and no casual adventure. Lives are at stake—perhaps all life. No stupid romantic suicide will help."

"How do you know what'll help?"

"I've got a couple of ideas."

Remis almost snarled at him. "Why should you have a mandate on heroism?"

Tashnark saw Rondan-El-Therill parry a stab from one of the monster's beaks.

"I'm not the hero here."

"I'm coming with you!"

"There's no time for this!"

"No, there isn't. So stop arguing. What magic have you got to fight the sorcerer?"

Tashnark's eyes searched hers. *What do I know of Bellarroth or myself?* he thought, suddenly afraid.

<Who said you'd be alone?>

He gasped, hearing the words again. Was Remis necessary for whatever was to happen?

"You might die," he said to her, desperation in his voice.

"So might we all."

No escape? No, he knew, there was none. "Oh god! What I wouldn't give to be drunk right now!"

"We have to go!"

The dilemma stirred his thoughts into turmoil. Suddenly he grabbed her and hugged her close. "Remis, I no longer know who I am. There are many things happening that I've kept secret—and facing the sorcerer lies at the heart of whatever's behind it all. I'm not even sure I'll be here when it's over—whichever way it goes. But if I am, I hope you'll...." He stuttered to a halt.

Remis pushed out of his embrace.

"Hope I'll what?"

"I don't know," he said. "I don't know."

iii.

Rondan-El-Therill's gray cat watched the demon from among the coils of a mooring-rope bunched on the deck of the *Spirit*. Its green eyes glowed fiercely when light from the conflict spilt into the shadows surrounding it, and in its muscles the tension of cunning anticipation contended with the need to wait.

It glanced across the deck to where Tashnark and Remis conferred with urgent gestures.

<Hurry. Hurry, or our way will be lost.>

The bulky Nahallhan looked up, startled, hearing the words

and stiffening against their familiarity.

<*"You?"*>

The cat's tail, unseen, twitched impatiently.

"Tashnark?" Remis gripped his arm, seeing outward awareness disappear from his face. "Tashnark? Are you alright?"

He stared at nothing, oblivious to her.

<*"Are you Tammenallor then?"*>

<*You know I am.*>

<*"Where are you?"*>

<*Nearby.*>

<*"How can you be nearby? You exist outside this world. You told me so yourself!"*>

<*Like Cormidthal? Like you?*>

<*"But in that place you're huge—like a world. How can you be here without being...obvious?"*>

<*Relativities. All things are governed by the vagaries of thought. What is big may be small, what is small may be big.*>

<*"If you exist, then the dreams I've been having—of Bellarroth, of Hanin, of giant monsters—they're memories."*>

<*Parallel moments. Dreams and memories. In the end there's no difference.* >

<*"Bullshit!"*>

"Tashnark!" yelled Remis.

The cat glanced to where the demon slashed out at Shaan, ethereal claws scoring the air as though it were flesh. They left a wound that bled fire onto the deck.

<*Take the woman with you. Perhaps she's important. She's as safe there as here, and may be of use. But go before it's too late. We can't allow death to interfere.*>

Tashnark shook his head, recovering from spiritual turmoil. He frowned. "It's against my better judgement."

"What is?" Remis watched him, afraid for his mind.

"Taking you. Come on."

He lowered himself over the bulwark and into the canoe. For a moment Remis hesitated, then she scrambled over the edge after him. They disappeared from view.

The cat unwound itself from the rope-shadows and stepped out onto the deck. The air around it was screaming and urgent with loosed Deep Power. The end was so close. Lithely the animal leapt to a vantage point nearer to the struggle, ready for the moment that must come.

<Be careful, Rondan-El-Therill.>

The Merilan warrior had moved in close to the demon, but now shuffled back out of the range of its claws and its fire, his sword forming a swiftly woven defensive barrier. The demon spat a curse across the night.

<Hurry, Bellarroth. The fragments come together and the Cerendar is restless to begin.>

Patient with age, the cat crouched low against the wood of the barrel where it sat and waited.

iv.

Halul was puzzled. There was no time to think, no time to hesitate, not now nor then. She had thrown herself into combat against the demon as a swimmer leaps quickly into a cold pond, to minimize the shock. Now she was floundering. The axe Gard-Pardel was shrieking for a taste of the demon—an E'ashalsinir-spawning rich in Dark life. But it yearned even more for the creature's distant master, knowing the monster to be an unre-ality, a surrogate for something greater. It knew that Worjaren Rehemon was near.

This divided attention was distracting. It made combat harder. Halul was finding it impossible to focus her energies on the one thing, but would begin movements that lost their logic at the very moment they were initiated, and those moments of disorientation were dangerous. They made her vulnerable, and opened a way for fear to enter.

Halul could also hear whispering somewhere nearby, a susurration that might have been words if there had been time to concentrate on them. She only sensed them when she wasn't thinking about them, and this too was perpetually unsettling her attack. She felt increasingly uneasy, as though there was something she was supposed to do, but which had been removed from her memory.

Thick, shadowy hide rose over her, lashing claws like a bony grapple, and a preternatural stench clogged her nostrils. She gagged. Knife-sharp yellow bone struck the deck where she'd been a moment before, and left a splintery scar and a wash of flame. Halul spun deftly, swinging the axe between herself and Shaan on her right and sending the blade horizontally toward the demon's belly. Red blisters of mucus and flesh at the point she had targeted suggested a multitude of worms moving beneath the surface of its skin. But then the blow was past, still swinging free, and she staggered to catch her balance. The demon had moved in the instant between impulse and impact.

More of its impossible garble, obscene like the foulest curses, burst out above her. Halul saw Shaan sidestep and thrust, but he too missed the creature and was put on the defensive. Rondan-El-Therill was hanging back, made cautious by the thing's erratic movement.

It's impossible, Halul thought. Skilled fighters were attacking the demon, on three sides, and still it was not hard pressed. Twice, three times hit, it fought on—for though their swords could wound it, a strike was not enough for victory.

The whispering turned to speech suddenly and Halul's mind involuntarily tried to understand it. It jerked into a background drone immediately. Expelling tension with a roar of impatience, she swiped at the demon's tail-head, whose jowls moved to mimic speech. Was that unnatural appendage the source of the whispering?

No end but their own—a moment of carelessness or fatigue— seemed at all likely to Halul. The prospect was like plunging into despair. The demon became a misty irrelevance to her, an ugly stain on the grayer night. She struck and struck and each strike was an impotent gesture for which she felt only scorn. An eye opened up like a grave and watched her, reading her thoughts and turning every move against her. She stumbled, pushed away as a claw descended and tore her breeches, thrust out her free arm to cushion the fall, and felt the wrist turn painfully.

Through the ache she looked up in time to see something— an iridescent globule—spit from the tail-head's thick lips and spin toward her. She turned her head aside, and the demon-mucus missed, sizzling across the watery deck like hot oil. But some of it, a mere droplet, splattered on her hand. She felt a cold numbness spread along her arm—a fire-ice insensitivity that made her arm buckle and dazed her like a blow to the head. The night flushed crimson.

<Now!>

Now? Drunkenly she swung her axe to drive off any threatened attack, kept awake at all only by Gard-Pardel's transferred passion. A dim part of her mind cried out in appeal, afraid of what might happen if she lost control of her will.

<Do it now!>

What's now? she thought, not questioning the existence of the voice, but rather its meaning.

But the voice was not speaking to her.

In her semi-blindness she saw Rondan-El-Therill suddenly step toward the demon and drive a sweeping blow at a length of neck, cutting it near where it joined the body. The demon screamed an obscenity and jerked backward. But the warrior didn't press his advantage. Instead, for an instant, he lowered his guard and simply gazed at the monster. The human-like tail-head swung around like a mace, crowing madly, and fastened its teeth on Rondan's throat. Still he didn't pull away. He tossed his sword across the deck and wound his arms around the demon-head, hugging it to his chest. Then he disappeared.

In cameo Halul saw the demon scream its rage in a way that might have been triumph or pain, while Shaan staggered back, shocked. In the moment before her own mind deadened and collapsed her ability to see anything, Halul's eyes focused along the deck to a movement on the periphery of the action.

It was the cat. Though darkness swept around it and kept Halul excluded from complete awareness, for a moment she saw it as it was. Its silhouette seemed to bulge, growing into something larger. Its fur became human-like skin, though thick and hard. In a vision Remis knew it as it soon might be: huge, dark, snakes sprouting like a collar around its neck, wings spreading outward from inhuman shoulders, vast-chested and impossible—a creature the size of a world. Cosmic winds whispered its esoteric name to her: *Tammenallor.*

But such a being was not for this world. She recognized in the same moment that this gigantic creature belonged on the other side of the world's skin; it was in that place it had attained its great size. Here it was smaller. In this world, it was no bigger than a cat.

Suddenly Halul could withstand the pressure no longer and her consciousness rebelled.

She fell back against the planks, succumbing to the poison of the demon's spittle.

V.

Arhl shrank into a corner of the deck, away from the hideous monstrosity the others were fighting. It repelled him in a manner he could not explain, and even though his cowardice was abhorrent to him, he could not overcome it in the face of the demon's unnatural presence.

The demon was something from his darkest nightmare—a grotesque parody of life that filled him with horror. In it he saw the end of existence. It was a blending of power and imagination created only to reap violence, something that destroyed meaning, leaving scars and emotional emptiness. It was what he had fled when he left his homeland on the journey that had brought him to Vesuula, and what he had hoped never to face again.

But in that instant he knew it was impossible to escape from despair. Despair was everywhere—the essence of life in the world. He had not escaped it, not for a moment. He had simply ignored it for a time, so that it had had to return to him in a form he could not ignore.

Now it had come to claim him at his end.

"Mother!"

He ran, screaming the word, his feet gouging through the light cover of snow and his eyes stripping the trees ahead. The movement there was broken by wind-driven rain, a misty veil that could not obscure his terror.

"Mother!"

His breath was irregular and came in deep bursts of fog that wisped away behind him. A red light diffused the forest and its coldness, creating an illusion of warmth.

The creature that held down his mother turned its hoggish snout in his direction, dripping blood and saliva like sweat across the gray snow-mud. His mother heaved and groaned under the thing's black grip.

Young Arhl Mogarni stopped as he saw it clearly, and his feet slid in the mush. He struggled for balance, unable to take his eyes from the ugly scene.

"Run, boy!" it grunted, as it reared up on its hind legs, a splash of gored flesh spinning away from the movement. The voice was harsh and unnatural coming from the beast's hard, warty mouth. As he stumbled, Arhl saw its eyes and felt the evil in them.

More than an animal, he thought. A thing from the Dark Shaman, sent to punish us.

"She violated the treaty, boy. And violators are mine to keep. This is my place and I am my own Law. Do you want to become like her?"

Its claw reached down and scooped a wad of bloody flesh from his mother's ravaged torso. Hideously, the body quivered and Arhl thought he heard a moan. Tears were streaming down his cheeks.

"Go away, boy. I have my feast. I'll collect you another time."

The youth turned and ran.

Arhl screamed, whether in his mind or aloud he couldn't tell. The memory—a grim distortion of the truth—stabbed pain through his body and he thrashed uncontrollably against the deck of the *Spirit*. Hands gripped him.

"Steady there, son!" His mother's voice, low and cold. Her fingers pressed into his arm. *"It is in your mind, Arhl. Don't let it defeat you."*

Her face was paler even than the palest member of his tribe, her cheeks gaunt, her eyes dark. Arhl had risen to his knees, but now he stood, pushing the ghost aside.

"Leave me alone!" he cried.

"Finish what you've started. Keep hold of the task that lies ahead." Mesmerized, he watched her bloodless lips mouthing the words that echoed in his skull.

"You died," he whispered, his own fingers pressing against his temples. "And I ran from the boar that ripped out your stomach. Perhaps, if I'd been braver, I might have saved you."

"You were a boy. Even if you'd been a man, you could not have kept me alive."

He growled, but the sound was weakened by emotion and transformed itself into a sob. "At least I might have slain the beast that took your life! Revenge is something."

She swept closer over the space he'd put between them, and he didn't move away. This time her arms embraced him, comforting. *"There's nothing you could have done that would have had meaning. Don't flail yourself over the past. She needs you now."*

Tears were streaming down his cheeks as they rested on her shoulder, but her final sentence made him glance up sharply.

"She?"

Dizziness hit him. He collapsed to his knees again.

"Steady there!" A sailor's voice, weak and natural. Arhl looked around, past the man, but his mother's ghost was nowhere. She was gone. Only her words lingered in his mind.

His eyes scanned the night. The demon hovered like a huge

moth drawn by the *Spirit*'s life. Its heads moved and turned in a weird slow-dance, though its claws were fast, and the effect was to confuse the mind and make it seem unreal, a nightmare.

Arhl searched for Remis and saw her further down the deck with the Nahallhan, talking vigorously. Emptiness pounded in the pit of his stomach. Then, as he watched, they disappeared over the bulwark. *Remis! Wait!* he tried to call, but wind thick with the demon's foul smells choked him and stifled his voice.

Instead he stumbled toward the spot where he had seen her, skirting around the demon as best he could. *Spirit* vibrated uneasily beneath his feet as waves pushed against the hull—but sounds retreated, making the struggle and the helpless cringing of the ship's crew seem more dreamlike and more unreal. He passed them without comment, and if they spoke he heard nothing. He was having trouble focusing his eyes. They stung and, against his will, turned the world into a blur. But he made himself keep going, concentrating on his purpose.

He reached the place where Remis had climbed into the night, and collapsed against the side-rail, peering out across the water. Darkness hid its details. *Remis!* he called, though only in his mind.

Gradually he picked out the canoe, a drifting silhouette on the oily surface of the sea. Two figures were in it and Arhl knew at once where they were going. *Gerargarth* was black against the channel's opening.

Without thinking, Arhl Mogarni stripped off his shirt and his boots, and climbed onto the rail. Sound was still a distant unreality. Ignoring the thing he feared more than death, the thing that called to him though he had blocked his ears to its crowing, he pushed himself up into a dive. *Remis*, he cried, *I will not let them take you, too.*

He plunged into the dark water.

vi.

It turned out that Remis' plans for Worjaren Rehemon and the *Gerargarth* were simple: she wanted to blow them both out of the water. When he heard her say so, Tashnark couldn't help a bitter laugh of derision.

"This man's a special being." He let the sweep of the oar suffer his fury. "More deadly than his acolytes, more powerful, perhaps, than the Saral. Remis, you can't possibly understand him. He doesn't even exist in this world."

"What do you mean he doesn't exist?"

"He's a phantom, an illusion. He exists on some other plane...a terrible place...."

"Where then?"

"On a monster...a thing of fire!" Words were useless. He couldn't make them adequate. Remis was looking at him as though he were mad.

"He's outside reality," he insisted.

"He's here, Tashnark—we've seen him, seen his power. If he's an illusion, he's like no illusion I've ever come across. He interacts with the world—so the distinction between reality and illusion becomes meaningless."

He paddled harder. "Except he can't die."

"How do you know all this?"

"He told me." Tashnark said it without thinking. As he heard his own words he cringed. "All right, say it's nonsense...a delusion of mine. But he's still powerful, too powerful for Shaan to handle. You're just a fledgling spellbinder. How will you manage this marvel?"

"I may be young, Tashnark, but I know my powers."

Ur-Teth save us from romantic fools! he thought. Remis was strong, determined, honest—but Tashnark was no longer sure that any of these things had any meaning in the light of Worjaren Rehemon and whatever it was he represented. *Why did I ever let her come?* He didn't want her to die. If he had to die himself, at least she should live.

"What then?" he said, glancing toward the ship's approaching bulk. It had dropped anchor where the bay-water was still deep. They'd reach it shortly, beyond hope of retreat.

Remis became earnest. She pushed her dark hair, which had become loose, back over her forehead. "Tashnark, I'm not as much a dolt as you seem to think. I know the sorcerer's powerful—and I know there's something else happening, something you can't tell me—"

"Go on!" he said impatiently. At the moment they were swinging around rough water churned up by a rocky spit. They were still in what would be almost complete darkness from the ship's deck. The *Gerargarth*'s sailors were gathered along the side of the ship that gave the clearest view of the distant *Spirit*. The canoe might be able to each the stern without being challenged. Might.

"I'm a spellbinder," Remis continued matter-of-factly, "and a good one. And that might help us. Worjaren Rehemon will expect direct power if he expects any attack at all. If I can place a hex of disruption along a large part of the ship's waterline, we can sink it easily. And we can get away. What do you think?

"Hex of disruption?"

"To disperse patches of matter...I can do it, Tashnark. It's a Low Depth binding. Not very spectacular but it'll let water in."

He sighed. It might work—though of course it wouldn't kill Cormidthal.

"Try it. But we're both fools. We should leave heroics to the heroes."

Tashnark became stonily silent and when Remis tried to speak he gestured for her to remain quiet. Abandoning the paddle, he dipped his hands in the water to push the canoe on. They moved slowly toward the *Gerargarth*'s black mass—a great beast on the waves, gently swaying as though breathing unevenly after a long journey from the ocean's depths. Nervous and urgently tense, Remis calmed herself by staring at the ripples that radiated from the edge of their canoe and from Tashnark's hands, watching each until it was lost in darkness and rougher seas. Yet her mind was alive with feared imaginings and half-formed ideas. She thought of Shaan fighting the demon, imagined his death and wondered what it would mean if he died. Would it mean that the Guardians had failed? Was Shaan the full extent of their endeavors against the Darkness threatened by the Cerendar and Worjaren Rehemon? What did Tashnark mean that the sorcerer was an illusion? None of it made sense. For a moment she saw Arban and the sailors die again and sobbed involuntarily. It was an image of all their fates for her.

Tashnark hushed her. They lay in the shadow of the carrack, tossed by crosswaves brokenly deflected from the hull. She glanced up at the dark, salt-encrusted planks, stained black with tar. They looked both ordinary and threatening. The one impression fed the other. But the deck above seemed quiet. "Do what you must," whispered Tashnark, close to her ear. There was dread in him, too. Remis could hear it. "I'm going up."

"No," she said, surprised. "You can't. It's too dangerous."

"You think I don't know?"

"But there's no need. Just help me here."

His eyes were distant, searching out the deck, though it was hidden from him by perspective. "Your plan won't kill Worjaren Rehemon, whatever it does to the ship," he said. "I told you. He's not really there...he's an illusion. It might distract him though, so I can get at him."

"You think you can kill him?"

"All I know is I'm supposed to try."

Remis didn't understand him, was afraid of his arguments, and glanced around, desperate for something to keep him with her. The sides of the ship were high, higher than the *Spirit*'s. "There's no way up. You'll be heard."

Tashnark was edging the canoe along the hull, keeping it from bumping against the barnacles. He gestured vaguely. "Hand-holds," he said, "like on the *Spirit*. I've had practice. Just work your magic. I'll worry about my own skin."

"So will I, no matter what you say."

He looked at her for a moment, his thoughts impenetrable. Remis felt unable to speak any more. It occurred to her then that perhaps any action was futile and that death was necessary. After all, why should the Dark Gods lose, simply because of their nature? Perhaps the threatened apocalypse was inherent in the world's existence. Perhaps this was its predetermined end.

"Don't let the canoe hit the hull," Tashnark said. "It'll make a hell of a noise. I'll be back."

She made no reply as his big hand gripped a hold above him and he pulled himself up. The canoe bobbed uneasily and Remis was forced to concentrate on keeping her balance. When she looked back he was already at the top. He gestured reassurance and she smiled as though she felt some elusive confidence that all would be well. Then he was gone over the rail.

She felt so helpless. Abandoned, she let panic squirm like some awakening chrysalis within her. Then, closing her eyes, she tried to calm her racing pulses and will quiet to her heart, hoping the momentary lapse would act as a catharsis and let her think.

But a voice broke her effort and let unrestrained fear flood over her as though it were a sea into which she fell. A deep, many-textured voice, distant yet close. She recognized it from the night they had fled through the streets of Vesuula. "Your friend is taken," it said. "Come up now yourself. I've been waiting for you."

A dark figure, faceless against the lighter sky, was leaning over the bulwark, its hand out to her as a threat or an offer of assistance. She cringed back automatically. Then she saw that others were there, pointing crossbows at her.

She glanced about, but there was nothing to use as a defense, and only the sea in which to hide, had she dared to move.

vii.

Perhaps Raaneon had never felt terror before. For a moment

the possibility opened in his mind, for what he felt now in the face of this demonic perversion was unquestionably terror—and it was more profound than any emotion he'd experienced before, even when his wife and child had died.

A surge of power made him stagger. He crashed against a bulkhead and collapsed painfully to one knee. "Are you okay?" asked Mallorin, grabbing at his arm.

"Yes," he managed. "Something hit me."

"It's the demon."

Lisian and Kari'ala. He never spoke of them, rarely thought of them. Doing so now made the pain real again, but it was too late to stop the recollection. Emotion jabbed him hard in the stomach—a physical blow.

Oh, yes, he had known such terror as this provoked by the demon. How could he have forgotten? It had been there then, and was back now. The blackest moment of his life.

The distorted crowing of the demon seemed to mingle with his memories, until suddenly they were indistinguishable.

There'd been no storm that night.

Raaneon waited in the candle-flicker of the large anteroom, feeling darkness like a tangible substance slithering about at the periphery of the light's glow. It was worse than a storm. Storms were natural. This darkness was something alien and it threatened him with unstated menace. He huddled into his cloak, though the air was not cold. He couldn't remember why he was here.

Movement. A scraping rush. He glanced up, startled.

"Daddy!"

For a moment he was unable to recognize the figure—a little girl, perhaps five years old. Curly, burnt-umber hair tumbled about her shoulders. He frowned. Was she talking to him? No, impossible. She was as much a mystery as his presence in this place. Yet he felt, oddly, that he belonged here, and that the girl belonged to him. There was no one else with them.

The girl stopped next to him, close, exuberant with familiarity. "Daddy, can I go outside?"

Kari'ala. His daughter.

"Outside? No Kari—no, you can't. It's dark."

She pouted and grabbed at his cloak. "But I'm bored, daddy. There's nothing to do in here. A man in a room said there was a playground out in the yard with swings and stuff and a pond that's got fish in it. I want to see it, daddy. When can we go home? Where's mummy?" The words came in a rush, as they often did, for Kari'ala was a very precocious child, full of whim and urgency.

"Kari, mummy's still busy with the doctor. She's very sick. You've got to help her by being a good girl. Come here and sit down quietly."

"I don't want to sit down."

"Well, you can't go outside. Is that clear?"

She nodded unenthusiastically and began to edge away.

Raaneon barely noticed. He was thinking of his wife Lisian— her gauntness, her increasing pain—and the grave solemnity of the healer attending her. Her sickness was lingering and puzzled the doctors. For months he had watched her growing feeble.

Thought of it made the darkness thicker and more evil.

A scream. He looked up, concentrating. The long corridor was empty and silent.

Where was Kari'ala?

Dark, profound terror stabbed into his chest as though he'd been punched in the heart and he jerked up into a tense crouch. Silence.

"Kari'ala!" he shouted.

His voice echoed along the gray, stone corridor, lingering in the shadows behind pillars and prying at doorways. The candle guttered uneasily.

He began to run—toward the exit, the 'outside' that Kari'ala had wanted to visit. "Kari'ala!" he called.

He plunged into the night. There was no wind, just an awful stillness that mocked him and made him frantic with worry. He hurried along a stone path that disappeared beneath a canopy of dark leaves and jagged branches. Who in their right mind would build a children's park near a pond?

"Kari'ala!"

The trees thinned. Ahead he could see the silhouettes of man-made structures in an open space that might be a park. There was someone there—no, two people. One was small. It had to be his daughter.

"Kari'ala!"

Who was she with? She was standing close, too close—as though the person was familiar to her. Who could it be?

"Kari'ala!"

As he drew near, the girl turned and looked at him, catching the fear in his voice and interpreting it as anger. She was uneasy, concerned because she had disobeyed him.

"It's all right, daddy," she said. "I'm with mummy."

The words didn't make sense. Raaneon stopped, confused, and looked at the other person. Shadows smoothed her features into a dim, half-formed strangeness for an instant, and then Raaneon saw the long hair, the sharp, intelligent features, the half-smiling lips that he knew so well.

"Lisian!" he said. "What are you doing out here?"

She grinned, grotesquely, and Raaneon felt his anger rise. But there was no time to let it grow. Lisian seemed to cringe with pain, stepping backward as though unaware of anything except her illness. Her eyes were pleading. She moaned as her feet stumbled against the rocky barrier around the edge of the pond.

"Watch out!" Raaneon screamed, noticing the slime-covered, oily water for the first time.

Lisian tripped and fell. Kari'ala shouted something.

The familiar face of his wife suddenly split apart as she broke the surface of the pond, and a mass of tendrils like giant worms burst out of her, staining the night red. Raaneon involuntarily jumped away, though he was already several paces from the spot where the oily blackness had consumed Lisian's torn body—but the tendrils splashed over Kari'ala like a wave and engulfed her. She cried out, her infant voice forlornly inhuman.

Raaneon stumbled against his retreat and tried to turn it into a wild grab for the little girl. But he was too late. The tendrils dragged her into the pond. Thrashing, while Raaneon leapt toward her, she disappeared beneath the weedy surface.

Raaneon was in the pond then, its water splashing around his knees. It was very shallow. Like a madman he flung himself into the murkiness, desperate to find his daughter, screaming and crying, tears as well as stagnant pond-water pouring down his cheeks.

He found nothing.

Strong hands gripped Raaneon's shoulders and shook him. He lashed out at whoever it was, shouting obscenities.

"Raaneon! Raaneon! It's me! Come on, man! It's Mallorin, your friend Mallorin!"

The words penetrated his madness. He opened his eyes, and the memory-nightmare had gone. Halul's apprentice? "Mallorin?"

"Yes. Are you all right?"

"I don't know...no, of course I'm not all right!"

Raaneon glanced around. The Demon was babbling dementedly and gouging at the *Spirit*'s deck. Shaan dodged one of its many claws, and squirmed out from among its thrashing tentacles. Raaneon felt his eyes irresistibly focus on the tail-head and it seemed to sneer at him across the distance between them. He forced himself to look away. "Half-memories," he said. "It's filling my mind with things from the past. But changing them... horrible!"

Mallorin nodded, as though he understood. "I've had the same. It's happening to all of us perhaps."

Raaneon looked back at Shaan, Halul and Rondan-El-Therill as they fought with the creature, dodging its blows and jostling for a strike at its vitals.

"How can they concentrate with that sort of stuff going on in their heads?"

"They're not like us," Mallorin said. "None of them!"

Raaneon recognized the truth of the statement. *But if it's true, what are they really?* he wondered.

"What are we going to do?"

Mallorin frowned. "About what?"

"About that thing! About them!"

"Nothing. We'll hide, we'll keep out of their way, we'll try to stay alive. You want to rush in there to help? When you know you'll get killed?"

"Magic then?"

"Arban's didn't do much good."

While Raaneon watched, the demon became furious—frustrated perhaps by its inability to kill these attackers—and began to rise into the thicker darkness. It stopped suddenly, straining to climb further, but it seemed to be held back. Raaneon wondered whether this was some power of Shaan's. The demon looked like it wanted to locate an easier target, to approach them from a steeper angle. *That's what I'd do*, Raaneon thought. But it merely resumed the battle.

"They seem locked together," he said.

"Much will be resolved here. My mistress has foreseen this moment for years and, indeed, has sought it out."

"What did she foresee?"

"I don't know exactly. A struggle over the Cerendar...she'd never explain."

Suddenly there was a change. The battle-tableau collapsed. Halul stumbled. She lost her footing and fell onto the deck. The demon lashed out at her, something like a spark of flame shooting from the tail-head and plowing across the boards. Then the woman was struggling back onto her feet. There was no control in her movements. It was as though she'd been hit.

"Mistress!"

Mallorin started forward, but Raaneon grabbed his arm. "No, Mallorin. There's something else happening."

Rondan-El-Therill had grabbed the demon. He was clinging to it as though to squeeze the life from it. While Raaneon watched, the warrior's form shimmered, as in the early stages of an illusion-transfer, and for an instant he was melting into the demon's rough hide. Then he was gone. Shaan cried out and stepped away in surprise.

The demon roared, its limbs and heads thrashing wildly. It seemed to be having a fit.

"What's happening?"

Mallorin broke out of Raaneon's grip and ran toward his mistress. There was a red fire-tinge staining everything, deck, sea and sky. It might have been subjective, a clouding of his eyes by rushing blood, but to Raaneon it seemed as though the air around the demon was swirling, bending into a maelstrom. The shapes of men and deck and ship's tackle were shredded and became floating ribbons of visual debris. Wind began to howl.

As Mallorin approached the moving cylinder of air he staggered, struggled against an opposing force for a moment, and then was flung away.

With that, movement began across the ship.

Those sailors still left on the *Spirit*—those who hadn't fled to shore—were scrambling for cover, leaping over the bulwarks or scurrying below deck. Raaneon could not hear their voices. His head was roaring with the wind.

He went to Mallorin and pulled him to his feet. The air had thickened. He felt as though he were forcing his way through mud.

"Can't get close!" Mallorin screamed. "I must help her."

"You can't!"

"I've got to!"

The *Spirit* shuddered, and then continued to vibrate beneath them.

"It's coming apart!"

Redness exploded forcelessly around them like an illusory fireball, turning Mallorin's hair to flame. Raaneon's sight washed into a speckled haze. "Come away! They'll have to look after themselves."

"I can't!"

The vibration jerked into a violent thrashing motion, ripping across the deck like an earthquake. They both stumbled, tossed aside, scrambling at each other in an instinctive attempt to grasp onto something as a prop. The cylinder of air was almost opaque, spinning grayish colors into a wall. The wind-roar was deafening.

Raaneon grabbed Mallorin and dragged him toward the prow. It was relatively easy. Wind currents were already pushing at them and flaying exposed skin into chafed sores. Any movement in the opposite direction eased the pain.

Raaneon felt renewed terror. He remembered the distorted dream in which memories of his dead wife and child had been turned to even more of a nightmare than it had been in reality. This was similar. Something distant, but profoundly *wrong*, was coming closer and closer each moment. He didn't want to be here when it arrived. Dread was like a vast emptiness in his chest.

"We've got to get away!"

Wind blew a mist of sea-spray into his eyes and he blinked them closed. In the darkness behind his eyelids, he saw something huge and terrible—a gigantic monster looming above them, gnarled and squirming with serpents. It was as large as a world. The darkness was encompassing wings.

He gasped and opened his eyes.

The vision was gone.

"E'ashalsinir!" he cried.

Mallorin gripped his upper arm with a force that was bruising. "What's that you say?"

"E'ashalsinir! I think...it was the Dark Gods! Or something like them. I saw them coming."

Mallorin let him go and stood staring into the raging wind-storm. When he spoke his voice was a whisper, but Raaneon heard him clearly.

"Then it's too late. The world's about to end."

Raaneon closed his eyes and watched it come.

viii.

When his rage and frustration passed somewhat, Tashnark began to notice things about the sorcerer. Interesting things. There was a tenseness and fatigue to his movements that reminded Tashnark of a hangover, and his eyes seemed less fiery than they'd been in the "dream" world, as though the life in them had been draining away over the years since he'd met Bellarroth on Tammenallor—how long ago? Who could know? Perhaps time was irrelevant there. When Worjaren Rehemon spoke, his voice was strong, but he spoke little and his eyes kept glazing over, as though his mind was required elsewhere.

Tashnark sensed that something had happened, something that had affected the sorcerer adversely. He wondered what it was, but refrained from asking, too uncertain of Remis' fate to risk creating unnecessary conflict.

Once he saw that Remis was safe, he let himself be led to a below-deck cabin—there was in fact little choice—and kept a critical eye on the sorcerer in case he might salvage from a chance moment some fleeting hope of effective action. He was relieved when Remis appeared docilely over the rail. Two crossbows and several pikes directed threateningly at his chest would've hindered him from making an assay of his luck, had Remis tried some cunning Power tactic. Both of them would have been instantly slain, most likely. But Remis seemed to realize this and came without giving trouble. The corner of her mouth twitched in acknowledgement as their eyes met.

Worjaren Rehemon gestured toward Tashnark. "Your weapon," he said, his square features moving minimally.

Slowly, Tashnark unsheathed his sword, touching the intertwined metal serpents on the hilt like familiar friends. On an impulse he said: "Take it!"

The sorcerer gazed at him commandingly. Tashnark remained defiant. Though only a fleeting sign showed on his face, uncertainty might have gripped the sorcerer's heart. He hesitated then edged a step closer, his robes shifting about his legs. His hand reached past the hilt-guard, forming a grip around the twisted metal.

But he did not take it.

"Something wrong?" sneered Tashnark.

The sorcerer's eyes searched his face but gave nothing. He smiled and pulled his hand away.

"You!" He pointed at one of his men. "Remove the weapon and take it to my cabin. It is foul with enemy sweat and I'd not soil my touch with it."

Used to the Lord's whims, the man snatched Tashnark's sword away without question and went before them toward the carrack's high stern. Tashnark molded his lips into a smirk.

"My Lord?" A well-weathered seaman approached and bowed slightly to the sorcerer. "What'd you want us to do about...the other matter?"

"Nothing. Watch and wait. When my agent is ready, it will return."

"Master?"

"Enough for now! I have other business to attend to."

"Aye, sir."

"Bring them both."

He strode into his cabin and the others followed. For the moment Tashnark felt unable to resist. He had to struggle hard to maintain his appearance of cynicism and carelessness and the effort drained any energy in him that might have been turned to cunning. The cold wind that swung across them from the open sea seemed to enter the cabin as they did, becoming subjective and threatening.

<*"What do I do now?"*> He spoke the words to the voice inside his mind, but silence was like abandonment. Had he been trapped into coming aboard the *Gerargarth*, trapped into giving himself into the sorcerer's hands? Had the voice been merely a lure?

Worjaren Rehemon's cabin closed about them. Tashnark looked up from staring at the floorboards and saw the bare, austere room. There was no sign of life having taken place in it. Only a chair and a rough-wood table—nothing else. "Leave us," the Lord said quietly to his men.

One of the men came forward anxiously. "Master, shouldn't some of us stay as a guard?"

"They're my guests, nothing more," the sorcerer said. "Don't bother me with your mothering. I have many private matters to discuss and no desire to air them before riff-raff." He paused. "Must I repeat myself?"

The men scrambled out. As they went, Tashnark considered leaping for his sword, which had been placed on the table—but it was on the far side of the sorcerer and he doubted his ability to get to it before Worjaren Rehemon acted. Even if he got it, what good would it do? He remembered the dream of Bellarroth's attack on Cormidthal. Futile.

Should he grapple the man with his bare hands then? For some reason the idea repelled him.

The cabin door slammed shut. "Tiresome, all this business of command and petty tyranny." Tashnark watched Worjaren Rehemon's lips as they released the words. He felt numb, disconnected. The words seemed the key to something important, though he could not see what.

"Then why do it?"

"Means to an end, my friend, as well you know."

"A terrible burden," Tashnark said sarcastically.

"Oh, there is authority that I enjoy, of course—where the power controlled is worth the effort. Have you considered the joy of necromantic conjuration? Commanding a demon such as this one is a sensual pleasure."

"It's foul," said Remis. Tashnark glanced at her, for an instant wondering who she was and what she was doing here—before memory kicked back in.

Worjaren Rehemon gestured agreement. "Yes, it *is* foul. Foul—and effective in its foulness."

"When we left the *Spirit*, your pet was at a standstill. Unexpected opposition, perhaps?"

"Just part of the game. That fight is over now."

Tashnark felt a stab of fear. Over? Did that mean the Saral was dead?

"Have you killed them?" Remis was pale and looked numbed. The sorcerer said nothing, and his silence seemed like confirmation.

Emptiness filled Tashnark's heart and for the first time he felt an almost welcome despair. Suddenly he wanted to lash out without care or understanding. He wanted drunkenly to abandon consequence, to deny everything, even Remis. What good was love to a man who saw no hope, who had lost touch with the world, failed to sustain trust and honor, who felt no surety that anything he thought about himself was real? Before him stood a man who should have died long ago, who had wielded his illicit life like a weapon, and had won success out of death. And what was left?

"Are they dead?" Remis asked the sorcerer again. He looked at her and smiled faintly.

"Dead?" Worjaren Rehemon gave a slight gesture of dismissal. Remis's eyes rose to watch his lips, as though hoping for some sign he was lying. "Yes, they're dead enough—as all in this luckless world are dead. We walk the earth, but what life is there that is free of the curse? Wish your comrades well in their new freedom."

Tashnark regarded Remis anxiously. Terrible pain trembled in her eyes. "Why do you worship death?" she said. "I don't understand you at all."

Worjaren Rehemon laughed. "Acknowledge that life is death's darker face and all becomes clear. There comes an end to strife, and morality is seen for what it is—the twitching of a corpse." Then his features hardened. He held his palm toward Remis, who shivered unnaturally. Her pupils slipped upwards behind her eyelids, leaving white orbs visible like lifeless marbles. Tashnark cried out and moved toward the sorcerer.

"Stay back!"

He stopped uncertainly. "What've you done to her?"

"Made her a ransom against your compliance." Worjaren Rehemon gestured once and Remis sank to the floor. "You're the real problem."

"Me?" Tashnark's muscles were knotted with tension. "Why are you so concerned about me?" he said. "What can I do with you, Cormidthal, that's worth a tinker's damn?"

He watched for the sorcerer's denial, but there was nothing, as though the name had been expected.

"Speak discreetly, friend." The sorcerer sat on the room's one chair. "On this ship, in this world, I am a phantom—Lord Worjaren Rehemon, Yanuran courtier. *Cormidthal* is far away."

"But you're Cormidthal? Answer that, sorcerer. The name's been haunting me for too long."

"I was Cormidthal once. Now I'm Worjaren Rehemon, that's all I can say. A tedious conceit—but a necessary one. In another time and place, perhaps I shall be Cormidthal again."

"Cormidthal three thousand years dead?"

"Three thousand years alive, rather. Death is gentler than life."

Tashnark put his hand to his head. It was cold and shaking. "I didn't want to believe it, I suppose. It gives me knowledge I shouldn't have, and certainly don't want. Is this immortality of yours a gift of the Dark Gods?"

"Dark Gods? No, the curse is a much greater Power than the E'ashalsinir can command."

"The Cerendar?"

"Of course."

"What is it, Cormidthal? What the hell is it for? The Cerendar has woven its way into all these disconnected lives and events, but I've seen it and it's nothing. Nothing at all. A stupid trinket."

"It's a nexus for Power. Ultimate Power. It doesn't have to *be* anything except that."

"And you want to control it? Like all the other fools?"

"I did. Not any more. Now I just want release. I want my life back."

"It's given you life for thousands of years! I'm starting to think your problem is greed."

"It's given me torment, not life. Now it will free me, so I am—here in the real world—no longer a phantom. Then I'll free it in turn."

"Free it from what?"

Suddenly Worjaren Rehemon staggered. Pain scarred his face as though as studded glove had struck him in the face. His eyes widened. "What...?"

Tashnark felt the disturbance, too, though not as pain. In him it was a surge of hope. He grabbed at the sorcerer, attempting to fling him aside while the fit was on him. But Worjaren Rehemon sidestepped, striking him hard across the arms.

The sorcerer stood clenching his fists, watching Tashnark regain his balance. "I thought *you* were my enemy, Bellarroth, but you are just as much a fake as I am. The threat comes from elsewhere."

"Elsewhere?"

"You're an irrelevancy and therefore will die."

An insubstantial hand of flame gripped Tashnark around the throat. He felt the hard gouging of fingers on his skin and the heat when it began to burn. He heard Remis gasping, and knew she was feeling it, too. He tried to thrash out at the sorcerer, but his muscles knotted. They were turning to bone, becoming more rigid moment by moment. A curse died in his lungs.

"When you meet the Death-God," Worjaren Rehemon said, "give him the name Bellarroth and curse Hanin that he wallowed so much in mysteries. Knowing more, you might have survived."

He drew the bonds tighter.

ix.

Crimson became wine-red and then blackened into old blood. Suddenly there was a stark gray light. A lantern? Halul sat up, staring at the faces around her as they stared back like gargoyles. She shook her head. "The cat!" she cried out. "What happened to the cat?"

One of the phantoms said: "Shut up, girl! You want to get us killed?"

"What cat?" muttered another—and the murmur of its voice became multiple and set up an eerie resonance around her.

The faces clarified and Halul recognized them. Comrades from long ago. Red Gatalmas, Te'rinald...others whose names she'd forgotten.... They were all dead now.

"You all right, Halul? What happened?" one said.

"I don't know. Must have tripped."

"On your pussy?" Sull laughed coarsely.

Movement shifted the gloom around her. Close-by stone walls on either side disappeared into darkness along a thin corridor.

Her awareness began to reform. "Where am I?" she whispered.

"See? She's lost her mind, Red."

But she knew. They were in the Temple of Zar-thang the Hideous, on the border of Hargin and the Werba'igal Territories. Halul was eighteen—an apprentice.

A long time ago?

No. Now.

She stood. "You can button your lip, Sull, or I'll cut out your bloody tongue."

"Promises, promises."

"Shut up, you two." Red Gatalmas, a large man for a thief and assassin, shoved Sull aside and glared at Halul in the lantern-light. "We're surrounded by dozens of the bastards...all bloody fanatics. If they find us, they'll slit our throats before we can blink. Let's keep the personalities for later, eh?"

They moved on, grumbles dying into the scraping of sandaled feet. Halul felt strange, as though she were being watched. It was not sinister, just unsettling. The imaginary watcher seemed very near, though it was not one of her companions.

Red Gatalmas had been hired by the burghers of a local village to kill off the High Priest of the Temple of Zar-thang the

Hideous—because of the Temple cult's undesirable interference in the bucolic life of the village. But the reason didn't matter to Red Gatalmas. He was a trained murderer and a professional fighter and it was generally only money that got him going. "Idealism doesn't fill your belly," he'd say, and he paid his dues to the truth of this axiom by never agreeing to a job that wasn't the highest paying on offer. His determination almost amounted to a religious conviction.

Red Gatalmas had gathered together a band of thieves to help plunder the temple while he went about his scheduled killing. Actually the burghers couldn't afford his normal fee. It had taken mention of the temple's treasury to secure his agreement.

Halul had been more like a hanger-on. She was an apprentice, little more, mistress to a friend of Red Gatalmas, a young man who had died on the gallows after a botched assassination attempt on the life of a regional governor. When this present expedition was organized, Halul had blustered her way into the party. The motivation for doing so had come in a dream, when a tall, dark figure appeared to her and told her it was necessary. In moments when she allowed herself the luxury of such whimsy, she imagined that the dark figure had been herself.

"It's just along this hall," Red Gatalmas whispered. Someone spoke but the words were lost in the shuffling silence. "I'm going off with Yagnol to get the old bugger," Red continued. "We'll cause a diversion or two. Should keep 'em out of your hair. Be careful. Okay?"

Mutterings of agreement.

Red Gatalmas and Yagnol plunged into a side corridor, the glow of their lantern disappearing at last around a corner. Sull cleared his throat. "Let's go—and be ready for bloody anything!"

The memory thinned into a nervous stumbling. Strange noises soaked through the walls and floors—indistinct sounds that were nothing, mere wisps of imagination. Halul moved slowly after the others, her mind sifting through images of past and future without holding on to anything definite. Sull growled a word or two at one of the men. Halul's foot clipped the edge of something soft that slid away before she could react. She ignored it. A sudden flurry ahead, splashed by light. "Bloody web!" There was a thud. Sull swore.

Disconnected images.

"Here. This is the door."

"It's locked!"

Scrapings, grunts. Metal on metal.

"Primitive mechanism! Only take me a moment."

Sull loomed into the light near her.

"Go down further and check it out, girl. Don't want to be snuck up on."

"Give me a lantern then."

"Just feel along the wall. We need the light here."

"Sull, you're a bastard."

"Yeah."

Darkness closed over her like a fog, containing her in a cell of isolation. Even sound was dulled. She continued along the corridor for perhaps fifty paces, then stopped and looked back. The passage must have curved, for she couldn't see anything except blackness.

"Sull!" she whispered, too quietly to be heard. Of course there was no response. Nervously she went back along the way she'd come, but after five minutes the dark hadn't changed.

"Sull!"

She moved faster. Still nothing. Then for a moment she imagined she was floating. The walls and floors melted from solid blackness into an immaterial haze. There was a forceless explosion of sickly light. It flushed the walls with redness, before fading. Halul stumbled and fell and as she did she reached out for support. There was nothing.

But she didn't strike the floor. Her fall became a headlong tumble into nothingness and she screamed.

The memory sagged.

She was surrounded by a raging turmoil of rushing grayness and splashes of anaemic color. The color stank. In it there were other figures—not Sull nor Red Gatalmas nor Te'rinald—but men she knew she would meet in latter days when the seeds of this night germinated and bore fruit.

And there was something huge, waiting for its time to arrive—a thing so vast she could not perceive it beyond an awareness of size. Waiting. Waiting. Impatient to begin.

Halul awoke.

She shook herself, squinting through the grainy air in an attempt to make her surroundings settle into a form that she understood.

She was in a large room with spiral pillars running along both sides, forming shadowy margins that hid ill-defined shapes. She stumbled off the central dais. The floor was wet. Her feet slid, making her movement unsteady. Kneeling, she looked closely at the stained tiles, running her hand across them. The moisture was thick and slimy. She sniffed her hand. Blood.

Suddenly the hall exploded with light and shadows rushed away into its corners. Halul blinked in the glare, forcing her eyes to see. The first thing she noticed were the bodies—her companions, torn to shreds, meat and intestine, the pieces flung around the hall. She couldn't recognize them, even as people, but she knew it was them. Her stomach heaved. "No!" she screamed.

Her voice echoed and re-echoed off the walls, contorting as it raced between the pillars and through the thick darkness that squeezed into the hall's peripheral spaces.

"No!"

The word became a syncopated cacophony. Halul screamed it again.

Then silence filled the space. She squeezed her eyes shut, unable to look at the remains of Sull and Red Gatalmas and the others, and for those moments remained like that, clenched into herself in a demented panic.

"You're next," said a deep oily voice behind her, a sound that seemed to come from far away, yet reverberated in the stone of the floor. Numb, Halul opened her eyes and turned.

The diseased light that had filled the hall was flowing from a creature squatting some twenty paces from her, beyond the dais—a creature so foul the sight of it made her stomach heave again. It was like a giant man in body, but its flesh was pale and covered in weeping sores, and the fat that made it so gross seemed to be oozing from split skin like greenish mud. A huge penis—a ropish, gnarled sack, facile and jaundiced, and leaking thick mucus—hung between its legs and twitched as the creature shifted. Its head was lumpy and so distorted it was almost impossible to see a face in its contours.

"You come into my Temple to murder my servants and steal my treasures and it seems only fair that your guts should decorate my walls. I require recompense for the slight you've inflicted on my reputation."

Halul felt her head thicken as the creature's foul smell dripped around her.

"Cat got your tongue?" the creature said and laughed. Laughter made its body squirm with runnels and shifting lumps of flesh.

It slid toward Halul, leaving a trail of blood and slime.

"Stay away from me!"

A viscous wad of mucus splattered at her feet. "This is my Temple, girl. I won't be ordered about in it. Certainly not by some pre-pubescent wench."

Halul moved back as the creature came closer. She couldn't get her mind to work, to seek ways out of this. It was too full of a perception of this thing's impossible existence. Was it one of the E'ashalsinir, incarnate here in this repulsive form?

"Who are you?"

"Who I am."

"What do you want?"

"I've come to give your life purpose, little Halul."

Hearing her name from the amorphous mouth of this horror almost made Halul choke. A sense of unreality filled her mind, like a sickness.

"How do you know who I am?"

It laughed again and was suddenly looming over her, its movement a grayish, yellow blur. She screamed and staggered away, afraid to turn her back on it to run, but hindered by her stumbling feet. With a final effort she found herself entering the darkness around the edge of the hall, welcoming it and dreading its unseen menace at the same time. Her foot hit something and she fell.

"You can't hide from a god!"

The creature swiped at a pillar and the stone crumbled into a shower of dust. Moisture from the creature's flesh sprayed Halul's cheeks. Panic became nausea.

She reached out, seeking leverage to push herself away—and her fingers touched steel. It was warm and injected an energy into her that was a mixture of hatred, desire and confidence. Instinctively she pulled back and the energy dissipated.

"You'll have to do something soon, little Halul...or the big, bad god will turn you to offal."

Then she heard other words, not the creature's, but words in her mind.

<Take the weapon. You'll need it. Gard-pardel, opener of the way. It has great hunger.>

She reached out again toward the touch of steel she had felt, and this time her fingers closed around a leather-embossed handle. A battle-axe. Strong emotions flowed into her.

<"What's it doing here?">

<This temple was built for it. It has been waiting for someone to take it. Waiting for you.>

Halul wanted to ask more, but her grip on her own will was crumbling away. She could no longer put the axe aside. Its passion was becoming hers. It cried out for the life of the monstrosity that haunted the Temple, desiring it with an intensity she couldn't resist. In that instant Halul failed to see where the Axe's reality ended and hers began.

She leapt up, screaming, this time with passion, not despair. The Axe filled her with Power.

The creature's foot swung toward her. Halul blocked its path with the Axe and where it touched, flesh turned black and peeled away.

She swept the Axe in an arch, driving the creature back. It cursed her, its voice a tangible force that pained all her senses. Then she turned the Axe upward and let its blade fall vertically across the creature's belly, which split open like a sack over-stuffed with mud, covering her with a gray torrent. The muck swirled about her. It made her sick and dizzy. She collapsed, holding tightly to the Axe as it drank in the dark force. For a moment she experienced the full intensity of the creature's distorted life.

It was too much. She had no strength to withstand the assault. Her mind crumbled.

* * * * * * *

"Halul! Are you all right?"

She opened her eyes. Shaan. His face was drawn and sickly, as though washed by light from the creature she had slain in her violated memory. Around them blackened air swirled, discolored by torn fragments of the faded past.

"What's happening?"

Beyond Shaan, the demon roared, epileptic with impotent anger and distress.

"We've been sealed off from the others. An enormous power transference is taking place. I think something wants to manifest itself."

"The sorcerer?"

"Something much worse."

Halul staggered up, aware of the weight of Gard-Pardel dragging on the strap at her waist. "Dark Gods?"

"Perhaps."

"What can we do?"

"You must guard the gateway."

"Gateway?"

"The demon. It is being used to find us. I must lend aid to the others. Though we are sealed from them, their fight is ours as well." Shaan reached into his pocket then held something out to Halul. It was small, like a carved stone. The Cerendar. "You must take this now."

"Me? Wouldn't it be safer with you?"

"I am not free to make the choices that must be made. I am a focus only, Halul—I cannot make decisions."

"That doesn't make sense. You've already made decisions, already affected things."

"I allowed them to happen. Like this demon, I'm a gateway for another power. Trust me and later you might understand." He dropped the artifact into Halul's fingers. It was light and insubstantial. "The Cerendar, too, has no magic. It's merely a focus. We can't understand what it is—because it's nothing. But Power deeper and infinitely more potent than the Raashyr's is at work here, and the Cerendar is its symbol."

"What greater power can there be?"

Shaan was already turning away, and said nothing, but a name leapt with certainty into Halul's mind—a truth she knew she had always known.

Junsar. The Creator.

X.

Death's face was not as ugly as Tashnark had feared. It was almost gentle—a benign friend who'd been away and now was back to bring relief from the tribulations that had run riot in the meantime. It did not want to punish Tashnark, accuse him of anything, or even to deprive him of life. It simply soothed like a cheery song or a glass of beer—and then offered to show him to a new resting place where everything would be just *fine*.

Tashnark no longer felt the constricting force that had squeezed his throat. Instead, he drifted in a peaceful oblivion, not even wondering who he was, where he was going or what he would find when he got there—a simple, mindless pleasure so close to utter relief, it filled him with gratitude.

Yet nothing lasts forever, not even death.

Suddenly, the sensation of drifting disappeared. Tashnark was aware of spiky grasses under his body and hard irregular undulations that heaved, distantly, as he lay on them waiting for the drift to continue. Something roared above, loud and raucous. The sound shook through to his bones and forced his eyelids to spring open.

The sky was on fire.

He sat up, startled, as feeling slammed into his chest and scalded his face. A monster so huge it blocked out the sky thundered past—a long way off, yet seeming close thanks to its enormous size. The wind of its movement flung him sideways, sent him tumbling, crashing across the weird, alien landscape. Alien, yes, but familiar, too. *I know this place*, he thought as he fell. *It's the landscape of my dreams. Tammenallor, Bellarroth's home. I'm dreaming again.*

Except this time, it was different. He hadn't become Bellarroth—instead he had remained Tashnark.

How that could be, he had no idea. Perhaps, if the Bellarroth dreams really had been *dreams*, his subconscious mind might simply have taken a different tack this time, casting him instead of Bellarroth as its protagonist. But he knew better than that; the *dreams* had been *memories*—memories of an alternative reality and a different self—so there was no question of subconscious manipulation. *Time and space bend in upon themselves.* What he knew did exist, however, was some type of cross-reality joining, as though Tashnark/Bellarroth was a single being existing across the two places, like an island part in and part out of the sea. Perhaps Worjaren Rehemon's attack on Tashnark had pushed his part of the island totally under the dark waters that had once held only Bellarroth. He had been forced into the secondary world.

But would he drown in it?

Another wave of heat slammed into him, sending him

tumbling again. Fear almost paralyzed him. Could he possibly survive this? And if he couldn't, would he die for real? That thought didn't comfort him. Instead he remembered Remis and what he felt for her, what that feeling might mean for the future and the different emphasis it gave to his existence. He wanted her, wanted to be with her—not here in another world, pummeled by shock waves from the passing of a monstrous being, not on the shoulders of a second monster, lost in impossible memories—and not dead either.

For a moment the fiery winds diminished. The withered, burnt grasses around him—hair-like strands that squirmed and thrashed against the winds—settled against him in the lull.

Obeying what began as a subconscious impulse his hand sought in his pocket for the coin Remis had enchanted days, weeks ago. Had she been serious in what she said? Had she made it into a charm—a talisman from which he could draw forth an image of the one he loved? Was it therefore a link to her? He hoped so, because it might be his only way back and if he didn't go back what would happen to Remis? What would happen to the world?

His fingers closed around the coin and with all his failing strength, he thought of Remis. For a few seconds nothing happened. Why wasn't it working? He loved her, he was certain, and thinking of his love was the goad that activated the charm— or so Remis had said. He suppressed the onset of panic. *Remis!* he cried. *Can you hear me?* Still the moments lingered, unresolved. He thought of her, pictured her in his mind. Scowling in the middle of *The Night Binge*. Speaking out against the Family man who had come to bully her. Defying Worjaren Rehemon's acolyte. Calmly struggling to avoid being swamped by the man's superior power. Berating Tashnark in the Temple. Talking passionately about spellbinding and its importance, her eyes alight with idealism. Refusing to take the easy road out of this chaos when it was offered to her. Demanding that she accompany him to face Worjaren Rehemon. Being forced into unconsciousness by the sorcerer's ancient power. Not giving up, always *caring*. Emotion rose from deep inside Tashnark in response, heading to the surface like a submarine behemoth. It burst through him, blazing more fiercely than the fires of the monster in the sky.

He cried out....

...and his own world came crashing back.

She was there—Remis. Comatose, but struggling—he could feel her struggle.

Worjaren Rehemon's grip was on Tashnark's neck. Choking. Killing him.

Tashnark forced himself to reach out, toward Remis, as the deck beneath him heaved.

xi.

Arhl had always been a good swimmer. Though he hadn't grown up on the coast, his wandering tribe had frequently settled near lakes and other large bodies of water, and his parents had taught him to negotiate them at every opportunity. He had helped his father fish whenever necessary; he had swum often, for enjoyment, with other children from the tribe. He had felt at ease with it—lake waters had generally been calm, clean and chilly, except on the rarest of occasions when storms had ripped across their surface.

The water he was in now was vastly different—salty, cut by unexpected currents, and unnaturally choppy. It drew him from his course, sometimes pushed against him fiercely. Arhl had torn off his boots the better to swim unrestricted and had no metal weapons to weigh him down. These precautions, along with a grim determination, let him move quickly despite the water's hindrance. His blacksmith arms, strengthened by his everyday work, gave each stroke extra power. Every now and then he'd stop, glance across the waves to the silhouette of the enemy ship, to re-orient himself. All he could think was: *Remis is there*—he should be there with her. This was the task his mother's ghost had laid upon him and it was his duty to obey. He had to reach Remis before their separation brought injury to her.

Yet despite his determined focus and the strength of his strokes, he was finding it increasingly difficult to concentrate. The currents in the bay were not the only ones that fought him. The world itself was being swept by waves of psychic disturbance. Snatches of power would burst into his mind, filling his thoughts with dark, evil imagery and churning his emotions into a frenzy. Sometimes the impact was so harsh it was all he could do not to blank out and drown. He had to exercise all the skills he'd learnt over the years to keep the currents back, to block out their roars. It was almost impossible. Yet somehow he managed.

As he approached the enemy ship, trying his best not to cause the sort of splashing that would draw attention, the psychic background became even more intense. It nearly overwhelmed him. Flailing desperately, he made it to the side of the ship and grabbed onto the rusted handholds he'd known would be there—just in time, for into his mind flooded terrible images, of burning flesh and huge monsters, of thick, dangerous darkness alive with sharp teeth and fury. Voices cried out—the sound of the dying. One of them he recognized: *Remis*. The realization energized him, and he pulled himself up. His slippery fingers slid on the metal. He clutched harder. In response the rung snapped, plunging him back into the sea. His leg scraped across barnacles on the hull, their jagged shells ripping his pants, slicing into his flesh. Blood swirled around him.

Remis!

A voice had spoken her name, urgently, desperately. Once again Arhl reached up, leaping, stretching beyond the broken rung to the one above it. It held.

Remis! Can you hear me?

The voice sounded frantic. Arhl pulled himself further, determined to reach the deck.

xii.

Because it confirmed her worst fears, Remis could not disbelieve Worjaren Rehemon's claim that Shaan and her friends were dead. Sorrow burned in her, forcing tears to her eyes and draining her strength. She did not want to fight, only to go quickly and mourn for them all.

Then her body was snatched from her and she felt isolated and distant. She couldn't move. Darkness overwhelmed her and her mind wouldn't work, even to form a thought of despair. Instead she heard voices. She thought one was Tashnark's—it called out to her, asking her for something...what? She couldn't quite hear. She strained harder.

Nothing.

Her concentration lagged again and the voices, even Tashnark's, became an incomprehensible murmur. The desire to die sprouted like a fungus and, when she tried to move but couldn't, she took refuge in misery and wept uncontrollably.

In her grief something stirred. *She sat alone on grass so thick and soft it was like a downy quilt beneath her. The light was warm and contentedly she watched grass-stalks and budding flowers as they swayed in the evening breeze. Then Shaan came to her and touched her cheek gently.*

"Don't be sad," he said.

"You're here. You haven't gone."

"I wouldn't abandon you. I'm your only hope."

She reached up and took his hand, but the touch of it wasn't the touch of healthy skin. It was cold and sticky and when she looked she was holding a torn stump, an arm smashed into pulp at the wrist, the hand gone.

"Shaan!" she cried.

Huge worms were breaking from his face, eating away the flesh. They whipped about in the air, firm in his skin as though they were an extension of his sinews.

Remis screamed and the world flared red.

"Remis!"

The natural, familiar voice seemed grotesque coming from the monstrosity before her.

"It's a lie, Remis. Don't believe it. This is a lie."

"But you're dead...all of you."

"No. Fight it. A delusion only." He reached out and touched her again and this time the hand was clean and alive. "See? There's no truth in these monstrous images."

His fingers moved across her cheek. She felt the abrasive softness of his touch raise an ache within her. This time his presence was not corrupted.

"I am still on the Spirit, *fighting the coming of doom—as are the others. The struggle is tenuous, the outcome uncertain. But you are in danger* now.*"*

"What must I do?" she asked.

"Listen for his voice."

"His voice? Who—?"

"Listen with your heart and you will know!"

She reached down into herself...and the sound that she heard susurrating through her pounding blood seemed to form words, clearer and clearer by the moment.

<"Remis? Can you hear me?">

Tashnark?

She felt his spirit reach out to her and she reached back, grabbing him, drawing him to her. The voices ebbed and flowed. Others joined them as she felt Tashnark drawing closer.

"When you meet the Death-God, give him the name Bellarroth...."

Words spoken with evil intent.

Her eyes jolted open. She was in a ship's cabin, squat upon the floor—before her a tall, ruthless man, and Tashnark struggling to reach her. With her mind she grasped his hand.

Power from somewhere far distant—channeled through Tashnark—boiled and swelled inside her.

Exulting, Remis burst the sorcerer's mind-grip as if shrugging an unwanted touch from her shoulder. Worjaren Rehemon started back. Tashnark was free. He sank to the floor, gasping for breath.

"Who are you?" said Worjaren Rehemon.

When Remis answered, it seemed to her it was in someone else's voice.

"I am no one. Who are you, sorcerer?"

"One unimpressed by your pitiful rebellion."

"Are you impressed by your own stupidity? Do you know what Powers you're meddling with? The world teeters at the edge of a bottomless chasm, while the E'ashalsinir gather at the gates of Hell, waiting for a path to open. Why give it to them?"

"What do I care? I've suffered long enough and only want my freedom. If the world has to suffer as well, it's only right it should. A proper recompense for sin."

"Suffered long enough? You don't know a thing about suffering—you've only suffered your own self-indulgence."

Remis was aware of the door opening.

"Kill her!" said Lord Worjaren Rehemon.

She tried to turn, but despite the strange power in her, she had little control over her physical movements. Her will had been released, but not her body.

"Kill her!"

Footsteps. Grunts.

"No!"

She heard the cabin door slam aside and smash against the wall. Violent movement, running. A man stumbled into her field of vision, tripped over the still-winded Tashnark, and collapsed heavily. Tashnark reached out as he did so and pounded the man on the back of the head.

Another man. This one held a long knife and his nose was bloodied.

More groans. Fighting.

Worjaren Rehemon tried to break away, but the Power-binding that held Remis incapable of movement held him as well. He cursed, struggled.

Two men fighting to incapacitate each other crashed past her.

Remis recognized one. It was Arhl. He was barefoot and looked like he was soaked. He must have swum here, following her.

"Enough!" screamed the sorcerer.

The anger in his tone made her gasp. She felt the link to distant power that had sustained her fading quickly and the change began to ache in her. She glanced at Worjaren Rehemon, conscious of his efforts to break free.

Suddenly fire leapt from his eyes and mouth, fire that came from as far away as the Power she'd been wielding—an alien, unnatural fire. It burst around her. The remains of her acquired strength held it off and she felt only the wind of its fury.

But now her strength was gone and the link severed.

The cabin was burning. Wood cracked and split. From somewhere else an explosion boomed and the ship beneath them shuddered. Worjaren Rehemon reached upward in a sweeping motion as though gathering force. His hands began to glow. Her pulses still racing, Remis sent a burst of power—her own unaided Power—through the flames to block the sorcerer's fireball before it left him. His eyes turned to her, aflame. She felt his will tear at her defenses, the blue-red shimmering globe suspended between their two wills.

Then Tashnark was there. He had crawled to the table, taken his sword and was staggering through the rising chaos toward the sorcerer. The flames burned more fiercely, streaming yellow tongues curling up around him. The heat was intense. He staggered and lashed out.

For a moment Remis thought she saw another figure with him, a red-haired giant dressed in roughly sewn leathers—but a blue light exploded around her and she was blinded. She supposed the red-haired giant was an illusion of the fire. Desperate, she rubbed the glare out of her eyes.

Worjaren Rehemon cried out something Remis guessed was a goad-word and white fire roared around him, obscuring her sight again. He leapt back as Tashnark's sword ripped through the flame. The blade turned, struck the hovering fireball and shed its force like a storm. Wind slashed through the cabin, knocking Remis down. The air was full of hurled wood, flame and clouds of burning oil. For a moment the last shreds of her strength cleared her sight, revealing a huge creature that towered out of the fire, rising high through the sundered roof. It loomed over the *Gerargarth* like a pall of smoke and ash, huge wings spreading outward and encircling the ship as if to gather up the fire.

Then Remis' ecstasy was past and in release her strength fell away. She was empty.

xiii.

Shedding the cat-form at last, Tammenallor/Shadow gathered to Itself the energies that had been dispersed so long ago, drawing upon all the gathered fragments of that distant, devastating cataclysm. It allowed the flames to sear away the vulnerable flesh of reality and replace matter with a body that could never again be hurt and confined. The Curse was not over, Tammenallor/Shadow knew that. But the escape had begun.

Soon Junsar would be at rest.

As Worjaren Rehemon's demon gave up the power that had created it, the shell of its form thrashed against the draining and into the emptiness something else began to flow. The new power was more profoundly hateful than even the demon had thought possible and for a moment it baulked.

Tammenallor/Shadow sensed the power and called to it. *<What you want is here. Come and get it!>*

The demon cried out a hideous lamentation, its pain unbearable. In a while, it knew, self-consciousness would disappear utterly and it would be transformed into a different being, a creature of distortion and fear—like itself, but more so than Life could support.

It was becoming an Ormsinir of the Dark God Huedaik.

It was becoming Eblamthezaik.

xiv.

Bellarroth struck the ground as though he'd fallen from a great height—but his consciousness cleared into awareness only then. In his mind there was a confusion of images, memories of things he had never done, things he had never seen done. There was a woman—her name was Remis—struggling to ward off a blaze of fiery Power, and men fighting—someone named Arhl Mogarni—and another he recognized as Cormidthal.

Flame surrounded Bellarroth, harsh, burning flame—but its agony was in his mind only. Pain wracked his body from the burning, but his flesh was not burnt. It remained whole. His clothes were incinerated but his body was not.

Elsewhere, he knew, he was fighting. As he gripped the serpent-hilt of his sword, he knew that another hand, a hand that impossibly belonged to himself, was gripping the same hilt in another world. He had a clear awareness of Tashnark in his mind, as though the experience was real, happening to him now. And he knew that in fact it was happening to him, as certainly as he knew he stood among Lucishnor's fires. Somehow he was in both places—and in both places Cormidthal was there, too.

Bellarroth glanced around, squinting through the red haze of flame.

"What are you doing here?" a voice said.

Bellarroth staggered against his pain toward the voice. Flames sneaked up through the soles of his feet, tearing at his bones.

"You should not be here."

"I'm here, whether I should be or not."

"Do you see what I have suffered," the voice roared. "Can you understand my desire to escape at any cost? Doesn't the pain fill you with compassion?"

It was intense, that pain. But there was too much knowledge in Bellarroth's head now, and more was filling him as the minutes passed. The knowledge was Tashnark's, but a reservoir of memory belonging to others was seeping into him as well. The sorrow was immense—the grief of a race.

Burning became a mere irritation.

"We can help each other, Bellarroth. Hanin was a fool. You need not be."

He could see Cormidthal now, a strong man made gaunt by fire.

"Together we could tame the Cerendar."

"Alone or together, we could only make the Cerendar into a weapon of destruction, and the result would be the world's end."

"At least that would free me."

Cormidthal gestured and magical flame intensified the fires of Lucishnor. Bellarroth felt it interweaving his muscles, scalding his lungs, blackening his heart.

He struck out with his sword. Cormidthal stepped back and the blade sliced the air, turning it into a pattern of swirling fire-currents.

"My hands have Deep Power enough to destroy you in all the worlds, boy!"

The sorcerer was beside him, grappling Bellarroth as he stumbled. They crashed to the ground. His fingers scraped at Bellarroth's throat.

Touch broke reality into a whirlpool of connected fragments.

* * * * * * *

—Sevthen Ulart-Tashnark stumbled through a raging mixture of earthly flame and Kharathahul fire, the smell of burning wood and pitch thick about him. His arm rose, carrying a sword—Bellarroth's sword.

—A woman—someone he loved—cried out as Deep Power raged in her, the blood of a cursed necromancer aching in her veins, eager for the Cerendar and peace.

—Black metal screamed for distorted blood. Like a sponge the Axe soaked up the energies that rushed around it, building

toward a consummation anticipated long before.

—A man, dying. His burning flesh carried the markings of a people who had fled Mikhalin at the beginning of the Great War, centuries ago.

—Unliving flesh, suspended in pain by a double-bladed dagger, lay unmoving amid furious tumult.

—Shaan, seed of the Raashyr, reached out with his Power to strengthen and comfort. He carried the stone-wizard Farhassin in his flesh—a legacy of Cormidthal's ancient enemy.

—A creature that for an instant was a cat, then a warrior named Rondan El-Therill, shed its form and became a towering Monster. It loomed through the fire and violence, knowing its time had come.

—Dark, elemental hatred bled into demon flesh.

* * * * * * *

All these images, in that moment of touching, exploded upon Cormidthal's mind, flowing through Bellarroth like an uncontrollable flood. Cormidthal felt a wave of consuming emotion and a chaos of experience that slashed his spirit and left a gaping wound.

He flung Bellarroth aside and staggered to his feet. His face was a mask of horror and confusion. His eyes turned to Bellarroth.

"Why is my freedom so unthinkable?" he said. "Why has such power built up against me? Answer, Hanin!"

<*There is no answer, Cormidthal. No answer except the reality of it.*>

"Who are you?"

<*I am Junsar the Creator, in these people and in these events. You have done the world a favor, Cormidthal. You have given me release from my bondage, a bondage that has wracked the world since time began. Now there can be healing.*>

"No! The freedom must be mine. I've suffered enough!"

<*Junsar has dwelt in the Cerendar, lost for all of history,*

since first he sought to use the seeds of creation, the kartoranth, to gain unlawful peace. Corrupted action brought distortion and distortion seals the exile continually. But there is no inevitability in distortion. Only life opens upon eternity.>

The Power around them gathered in fury and fire rushed through their bones.

<You think you've suffered, Cormidthal? Let me show you suffering.>

A hand of flame reached out of the chaos and touched Cormidthal's forehead. He screamed, a primal scream that stripped away his cynicism, his hatred, even his despair. In his scream there was a world of pain that transcended anything ever experienced by a single man.

But Bellarroth understood what it was that Cormidthal had felt in that endless moment: the agony of every creature in Tharenweyr, agony that was physical pain and deep sorrow, agony that was loss and loneliness and despair. It was suffering that encompassed all suffering, and its profundity was more than he could bear.

Bellarroth knew—because he felt it, too.

XV.

Dark Power was coming. Raaneon could sense it. The demon, Shaan and Halul had disappeared from view completely, lost in a gray tornado that was ripping the ship into driftwood and ashes. In a panic he dragged Mallorin through the shallow water onto the beach, forcing him away from the manifestation.

"I must help," Mallorin said weakly.

"There's nothing we can do."

Even the grayness was taking form now. That form was something Raaneon did not want to see and he forced himself to look away and to join the rush of sailors up the wet sand toward the comforting darkness of the distant scrub. "Come on, Mallorin! Don't be a fool!"

Behind them, the tumult had become a raging wind, so loud Raaneon could hear little else. A sudden gust at his back made him stumble and he fell into the sand. He looked toward the ship. An indistinct shape was forming, a shape that suggested the demon, but suggested something else as well.

Sudden movement at the water's edge caught his eye. A small figure was running up the beach toward him. He gasped as he saw it, rejecting it instantly. It was Kari'ala, her babyish face smashed into a twisted mask.

Raaneon's mind began spinning with distorted memories he couldn't control. He thrashed against the sand.

"Raaneon!" Mallorin dragged him to his feet. "Don't look at it! You're right. There's nothing we can do."

Raaneon screamed again, with such passion that pain burnt in his lungs.

"Come on, Raaneon!"

The images spun away from him, pain anchoring his mind to something concrete. "I'm all right," he said. "It was like the demon, only worse."

"Yes. Come on."

The sand had become a thick mud, gripping his feet and sucking him down. Again he glanced back, involuntarily, and saw that the gray whirlpool was spreading, moving toward them and tearing the water, the beach, the sky into fractured streams of color.

"Where can we go?"

"Away from it, that's all!"

The spreading wind caught them almost at once. Raaneon felt himself lifted up and thrown violently forward. Again hideous images filled his mind, but he was more prepared this time and could force them aside. Then he tripped and his hands sank into the sand, cushioning his fall. He welcomed the distraction.

But at once he was aware that the sand was moving, not simply under the pressure of the wind, but of itself, as though it had acquired a life of its own. Something buried below him was struggling to the surface.

He leapt up, stumbling a few paces. Mallorin tried to hold onto him. "What's the matter now, damn it?"

"The sand. It moved."

A large gray-brown shell became visible, yellow grains running from it on all sides like water. Beneath it there were spindly orange legs.

"Some sort of crab!"

Raaneon could see it clearly now. The end where the crab's eyes should have been was bulging obscenely, sprouting a gnarled form that looked like a bird's head but wasn't. The creature tried to scuttle across the sand and its legs twisted, becoming tangled with new ones that were clawing out of the shell. It fell—writhing, changing....

"What's happening!" cried Raaneon.

"It's that thing!" Mallorin gestured toward the massive shape forming over the ship, "That Dark God or whatever it is...." Mallorin's grip on Raaneon was so tight it was bruising him. "...It's doing this, isn't it? It's doing this."

"Probably. How should I know?"

For a moment Raaneon had a disturbing vision of Mallorin. His face was distorting into a parody of itself, bogus heads growing from his chest....

"Let's just get away!" he yelled against the roaring wind. "As far away as we can!"

xvi.

Tashnark felt the change in Worjaren Rehemon even as it happened. The sorcerer had stopped struggling.

Automatically he shoved hard at the man's shoulder and Worjaren Rehemon staggered backwards, lost to an explosion of fire that swept across the cabin floor. Tashnark gripped the serpent-hilt of his sword, drawing himself into a battle-ready stance. The flames roared and tore at his skin.

* * * * * * *

Pulsing with energy being drawn into it from the flames around him, the sword writhed in Bellarroth's hand. It stung his spirit, filling him with an expansive awareness that frightened him and hindered his power to act. There was no rational understanding in that awareness, just a perception of breadth and profundity.

Yet in that expanse there was knowledge, too, and it rushed into him as he breathed. His mind had been stripped of memory once again, but it was not to be left that way. He was an empty container, its contents incinerated—and selective knowledge was being reformed in the ashes.

Tashnark. He was aware of Tashnark, and that this person from another world was himself.

He also knew of Lucishnor and Tammenallor. He knew what they were and understood it was they who had orchestrated not simply these events, but his own existence. Hanin was dead. He had given the Kharathahul the dedication and moral strength needed for the future, but mortality had taken him and he had departed into darkness after creating his warrior.

The sword was his legacy. It was formed of Lucishnor's fires and Tammenallor's strength, formed to cut away error and to leave a healthy wound on the flesh of Time—a wound that gave hope of healing.

He knew of Cormidthal, too, but Cormidthal was more than just a tyrant cursed by his own folly to an unliving torment. Cormidthal was a focus of Distortion—a man with will and passion, yes, but a man in whose actions fate had been concentrated and refined. Part chance, part desperate gambit, he was a nexus for dark currents in the world. In him was focused the hope of life or death.

There was memory of pain and suffering, too—diverse, profound sorrow that was the burden of time and mortality. Cormidthal and Bellarroth had both felt it and the horror and pity of it remained indelibly scarred in their minds.

* * * * * * *

Shadow shimmered near Bellarroth, threatening to emerge from the wall of flame. He turned his sword to defense.

* * * * * * *

Worjaren Rehemon didn't attack. On the contrary he seemed drained of any desire to move at all and stood there immune to the chaos around him.

Tashnark was conscious that Bellarroth faced Cormidthal in the alien place. Memory of suffering oppressed his mind, so that even his concern for Remis had dwindled to a peripheral tension nagging at the edge of his awareness. His instincts told him to confront Worjaren Rehemon now, while the sorcerer was disoriented and dispirited, but like the sorcerer he could not draw himself back from the intense world-sorrow in order to continue with normal conflict. Nothing seemed normal now. An existential empathy had engulfed them both.

* * * * * * *

Both Tashnark and Bellarroth, their perceptions coinciding into a single vision, knew what Power lay embedded in these events.

Tammenallor and Lucishnor—and other Monstrous beings that had no name—were distortions of Junsar's Spirit, divided and cursed by exile to exist on the fringes of the Real. Now Reality was drawing them back into time and convergence was about to begin.

Just as Cormidthal was the focus of Distortion, Tashnark had become the focus of Healing.

He felt his personality crumble. Wind swept through the flame, carrying ash and dust in a vast storm that was only partly objective. It drew Tashnark into it—and for a moment he was lost.

* * * * * * *

Cormidthal stood unmoving. Small convulsions passed over his body. Bellarroth recognized what they were in the instant before he, too, was taken by the storm.
Cormidthal wept.

xviii.

"Let me out of here!" Sire Thargonal concentrated all the anger in his corpulent body and screamed yet again, his throat aching with the panic that lay behind the words. "Open this door!"

The Vesuulan aristocrat had been screaming for what seemed like hours, screaming and pounding on the cabin door, but neither the screaming nor the pounding had had any effect except to make his voice hoarse, lacerate his fists, and increase his level of anxiety. He had even tried to break down the door with a chair.

"Let me out!"

The ship shook beneath his feet, throwing him against a wall. He leaned there, gasping, trying to control the pain that squeezed his heart. He was deeply afraid. It was not the sea that was making the ship quiver, but something Thargonal didn't want to believe in. At first he'd thought it was Worjaren Rehemon, and that would've been acceptable—though it worried him that Worjaren Rehemon's actions were sometimes rash and indiscriminate in their targets. But there was something else going on, something he didn't understand. The waves of power sweeping over him at intervals carried a cargo of mental images both obscene and hateful, and the effort to keep them at bay wore him down. He felt as though he were going mad. When he was quiet, distant cries leaked into the cabin, cries full of terror and dismay.

"Please!" He wept out the sounds, so mingled with sobs and

gasps they were unrecognizable. "Please let me out!"

He was afraid the ship would sink and in their scramble for safety his captors would forget about him and let him drown. He was afraid they had determined to kill him all along and the storm they seemed to have run into would give them the excuse to carry out their plan. He was afraid there was something out there neither his captors nor Worjaren Rehemon could control, and that something would inflict a pain worse than death upon him.

In this, he was right.

The floor buckled under his feet. As he staggered, a movement in the corner of the room attracted his eye. There was a gap in the boards there that seemed to have widened, oozing shadow like a thick tar. Before he could really grasp what was happening the shadow become solid and slithered out into full view. Thargonal let a shudder of revulsion pass over him. He backed away from the thing, too afraid to say anything or to call for help. *What's happening?* his mind cried. *What do you want of me?*

The shadow coming from the gap in the boards was dark green and wetly sleek, long and thin, moving over the floor as though swimming. It might have been seaweed or a watersnake, but it was also multi-stranded and each of the strands seemed to end in a face, a miniature human face that scowled and snarled and bared tiny pinprick teeth. As it moved further into the room some of the faces saw Thargonal and grinned at him. He thought he could hear voices, very shrill and very distant, calling him in words he couldn't understand. His back hit the opposite wall and stopped his retreat.

"Get away from me!" he shrieked. "I'm a High-Lord of Vesuula. You have no right to touch me."

More and more heads, all attached to slithering knots of fiber, were folding out of the shadowy darkness, twisting toward him like a tide of insanity. In a panic Thargonal grabbed at a piece of the busted chair he had tried to use to batter down the door, and waved it threateningly. "Stay back!"

The thing ignored him. It was so close now he could feel the chill of its moist breath latching onto his skin and fraying his nerves. Wind had increased in the cabin as well, a bleak, putrid wind that was not stopped by walls and ceilings. It swirled toward him, shredding the wood of the ship and roaring loudly. Beneath the roar he could hear the tiny voices of the impossible creature.

He struck out at the thing, crushing some of its heads into a green smear across the floorboards. He lifted his boot and stamped down on another knot of squirming fibers. The calling turned to cries of pain. He stamped again, and again, until his boot was slimy with gore and he slid and nearly fell headlong into the dark tangle. With his club he beat one face into pulp, then another. Thargonal felt little drops of wetness splatter up his arm, but he kept up the motion. It became compulsive and it was a while before he could make himself stop.

By that time the air was a solid fog, raging about him like a hurricane. It came from beyond the cabin walls, indifferent to them, spinning around him, and out the opposite side. The sound was deafening, a terrible mixture of wind-roar and thousands of screaming voices.

As he became fully aware of it, the wind tossed him off his feet. He felt its force as a blow not only to his body, but also to his spirit. His mind was flooded with images of horror and distortion that made his muscles convulse and wrenched his chest painfully. He screamed, his thoughts disappearing into the spinning gray chaos.

Desperately he reached out to brush away the swirling air—and saw his hand fumble and weave trails of fog into fantastical shapes. Pain welled up in him, an irresistible pressure that seemed to be bloating his body until he thought he'd burst. To his horror he saw his fingers changing, bulging, extending into writhing serpent-like creatures. Eyes pushed up through the cracking skin and wounds were slashed across the tips that became mouths full of teeth and whipping, pointed tongues.

Screaming, he smashed his hand against the wall.

xix.

Shaan's act had filled Halul with numbing fear, an emotion so gently debilitating that she found it hard to fight. And that name? *Junsar!* Was that primitive deity really the cause of all this fury? It seemed so remote. In legend and religious observance, Junsar was one of the Hiannel—ancient beings who were supposed to have been created by Erellinarth to give the world its form; its construction workers, as it were. Junsar's name was perhaps the most familiar, for he/she had warped the world and given birth to the curse that produced the Dark Gods and other monsters, the curse that distorted reality and led it firmly toward a foretold apocalyptic Death. Junsar's name was synonymous with *Doom.*

Halul felt the small hardness of the Cerendar in her hand. She held it up and looked at its ornate surface. There was no sign that it was more than an ordinary piece of sculptured rock, but suddenly Halul knew exactly what the Cerendar was.

In those early times of legend, when Erellinarth sank down into Matter from Universal Chaos—to sleep out the times and await reformation—the husks of the creational Seed from which the world grew were to be placed one at His head and one at His feet, to confine the space and govern the world's growth while he slept. These husks were called Kartoranth. But, it was said, one of the Hiannel—overcome by fear—stole the Kartoranth from the world's nether end, hoping to use it to construct a safe abode for himself. The result was chaos. The processes of Time were warped and the world riddled by distortion, and though the Head-Kartoranth's energies sought to draw Life into a unified Form, there was no stability and the work had been doomed to fail.

The one who stole the Kartoranth? Junsar, of course.

That is what I hold in my hand, Halul thought, her pulses racing. *The lost Seed-husk, the missing Kartoranth casing—an unworldly power fashioned by fear into a gleam of hope.*

And on the heels of that insight came another. The Seed of legend, from which the world grew, was not a seed as such, but a paradigm, on the basis of which all form would be based. Encoded into the essential rock of reality, it had became the two objects they called Cerendar, which would define the extreme limits of the world and thus resist the forces of Chaos that sought to tear Tharenweyr apart. This Cerendar, then, the lost one, had been intended to define the lower limit of Creation's original structure—a fragment of primal memory that contained its ultimate form. Removing it from its position had destabilized everything. But here, now, it had drawn the fragments of apocalypse together—could that be an accident? Or was Junsar himself, regretting his actions, behind this incredible convergence of forces? Had he all along been manipulating a finish to the process of decay initiated by the Cerendar's removal during Creation? Most awfully of all, did he intend that the artifact should return to the spot from which it had been stolen, taken there by the Dark Gods themselves?

Were the Dark Gods to be the unknowing architects of their own reformation and the world's renewal?

Halul breathed deeply, trying to contain her excitement and fear. This was knowledge not even the Raashyr had been granted. But it had been given to her and now fate itself rested in her hands. The future was hers.

There was a sudden increase in the wind's turmoil. A roaring explosion, of a kind that followed the completion of a Spell of Spatial Displacement, ripped through the air, forcing it into a flurry of movement. Halul glanced toward the demon and saw it bulging and growing, losing the knotted harshness that characterized demonic creatures and becoming more stable and more absolute. Fierce bird-like heads replaced the demon's indeterminate faces and the body became firm and solid as rock. The tail-head withered and was transformed into a spiked weapon.

Eblamthezaik, Halul thought with awe, recognizing the features of Huedaik's Ormsinir from images she had seen during her journeys. Had Eblamthezaik's form been reflected in the decoration of the Temple of Zar-thang the Hideous? She couldn't recall.

It was her last moment of rational thought. As the Ormsinir materialized, the passion of Gard-Pardel reached out to Halul, even though she was not holding its handle, and the hysteria of the Axe's lust wiped her own mind away. She gripped the oiled leather and drew the weapon from its thong. It was screaming for the Ormsinir's life.

Halul leapt into action, twirling the battle-axe as she ran at the Dark God servant, all thought of personal safety lost in the fury. Nothing could stop her. She had become a movement in the raging storm of twisted images, a wisp of gray fog, a shudder in the tortured air.

Eblamthezaik, caught in a moment of disorientation, realized that something was wrong only as Halul reached Its side. With god-like vision It saw not a woman and a black-metal battle-axe, but the Power-form of a creature so huge its body obscured the sky—a concentration of Deep Power more extensive than even the Godling had ever experienced.

For a moment the Ormsinir did not see the Distortion and lust of the creature and thought that a Raashyr-Lord had come to drive It away. It reached out to find another target for Its still-materializing energies and felt the obscene power of Worjaren Rehemon.

You are our servant now, as always, It whispered.

Halul's Axe sliced through the grayness and power-tense flesh, drinking the dark life of the creature in an ecstasy of hatred.

But it was the dark-life of the demon—not the Ormsinir. The Ormsinir had already fled.

XX.

You are our servant now, as always.
Worjaren Rehemon heard the words and instantly under-

stood the implications of them, even while he fought with his own raging emotions. His mind was uncharacteristically turbulent, trying to assimilate the vast barrage of knowledge that had come to him during the last few moments. But those words hardened him and gave him control of his thoughts.

Below everything, the world's pain still clung to his bones, the echoes of its pitiful lamentation more than he could bear.

You are our servant now, as always.

The first traces of the Ormsinir's transference touched his soul like a dagger to the heart.

<Should the Ormsinir take you, Cormidthal, should it become you, it will become Lucishnor as well. A pathway has been opened into the Cerendar, into Creation's Seed, and taking it, the E'ashalsinir will govern fate forever. Your evils give them access, and the result will be a world in which distortion is eternal. Can you imagine that? You have felt the world's pain, but can you bear the pain of immortal Erellinarth as he dies, forever?>

"How can I stop it?" he cried.

<The sword was forged in Lucishnor's flames and hewn from Tammenallor's flesh. But the sacrifice must be yours.>

Contemplation of alternatives was impossible. The pain of hesitation would be absolute.

Worjaren Rehemon turned through the flames to Sevthen Ulart-Tashnark and spoke urgently. "Slay me!" he said.

xxi.

"Slay me!"

Bellarroth drew back, suspicious of Cormidthal's words.

"Slay me!" the ancient lord repeated, his voice desperate. "There's no time for doubt."

Something was happening to him. As Bellarroth watched, his face contorted, bulging outward, tensing with struggle.

When he spoke again, his voice was forced between clenched teeth.

"I—can't—hold—it—back."

* * * * * *

Confusion made Tashnark groan. Worjaren Rehemon's command had thrown him, but more than that, their shared experience of the world's pain lingered in his limbs and in his mind, and denied him the power to kill.

"I can't!" he said, seeing the sorcerer's desperation.

"You—must!"

Worjaren Rehemon's body was twisting out of shape, bending and writhing in its resistance.

<The sacrifice must be yours.>

Abruptly Worjaren Rehemon gestured at Tashnark and cried out a string of dark syllables. Deep Power rushed from his hands. Thinking himself attacked, Tashnark moved the sword into a defensive position in front of his body, but magic-power gripped the steel and wrenched it from his fingers.

* * * * * *

Bellarroth watched helplessly as the blade tore into Cormidthal's heart, drawing Lucishnor's flames after it. The ancient lord began to burn.

* * * * * *

A fierce combustion that exploded from the sorcerer's body flung Tashnark aside. He hit the burning deck and rolled away.

When he looked back, Worjaren Rehemon was gone.

xxii.

A shadow detached itself from the textured darkness of the

bush and came toward them across the sand. Raaneon looked up in time to see it and knew at once it wasn't human. Its movement was stiff and awkward, as though it found walking difficult—and when he caught sight of its more stable outline against the tossing violence of the trees he saw that it was bloated and knotted and seemed to have two heads.

Wind lifted sand around them in a blinding cloud.

"Quickly!" He grabbed Mallorin and dragged him to the side, hoping to avoid the oncoming monstrosity, whatever it was. From somewhere in the swirling darkness he heard a human voice call out and a sound that might have been an extended groan of agony.

Suddenly his foot struck an object on the sand dune and he stumbled. Mallorin fell, but Raaneon held his arm and pulled him up. He looked back. Though sand was thick in the air around it, he could tell the object was a corpse—one of the sailors. The man's head had been torn from his body and even as Raaneon watched a new one began to emerge from the gore and splintered bone, screaming the whole time. It was like a dog's head. The torso was distorting, too—a clawed arm tearing through the man's shirt as it grew out from the small of his back.

Revolted, Raaneon pushed Mallorin away, suddenly aware of a monstrous shadow looming through the wind. "Run!" he cried.

They reached the top of the dune and sprinted into a hollow on the far side of it. Sandalwood trees, spindly and tangled, grew at angles from the shifting sand, covering them in a woven blanket of shadow.

Raaneon could feel corruption tugging at the edge of his mind, a grim current of dark power that urged his spirit toward distortion. It was in the air that spun around them, in the earth beneath their feet, in life itself—a potential that any moment of despair could fulfil. The Dark God creature manifesting on their ship was stimulating distortion in the world around it and only Raaneon's tenuous grip on his own *integrity* held the corruption back from completely absorbing him.

Then he noticed that Mallorin was gasping, breathing heavily as his body twitched.

"Fight it, Mallorin!" he screamed. "Fight it or it'll take you!"

"I can't."

Mallorin buckled over. For a moment his eyes searched Raaneon's face, desperation reaching out from the depths of his skull. His mouth twitched.

"Mistress?" he groaned.

Raaneon grabbed his shoulders. "Don't, Mallorin! Don't give in!"

The wind was strong, tearing at the trees and slashing sight of the island into a blur. Mallorin looked around, as if an unheard voice had drawn his attention. Something began to expand from his shoulder. His coat tore.

"Mallorin!" Raaneon pulled him close, trying to protect him with his own determination. "Don't let it happen! It doesn't have to be this way."

Mallorin's body was struggling against the wizard's grip now. A spidery lump, black and greasy with blood, pushed through his shirt and wrapped itself around Raaneon's arm. Though it was moving, there was no warmth in it. An eye opened on its surface.

At that moment the wind dropped away. Raaneon barely noticed that stillness had swept in around him and that the roaring in his ears was only a lingering memory. Mallorin's body had gone limp. The sudden weight pulled on Raaneon's arms and the body dropped to the sand.

"Mallorin!" he cried. Kneeling beside the apprentice, he grabbed him and shook furiously.

"Mallorin! Don't give in! Don't give in!"

Except for Raaneon's voice, the night was silent.

xxiii.

Clutched in Halul's hand, the Cerendar—which she alone

knew to be the lost Kartoranth, stolen by Junsar in the early days of Creation—began to glow. Suddenly standing now at the center of a vast network of Deep Power—a network reaching outward from within the tiny object and encompassing all the currents of reality—Halul felt its activation as a moment of unity and renewal.

Gard-Pardel was gone, absorbed back into the Cerendar, but Halul no longer needed it. She knew what must be done.

"Eblamthezaik!" she called. The power of the Cerendar reached out, grabbed the Ormsinir and made it appear before her.

"Who are you?" the Being said, unnerved that it had been helpless against the force that had drawn it to this spot.

"I am no one, but the Cerendar has opened to me."

The Ormsinir's heads strained forward, as Halul held out her hand and revealed the artifact. It was no longer glowing.

"We would have it!" said the Ormsinir.

"Then take it. I offer it to you."

The Dark God servant hesitated, not understanding the woman's words and suspecting treachery.

"First you stand against us, wielding the Raashyr's power— and when we are forced to retreat, defeated as we are never defeated, then you call us back to give us what we want— without fight or compunction. There is trickery here, though we cannot see it."

"No tricks. I offer you what you and your Master desire. The Cerendar—All-Power."

The Ormsinir gestured and the Cerendar rose from Halul's hand. It floated slowly toward Eblamthezaik, until the Being reached out with one huge claw and took the artifact from the air.

"Yes," It said, "no tricks."

One of Its heads turned toward Halul and she thought that perhaps It would kill her now. She would have no defense should It try, but that was not important.

"We return to Nalim-Tar at the far end of the world, where

the Master waits, and the return shall mark the beginning of humanity's transformation. You have betrayed all the world, human. Can you live with that knowledge?"

Halul smiled. It was difficult, but she managed it with some effort. "Of course. I want to be there as it happens."

"There is true darkness in your heart," the Ormsinir said, Its voice coming from all around her. "You have gained a place of honor in our world of ruin. Follow me!"

"I would say one last farewell," she said.

The Being gestured compliance.

* * * * * * *

Suddenly Halul was standing on the deck of the *Spirit*, gazing out across Sororon as light crept over its cliffs. It was bleak and cold.

"What have you done?" said Shaan, beside her.

She held out her hands—and they were empty. On one of them a distorted Star pattern was burnt into the palm.

"Don't worry," she said. "Though the Dark Ones have it, everything will be for the best." Then she faded into the air as though she had been a memory all along.

CHAPTER EIGHT
ASHES

i.

Fire dwindled into darkness for Remis. While her companions fought off the influences of Worjaren Rehemon and the
Ormsinir, she lay in a bubble of protection, cradled by her own
inner strength. She did not dream, she did not think, she did
not feel—for a brief time she was outside history, gathering
renewed energy and healing emotional wounds.

Suddenly there were images in the darkness and Remis's
mind snapped to attention. At first they were fragmented and
insecure, sliding her awareness in and out of thought and
feeling—but at last her surroundings firmed and her drift was
halted. *Where's Tashnark?* she wondered and concern nudged
her fully awake. She felt as though she glanced up and found a
dim, shadowy figure standing above her, its square-cut beard
and gaunt features distantly familiar. She might have spoken to
the figure, but she blinked and the shadows moved about her,
plunging her into a dream.

*She was a novitiate again, an adolescent reading in the
College Library. The works she was reading were not the* Ancient
Texts of the Deep Arts *nor the prescribed* Lore of the Hassur
Fathers. *Instead she poured over* Tales of the Ancient Heroes,
*thrilling in the adventure and aglow with romance. She read of
Karoath, who fought the Beast of Peral-Swahn and saved a city
from annihilation; she imagined the thoughts of Shalidas the*

Thriselian, who denied the demon Yolig passage into her soul, and thus guaranteed the continuance of the Thrisel race; she wept as Koreeli the Maid wove a shroud for her father from the very sinews of her life. The stories filled her with a desire that was almost pain.

But memory soon distorted. The book trembled in her fingers and one of the pictures in it—a wood-cut of Moredlin el-Therill slaying a rampaging giant—was suddenly moving on the page, the muscles of the huge monster straining to reach out of the book. The giant's leg rose and its foot came down on Moredlin and his horse, crushing both to a red stain. Blood dripped off the parchment onto Remis' hand. She started violently and tossed the book aside.

When she tried to rise, to escape the images, she merely fractured it. Now she saw a tall but stocky figure, archaically dressed, striding hurriedly along narrow streets, his manner earnest. This was different from the previous dream—more solid, like a memory. The man came to a salt-filthied dock and a moored vessel of a kind unfamiliar to Remis, all curves and metal-filigree. Hastily he strode up the ramp onto the ship's deck, where a bushily bearded sailor met him. "Do you have it?" he said.

"My friend, do you doubt me?" The seaman gestured effusively. "I lost two dozen men to pirates and monstrous beasts; I saw marvels and horrors unparalleled. Steel-men that shoot fire like wizards, but no spells uttered. Cities derelict, now the home of hideous creatures and obscene men. I went all right, following your directions; I dared the Dead Lands for you, and by the Belly of Hisast, I found what you seek—"

"Are you sure?"

"Three years and half my life. Yes, I'm sure."

The two men went below deck into a sordid darkness. The seaman fetched a small iron box and slammed it on the table. "There, take it. But before you go to do whatever you would with it, first tell me two things: how did you know where it would be, if you have never been to Mikhalin—and why do you want it so much that you would pawn me the larger part of your fortune to get it?"

The tall man laughed, almost joyously. "I'll answer neither question. Such questions are not in our bargain. A million gold coins—that was the price of your service. You are a rich man now, Orkarl. Why waste time over knowledge you might regret?"

The seaman shrugged. "You are a rich man, Lord Valarl, yet you waste time over such knowledge. Still, begrudge me the truth, and I'm content to be ignorant. You'll not see me again."

Checking the contents of the box, and grinning over what he saw, Valarl gave the seaman a sizeable bag and said: "Final payment." He turned away and was gone into the night, disappearing along the alleys beyond the dock.

Then Remis dreamt/remembered Valarl in a large chamber, speaking sorceries across a symbol-scarred floor, his eyes ablaze. A shape appeared to him in a haze of fire and it spoke. "It has been retrieved?" the shape hissed.

"Yes, lord, it is here with me now. The directions you gave were accurate."

"Of course. I know my own land."

"A land long dead, Master."

"Now, but not then. Then I was a mighty ruler, and Mikhalin a kingdom of unsurpassed glory. But that was long ago, as you have said—and I was free. Enough. If you really do have the Cerendar, perhaps I'll be free again."

"I have it."

"Then you must do as I have instructed. It holds me back from life—but its power can destroy the cage if we are more cunning than it is. The link fades. Go!"

The sorcery died. Valarl stood and left the chamber, clutching the metal box to his heart.

* * * * * * *

Remis groaned with the shock of spiritual disruption—

another dream-memory.

* * * * * * *

Valarl and a youthful assistant with dark, pinched features were in a sparsely furnished room, where dark, sinister hangings and necromantic charms broke the candlelight into ill-defined shadows. A young man, naked, lay stretched on an altar. He was alive, though prone, his torso moving gently as he breathed.

A curved, double-bladed dagger hung suspended in a hollow pyramid on a bench nearby. Valarl spoke forbidden words over it, and with his power etched symbols onto the blades. For a moment the dagger glowed dully. Valarl reached into the pyramid structure, removing the totem from its magical cradle. He then stood over the young man, who did not react and was probably unconscious. He raised the dagger.

Something made him stop and glance back over his shoulder. He stared into the shadows.

The assistant asked him if something was wrong.

"I felt a disturbance...," Valarl said after a moment. Then "No, it was nothing."

He turned back to the job at hand and plunged the dagger into the young man's chest.

The body shuddered, pinned under the dagger's enchantment. Valarl held tightly to the hilt, forcing it down until there was no more resistance. All the while the acolyte repeated mystical phrases.

"It's done, Koth," Valarl said. "He's dead."

He stepped back, releasing his hold on the dagger. The young man did not move, nor was his chest swelling with breath any more.

"Now the test." Valarl reached back to the dagger and grasped the hilt. He pulled it from the bloody flesh.

"Rise!" he commanded.

Immediately the corpse stood and came to him.

"See, Koth," said Valarl, "see how skillfully I create a path of safety where History has denied it for so long. With this living corpse I will perform a work never successfully achieved in any age before this. My name will be remembered, Koth."

"How is this dead man of use, master?"

Valarl opened a small metal box that he produced from its hiding place in his robes. "This is the famed Cerendar, Koth. All-Power...so called. In the past, attempts to use it have released doom upon the controller—for it hates Life and cannot bear Life's touch. But now Death shall seduce its power, while I remain safely hidden behind this undead creature. The creature shall be the target of any curse."

And so the necromancer took the box and gave it to the undead youth. In a stern voice he instructed the creature how to act and how to work the spells to seal the Cerendar to his bondage. But there was no safety for Valarl or for the world in this stratagem. As the undead youth did its part, a fierce light arose from the box and in a moment the creature was burnt away to ash. Horror and mortal fear swept across Valarl's face. He screamed and was gathered into the aura of light. The Cerendar disappeared from the metal box and in its place was a living heart—Valarl's—that beat steadily in the dimness that then descended over the chamber. Valarl collapsed onto the floor.

Silence hung in the room and for an instant it seemed as though the Cerendar would be satisfied that its curse end there. Koth, stunned, was breathing slowly, praying that he would be spared. His own heart beat once...twice...three times....

Suddenly a wave of energy flooded through the room, emanating from nowhere and everywhere. The stone floor heaved and buckled as it passed.

Koth had heard the legends of the Cerendar. He remembered that violation of the artifact was believed to initiate an apocalyptic fury that could devastate the world, and as the wave of energy swept around him he imagined it had begun.

He turned and ran from the chamber.

But outside, the world waited in mundane anticipation....

Others came to the necromancer's room and they took Valarl and conveyed him to the sunken crypt where the rest of his family had been laid. In this place the metal box was also secreted, for there was no understanding in these people, only superstition and fear.

In her dreams Remis heard: *a voice, distant and powerless, that echoed in the chamber of sorcery where many times before Valarl had opened a channel through to an impossible place of monstrous fire and hated exile. The voice called for Valarl, commanded him, but at last understood that the endeavor had failed and that again the Cerendar had brought doom. Desperately the voice, gaining in strength as the days passed, sought out the acolyte Koth where he was hiding in Valarl's halls, and instructed him to go to the tomb of Valarl to regain the Cerendar. Koth trembled and was afraid.*

"It will kill me, great master."

"I will kill you even more surely and much more painfully," the voice said. It commanded Koth to take the ritual dagger that Valarl had enchanted and to use it to pry the Cerendar from the corpse's flesh. *"Unless Power is used on it, the Cerendar will not harm you."*

In the dimness of the tomb Koth opened Valarl's coffin, and cut into the body with the dagger's double edge. Its points scored through bloodless flesh, which shriveled away from the magic as though in fear. The acolyte removed the Cerendar from the dark incision. Suddenly the corpse moved, grabbing at Koth's throat and reaching for the artifact. Koth backed away, thrashing out with the knife. It sank deep into Valarl's flesh and the undead creature dropped as suddenly as it had risen.

Obsessed with guilt and with the Cerendar, Koth abandoned the tomb and, half insane, butchered the remaining members of Valarl's family, burning the ancestral home and destroying the sorcerous emblems Valarl had used to invoke Cormidthal's voice. Then Koth fled from the island—which was called Eneth and later Reyad—and was lost to the voice's influence.

In her dream Remis heard the voice curse and call help-lessly for aid and at last fade away like a desert wind. Dirt on stone slid under her movements, making her jerk open her eyes, disoriented. Light was gray and dim.

"Hurry, Koth, the time-cycle is at its optimum point and we can't afford delay. Necromancy is no simple wizard's trick." The voice was light, but underlying tension made its inflections sharp.

Clattering of crucibles and shuffling movement. Pages rustling.

"I don't understand why we must do this, master."

"You don't need to, Koth. Enough to follow instructions. We are about to become part of a greatness we have till now never dreamt might be possible."

Remis pushed herself off the floor. She was behind some crates and a large statue whose shape she couldn't determine. Candlelight flickered into crevices and was scattered as an uncertain stain across the ceiling. *Impossible!* she thought. *How can I be here?*

She glanced at her limbs. They seemed to be hers, rather than those of someone she had invaded in her sleep.

More noises of spell-preparation. The stronger voice began intoning an incomprehensible chant. After a moment the second voice joined in. The rhythms made Remis drowsy, weaving into her consciousness like breezes through a forest glade. She had to fight to stop herself from drifting away.

Cautiously she eased herself toward the top of the crate, where a gap between it and another by its side might allow her to see through into the room. Her shoe scraped on the stone floor, making her freeze. But the chants continued, leaving her unnoticed.

Light in the room was dim and variegated. At first she could distinguish little in the shifting darkness visible through the narrow slit, and she squinted, concentrating on an angular patch of lighter coloring. Gradually it took shape, a man's back. It was moving in a sort of swaying motion—spell-dance, as the type of ritual had once been called. Then the figure turned so that Remis could see its face. As she expected, it was familiar, gaunt, square-bearded, the face that had appeared to her as she slept in her room in Koerpel-Na, at the beginning of her involvement in these events—so long ago, it seemed.

"Continue the chant, Koth," Valarl said.

He reached out of sight, and when his hand came back it held a double-bladed dagger.

Remis tensed.

Somewhere in this moment was a key to the future.

Remis' mind filled with possibility. Should she interfere with Valarl's ritual, stopping him from creating the undead thing? Should she steal the Cerendar from him? She clenched her fists against panic, aware that there would be no second chance. What was the answer then? There was nothing to guide her—no clue from whomever, or whatever, had sent her here.

Valarl raised the dagger, ready to plunge it into the unseen youth Remis knew would lie just out of her sight. There was no time to consider. She decided to follow her instincts.

She stepped from behind the crates into the dim light shed by Valarl's ceremonial candles. "Valarl!" she cried, "Stop!"

Valarl hesitated. His face, intense with magical passion, glared in her direction, but he did not see her. His eyes looked through her.

"What is it, master?" Koth was gazing hollow-eyed into the shadows.

"I felt a disturbance...no, it was nothing."

The necromancer turned back to his sacrifice.

"Valarl!" Remis screamed, going closer. It was impossible for him not to see her now, not to hear her clearly and to feel her presence. "Valarl, if you do this, you will suffer terribly for it. I've seen the results!"

His hands drove the dagger downward. The youth's bare chest split under the knifepoint and blood welled up around the hilt. The corpse thrashed and struggled and Remis dropped her eyes from sight of it. She had already seen the killing, but that had been a dream. Now she was part of it.

The sounds of struggle died away at last. Remis looked up as Valarl stepped back from the corpse, hands red with blood.

"It's done, Koth. He's dead." He raised his bloody hands in a gesture of acceptance. "Now the test."

Remis moved up to him, reaching out, trying to touch him. Desperation was clawing at her heart. "Valarl, listen to me. I'm your descendant and I've been sent through time to warn you. Don't go on with this."

He did not react to her at all now. Remis looked around at Koth, who was staring fearfully at the youth's corpse.

"Why can't you hear me?" she yelled, frustration like pain in her chest.

Valarl reached toward the dagger. His fingers enclosed the hilt in a tense grip.

Remis grabbed at his wrist, hoping to drag his hand away. But the air held her off and she could not touch him. "Why are you stopping me?" she screamed. "What's the point in sending me here if I can't do anything?"

Time seemed to slow. She felt Deep Power ensnare each moment and endow it with a reluctance to pass. Valarl's pull on the dagger was agonisingly minute.

This strangeness calmed Remis' frustrations. Clearly she could not stop Valarl's actions, and once she accepted that limitation, she saw the logic behind it. She was from the future, projected into a key moment from the past and unable to change it, because if she changed it, the future that she knew would change too, and she would not be in a position to change anything. Perhaps, in a changed future, she would not even exist. Perhaps the forces that were working to free the future would be thwarted...perhaps the Dark Gods would win without opposition. Who could say? If she'd been sent back into the past to do something it was not to change the event, for to do so opened up too many dangers, too many paradoxes. No, there was something else.

She glanced at Valarl's hand, dragging at the dagger. The

corpse's flesh was pulling upward as the blade slowly withdrew.

Not to change the event, perhaps, but to understand it. This was the moment that created the undead creature at the center of the future events—and for her to be here at the point of creation, a Spellbinder with trained analytic skills, was an opportunity no magic-worker was ever given in the course of normal magical research. She could study the form and nature of the necromancy first hand, from within. The understanding it would give her would let her return to her own time and unravel the curse there.

Assuming she could survive the trauma of such empathy.

She moved away slightly, determined to succeed, and began her own analytic spells. Her spirit entered Valarl's hand, the dagger, the flesh of the dead youth. She became lost in the gathering storm.

"Rise!" Valarl commanded and she felt the undead pain stir in her limbs. It had begun.

ii.

Across the dark waters of the bay the *Gerargarth* was still burning. Half sunk and broken, it released palls of smoke like black steam that rose above the wreck and joined with the morning's natural haze. The glow stained the sea in fragmented lines, and waves, washing on the shore as a residue of the storm's passing, carried debris from the ship but none of its flame. Occasional spits of rain and fine ash were all that was left to disturb the new day.

A few survivors had gathered wood from the dunes and the brush land beyond them and built fires. Tashnark watched them from a distance, staying away because he was afraid to find out who they were. Arhl was dead—he knew that. His friend had been incinerated in the sorcerer's cabin on the *Gerargarth*. But what of the others? Especially Remis. He hadn't been able to find her. After Cormidthal's death, most of the fires had died, and Tashnark had searched for her unsuccessfully, with escalating desperation—before he was forced to leap from the ship and swim for shore. By then, the immunity he had had to Cormidthal's fire had left him, and he was badly singed. He was terrified for Remis, not wanting to lose her—desperate not to lose her—but his emotions would not let him come to grips with the possibility of her death. Instead specific concern became general and his mind sank into confusion.

Remembered violence and continuing fear colored all his thoughts. The island's present stillness seemed a lure to trick him and a cloak to hide confusion and distress. He just sat on the damp sand among the litter and ruin, as he had for some time, and watched the smoke and the flaring fires. Perhaps he was in shock. He couldn't tell.

Absently he swatted at a sandfly and the force of his blow ploughed it deep into the dune.

How could he be Bellarroth? He was Sevthen Ulart-Tashnark, born in Zogran thirty-seven years ago, formed in the womb of Eresteyin Par-Sevthen and of the seed of Horthas Ulart-Sevthen, slaver and Nahallhan Oath-breaker. He had brothers, skills, memories. Impulsively, he reviewed them all in his mind, as if to regiment the force of their truth. His fingers felt the knots of the plaits—tattered now, and unraveling—and searched out the Nahallhan broach that secured the collar of his shirt. These things spoke of his Nahallhan blood. How could he, who owned them, be Bellarroth—an otherworldly hero who fought horrors on a monster's back and fled to Tharenweyr under the pressure of an ancient curse, the same curse that had kept Cormidthal alive for several thousand years?

The Cerendar artifact was the key to understanding; he knew that now. Though much of what had happened during the brief chaos of his fight against Cormidthal had receded into a mental fog, of that one thing he was sure. His life had become entwined with the artifact's history; Cormidthal had sought it as an escape from his self-created prison; they had struggled always in the shadow it cast. He knew that the ancient Lord had damned himself by some injudicious use of the Object, invoking a power that broke Mikhalin and threw the world into apocalypse. But had the wizard Hanin been caught in the wave of fury and in that impossible exile given life to a soul that was his own, be it called Bellarroth or Sevthen Ulart-Tashnark?

It would seem so, yet surely it was impossible. It made no sense—even though, for a while, he had accepted the strange fate, and because of that acceptance his clouded mind still held memories of Junsar. He caught an image of the ancient Creator gathering together the fragments of His scattered being, focusing them into a moment of conflict. Tammenallor was one such fragment. But how could Tashnark know these things if he was whom he had always seemed to be?

Were memories of Zogran and childhood, exile in Vesuula, adolescence and growth, disillusionment and resolve, all some terrible lie that must now reach an end? Must he abandon the name 'Tashnark' and take on the memories, as yet obscure, of some phantasmal warrior?

He grabbed at a piece of driftwood and found that his fingers crushed it. The destruction shocked him like a new revelation, momentarily forcing him back into the world. As though it were something bizarre found upon the beach, he looked at his arm and thought: *Is this arm Bellarroth's?*

There was a movement near him and he looked around languidly, no longer concerned by dangers. It was a gray cat—Rondan-El-Therill's gray cat. Something stirred in his mind, a memory, or an awareness.

The cat stopped about two paces from him and stared out to where the *Gerargarth* lay. Suddenly the ship shifted and a huge air-bubble burst into waves on the surface. Then the *Gerargarth* slid down into the waters until, caught on a reef, it settled with only parts of the forecastle protruding above the sea as a sign of its passing.

<Self-pity does not suit you>, a familiar internal voice whispered.

"Where were you?" said Tashnark, aloud.

<Busy, but always here. How could I be elsewhere?>

"I don't understand."

<You understand everything. You simply won't accept it.>

Tashnark glanced around angrily. The cat was staring at him, its eyes like slivers of light brighter even than the dawn.

Was the cat the source of the voice?

"You can talk," he said to it. He felt that his mind had become unhinged, but he was afraid to move away and break the illusion.

<After a fashion. I am Tammenallor. Why shouldn't you hear me if I want to be heard? You've existed so long on my shoulders I feel I know your innermost soul.>

"Tammenallor? You?"

<This cat form is simply an extension of myself into your reality. It's nothing. An artifice, like Cormidthal's.>

"Are all cats monsters from another world?"

<Perhaps.> *The voice sounded amused.*

"And Rondan-El-Therill?"

<He existed only in my mind and appeared as I willed it. A convenient illusion, to accompany me as I made my plans. He is gone now.>

"And what am I? Another illusion?"

<Do you feel like an illusion? Is your pain an illusion's pain? Rondan-El-Therill felt none.>

"Don't give me riddles! Give me a clear-cut answer, damn it!"

<A clear answer? There are none available. The world doesn't like certainty. But if you find you're not what you thought you were, why should you feel compelled to reject the past as a consequence? The old and the new are always akin. I'm a cat, and I'm Tammenallor. Tammenallor is Junsar, and Junsar is Erellinarth. Fragments, divided but never for eternity. The world will be healed, Tashnark, or it will be destroyed. But destruction is not eternal. Only life is eternal, and though your fragment of life takes many forms—it's always yours.>

"What about Bellarroth?"

<He, who is also yourself, was a creation of my reality, the reality of vast spaces and cosmic monsters. For a time this reality was transcended. You had several aspects—as had I and as had Cormidthal. And though this may seem to violate reality as you know it, incontrovertible laws are human constructs and never absolute. What happened was necessary. The intention could have failed, but the deed was necessary. We were all caught up in conflict much greater than ourselves.>

"And now?"

<Now time is freed, at least for the moment. The future will continue, for good or ill. It won't be my responsibility.>

"But you're still here?"

<I returned to tell you this: you are yourself and always were. You should simply accept that this is so, and be happy with whatever you can add to the world. But it's hard, and you were used more thoroughly than most. Consequently, by way of recompense, I make you an offer. When I go back to the Cerendar—when I become part of it again—I'll take with me your memory of these things, if you want me to. You will remain Tashnark. And only Tashnark. You'll remember nothing of the last few weeks, except that you were caught up in a terrible conflict and survived. No Bellarroth, no Hanin, no Cormidthal, no Tammenallor, no Junsar. Do you want that?>

For a moment Tashnark was silent, remembering. Of all the names, there was one he didn't wish to forget.

"No," he said at last, "I don't want that. The memories are mine. I'll keep them."

The cat rose and began sauntering along the sand.

"Is that all?"

The cat did not stop, but the voice said: *<Look behind you.>*

Involuntarily Tashnark turned. Someone lay sprawled on the damp sand, washed up on the beach like so much flotsam. Remis? He ran to her and knelt, checking for signs of life. She was breathing steadily.

"Thank the—" he began.

But was this the work of gods?

When he looked back along the beach, the cat had gone.

iii.

Fire spluttered, spitting moisture from the damp wood. Its warmth seemed tenuous, dissipated easily by stray breezes off the sea. It gave little comfort. Those huddled around it were waiting, perhaps for a touch of that elusive warmth, perhaps for something even less tangible.

When Tashnark appeared over the beach, disheveled and wet and carrying Remis, only Shaan stepped out of the fire's glow to meet him. "You survived," he commented. Tashnark couldn't tell if his tone expressed surprise, foreknowledge or indifference.

"Maybe. I haven't decided yet."

"And Remis?"

"She's fine. Unconscious, but alive."

"Then we can do no more. It's over."

Tashnark looked into the Saral's clear eyes, seeing not youth, but his ancient, powerful immortality. There was impotence, too, and *that* surprised him.

"Is it?" he said.

Shaan reached out and touched his shoulder. "For you and Remis, yes. There's only the grief of loss to endure.... And more losses to come."

"How many died?"

"Too many. Few could withstand the E'ashalsinir corruption. Even my presence couldn't hold it off. I'd hoped it might."

"I saw a corpse." Tashnark indicated direction with a movement of his head. "It was hideous. Had something like a snake—a huge one and dead, of course—sprouting from its chest. They're all like that?"

"Not all. But many, yes. Lay Remis near the fire!"

As he nodded and moved toward the group sitting about the fire, Tashnark let his eyes scan the faces, looking for familiar signs. Captain Werrinlit nodded at him dully and a few others glanced up. He knew one or two by sight. Feeling emotion thick in his throat, he lowered Remis to the sand then knelt beside her for a moment, watching her calm breathing.

At least she's still here, he thought. *I couldn't have stood it otherwise.* And it was not simply friendship that had fostered the ache in him. It was something much deeper.

Shaan crouched beside him. Tashnark felt the Saral's firm grip on his shoulder. "Raaneon lives," he said gently. "He sits there...." He gestured. "...in the gloom, in mourning and afraid. Not Mallorin, however. Perhaps it's as well."

"Mallorin's gone?"

"Yes. Dead. He couldn't deny the Dark God Spirit and the struggle killed him. Raaneon was there. He's coping."

"Where's Mallorin's mistress then?"

"Lost."

"Lost? She didn't have a map of the island. That was careless of her."

Shaan frowned at Tashnark's sardonic humor. "Lost," he repeated firmly.

Tashnark caught something in the Saral's voice this time, though he didn't question it. Later perhaps.

"Arhl was killed during the fight," he commented instead, feeling the sadness of that fact scratch across his heart, bleeding all humor from him. He looked at Shaan. "I liked him—stupid superstitious hulk that he was. He was a good man. He should have survived this. Why couldn't the Guardians have done something useful for a change, and saved those who deserve to be in the world?"

"They were helpless, my friend. This struggle took place in places far outside their sphere of influence." Shaan ran his hands through his tangled hair. "The Raashyr have been increasingly limited by the forces at work in reality. Fate and Time shut them out, forcing them to act indirectly, through human lives. They're as much slaves of Fate as you or I. They've never understood what the Cerendar is."

"And do you?"

"I am one with them. Therefore I'm just as ignorant."

Shaan's glance seemed to score across Tashnark's mind. Perhaps he wanted to see into Tashnark's soul, knowing there was something there closed to himself, but hoping the Nahallhan would open it to him. Tashnark said nothing, but the Saral was right. From his special position in the chaos, Tashnark had seen it all, and he knew. He knew that the Cerendar was the lost Kartoranth, the Seed-husk that Junsar stole at the beginning of time. He knew it was All-Power indeed, for it was intended to re-form Life in the midst of the God's Death. When the Kartoranth was removed from its proper place, Fate became distorted and the artifact's power frustrated. Attempts to use it had made its power monstrous. He knew all this.

But he said nothing—this was hidden knowledge that, for the world's sake, had to remain hidden. He didn't know why, but he couldn't speak of it. When he tried, the words slipped back into his throat before they could emerge. No, if Junsar had wanted it known, he would have done the speaking himself. He was clearly telling Tashnark to keep his mouth shut.

Tashnark unclenched his fist against this conspiracy of mystery. "Where's the Cerendar now?" he asked.

Shaan turned partly away, ensuring that no one except Tashnark would hear. "The Dark God servant has it. Halul gave it to the Creature."

Tashnark stood, surprised and for a moment fearful.

"Halul gave it to the E'ashalsinir? After we fought so hard to stop them getting it? I thought that's what this was all about! What possessed her?"

"I can only think that Evil was too strong for her. I thought she was the safest. But I made a mistake. This is my responsibility. As for her motive, we can never ask now. She's disappeared. Gone, perhaps, with the Creature to its home at the end of the world."

"It's all been for nothing?"

Shaan rubbed his palm over his forehead. "So it seems."

"Are we doomed?" But even as he spoke, Tashnark knew they weren't doomed. Quite the opposite, in fact. Suddenly, in that moment, the reality of the Cerendar's nature connected in his mind with knowledge of Halul's apparent treachery—and he understood. She had known the truth, perhaps because of the special relationship she had with Junsar through her Axe. As it drank Dark Life, so it let her see into the soul of Corruption—a gateway to knowledge. She'd acted in the way Junsar wanted—Tashnark knew that, instinctively. Perhaps she was the only one who could have done it. How could any of them have handed the Cerendar to the Dark Gods, being unable to see into the heart of corruption? Understanding wasn't the same as acting. But Tashnark understood that the Cerendar was the Kartoranth—the source of true Form—and that it belonged at the end of the world, the place from which it was taken during the time of Creation, the place of Distortion where the Dark Gods had been born. Like the Guardians, the Dark Servant knew the Cerendar only as Power and had been more than willing to take it back to Its Masters in Nalim-Tar. They believed it would give them victory over Life.

And the implications of that? Despite himself Tashnark laughed.

"There's no humor in it, Tashnark," said Shaan sadly. "This is a dark time...an end to many hopes."

"There's always humor, Saral...life's full of irony."

What he saw, and Shaan didn't, was that by taking the Cerendar into their home the Dark Gods were destroying themselves. No, that was wrong. Not destroying, but *healing* themselves...and the world as well. The Ormsinir had taken the Kartoranth back to the heart of Tharenweyr's Corruption, to Nalim-Tar...to its own beginning. That was where it was supposed to be, where it had always belonged. The pattern of Life within the world would be re-established. As prophecied, the gates of Nalim-Tar would be opened all right, not to a flood of evil, but to waves of renewal.

How long would it take to begin, he wondered?

"And what part did Worjaren Rehemon play in all this?" Tashnark asked, wishing he could explain his awareness to Shaan, to relieve the Saral's burden and free Halul from the taint of treachery. But Junsar said no. This was knowledge it was not Tashnark's to give.

"I'd guess his manipulations formed some sort of added threat. It seems pointless now. You, perhaps, have more idea of that than I."

Tashnark glanced across Sororon's smashed hinterland and for a moment watched sea-birds glide out of sight behind a bank of mist. He breathed in the sea-salt tang, aware of the scent of blood that tainted it.

"Yes," he said, "Perhaps I do."

iv.

Remis awoke while Tashnark and Shaan were talking. She didn't move, just lay there listening to the rhythm of their words, gathering her strength and recalling what she had learnt. After a while she stirred, attracting Tashnark's attention.

"Decided to come back to us, have you?" he said, squatting beside her and helping her up.

"I've been a long way off—a long way in the past."

"Eh?"

"It doesn't matter. I'll explain later."

He grinned and hugged her against his chest. She returned the embrace.

* * * * * * *

Later, they built funeral pyres and burnt as many of the dead as they could gather from along the foreshores. The smoke rose blackly into the low, misty sky. It was a grim and demoralising aftermath to what had seemed at first a miraculous survival, but there was strength to be gained from the effort and from the rites of passing performed for lost friends.

Tashnark went with Remis on board the crippled *Spirit*, looking for Valarl's corpse. While he was on the ship, he climbed below deck to see what had happened to Sire Thargonal—and regretted doing so once he found him. The Vesuulan aristocrat was dead, of course, but twisted so out of shape he was barely recognizable as human. It seemed too grotesque a fate even for his crimes.

Tashnark returned to Remis and found her in a trance next to the inert form of undead Valarl. She was muttering spell-wordings. He sat near her and waited.

After some twenty minutes she turned to him. "It's done. I've unlocked the invulnerability that seals him from death."

"We can pull out the dagger and he won't get up?"

"He's still undead and the dagger holds him. But we can free him with fire."

She stood, pushed Tashnark away from the corpse, and cast her spell. Fire sprang up around the gray-fleshed limbs.

"Even the fact he's a desiccated old relic doesn't make him good kindling," Tashnark commented wryly. "He's not burning."

"Get his heart. Put it on the fire."

The box with the living heart in it had been placed in a nearby cabinet. Tashnark found it was still there, so he took it out and flipped open the lid. The heart pulsed in the shadows.

"Creepy," he growled.

"On the fire!" said Remis urgently.

With a flourish, Tashnark emptied the heart onto the flames that curled around Valarl's body. He watched in fascination as first the heart and then the corpse began to burn, succumbing to the heat. For a moment Valarl was a glowing skeletal specter, then there were only ashes where he had been—and a blackened dagger that clattered onto the singed wood of the floor.

* * * * * * *

Remis gathered up Valarl's dust and performed the Death

Rites for him on the shore. While the day's light suffused the thick cloudbanks that covered Sororon, she raised a wind and blew the ashes out across the bay. They drifted seaward and gradually settled onto the choppy waters.

"What now?" said Tashnark.

"I guess someone will find us and we'll go back to Koerpel-Na. See how things stand."

"There'll probably be trouble from the Supreme Council."

"Probably. I'm not sure I care."

"Who wants a peaceful life, eh?" Tashnark laughed and put his arm around her shoulders.

She smiled wanly. "After that I suppose we wait for the world to end."

"Perhaps it won't end so easily. There's plenty to live for."

She looked up at him. "Is there? Such as?"

For a long moment Tashnark stared into her deep, compelling eyes. He wanted to explain many things—how he felt, what she meant to him—but as always no worthwhile words came. Instead he drew her closer.

She reached up between their touching bodies, putting her hand over his mouth.

"Not now," she whispered.

Hurt, he pulled back, letting her fingers trail off him. "Why not? I know I stink of sweat and demon shit, but surely—?" he began.

Remis interrupted. "I feel lots of things, Tashnark, perhaps even the things you want me to feel. But now's not the right time, that's all."

"We survived. Is there a better time?"

"We've been through too much. And if what Shaan says is true, then the Dark Gods have gained a power greater than any other that's ever existed in the world. If they find a way to use it, they'll sweep us all aside with it; if they don't, the attempt will create a curse that may still be the end of us, perhaps forever."

"I think you're being overly pessimistic."

"What else is there to be?" Remis felt tears forming and

resisted them, letting them become anger instead. "How could Halul do this to us...to the world? She's destroyed our hopes... everything."

"Perhaps she could see what needed to be done, more clearly than the Guardians even. After all, the Raashyr knew nothing about the Cerendar and its true nature."

"What do you mean, its true nature? What do you know about it?"

He took her hand in his. "You can't give in to despair, Remis—that's what I know. There's always the chance we just can't see far enough to predict how it'll all pan out. Trust me." He grinned, leaning close again, breathing her scent. "Can't you see the truth of it in my eyes?"

Remis held his stare, then her lips twisted into something between a sneer and a smirk. "What I see is someone who'd rather stay ignorant than live with an unpalatable truth."

"Truth is something I've been forced to own up to, like it or not. These last few days have been...educational."

Remis detected something in his voice. It made her pause.

"Tell me what you know then." He didn't respond, so she paced away from him, rubbing her hand through her knotted hair. "Life was disappointing enough before this, Tashnark. I don't think I can settle down to face the old social pressures while this...." She waved her hand at the shattered island. "...this remains unresolved."

"Forget it, for god's sake," he growled.

"Forget it?"

"Sure."

"How?"

"It's easy. Alcohol. Sex. The occasional brawl."

She grabbed his arm. "Tell me something that will stop me from leaving here—now, and heading south...beyond Vesuula. Going further, into the darkness. Why shouldn't I follow Halul, face the Dark Gods, try to do something that will make it all better? Talk me out of it, Tashnark! Tell me what you know!"

"Nothing. I don't know a thing."

"You know something all right. I can almost taste it on you."

Tashnark swallowed nervously, feeling the pressure squeezing on his heart. "I...."

"And don't lie to me."

"I *can't* tell you."

"Tell me, Tashnark. Please!"

He closed his eyes, concentrating his thoughts. *Let me say something*, he hissed at the sense of infinite space within him that he interpreted as Junsar. *Please*. Words burgeoned in his mind, fomenting, becoming an irresistible flood. *Let me speak to her.*

When words came, they came in a rush, so much so that he groaned in surprise. "I found out that I belong here, in this world," he managed, feeling the emptiness retreat. He stopped, breathing gently to calm himself. When he spoke again, his speech was measured. "I found out that caring for people... loving them...loving *you*...is what makes me real." He leaned toward her, his voice a whisper. "I know what I am. And I know what the Cerendar is."

"What is it then?"

"A thread that runs through reality, binding it together. And like Halul, I know that sometimes you can give evil enough *thread*, if not rope, to hang itself."

Remis drew back. "I don't see—"

"The Cerendar belongs at the end of the world, Remis. There's an emptiness there, a vast unresolved potential that the Cerendar will mend."

"But the Dark Gods—"

"It won't do what the Dark Gods want...believe me! When has the Cerendar ever done what its wielders wanted it to do? Rehemon found that out as surely as I did."

Remis gave no reply, but her slender fingers gripped his callused ones strongly.

"I hope you're right," she said at last.

After a moment, Tashnark gathered words from some buried memory and whispered:

"Fragments of a broken land
linger unrequited
in patterns of destruction.

Life-blood, aching flesh—
dust blown freely from the ruined land—
cry,
so we will hear the call
and the world will grow—
Into Life."

He knew the words came from another's memories, and for a moment saluted their origin. "See you 'round, Bellarroth," he muttered.

"What?" said Remis, startled.

"Nothing. I was just talking to myself."

AFTERWORD

It has been a long process getting this book to print. Despite endless revisions and many difficulties, I have always (with only occasional moments of self-doubt) believed in it—believed in its worth, believed in its uniqueness and believed that literary and thematic complexity need not be considered a negative in the writing of fantasy.

Many people have helped me with encouragement and advice. Foremost in this regard is Jack Dann, who read the manuscript, appreciated it and subsequently championed it whenever possible. Though I barely knew him at the time, he took it upon himself to do a complete structural edit—a mammoth task and an expression of sheer generosity that I loved him for and still do. It is thanks to his encouragement that I continued working on the novel when the prospects for it seemed bleak. In no small measure it is due to him that it is being published now.

I'd like to thank my wonderful partner Cat Sparks, who kept prodding me to stop whingeing and to get on with it, and my one-time agent Fran Bryson, who made me undertake some very simple but very astute revisions—the story became all the better for them. I'd also like to thank those who in one way or another had some impact on the development of the novel, whether they knew it or not, including: Bill Congreve, Keith Stevenson, Margaret Curtis, Graham Wykes, Veronica Curtis, Trevor Hood and Alan Bingham. I'm sure there are others, but many years have passed since it all began and time blurs memory. If I've neglected to mention you, please accept my apologies as well as my sincere thanks.

Thanks as well to my editor, Rob Reginald of Borgo Press, and cover artist Bob Eggleton, whose superb artwork adorns the cover of this edition.

I'd also like to acknowledge the many cats I've known, who brought (and still bring) an alien grandeur into my mundane life—and I especially remember Shadow, who lies behind the character of the same name in the novel.

Finally, thanks to poet and artist William Blake, whose prophecies and nascent fantasy novels inspired me and whose ideas lie behind the metaphysical and metaphorical structure of Tharenweyr itself.

For more on *Fragments of a Broken Land*, as well as stories about Tharenweyr and the characters in the novel, visit the website at

http://fragmentsnovel.undeadbackbrain.com/

—Robert Hood,
Wollongong, Australia
January 2012

ABOUT THE AUTHOR

Described by best-selling author Sean Williams as "Australia's master of dark fantasy," **ROBERT HOOD** has had a prolific and long-running career producing work that is "absolutely luminous, unnerving, and original" (prize-winning author and anthologist Jack Dann). His crime, dark fantasy, and science fiction short stories have been published in major genre magazines and anthologies worldwide, from *Alfred Hitchcock's Mystery Magazine* and *The Year's Best Horror Stories XIX* to *Exotic Gothic 4* and *Zombie Apocalypse!* Many have found their way into his own collections—*Day-Dreaming on Company Time*, *Immaterial: Ghost Stories*, and *Creeping in Reptile Flesh*. Hood is also the author of the critically acclaimed novel *Backstreets*, and the YA supernatural series *Shades*. As well as writing children's books, plays, and award-winning film commentary, he is co-editor of the renowned *Daikaiju! Giant Monster Tales* anthology and its sequels. His main website is roberthood.net, and he maintains a writing news blog at robert-hoodwriter.com. More information on *Fragments of a Broken Land: Valarl Undead* is available at

http://fragmentsnovel.undeadbackbrain.com/

www.ingramcontent.com/pod-product-compliance
Lightning Source LLC
Chambersburg PA
CBHW022204030726
47494CB00019B/185